P9-AOY-408

THE BIG U

Vintage Books

A Division of Random House · New York

THE BIG U

Neal Stephenson

A VINTAGE ORIGINAL
September 1984
First Edition

Copyright © 1984 by Neal Town Stephenson
All rights reserved under International and Pan-American Copyright Conventions. Published in the United States by Random House, Inc., New York, and simultaneously in Canada by Random House of Canada Limited, Toronto.

LIBRARY OF CONGRESS CATALOGING IN PUBLICATION DATA
Stephenson, Neal.
The big U.

I. Title.
PS3569.T3868B5 1984 813'.54 84-40023
ISBN 0-394-72362-7

Manufactured in the United States of America

to John Forssman

"WHEN I THINK OF THE MEN WHO WERE MY TEACHERS, I REALIZED THAT MOST OF THEM WERE SLIGHTLY MAD. THE MEN WHO COULD BE REGARDED AS GOOD TEACHERS WERE EXCEPTIONAL. IT'S TRAGIC TO THINK THAT SUCH PEOPLE HAVE THE POWER TO BAR A YOUNG MAN'S WAY."

—German political figure Adolf Hitler, 1889–1945
(from *Hitler's Secret Conversations, 1941–44,* translated by Norman Cameron and R. H. Stevens)

I am indebted to the following people for the following things:

My parents for providing several kinds of support.

Edward Gibbon, for writing *The Decline and Fall of the Roman Empire.*

Julian Jaynes, for writing *The Origin of Consciousness in the Breakdown of the Bicameral Mind.*

William Blake and William Butler Yeats, for providing Pertinax with inspiration.

Kathrin Day Lassila, for numerous and thoughtful disagreements.

Gordon Lish, for the most productive rejection slip of all time.

Gary Fisketjon, for buying me a beer in the Top Hat in Missoula, Montana, on July 1, 1983, and other services beyond the call of editorial duty.

—N. T. S.

THE
GO BIG RED
FAN

The Go Big Red Fan was John Wesley Fenrick's, and when ventilating his System it throbbed and crept along the floor with a rhythmic chunka-chunka-chunk. Fenrick was a Business major and a senior. From the talk of my wingmates I gathered that he was *smart*, yet *crazy*, which helped. The description *weird* was also used, but admiringly. His roomie, Ephraim Klein of New Jersey, was in Philosophy. Worse, he was found to be smart *and* weird *and* crazy, intolerably so on all these counts and several others besides.

As for the Fan, it was old and square, with a heavy rounded design suitable for the Tulsa duplex window that had been its station before John Wesley Fenrick had brought it out to the Big U with him. Running up one sky-blue side was a Go Big Red bumper sticker. When Fenrick ran his System—that is, bludgeoned the rest of the wing with a record or tape—he used the Fan to blow air over the back of the component rack to prevent the electronics from melting down. Fenrick was tall and spindly, with a turkey-like head and neck, and all of us in the east corridor of the south wing of the seventh floor of E Tower knew him for three things: his seventies rock-'n'-roll souvenir collection, his trove of preposterous electrical appliances, and his laugh—a screaming hysterical cackle that would ricochet down the long shiny cinderblock corridor whenever something grotesque flashed across the 45-inch screen of his Video System or he did something especially humiliating to Ephraim Klein.

Klein was a subdued, intellectual type. He reacted to *his* victories with a contented smirk, and this quietness gave some residents of EO7S East the impression that Fenrick, a roomie-buster with many a notch on his keychain, had already cornered the young sage. In fact, Klein beat Fenrick at a rate of perhaps sixty percent, or whenever he could reduce the conflict to a rational discussion. He felt that he should be capable of better against a power-punker Business major, but he was not taking into account the animal shrewdness that enabled Fenrick to land lucrative oil-company internships to pay for the modernization of his System.

Inveterate and cynical audio nuts, common at the Big U, would walk into their room and freeze solid, such was Fenrick's System, its skyscraping rack of obscure black slabs with no lights, knobs or switches, the 600-watt Black Hole Hyperspace Energy Nexus Field Amp that sat alone like the Kaaba, the shielded coaxial cables thrown out across the room to the six speaker stacks that made it look like an enormous sonic slime mold in spawn. Klein himself knew a few things about stereos, having a system that could reproduce Bach about as well as the American Megaversity Chamber Orchestra, and it galled him.

To begin with there was the music. That was bad enough, but Klein had associated with musical Mau Maus since junior high, and could inure himself to it in the same way that he kept himself from jumping up and shouting back at television commercials. It was the Go Big Red Fan that really got to him. "Okay, okay, let's just accept as a given that your music is worth playing. Now, even assuming that, why spend six thousand dollars on a perfect system with no extraneous noises in it, and then, *then*, cool it with a noisy fan that couldn't fetch six bucks at a fire sale?" Still, Fenrick would ignore him. "I mean, you amaze me sometimes. You can't think at all, can you? I mean, you're not even a sentient being, if you look at it strictly."

When Klein said something like this (I heard the above one night when going down to the bathroom), Fenrick would look up at him from his Business textbook, peering over the wall of bright, stolen record-store displays he had erected along the room's centerline; because his glasses had slipped down his long thin nose, he would wrinkle it, forcing the lenses toward the desired altitude, involuntarily baring his canine teeth in the process and causing the stiff spiky hair atop his head to shift around as though inhabited by a band of panicked rats.

"You don't understand real meaning," he'd say. "You don't have a monopsony on meaning. I don't get meaning from books. My meaning means what it means to me." He would say this, or something equally twisted, and watch Klein for a reaction. After he had done it a few times, though, Klein figured out that his roomie was merely trying to get him all bent out of shape—to freak his brain, as it were—and so he would drop it, denying Fenrick the chance to shriek his vicious laugh and tell the wing that he had scored again.

Klein was also annoyed by the fact that Fenrick, smoking loads of parsley-spiked dope while playing his bad music, would forget to keep an eye on the Go Big Red Fan. Klein, sitting with his back to the stereo, wads of foam packed in his ears, would abruptly feel the Fan *chunk* into the back of his chair, and as he spazzed out in hysterical surprise it would sit there maliciously grinding away and transmitting chunka-chunka-chunks into his pelvis like muffled laughs.

If it was not clear which of them had air rights, they would wage sonic wars.

They both got out of class at 3:30. Each would spend twenty minutes dashing through the labyrinthine ways of the Monoplex, pounding fruitlessly on elevator buttons and bounding up steps three at a time, palpitating at the thought of having to listen to his roommate's music until at least midnight. Often as not, one would explode from the elevator on E07S, veer around to the corridor, and with disgust feel the other's tunes pulsing victoriously through the floor. Sometimes, though, they would arrive simultaneously and power up their Systems together. The first time they tried this, about halfway through September, the room's circuit breaker shut down. They sat in darkness and silence for above half an hour, each knowing that if he left his stereo to turn the power back on, the other would have his going full blast by the time he returned. This impasse was concluded by a simultaneous two-tower fire drill that kept both out of the room for three hours.

Subsequently John Wesley Fenrick ran a fifty-foot tri-lead extension cord down the hallway and into the Social Lounge, and plugged his System into that. This meant that he could now shut down Klein's stereo simply by turning on his burger-maker, donut-maker, blow-dryer and bun-warmer simultaneously, shutting off the room's circuit breaker. But Klein was only three feet from the extension cord and thus could easily shut Fenrick down with a tug. So these tactics were not resorted to; the duelists preferred, against all reason, to wait each other out.

Klein used organ music, usually lush garbled Romantic masterpieces or what he called Atomic Bach. Fenrick had the edge in system power, but most of that year's music was not as dense as, say, Heavy Metal had been in its prime, and so this difference was usually erased by the thinness of his ammunition. This did not mean, however, that we had any trouble hearing him.

The Systems would trade salvos as the volume controls were brought up as high as they could go, the screaming-guitars-from-Hell power chords on one side matched by the subterranean grease-gun blasts of the 32-foot reed stops on the other. As both recordings piled into the thick of things, the combatants would turn to their long thin frequency equalizers and shove all channels up to full blast like Mr. Spock beaming a live antimatter bomb into Deep Space. Finally the filters would be thrown off and the loudness switches on, and the speakers would distort and crackle with strain as huge wattages pulsed through their magnet coils. Sometimes Klein would use Bach's "Passacaglia and Fugue in C Minor," and at the end of each phrase the bass line would plunge back down home to that old low C, and Klein's sub-woofers would pick up the temblor of the 64-foot pipes and magnify it until he could watch the naked speaker cones thrash away at the air. This particular note happened to be the natural resonating frequency of the main hallways, which were cut into 64-foot, 3-inch halves by the fire doors (Klein and I measured one while drunk), and therefore the resonant frequency of every other hall in every other wing of all the towers of the Plex, and so at these moments everything in the world would vibrate at sixteen cycles per second; beds would tremble, large objects would float off the edges of tables, and tables and chairs themselves would buzz around the rooms of their own volition. The occasional wandering bat who might be in the hall would take off in random flight, his sensors jammed by the noise, beating his wings against the standing waves in the corridor in an effort to escape.

The Resident Assistant, or RA, was a reclusive Social Work major who, intuitively knowing she was never going to get a job, spent her time locked in her little room testing perfumes and watching MTV under a set of headphones. She could not possibly help.

That made it my responsibility. I lived on E07S that year as faculty-in-residence. I had just obtained my Ph.D. from Ohio State in an interdisciplinary field called Remote Sensing, and was a brand-shiny-new associate professor at the Big U.

Now, at the little southern black college where I went to school, we had no megadorms. We were cool at the right times and academic at the right times and we had neither Kleins nor Fenricks. Boston University, where I did my Master's, had pulled through its crisis when I got there; most students had no time for sonic war, and the rest vented their humors in the city, not in the dorms. Ohio State was nicely spread out, and I lived in an apartment complex where noisy shit-for-brains undergrads were even less welcome than tweedy black bachelors. I just did not know what to make of Klein and Fenrick; I did not handle them well at all. As a matter of fact, most of my time at the Big U was spent observing and talking, and very little doing, and I may bear some of the blame.

This is a history, in that it intends to describe what happened and suggest why. It is a work of the imagination in that by writing it I hope to purge the Big U from my system, and with it all my bitterness and contempt. I may have fooled around with a few facts. But I served as witness until as close to the end as anyone could have, and I knew enough of the major actors to learn about what I didn't witness, and so there is not so much art in this as to make it irrelevant. What you are about to read is not an aberration: it can happen in your local university too. The Big U, simply, was a few years ahead of the rest.

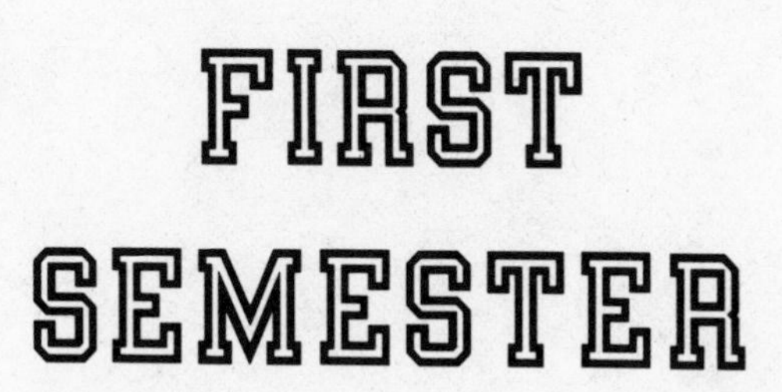
FIRST
SEMESTER

September

On back-to-school day, Sarah Jane Johnson and Casimir Radon waited, for a while, in line together. At the time they did not know each other. Sarah had just found that she had no place to live, and was suffering that tense and lonely feeling that sets in when you have no place to hide. Casimir was just discovering that American Megaversity was a terrible place, and was not happy either.

After they had worked their way down the hall and into the office of the Dean of the College of Sciences and Humanities, they sat down next to each other on the scratchy Dayglo orange chairs below the Julian Didius III Memorial Window. The sunlight strained in greyly over their shoulders, and occasionally they turned to look at the scene outside.

Below them on one of the Parkway off-ramps a rented truck from Maryland had tried to pass under a low bridge, its student driver forgetting that he was in a truck and not his Trans-Am. Upon impact, the steel molding that fastened the truck's top to its sides had wrapped itself around the frame of a green highway sign bolted to the bridge. Now the sign, which read:

AMERICAN MEGAVERSITY

VISITOR PARKING

SPORTS EVENTS

EXIT 500 FT.

was suspended in the air at the end of a long strip of truck that had been peeled up and aside.

A small crowd of students, apparently finished with all their line-waiting, stood on the bridge and beside the ramp, throwing Frisbees and debris into the torn-open back of the truck, where its renters lounged in sofas and recliners and drank beer, and threw the projectiles back. Sarah thought it was idiotic, and Casimir couldn't understand it at all.

Out in the hallway, people behind them in the line were being verbally abused by an old derelict who had penetrated the Plex security system. "The only degree you kids deserve is the third degree!" he shouted, waving his arms and staggering in place. He wore a ratty tweed jacket whose elbow patches flapped like vestigial wings, and he drank in turns from a bottle of Happy's vodka and a Schlitz tall-boy which he kept holstered in his pockets. He had the full attention of the students, who were understandably bored, and most of them laughed and tried to think of provocative remarks.

As the drunk was wading toward them, one asked another how her summer had been. "What about it?" asked the derelict. "Fiscal conservatism? Fine in theory! Tough, though! You have to be tough and humane together, you see, the two opposites must unite in one great leader! Can't be a damn dictator like S. S. Krupp!"

This brought cheers and laughter from the upperclassmen, who had just decided the drunk was a cool guy. Septimius Severus Krupp, the President of American Megaversity, was not popular. "Jesus Christ!" he continued through the laughter, "What the hell are they teaching you savages these days? You need a spanking! No more circuses. Maybe a dictator is just what you need! Alcibiades! Pompilius Numa! They'd straighten things out good and fast."

Sarah knew the man. He liked to break into classes at the Big U and lecture the professors, who usually were at a loss as to how to deal with him. His name was Bert Nix. He had taken quite a shine to Sarah: for her part, she did not know whether or not to be scared of him. During the preceding spring's student government compaign, Bert Nix had posed with Sarah for a campaign photo which had then appeared on posters all over the Plex. This was just the kind of thing that Megaversity students regarded as a sign of greatness, so she had won, despite progressive political ideas which, as it turned out, nobody was even aware of. This was all hard for Sarah to believe. She felt that Bert Nix had been elected President, not the woman he had appeared with on the campaign poster, and she felt obliged to listen to him even when he simply jabbered for hours on end. He was a *nice* lunatic, but he was adrift in the Bert Nix universe, and that stirred deep fears in Sarah's soul.

Casimir paid little attention to the drunk and a great deal to Sarah. He could not help it, because she was the first nice-seeming person, concept or thing he had found in his six hours at the Big U. During the ten years he had spent saving up money to attend this school, Casimir had kept himself sane by imagining it. Unfortunately, he had imagined quiet talks over brunch with old professors, profound discussions in the bathrooms, and dazzling, sensitive people everywhere just waiting to make new friends. What he had found, of course, was American Megaversity. There was only one explanation for this atmosphere that he was willing to believe: that these people *were* civilized, and that for amusement they were acting out a *parody* of the squalor of high school life, which parody Casimir had been too slow to get so far. The obvious explanation—that it was really this way—was so horrible that it had not even entered his mind.

When he saw the photo of her on the back page of the back-to-school edition of the *Monoplex Monitor*, and read the caption identifying her as Sarah Jane Johnson, Student Government President, he made the most loutish double take between her and the photograph. He knew that she knew that he now knew who she was, and that was no way to start a passionate love affair. All he could do was to make a big show of reading about her in the *Monitor*, and wait for her to make the first move. He nodded thoughtfully at the botched quotations and oversimplifications in the article.

Sarah was aware of this; she had watched him page

slowly and intensely through the paper, waiting with mild dread for him to get to the back page, see the picture and say something embarrassing. Instead—even more embarrassing—he actually read the article, and before he reached the bottom of the page, the student ahead of Sarah stomped out and she found herself impaled on the azure gaze of the chief bureaucrat of the College of Sciences and Humanities. "How," said Mrs. Santucci crisply, "may I help you?"

Mrs. Santucci was polite. Her determination to be decent, and to make all things decent, was like that of all the Iranian Revolutionary Guards combined. Her policy of no-first-use meant that as long as we were objective and polite, any conversation would slide pleasantly down greased iron rails into a pit of despair. Any first strike by *us*, any remarks deemed improper by this grandmother of twenty-six and player of two dozen simultaneous bingo cards, would bring down massive retaliation. Sarah knew her. She arose primly and moved to the front chair of the line to look across a barren desk at Mrs. Santucci.

"I'm a senior in this college. I was lucky enough to get an out-of-Plex apartment for this fall. When I got there today I found that the entire block of buildings had been shut down for eight months by the Board of Health. I went to Housing. Upon reaching the head of that line, I was told that it was being handled by Student Affairs. Upon reaching the head of the line there, I was given this form and told to get signatures at Housing and right here . . ."

Mrs. Santucci reached out with the briskness that only old secretaries can approach and seized the papers. "This form is already signed," she informed Sarah.

"Right. I got that done at about one o'clock. But when I got to my new temporary room assignment it turned out to be the B-men's coffee lounge and storeroom for the northeast quad of the first sublevel. It is full of B-men all the time. You know how they are—they don't speak much English, and you know what kinds of things they decorate their walls with"—this attempt to get Mrs. Santucci's sympathy by being prissy was not obviously successful—"and I can't possibly live there. I returned to Housing. To change my room assignment is a whole new procedure, and I need a form from you which says I'm in good academic standing so far this semester."

"That form," Mrs. Santucci noted, "will require signatures from all your instructors."

"I know," said Sarah. All was going according to plan and she was approaching the center of her pitch. "But the semester hasn't started yet! And half my courses don't even have teachers assigned! So, since I'm a senior and my GPA is good, could the Dean okay my room change without the form? Doesn't that make sense? Sort of?" Sarah sighed. She had broken at the end, her confidence destroyed by Mrs. Santucci's total impassivity, by those arms folded across a navy-blue bosom like the Hoover Dam, by a stare like the headlights of an oncoming streetsweeper.

"I'm sure this is all unnecessary. Perhaps they don't know that their lounge has been reassigned. If you can just explain matters to them, I'm sure that Building Maintenance will be happy to accommodate you."

Sarah felt defeated. It had been a nice summer, and while away she had forgotten how it was. She had forgotten that the people who ran this place didn't have a clue as to how reality worked, that in their way they were all as crazy as Bert Nix. She closed her eyes and tilted her tense head back, and the man in the chair behind her intervened.

"Wait a minute," he said righteously. His voice was high, but carried conviction and reasonable sensitivity. "She can't be expected to do that. Those guys don't even speak English. All they speak is Bosnian or Moldavian or something."

"Moravian," said Mrs. Santucci in her Distant Early Warning voice, which was rumored to set off burglar alarms within a quarter-mile radius.

"The language is Crotobaltislavonian, a modern dialect of Old Scythian," announced Sarah, hoping to end the conflict. "The B-Men are refugees from Crotobaltislavonia."

"Listen, I talk to Magrov all the time, and I say it's Moravian." Sarah felt her body temperature begin to drop as she chanced a direct look at Mrs. Santucci.

Trying to sound prim, Sarah said, "Have you ever considered the possibility that you are confusing *Magrov* with *Moravian?*" Seeing the look on Mrs. Santucci's face, she then inhaled sharply and shifted away. Just as the old bureaucrat's jaw was starting to yawn, her chest rising like the return of Atlantis, Casimir Radon leaned way across and yanked something out of Sarah's lap and—in a tone so arresting that it was answered by Bert Nix outside—exclaimed, "Wait a minute!"

Casimir was meek and looked like a nerd and a wimp, but he was great in a crisis. The lost continent subsided and Mrs. Santucci leaned forward with a dangerous frown. Out in the hallway the exasperated Bert Nix cried, "But there's no more minutes to wait! To save the Big U we've got to start now!"

Casimir had taken Sarah's room assignment card from the stack of ammunition on her lap, and was peering at it like a scientific specimen. It was an IBM card, golden yellow, with a form printed on it in yellow-orange ink. In the center of the form was a vague illustration of the Monoplex, looking decrepit and ruined because of the many rectangular holes punched through it. Along the top was a row of boxes labeled with tiny blurred yellow-orange abbreviations that were further abbreviated by rectangular holes. Numbers and letters were printed in black ink in the vicinity of each box.

Bert Nix was still carrying on outside. "Then fell the fires of Eternity with loud & shrill Sound of loud Trumpet thundering along from heaven to heaven, A mighty sound articulate Awake ye dead & come To Judgement from the four winds Awake & Come away Folding like scrolls of the Enormous volume of Heaven & Earth With thunderous noises & dreadful shakings rocking to & fro: The heavens are shaken & the Earth removed from its place; the foundations of the eternal Hills discovered; The thrones of Kings are shaken they have lost their robes and crowns . . . and that's what poetry is! Not the caterwaulings of the Unwise!"

Finally, Casimir looked relieved. "Yeah, I thought that might be it. You were reading this number here. Right?" He got up and stood beside Sarah and pointed to her temporary room number.

"Sure," said Sarah, suddenly feeling dreadful.

"Well," said Casimir, sounding apologetic, "that's not what you want. Your room is not identified by room number, because some rooms repeat. It's identified by door number, which is unique for all doors. This number you were looking at isn't either of those, it's your room ID number, which has to do with data processing. That ID number refers to your actual door number, incorrectly called room number. It is the middle six digits of this character string here. See?" He masked the string of figures between the dirty backward parenthesis of his thumbnails. "In your case we have E12S, giving tower, floor and wing, and then 49, your actual room number."

Sarah did not know whether to scream, apologize or drop dead. She shoved her forms into her knapsack and stood. "Thank you for your trouble, Mrs. Santucci," she said quickly. "Thank you," she said to Casimir, then snapped around and headed for the door, though not fast enough to escape a withering *harrrumph* from Mrs. Santucci. But as she stepped into the hallway, which in order to hold down utility costs was dimly lit, she saw a dark and ragged figure out of the corner of her eye. She looked behind to see Bert Nix grab the doorframe and swing around until he was leaning into the office.

"Listen, Genevieve," he said, "she doesn't need any of your phlegm! She's President! She's my friend! You're just a doorstop!" As much as Sarah wanted to hear the rest of this, she didn't have the energy.

Casimir was left inside, his last view of Sarah interrupted by the dangling figure of the loony, caught in a crossfire he wanted no part of.

"I'll call the guards," said Mrs. Santucci, who for the first time was showing uneasiness.

"Today?" Bert Nix found this a merry idea. "You think you can get a guard today?"

"You'd better stop coming or we'll keep you from coming back."

His eyes widened in mock, crimson-rimmed awe, "Ooh," he sighed, "that were terrible. I'd have no reason to live." He pulled himself erect, walked in and climbed from the arm of Casimir's chair to the broad slate sill of the window. As Mrs. Santucci watched with more terror than seemed warranted, the derelict swung one window open like a door, letting in a gust of polluted steam.

By the time he was leaning far outside and grinning down the seventy-foot drop to the Parkway and the interchange, she had resolved to try diplomacy—though she motioned that Casimir should try to grab his legs. Casimir ignored this; it was obvious that the man was just trying to scare her. Casimir was from Chicago and found that these Easterners had no sense of humor.

"Now, Pert," said Mrs. Santucci, "don't give an old lady a hard time."

Bert Nix dropped back to the sill. "Hard time! What do you know about hard times?" He thrust his hand through a hole in his jacket, wiggling his long fingers at her, and wagging his out-of-control tongue for a few seconds. Finally he added, "Hard times make you strong."

"I've got work to do, Pert."

This seemed to remind him of something. He closed the window and cascaded to the floor. "So do I," he said, then turned to Casimir and whispered, "That's the Julian Didius III Memorial Window. That's what I call it, anyway. Like the view?"

"Yeah, it's nice," said Casimir, hoping that this would not become a conversation.

"Good," said the derelict, "so did J. D. It's the last view he ever saw. Couldn't handle the job. That's why I call it that."

The giggling Bert Nix ambled back into the hall, satisfied, pausing only to steal the contents of the office wastebasket.

Through most of this Casimir sat still and stared at the faded German travel poster on the wall. Now he was really in the talons of Mrs. Santucci, who had probably shifted into adrenaline overdrive and was likely to fling her desk through the wall. Instead, she was perfectly calm and professional. Casimir disliked her for it.

"I'm a junior physics major and I transferred in from a community college in Illinois. I know the first two years of physics inside and out, but there's a problem. The rules here say physics courses must include 'socioeconomic contexts backgrounding,' which I guess means it has to explain how it fits in with today's something or other . . ."

"In order to context the learning experience with the *real* world," said Mrs. Santucci gravely, "we must include socioeconomic backgrounding integral with the foregrounded material."

"Right. Anyway, my problem is that I don't think I need it. I'm not here to give you my memoirs or anything, but my parents were immigrants, I came from a slum, got started in electronics, sort of made my own way, saw a lot of things, and so I don't think I really need this. It'd be a shame if I had to start all over, learning, uh, foregrounded material I already know."

Mrs. Santucci rolled her eyes so that the metal-flake blue eyeshadow on her lids flashed intermittently like fishing lures drawn through a murky sea. "Well, it has been done. It must be arranged with the curriculum chair of your department."

"Who is that for physics?"

"Distinguished Professor Sharon," she said. Bulging her eyeballs at Casimir, she made a respectful silence at the Professor's name, daring him to break it.

When Casimir returned to consciousness he was drifting down a hallway, still mumbling to himself in astonishment. He had an appointment to meet *the* Professor Sharon. He would have been ecstatic just to have sat in on one of the man's lectures!

Casimir Radon was an odd one, as American Megaversity students went. This was a good thing for him, as the Housing people simply couldn't match him up with a reasonable roommate; he was assigned a rare single. It was in D Tower, close to the sciences bloc where he would spend most of his time, on a floor of single rooms filled by the old, the weird and the asinine who simply could not live in pairs.

In order to find his room he would have to trace a mind-twisting path through the lower floors until he found the elevators of D Tower. So before he got himself lost, he went to the nearest flat surface, which was the top of a large covered wastebasket. From it he cleared away a few Dorito bags and a half-drained carton of FarmSun SweetFresh brand HomeLivin' Artificial Chocolate-Flavored Dairy Beverage and forced them into the overflowing maw below. He then removed his warped and sweat-soaked Plex map (the Plexus) from his pocket and unfolded it on the woodtoned Fiberglass surface.

As was noted at the base of the Plexus, it had been developed by the AM Advanced Graphics Workshop. Rather than presenting maps of each floor of the Plex, they had used an Integrated Projection to show the entire Plex as a network of brightly colored paths and intersections. The resulting tangle was so convoluted and yet so clean and spare as to be essentially without meaning. Casimir, however, could read it, because he was not like us. After applying his large intelligence to the problem for several minutes he was able to find the most efficient route, and following it with care, he quickly became lost.

The mistake was a natural one. The elevators, which were busy even in the dead of night, were today clogged with catatonic parents from New Jersey clutching beanbag chairs and giant stuffed animals. Fortunately (he thought), adjacent to each elevator was an entirely unused stairwell.

Casimir discovered shortly afterward that in the lower floors of the Plex all stairwell doors locked automatically from the outside.

I discovered it myself at about the same time. Unlike Casimir I had been in the Plex for ten days, but I had spent them typing up notes for my classes. It is unwise to prepare two courses in ten days, and I knew it. I hadn't gotten to it until the last minute, for various reasons, and so I'd spent ten days sitting there in my bicycling shorts, drinking beer, typing, and sweating monumentally in the fetid Plex air. So my first exposure to the Plex and its people really came that afternoon, when I wandered out into the elevator lobby and punched the buttons. The desperate Tylenol-charged throngs in the elevators did not budge when the doors opened, because they couldn't. They stared at me as though I were Son of Godzilla, which I was used to, and I stared at them and tried to figure out how they got that way, and the doors clunked shut. I discovered the stairways, and once I got below the bottom of the tower and into the lower levels, I also found that I was locked in.

For fifteen minutes I followed dimly lit stairs and corridors smelling of graffiti solvent and superfluous floor wax, helplessly following the paths that students would take if the Plex ever had to be evacuated. Through little windows in the locked doors I peered out of this twilight zone and into the different zones of the Plex—Cafeteria, Union, gymnasia, offices—but my only choice was to follow the corridors, knowing they would dump me into the ghetto outside. At last I turned a corner and saw the wall glistening with noisy grey outside light. At the end of the line, a metal door swung silently in the breeze, emblazoned thus: FIRE ESCAPE ONLY. WARNING—ALARM WILL SOUND.

I stepped out the door and looked down a long, steep slope into the canyon of the Turnpike.

The American Megaversity Campustructure was three blocks on a side, and squatted between the Megalopolitan Turnpike on the north and the Ronald Reagan Parkway on the south. Megaversity Stadium, the only campus building not inside the Plex proper, was to the west, and on the east was an elaborate multilevel interchange interconnecting the Pike, the Parkway, the Plex and University Avenue. The Pike ran well below the base of the Plex, and so as I emerged from the north wall of the building I found myself atop a high embankment. Below me the semis and the Audis shot past through the layered blue monoxide, and their noises blended into a waterfall against the unyielding Plex wall. Aside from a few wretched weeds growing from cracks in the embankment, no life was to be seen, except for Casimir Radon.

He had just emerged from another emergency exit. We saw each other from a hundred feet apart, waved and walked toward each other. As we converged, I regarded a tall and very thin man with an angular face and a dense five-o'clock shadow. He wore round rimless glasses. His black hair was in disarray as usual; during the year it was to vary almost randomly between close-cropped and shoulder-length. I soon observed that Casimir could grow a shadow before lunch, and a beard in three days. He and I were the same age, though I was a recent Ph.D. and he a junior.

Later I was to think it remarkable that Casimir and I should emerge from those fire doors at nearly the same moment, and meet. On reflection I have changed my mind. The Big U was an unnatural environment, a work of the human mind, not of God or plate tectonics. If two strangers met in the rarely used stairways, it was not unreasonable that they should turn out to be similar, and become friends. I thought of it as an immense vending machine, cautiously crafted so that any denomination too ancient or foreign or irregular would rattle about randomly for a while, find its way into the stairway system, and inevitably be deposited in the reject tray on the barren back side. Meanwhile, brightly colored graduates with attractively packaged degrees were dispensed out front every June, swept up by traffic on the Parkway and carried away for leisurely consumption. Had I understood this earlier I might have come to my senses and immediately resigned, but on that hot September day, with the exhaust abrading our lungs and the noise squashing our conversation, it seemed worthwhile to circle around to the Main Entrance and give it another try.

We headed east to avoid the stadium. On our right the wall stretched up and away for acres in a perfect cinderblock grid. After passing dozens of fire doors we came to the corner and turned into the access lot that stretched along the east wall. Above, at many altitudes, cars and trucks screeched and blasted through the tight curves of the interchange. People called it the Death Vortex, and some claimed that parts of it extended into the fourth dimension. As soon as it had been planned, the fine old brownstone neighborhood that was its site plummeted into slumhood; Haitians and Vietnamese filled the place up, and the feds airproofed the buildings and installed giant electric air filters before proceeding.

Here on the access lot we could look down a long line of loading docks, the orifices of the Plex where food and supplies were ingested and trash discharged, serviced by an endless queue of trucks. The first of these docks, by the northern corner, was specially designed for the discharge of hazardous wastes produced in Plex labs and was impressively surrounded by fences, red lights and threatening signs. The next six loading docks were for garbage trucks, and the rest, all the way down to the Parkway, for deliveries. We swung way out from the Plex to avoid all this, and followed the fence at the border of the lot, gazing into the no-man's-land of lost mufflers and shredded fanbelts beyond, and sometimes staring up into the Plex itself.

The three-by-three block base had six stories above ground and three below. Atop it sat eight 25-story towers where lived the 40,000 students of the university. Each tower had four wings 160 feet long, thrown out at right angles to make a Swiss cross. These towers sat at the four corners and four sides of the base. The open space between them was a huge expanse of roof called Tar City, inhabited by great machines, crushed furniture thrown from above, rats, roaches, students out on dares, and the decaying corpses of various things that had ventured out on hot summer days and become mired in the tar. All we could see were the neutral light brown towers and their thousands and thousands of identical windows reaching into the heavens. Even for a city person, it was awesome. Compared to the dignified architecture of the old brownstones, though, it caused me a nagging sense of embarrassment.

The Vortex whose coils were twined around those brownstones threw out two ramps which served as entrance and exit for the Plex parking ramp. These ran into the side of the building at about third-story level. To us they were useless, so we continued around toward the south side.

Here was actually some green: a strip of grass between the walk and the Parkway. On this side the Plex was faced with darker brown brick and had many picture windows and signs for the businesses of the built-in mall on the first floor. The Main Entrance itself was merely eight revolving doors in a row, and having swished through them we were drowned in conditioned air, Muzak, the smell of Karmel Korn and the idiotic babble of penny-choked indoor fountains. We passed through this as quickly as possible and rode the long escalators ("This must be what a ski lift is like," said Casimir) to the third floor, where a rampart of security booths stretched across our path like a thruway toll station. Several of the glass cages were occupied by ancient guards in blue uniforms, who waved us wearily through the turnstiles as we waved our ID cards at them. Casimir stopped on the other side, frowning.

"They shouldn't have let me in," he said.

"Why?" I asked. "Isn't that your ID?"

"Of course it is," said Casimir Radon, "but the photo is so bad they had no way of telling." He was serious. We surveyed the rounded blue back of the guard. Most of them had been recruited out of Korea or the Big One. The glass cages of the Plex had ruined their bodies. Now they had become totally passive in their outlook; but, by the same token, they had become impossible to faze or surprise.

We stepped through more glass doors and were in the Main Lobby.

The Plex's environmental control system was designed so that anyone could spend four years there wearing only a jockstrap and a pair of welding goggles and yet never feel chilly or find the place too dimly lit. Many spent their careers there without noticing this. Casimir Radon took less than a day to notice the pitiless fluorescent light. Acres of light glanced off the Lobby's polished floor like sun off the Antarctic ice, and a wave of pain now rolled toward Casimir from near the broad vinyl information desk and washed over him, draining through a small hole in the center of his skull and pooling coldly behind his eyes. Great patches of yellow blindness appeared in the center of his vision and he coasted to a stop, hands on eyes, mouth open. I knew enough to know it was migraine, so I held his skinny arm and led him, blind, to his room in D Tower. He lay cautiously down on the naked plastic mattress, put a sock over his eyes and thanked me. I drew the blinds, sat there helplessly for a while, then left him to finish his adjustment to the Big U.

After that he wore a uniform of sorts: old T-shirt, cutoffs or gym shorts, hightop tennis shoes ("to keep the rats off my ankles") and round purple mountain-climbing goggles with leather bellows on the sides to block out peripheral light. He was planning such a costume as I left his room. More painfully, he was beginning to question whether he could live in such a place for even one semester, let alone four. He did not know that the question would be decided for him, and so he felt the same edgy uncertainty that nagged at me.

Some people, however, were quite at home in the Plex. At about this time, below D Tower in the bottom sublevel, not far from the Computing Center, several of them were crossing paths in a dusty little dead end of a hallway. To begin with, three young men were standing by the only door in the area, taking turns peering into the room beyond. The pen lights from their shirt pockets illuminated a small windowless room containing a desk, a chair and a computer terminal. The men stared wistfully at the latter, and had piled their math and computer textbooks on the floor like sandbags, as though they planned a siege. They had been discussing their tactical alternatives for getting past the door, and had run the gamut from picking the lock to blowing it open with automatic-weapon bursts, but so far none had made any positive moves.

"If we could remove that window," said one, a mole-faced individual smelling of Brut and sweat and glowing in a light blue iridescent synthetic shirt and hi-gloss dark blue loafers, "we could reach in and unlock it from inside."

"Some guy tried to get into my grandma's house that way one time," recalled another, a skinny, long-haired, furtive fellow who was having trouble tracking the conversation, "but she took a sixteen-ounce ball-peen hammer and smashed his hand with it. He never came back." He delivered the last sentence like the punchline to a *Reader's Digest* true anecdote, convulsing his pals with laughter.

The third, a disturbingly 35-ish looking computer science major with tightly permed blond hair, eventually calmed down enough to ask, "Hey, Gary, Gary! Did she use the ball end or the peen end?"

Gary was irked and confused. He had hoped to impress them by specifying the weight of the hammer, but he was stumped by this piece of one-upsmanship; he didn't know which end was which. He radiated embarrassment for several seconds before saying, "Oh, gee, I don't know, I think she probably used both of 'em before she was done with the guy. But that guy never came back."

Their fun was cut short by a commanding voice. "A sixteen-ounce ball-peen hammer isn't much good against a firearm. If I were a woman living alone I'd carry a point thirty-eight revolver, minimum. Double action. Effective enough for most purposes."

The startling newcomer had their surprised attention. He had stopped quite close to them and was surveying the door, and they instinctively stepped out of his way. He was tall, thin and pale, with thin brown Brylcreemed hair and dark red lips. The calculator on his hip was the finest personal computing machine, and on the other hip, from a loop of leather, hung a fencing foil, balanced so that its red plastic tip hung an inch above the floor. It was Fred Fine.

"You're the guy who runs the Wargames Club, aren't you," asked the blond student.

"I am Games Marshall, if that's the intent of your question. Administrative and financial authority are distributed among the leadership cadre according to the Constitution."

"The Wargames Club?" asked Gary, his voice suffused with hope. "What, is there one?"

"The correct title is the Megaversity Association for Reenactments and Simulations, or MARS," snapped Fred Fine. Still almost breathless, Gary said, "Say. Do you guys ever play 'Tactical Nuclear War in Greenland?' "

Fred Fine stared just over Gary's head, screwing up his face tremendously and humming. "Is that the earlier version of 'Martians in Godthaab,' " he finally asked, though his tone indicated that he already knew the answer.

Gary was hopelessly taken aback, and looked around a bit before allowing his gaze to rest on Fred Fine's calculator. "Oh, yeah, I guess. I guess 'Martians in Godthaab' must be new."

"No," said Fred Fine clearly, "it came out six months ago." To soften the humiliation he chucked Gary on the shoulder. "But to answer your question. Some of our plebes—our novice wargamers—do enjoy that game. It's interesting in its own way, I suppose, though I've only played it a dozen times. Of course, it's a Simuconflict product, and their games have left a lot to be desired since they lost their Pentagon connections, but there's nothing really wrong with it."

The trio stared at him. How could he know so much?

"Uh, do you guys," ventured the blue one, "ever get into role-playing games? Like Dungeons and Dragons?"

"Those of us high in the experiential hierarchy find conventional D and D stultifying and repetitive. We prefer to stage live-action role-playing scenarios. But that's not for just anyone."

They looked timidly at Fred Fine's fencing foil and wondered if he were on his way to a live-action wargame at this very moment. For an instant, as he stood in the dim recess of the corridor, light flickering through a shattered panel above and playing on his head like distant lightning, his feet spread apart, hand on sword pommel, it seemed to them that they beheld some legendary hero of ancient times, returned from Valhalla to try his steel against modern foes.

The mood was broken as another man suddenly came around the corner. He brushed silently past Fred Fine and nearly impaled Gary on a key, but Gary moved just in time and the new arrival shoved the key home and shot back the deadbolt. He was tall, with nearly white blond hair, pale blue eyes and a lean but cherubic face, dressed in cutoffs and a white dress shirt. Shouldering through them, he entered the little room.

Fred Fine reacted with uncharacteristic warmth. "Well, well, well," he said, starting in a high whine and dropping in pitch from there. I had Fred Fine in one of my classes and when in a good mood he really did talk like Colonel Klink; it took some getting used to. "So they haven't caught up with you and your master key yet, eh, Virgil? Very interesting."

Virgil Gabrielsen turned smoothly while stepping through the doorway, and stared transparently through Fred Fine's head. "No," he said, "but I have plenty of copies anyway. They aren't about to change every lock in the Plex on my account. The only doors this won't open are in the hazardous waste area, the Administration Bloc, Doors 1253 through 1778 and 7899 to 8100, which obviously no one cares about, and Doors 753, 10100 and the high 12,500's, and I'm obviously not going to go ripping off vending-machine receipts, am I?" At this the three friends frowned and looked back and forth. Virgil entered the room and switched on the awesomely powerful battery of overhead fluorescent lights. Everything was somewhat dusty inside.

"No rat poison on the floor," observed Fred Fine. "Dusty. Still keeping the B-men out, eh?"

"Yeah," said Virgil, barely aware of them, and began to pull things from his knapsack. "I told them I was doing werewolf experiments in here."

Fred Fine nodded soberly at this. Meanwhile, the three younger students had invited themselves in and were gathered around the terminal, staring raptly into its printing mechanism. "It's just an antique Teletype," said the blue one. He had already said this once, but repeated it now for Fred Fine. "However, I really like these. Real dependable, and lots of old-fashioned class despite an inferior character menu." Fred Fine nodded approvingly. Virgil shouldered through them, sat before the terminal and, without looking up, announced, "I didn't invite any of you in, so you can all leave now."

They did not quite understand.

"Catch my drift? I dislike audiences."

Fred Fine avoided this by shaking his head, smiling a red smile and chuckling. The others were unmanned and stood still, waiting to be told that Virgil was kidding.

"Couldn't we just sit in?" one finally asked. "I've just got to XEQ one routine. It's debugged and bad data tested. It's fast, it outputs on batch. I can wait till you're done."

"Forget it," said Virgil airily, scooting back and nudging him away. "I won't be done for hours. It's all secret Science Shop data. Okay?"

"But turnover for terminals at CC is two hours to the minus one!"

"Try it at four in the morning. You know? Four in the morning is a great time at American Megaversity. Everything is quiet, there are no lines even at the laundry, you can do whatever you want without fucking with a mob of freshmen. Put yourselves on second shift and you'll be fine. Okay?"

They left, sheeshing. Fred Fine stopped in the doorway, still grinning broadly and shaking his head, as though leaving just for the hell of it.

"You're still the same old guy, Virgil. You still program in raw machine code, still have that master key. Don't know where science at AM would be without you. What a *wiz*."

Virgil stared patiently at the wall. "Fred. I told you I'd fix your MCA and I will. Don't you believe me?"

"Sure I do. Say! That invitation I made you, to join MARS anytime you want, is still open. You'll be a Sergeant right away, and we'll probably commission you after your first night of gaming, from what I know of you."

"Thanks. I won't forget. Goodbye."

"Ciao." Fred Fine bowed his thin frame low and strode off.

"What a creep," said Virgil, and ferociously snapped the deadbolt as soon as Fred Fine was almost out of earshot.

Removing supplies from the desk drawer, he stuffed a towel under the door and taped black paper over the window. By the terminal he set up a small lamp with gel over its mouth, which cast a dim pool of red once he had shut off the room lights.

He activated the terminal, and the computer asked him for the number of his account. Instead of typing in an account number, though, Virgil typed: FIAT LUX.

Later, Virgil and I got to know each other. I had problems with the computer only he could deal with, and after our first contacts he seemed to find me interesting enough to stay in touch. He began to show me parts of his secret world, and eventually allowed me to sit in on one of these computer sessions. Nothing at all made sense until he explained the Worm to me, and the story of Paul Bennett.

"Paul Bennett was one of these computer geniuses. When he was a sophomore here he waltzed through most of the secret codes and keys the Computing Center uses to protect valuable data. Well, he really had the University by the short hairs then. At any time he could have erased everything in the computer—financial records, scientific data, expensive software, you name it. He could have devastated this university just sitting there at his computer terminal—that's how vulnerable computers are. Eventually the Center found out who he was, and reprimanded him. Bennett was obviously a genius, and he wasn't malicious, so the Center then went ahead and hired him to design better security locks. That happens fairly often—the best lock-designers are people who have a talent for picking locks."

"They hired him right out of his sophomore year?" I asked.

"Why not? He had nothing more to learn. The people who

were teaching his classes were the same ones whose security programs he was defeating! What's the point of keeping someone like that in school? Anyway, Bennett did very well at the Center, but he was still a kid with some big problems, and no one got along with him. Finally they fired him.

"When they fire a major Computing Center employee, they have to be sneaky. If they give him two weeks' notice he might play havoc with the computer during those two weeks, out of spite. So when they fire these people, it happens overnight. They show up at work and all the locks have been changed, and they have to empty out their desks while the senior staff watch them. That's what they did to Paul Bennett, because they knew he was just screwed up enough to frag the System for revenge."

"So much for his career, then."

"No. He was immediately hired by a firm in Massachusetts for four times his old salary. And CC was happy, because they'd gotten good work out of him and thought they were safe from reprisals. About a week later, though, the Worm showed up."

"And that is—?"

"Paul Bennett's sabotage program. He put it into the computer before he was fired, you see, and activated it, but every morning when he came to work he entered a secret command that would put it on hold for another twenty-four hours. As soon as he stopped giving the command, the Worm came out of hiding and began to play hell with things."

"But what good did it do him? It didn't prevent his being fired."

"Who the hell knows? I think he put it in to blackmail the CC staff and hold on to his job. That must have been his original plan. But when you make a really beautiful, brilliant program, the temptation to see it work is just overwhelming. He must have been dying to see the Worm in action. So when he was fired, he decided, what the hell, they deserve it, I'll unleash the Worm. That was in the middle of last year. At first it did minor things such as erasing student programs, shutting the System down at odd times, et cetera. Then it began to worm its way deeper and deeper into the Operator —the master program that controls the entire System—and wreak vandalism on a larger scale. The Computing Center personnel fought it for a while, but they were successful for only so long. The Operator is a huge program and you have to know it all at once in order to understand what the Worm is doing to it."

"Aha," I said, beginning to understand, "they needed someone with a photographic memory. They needed another prodigy, didn't they? So they got you? Is that it?"

At this Virgil shrugged. "It's true that I am the sort of person they needed," he said quietly. "But don't assume that they 'got' me."

"Really? You're a free lance?"

"I help them and they help me. It is a free exchange of services. You needn't know the details."

I was willing to accept that restriction. Virgil had told me enough so that what he was doing made sense to me. Still, it was very abstract work, consisting mostly of reading long strings of numbers off the terminal and typing new ones in. On the night I sat in, the Worm had eaten all of the alumni records for people living in states beginning with "M." ("M!," said Virgil, "the worst letter it could have picked.") Virgil was puttering around in various files to see if the information had been stored elsewhere. He found about half of Montana hidden between lines of an illegal video game program, retrieved the data, erased the illegal program and caused the salvaged information to be printed out on a string of payroll check forms in a machine in the administrative bloc.

On this night, the first of the new school year, Virgil was not nobly saving erased data from the clutches of the Worm. He was actually arranging his living situation for the coming year. He had about five choice rooms around the Plex, which he filled with imaginary students in order to keep them vacant—an easy matter on the computer. To support his marijuana and ale habits he extracted a high salary from various sources, sending himself paychecks when necessary. For this he felt neither reluctance nor guilt, because Fred Fine was right: without Virgil, whose official job was to work in the Science Shop, scientific research at the Big U would simply stop. To support himself he took money from research accounts in proportion to the extent they depended on him. This was only fair. An indispensable place like the Science Shop needed a strong leader, someone bold enough to levy appropriate taxes against its users and spend the revenues toward the ends those users desired. Virgil had figured out how to do it, and made himself a niche at the Big U more comfortable than anyone else's.

Sarah lived in a double room just five floors above me and Ephraim Klein and John Wesley Fenrick, on E12S—E Tower, twelfth floor, south wing. The previous year she had luxuriated in a single, and resolved never to share her private space again; this double made her very angry. In the end, though, she lucked out. Her would-be roommate had only taken the space as a front, to fake out her pay-rents, and was actually living in A Tower with her boyfriend. Thus Sarah did not have to live four feet away from some bopper who would suffer an emotional crisis every week and explore the standard uses of sex and drugs and rock-and-roll in noisy experimental binges on the other side of the room.

Sarah's problem now was to redecorate what looked like the inside of a water closet. The cinderblock walls were painted chocolate brown and absorbed most light, shedding only the garish parts of the spectrum. The shattered tile floor was gray and felt sticky no matter how hard she scrubbed. On each side of the perfectly symmetrical room, long fluorescent light fixtures were bolted to the walls over the beds, making a harsh light nearby but elsewhere only a dull greenish glow. After some hasty and low-budget efforts at making it decent, Sarah threw herself into other activities and resigned herself to another year of ugliness.

On Wednesday of the term's second week there was a wing meeting. American Megaversity's recruitment propaganda tried to make it look as though the wings did everything as a jolly group, but this had not been true on any of Sarah's previous wings. This place was different.

When she had dragged her duffel bags through the stairwell door on that first afternoon, a trio of well-groomed junior matrons had risen from a lace-covered card table in the lobby, helped her with the luggage, pinned a pink carnation on her sweaty T-shirt and welcomed her to "our wing." Under her pillow she had found a "starter kit" comprising a small teddy bear named Bobo, a white candle, a GOLLYWHATAFACE-brand PERSONAL COLOUR SAMPLER PACQUET, a sack of lemon drops, a red garter, six stick-on nametags with SARA written on them, a questionnaire and a small calligraphied Xeroxed note inviting her to the wing meeting. All had been wrapped in flowery pastel wrapping paper and cutely beribboned.

Most of it she had snarlingly punted into the nether parts of her closet. The wing meeting, however, was quasi-political, and hence she ought to show up. A quarter of an hour early, she pulled on a peasant blouse over presentable jeans and walked barefoot down the hall to the study lounge by the elevator lobby.

She was almost the last to arrive. She was also the only one not in a bathrobe, which was so queer that she almost feared she was having one of those LSD flashbacks people always warn you about. Her donut tasted like a donut, though, and all seemed normal otherwise, so it was reality—albeit a strange and distant branch thereof.

Obviously they had not all been bathing, because their hair was dry and their makeup fresh. There were terry robes, silk robes, Winnie-the-Pooh robes, long plush robes, plain velvety robes, designer robes, kimonos and even a few nightshirts on the cute and skinny. Also, many slippers, too many of them high-heeled. Once she was sure her brain was okay, she edged up to a nearby wingmate and mumbled, "Did I miss something? Everyone's in bathrobes!"

"Shit, don't ask me!" hissed the woman firmly. "I just took a shower, myself."

Looking down, Sarah saw that the woman was indeed

clean of face and wet of hair. She was shorter than average and compact but not overweight, with pleasant strong features and black-brown hair that fell to her shoulders. Her bathrobe was short, old and plain, with a clothesline for a sash.

"Oh, sorry," said Sarah. "So you did. Uh, I'm Sarah, and my bathrobe is blue."

"I know. President of the Student Government."

Sarah shrugged and tried not to look stuck-up.

"What's the story, you've never lived on one of these floors?" The other woman seemed surprised.

"What do you mean, 'one of these floors?' "

She sighed. "Ah, look. I'm Hyacinth. I'll explain all this later. You want to sit down? It'll be a long meeting." Hyacinth grasped Sarah's belt loop and led her politely to the back row of chairs, where they sat a row behind the next people up. Hyacinth turned sideways in her chair and examined Sarah minutely.

The Study Lounge was not a pretty place. Designed to be as cheery as a breath mint commercial, it had aged into something not quite so nice. Windows ran along one wall and looked out into the elevator lobby, where the four wings of E12S came together. It was furnished with the standard public-area furniture of the Plex: cubical chairs and cracker-box sofas made of rectangular beams and slabs of foam covered in brilliant scratchy polyester. The carpet was a membrane of compressed fibers, covered with the tats and cigarette-burns and barfstains of years. Overhead, the ubiquitous banks of fluorescent lights cheerfully beamed thousands of watts of pure bluish energy down onto the inhabitants. Someone was always decorating the lounge, and this week the theme was football; the decorations were cardboard cutouts of well-known cartoon characters cavorting with footballs.

The only other nonrobed person in the place was the RA, Mitzi, who sat bolt upright at the lace-covered card table in front, left hand still as a dead bird in her lap, right hand three inches to the side of her jaw and bent back parallel to the tabletop, fingers curled upward holding a ballpoint pen at a jaunty but not vulgar forty-five-degree angle. She bore a fixed, almost manic smile which as far as Sarah could tell had nothing to do with anything—charm school, perhaps, or strychnine poisoning. Mitzi wore an overly formal dress and a kilogram of jewelry, and when she spoke, though not even her jawbone moved, one mighty earring began to swing violently.

Among other things, Mitzi welcomed new "members." There were three: another woman, Hyacinth and Sarah, introduced in that order. The first woman explained that she was Sandi and she was into like education and stuff. Then came Hyacinth; she was into apathy. She announced this loudly and they all laughed and complimented Hyacinth on her sense of humor.

Sarah was introduced last, being famous. "What are you into, Sarah Jane?" asked Mitzi. Sarah surveyed the glistening, fiercely smiling faces turned round to aim at her.

"I'm into reality," she said. This brought delighted laughter, especially from Hyacinth, who screamed like a sow.

The meeting then got underway. Hyacinth leaned back, crossed her arms and tilted her head back until she was staring openmouthed at the ceiling. As the meeting went on she combed her hair, bit her nails, played with loose threads from her robe, cleaned her toes and so on. The thing was, Sarah found all of this more interesting than the meeting itself. Sarah looked interested until her face got tired. She had spoken in front of groups enough to know that Mitzi could see them all clearly, and that to be obviously bored would be rude. Sometimes politeness had to give way to sanity, though, and before she knew it she found herself trying to swing the tassels at the ends of her sleeves in opposite directions at the same time. Hyacinth watched this closely and patted her on the back when she succeeded.

Mainly what they were doing was filling a huge social calendar with parties and similar events. Sarah wanted to announce that she liked to do things by herself or with a few friends, but she saw no diplomatic way of saying so. She did resurface for the discussion of the theme for the Last Night Party, the social climax of the semester: Fantasy Island Nite.

"Wonder how they're going to tell it apart from all the other nights," grumbled Hyacinth. Nearby wingmates turned and smiled, failing to understand but assuming that whatever Hyacinth said must be funny.

Another phase of the social master plan was to form an official sister/brother relationship with the wing upstairs, known as the Wild and Crazy Guys. This in turn led to the wing-naming idea. After all, if E13S had a name for itself, shouldn't E12S have one too? Mari Meegan, darling of the wing, made this point, and "Yeah!"s zephyred up all around.

Sarah was feeling pretty sour by this point but said nothing. If they wanted a name, fine. Then the ideas started coming out: Love Boat, for example.

"We could paint our lobby with a picture of the Love Boat like it looks at the start of the show, and we could, you know, do everything, like parties and stuff, with like that kind of a theme. Then on Fantasy Island Nite, we could pretend the Boat was visiting Fantasy Island!"

This idea went over well and the meeting broke up into small discussions about how to apply this theme to different phases of existence, Finally, though, Sarah spoke up, and they all smiled and listened. "I'm not sure I like that idea. There are plenty of creeps on the floor already, because we're all-female. If we name it Love Boat, everyone will think it's some kind of outcall massage service, and we'll never get a break."

Several seconds of silence. A few nods were seen, some "yeah"s heard, and Love Boat was dead. More names were suggested, most of them obviously dumb, and then Mari Meegan raised her hand. All quieted as her fingernails fluttered like a burst of redhot flak above the crowd. "I know," she said.

There was silence save for the sound of Hyacinth's comb rushing through her hair. Mari continued. "We can call ourselves 'Castle in the Air.' "

The lounge gusted with oohs and aahs.

"I like that."

"You're so creative, Mari."

"We could do a whole Dark Ages theme, you know, castles and knights and shining armor."

"That's nice! Really nice!"

"Wait a sec." This came from Hyacinth.

At this some of the women were clearly exasperated, looking at the ceiling, but most wore expressions of forced tolerance.

Hyacinth continued flatly. "Castle in the Air is derogatory. That mean's it's not-nice. When you talk about a castle in the air, you mean something with no basis in reality. It's like saying someone has her head in the clouds."

They all continued to stare morosely, as though she hadn't finished. Sarah broke in. "You can call it anything you want. She is just making the point that you're using an unflattering name."

Mari was comforted by two friends. The rest of them defended the name, nicely. "I never heard that."

"I think it sounds nice."

"Like a Barry Manilow song."

"Like one of those little Chinese poems."

"I always thought if your head was in the clouds, that was nice, like you were really happy or something. Besides, castles are a neat theme for parties and stuff—can't you see Mark dressed up like a knight?" Giggles.

"And this way we can call ourselves the *Airheads!*" Screams of delight. Hyacinth's objection having been thus obliterated, Castle in the Air was voted in unanimously, with two abstentions, and it was decided that paints and brushes would be bought and the wing would be painted in this theme during the weeks to come. Presently the meeting adjourned.

"We've got forty minutes until the Candle Passing," observed Mitzi, "and until then we can have a social hour. But not a whole hour."

The meeting dissolved into chattering fragments. Sarah leaned toward Hyacinth to whisper in her ear, and Hyacinth tensed. They had been whispering to each other in turns for the last half hour, and as both had ticklish ears this had caused much hysterical lip-biting and snorting. Sarah did not really have to whisper now, but it was her turn. "What candle passing?" she asked.

Hyacinth's attempt to whisper back was met by violent resistance from Sarah, so they laughed and made a truce. "It's kind of complicated. It means something personal happened between someone and her boyfriend, so everyone else has to know about it. Listen. We've got to escape, okay?"

"Okay."

"Go to Room 103 when the alarm sounds."

"Alarm?" But Hyacinth was already gliding out.

Sarah was quickly trapped in a conversation group including Mitzi and Mari. She accepted a cup of Kool-Aid/vodka punch and smiled when she could. Everyone was being nice to her in case she felt like an idiot for having said those things during the meeting. Mari asked if her boyfriend helped out with the hard parts of being President and Sarah had to say that just now she didn't have a boyfriend.

"Ahaa!" said everyone. "Don't worry, Sarah, we'll see what we can come up with. No prob, now you're an Airhead."

Sarah was groping for an answer when the local smoke alarm howled and the Airheads moaned in disappointment. As they all trooped off to their rooms to make themselves a little more presentable, Sarah headed for Room 103, following a heavy trail of marijuana smoke with her nose. As this was only the smoke alarm, only the twelfth floor would be evacuated.

Hyacinth pulled Sarah into the room and carefully fitted a wet reefer to her lips. It was dark, and a young black woman was slumped over a desk asleep, stereo on loud. Hyacinth went to the vent window and released an amazing primal scream toward F Tower. After some prompting from her hostess, Sarah gave back the joint and followed suit. Hyacinth's sleeping roommate, Lucy, sat up, sighed, then went over and lay down on her bed. Sarah and Hyacinth sat on Hyacinth's bed and drank milk from an illegal mini-fridge in the closet.

They silently finished the joint, shaking their heads at each other and laughing in disbelief.

"Ever done LSD?" asked Sarah.

"No. Why? Got some?"

"Oh, jeez, I wasn't suggesting it. I was going to say, for a minute there I thought I was back on it. That's how unreal those people are to me."

"You think they're strange?" said Hyacinth. "I think they're very normal."

"That's what I'm afraid of. Your room is pretty nice; I feel very much at home here." It was a nice room, one of the few Plex rooms I ever saw that was pleasant to be in. It was full of illegal cooking appliances and stashes of food, and the walls had been illegally painted white. Wall hangings and plants were everywhere.

"Well, we were in the Army—Lucy and me," said Hyacinth, carefully fitting a roach clip. "That's almost like LSD."

By now their wing had been evacuated, and a couple of security guards were plodding up and down the hallways pretending to inspect for sources of smoke. Sarah and Hyacinth leaned together and spoke quietly.

"You're not real presidential," said Hyacinth. "People like you aren't supposed to take LSD."

"I don't take it anymore. See, back when I was about fourteen, my older sister was really into it, and I did it a few times."

"Why'd you stop?"

Sarah squinted into the milk carton and said nothing. Outside, the guards cursed to each other about students in general. Sarah finally said, "I kept an eye on my sister, and when she got cut loose completely—lost track of what was real and stopped caring—I saw it wasn't a healthy thing."

"So now you're President. I don't get it."

"The important thing is to get your life anchored in something. I think you have to make contact with the world in some way, and one way is to get involved."

"Student government?"

"Well, it beats MTV."

A guard beat on their door, attracted by the stereo-noise.

"Screw off," said Hyacinth in a loud stage whisper, flipping the bird toward the door. Sarah put her face in her hands and bent double with suppressed laughter. When she recovered, the guard had left and Hyacinth was smiling brightly.

"Jeezus!" said Sarah, "you're pretty blatant, aren't you?"

"If it's the quiet, polite type you want, go see the Airheads."

"You've lived with people like this before. Why don't they kick you off the wing?"

"Tokenism. They have to have tokens. Lucy is their token black, I'm their token individual. They love having a loudmouth around to disagree with them—makes them feel diverse."

"You don't think diplomacy would be more effective?"

"I'm not a diplomat. I'm me. Who are you?"

Instead of answering this difficult question, Sarah leaned back comfortably against the wall and closed her eyes. They listened to music for a long time as the Airheads breezed back onto the wing.

"I'd feel relaxed," said Sarah, "except I'm actually kind of guilty about missing the Candle Passing."

"That's ridiculous."

"You're right. You can say that and be totally sure of yourself, can't you? I admire you, Hyacinth."

"I like you, Sarah," said Hyacinth, and that summed it up.

In the Physics Library, Casimir Radon read about quantum mechanics. The digital watch on the wrist of the sleeping post-doc across the table read 8:00. That meant it was time to go upstairs and visit Professor Emeritus Walter Abraham Sharon, who worked odd hours. Casimir was not leaving just yet, though. He had found that Sharon was not the swiftest man in the world, and though the professor was by no means annoyed when Casimir showed up on time, Casimir preferred to come ten minutes late. Anyway, in the informal atmosphere of the Physics Department, appointments were viewed with a certain Heisenbergian skepticism, as though being in the right place at the right time would involve breaking a natural law and was therefore impossible to begin with. Outside the picture windows of the library, the ghettos of the City were filled with smoky light, and occasionally a meteor streaked past and crashed in flames in the access lot below. They were not actual meteors, but merely various objects soaked in lighter fluid, ignited and thrown from a floor in E Tower above, trailing fire and debris as they zoomed earthward.

Casimir found this perversely comforting. It was just the sort of insanity he hadn't been able to get away from during his first week at American Megaversity. Soon the miserable Casimir had taken me up on my offer to stop by at any time, showing up at my door just before midnight, wanting to cry but not about to. I took coffee, he took vodka, and soon we understood each other a little better. As he explained it, no one here had the least consideration for others, or the least ability to think for themselves, and this combination was hard to take after having been an adult. Nor had academics given him any solace; owing to the medieval tempo of the bureaucracy, he was still mired in kindergarten-level physics. Of course he could speed these courses up just by being there. Whenever a professor asked a question, rhetorical or not, Casimir shouted the answer immediately. This earned him the hatred and awe of his classmates, but it was his only source of satisfaction. As he waited for his situation to become sensible, he sat in on the classes he really wanted to take, in effect taking a double load.

"Because I'm sure Sharon is going to bring me justice," Casimir had declared, raising his voice above a grumble for the first time. "This guy makes sense! He's like you, and I can't understand how he ended up in this place. I never thought I'd be surprised by someone just because he is a sensible person and a good guy, but in this place it's a miracle. He cares about me, asks questions about my life—it's as though discovering what's best for me is a research project we're working on as a team. I can't believe a great man like him would care." Long, somber pause. "But I don't think even he can make up for what's wrong with this place. How about you, Bud? You're normal. What are you doing here?" Lacking an answer, I changed the subject to basketball.

A trio of meteors streaked across the picture windows and it was 8:10. Casimir returned his book and exited into the dark shiny hall. He was now at the upper limit of the Burrows, the bloc of the Plex that housed the natural sciences. Two floors above him, on the sixth and top floor of the base, was Emeritus Row, the plush offices of the academic superstars. He made his way there leisurely, knowing he was welcome.

Emeritus Row was dark and silent, illuminated only by the streak of warm yellow splashed away from Sharon's door. Casimir removed his glacier glasses. "Come in," came the melodious answer to his knock, and Casimir Radon entered his favorite room in the world.

Sharon looked at him with raised eyebrows. "Vell! You haff made a decision?"

"I think so."

"Let's have it! Leaving or staying? For the sake of physics I hope the latter."

Casimir abruptly realized he had not really made up his mind. He shoved his hands into his pockets and breathed deeply, a little surprised by all this. He could not keep a smile from his face, though, and could not ignore the hominess of Sharon's chaotic office. He announced that he was going to stay.

"Good, good," Sharon said absently. "Clear a place to sit." He gestured at a chair and Casimir set about removing thirty pounds of high-energy physics from it. Sharon said, "So you've decided to cross the Rubicon, eh?"

Casimir sat down, thought about it, and said with a half grin, "Or the Styx, whichever the case may be."

Sharon nodded, and as he did a resounding thump issued from above. Casimir jumped, but Sharon did not react.

"What was that?" Casimir asked. "Sounded big."

"Ach," said Sharon. "Trowing furniture again, I should guess. You know, don't you, that many of our students are very interested in the physics of falling bodies?" He delivered this, like all his bad jokes, slowly and solemnly, as though working out long calculations in his head. Casimir chuckled. Sharon winked and lit his pipe. "I am given to understand, from grapevine talk, that you are smarter than all of our professors except for me." He winked again through thick smoke.

"Oh. Well, I doubt it."

"Ach, I don't. No correlation between age and intelligence! You're just afraid to use your smarts! That's right. You'd rather suffer—it is your Polish blood. Anyway, you have much practical experience. Our professors have only book experience."

"Well, it's the book experience I want. It's handy to know electronics, but what I really like is pure principles. I can make more money designing circuits, if that's what I want."

"Exactly! You prefer to be a poor physicist. Well, I cannot argue with you wanting to know pure things. After all, you are not naïve, your life has been no more sheltered than mine."

Embarrassed, Casimir laughed. "I don't know about that. I haven't lived through any world wars yet. You've lived through two. I may have escaped from a slum, but you escaped from Peenemunde with a suitcase full of rocket diagrams."

Sharon's eyes crinkled at the corners. "Yet. A very important word, *nicht wahr?* You are not very old, yet."

"What do you mean? Do you expect a war?"

Sharon laughed deeply and slowly. "I have toured your residential towers with certain students of mine, and I was reminded of certain, er, locations during the occupation of the Sudetenland. I think from what I see"—the ceiling thumped again, and he gestured upward with his pipestem —"and hear, that perhaps you are in a war now."

Casimir laughed, but then sucked in his breath and sat back as Sharon glowered at him morosely. The old professor was very complicated, and Casimir always seemed to be taking missteps with him.

"War and violence are not very funny," said Sharon, "unless they happen to you—then they are funny because they haff to be. There is more violence up there than you realize! Even speech today has become a form of violence—even in the university. So pay attention to that, and don't worry about a war in Europe. Worry about it here, this is your home now."

"Yes, sir." After pausing respectfully, Casimir withdrew a clipboard from his pack and put it on Sharon's desk. "Or it will be my home as soon as you sign these forms. Mrs. Santucci will tear my arms off if I don't bring them in tomorrow."

Sharon sat still until Casimir began to feel uncomfortable. "*Ja,*" he finally said, "I guess you need to worry about forms too. Forms and forms and forms. Doesn't matter to me."

"Oh. It doesn't? You aren't retiring, are you?"

"*Ja*, I guess so."

Silently, Sharon separated the forms and laid them out on the Periodic Table of the Elements that covered his desk. He examined them with care for a few minutes, then selected a pen from a stein on his desk, which had been autographed by Enrico Fermi and Niels Bohr, and signed them.

"There, you're in the good courses now," he concluded. "Good to see you are so well Socioeconomically Integrated." The old man sat back in his chair, clasped his fingers over his flat chest, and closed his eyes.

A thunderous crash and Casimir was on the floor, dust in his throat and pea gravel on his back. Rubble thudded down from above and Casimir heard a loud inharmonious piano chord, which held steady for a moment and moaned downward in pitch until it was obliterated by an explosive splintering crack. More rubble flew around the room and he was pelted with small blocks. Looking down as he rubbed dust from his eyes he saw scores of strewn black and white piano keys.

Sharon was slumped over on his desk, and a trickle of

blood ran from his head and onto the back of his hand and puddled on the class change form beside his pipe. Gravel, rainwater and litter continued to slide down through the hole in the ceiling. Casimir alternately screamed and gulped as he staggered to his feet. He waded through shattered ceiling panels and twisted books to Sharon's side and saw with horror that the old man's side had been pierced by a shard of piano frame shot out like an arrow in the explosion. With exquisite care he helped him lean back, cleared the desk of books and junk, then picked up his thin body and set him atop the desk. He propped up Sharon's head with the 1938 issues of the *Physical Review* and tried to ease his breathing. The head wound was superficial and already clotting, but the side wound was ghastly and Casimir did not even know whether to remove the splinter. Blood built up at the corners of Sharon's mouth as he gasped and wheezed. Brushing tears and dirt from his own face, Casimir looked for the phone.

He started away as a small bat fluttered past.

"Troglodyte! No manners! This is what you're supposed to see!" Casimir whirled to see Bert Nix plunging from the open door toward Sharon's desk. Casimir tried to head him off, fearing some kind of attack, but Bert Nix stopped short and pointed triumphantly to Sharon. Casimir turned to look. Sharon was gazing at him dully through half-shut eyes, and weakly pounding his finger into a spot on the tabletop. Casimir leaned over and looked. Sharon was pointing at the Table of the Elements, indicating the box for Oxygen.

"Oxygen! Oh two! Get it?" shouted Bert Nix.

Bill Benson, Security Guard 5, was arguing with a friend whether it was possible that F.D.R. committed suicide when the emergency line rang. He let it ring four times. Since ninety-nine calls out of a hundred were pranks, by letting each one ring four times he was delaying the true emergency calls by an average of only four one-hundredths of a ring apiece—nothing compared with the time it took to respond. Anyway, he was fed up with kids getting stoned at parties and falling down on the way out to barf and spraining their wrists, then (through some miracle of temporary clearheadedness) calling Emergency and trying to articulate their problems through a hallucinogenic miasma while monster stereos in the background threatened to uncurl his phone cord. Eventually, though, he did pick up the phone, holding the earpiece several inches from his head in case it was another of those goddamn Stalinist whistle-blasters.

"Listen," came the voice, sounding distant, "I've got to have some oxygen. Do you have some there? It's an emergency!"

Oh, shit, Did he have to get this call every night? He listened for a few more seconds. "It's an oxygen freak," he said to his friend, covering the mouthpiece with his hand.

"Oxygen freak? What do they do with oxygen?"

Benson swung his feet down from the counter, put the receiver in his lap, and explained. "See, nitrous oxide, or laughing gas, is the big thing. They breathe it through masks, like for surgery. But if you breathe it pure you'll kick in no time, because you got to have oxygen. And they are so crazy about laughing gas they don't want to take off that mask even to breathe, so they like to get some oxygen to mix with it so that they can sit there all goddamn night long and breathe nothing else and get blasted out of their little minds. So we always get these calls."

He picked up the receiver again, took a puff on his cigar, exhaled slowly. "Hello?" he said, hoping the poor gas-crazed sap had hung up.

"Yeah? When will it be here?"

"Cripes!" Bill Benson shouted, "look, guy, hang it up. We don't have any and you aren't allowed to have it."

"Well, shit then, come up here and help me. Call an ambulance! For God's sake, a man's dying here."

Some of these kids were such cretins, how did they make it into college? Money, probably. "Listen, use your head, kid," he said, not unkindly. "We're the Emergency Services desk. We can't leave our posts. What would happen if there was an emergency while we were gone?"

This was answered by silence; but in the background,

Benson could just make out another voice, which sounded familiar: "You should have listened to what he was trying to tell you! He wasn't farting around! We had to sack the Cartography Department to afford him. And you don't listen!"

"Shut up!" shouted the gas freak.

"Hey, is that Bert? Is that Bert Nix on the phone?" asked Bill Benson. "Where are you, kid?"

"Emeritus Row!" shouted the kid, and dropped the phone. Bill Benson continued to listen after the BONKITY-BONK of the phone's impact, trying to make sure it was really good old Bert Nix. I think he heard this poem; on the news, he claimed he heard *a* poem, and it could well have been this, which Bert Nix quoted regularly and liked to write on the walls:

Tenuring and tenuring in the ivory tower!
The flagon cannot fill the flagoneers.
Krupp cuts a fart! The sphinxter cannot hold
Dear academe, our *Lusitania*, recoils.
The time-limned dons are noosed. With airy webs
The cerebrally infarcted bring me down.
The East affects conscription, while the curst
Are gulled with Fashionate Propensities.

Shrilly, sum reevaluation is demanded.
Earlier-reckoned commencement is programmed!
What fecund mumming! Outly ward those words hard
When a glassed grimace on an animal Monday
Rumbles at night; unaware that the plans aren't deserved
Escapists' lie-panoply aims to head off the Fan.
A sign frank and witless as the Sun
Is mute in the skies, yet from it are shouted
Real shadows of endogenous deserted words.
The concrete drops down in; but know I now
That thirty-storied stone steel keeps
When next the might of Air are rooks unstable.
What buff beast, its towers coming down deglassed
Slumps amid Bedlam in the morn?

"Holy shit!" cried Bill Benson. "Bert? Is that you? Hell, maybe something's up. Sam, punch me onto line six there and I'll see if I can raise the folks down at nine-one-one."

Casimir was careening through the halls, cursing himself for having had to leave Sharon alone with a derelict, adrenaline blasting through him as he imagined coming back to find the old man dead. He didn't know how he was going to open the door when he got where he was going, but at the moment it did not matter because no slab of wood and plastic, it seemed, could stand in his way. He veered around a corner, smashing into a tall young man who had been coming the other way. They both sprawled dazed on the floor, but Casimir rolled and sprang to his feet and resumed running. The man he had collided with caught up with him, and he realized that it was Virgil Gabrielsen, King of the Burrows.

"Virgil! Did you hear that?"

"Yeah, I was coming to check it out. What's up?"

"Piano fell into Sharon's office . . . pierced lung . . . oxygen."

"Right," said Virgil, and skidded to a stop, fishing a key from his pocket. He master-keyed his way into a lab and they sent a grad student sprawling against a workbench as they made for the gas canisters. Casimir grabbed a bottle-cart and they feverishly strapped the big cylinder onto it, then wheeled it heavily out the door and back toward Sharon.

"Shit," said Virgil, "no freight elevator. No way to get it upstairs." They were at the base of the stairs, two floors below Sharon. The oxygen was about five feet tall and one foot in diameter, and crammed with hundreds of pounds of extremely high-pressure gas. Virgil was still thinking about it when Casimir, a bony and unhealthy looking man, bear-hugged the canister, straightened up, and hoisted it to his shoulder as he would a roll of carpet. He took the stairs two at a time, Virgil bounding along behind.

Shortly, Casimir had slammed the cylinder down on the floor near Sharon. Bert Nix was holding Sharon's hand, mumbling and occasionally making the sign of the cross. As Virgil closed the door, Casimir held the top valve at arm's length, buried one ear in his shoulder, and opened it up. Virgil just had time to plug his ears.

The room was inundated in a devastating hiss, like the shriek of an injured dragon. Casimir's hands were knocked aside by the fabulously high pressure of the escaping oxygen. Papers blizzarded and piano keys skittered across the floor. Ignoring it, Bert Nix stuffed Kleenex into Sharon's ears, then into his own.

In a minute Sharon began to breathe easier. At the same time his pipe-ashes burst into a small bonfire, ignited by the high oxygen levels. Casimir was making ready to stomp it out when Virgil pushed him gently aside; he had been wise enough to yank a fire extinguisher from the wall on their way up. Once the fire was smothered, Virgil commenced what first aid was possible on Sharon. Casimir returned to the Burrows and, finding an elevator, brought up more oxygen and a regulator. Using a garbage bag they were able to rig a crude oxygen tent.

The ambulance crew arrived in an hour. The technicians loaded Sharon up and wheeled him away, Bert Nix advising them on Sharon's favorite foods.

I passed this procession on my way there—Casimir had called to give me the news. When I arrived in the doorway of Sharon's office, I beheld an unforgettable scene: Virgil and Casimir knee-deep in wreckage; a desk littered with the torn-open wrappers of medical supplies; Virgil holding up a sheaf of charred, bloodstained, fire-extinguisher-caked forms; and Casimir laughing loudly beneath the opened sky.

October

At the front of the auditorium, Professor Embers spoke. He never lectured; he spoke. In the middle of the auditorium his audience of five hundred sat back in their seats, staring up openmouthed into the image of the Professor on the nearest color TV monitor. In the back of the auditorium, Sarah sat in twilight, trying to balance the Student Government budget.

"So grammar is just the mode in which we image concepts," the professor was saying. "Grammar is like the walls and bumpers of a pinball machine. Rhetoric is like the flippers of a pinball machine. You control the flippers. The rest of the machine—grammar—controls everything else. If you use the flippers well, you make points. If you fail to image your concepts viably, your ball drops into the black hole of nothingness. If you try to cheat, the machine tilts and you lose—that's like people not understanding your interactions. That's why we have to learn Grammar here in Freshman. That, and because S. S. Krupp says we have to."

There was a pause of several seconds, and then a hundred or so people laughed. Sarah did not. Unlike the freshmen in the class, who thought Professor Embers was a cool guy, Sarah thought he was a bore and a turkey. He continued to speak, and she continued to balance.

This was the budget for *this* semester, and it was supposed to have been done *last* semester. But last semester the records had been gulped by a mysterious computer error, and now Sarah had to reconstruct them so that the government could resume debate. She had some help from me in this, though I don't know how much good it did. We had met early in the year, at a reception for faculty-in-residence, and later had a lunch or two together and talked about American Megaversity. If nothing else, my suite was a quiet and pleasant enough place where she could spread her papers out and work uninterrupted when she needed to.

She could also work uninterrupted in her Freshman English class, because she was a senior English major with a 3.7 average and didn't need to pay much attention.

Her first inkling that something was wrong had been in midsummer, when the megaversity's computer scheduling system had scheduled her for Freshman English automatically, warning that she had failed to meet this requirement during her first year.

"Look," she had said to the relevant official when she arrived in the fall, "I'm an English major. I know this stuff. Why are you putting me in Freshman English?"

The General Curriculum Advisor consulted little codes printed by the computer, and looked them up in a huge computer-printed book. "Ah," he said, "was one of your parents a foreign national?"

"My stepmother is from Wales."

"That explains it. You see." The official had swung around toward her and assumed a frank, open body-language posture. "Statistical analysis shows that children of one or more foreign nationals are often gifted with Special Challenges."

Sarah's spine arched back and she set her jaw. "You're saying I can't speak English because my stepmother was Welsh?"

"Special Challenges are likely in your case. You were mistakenly exempted from Freshmen English because of your high test scores. This exemption option has now been retroactively waived for your convenience."

"I don't want it waived. It's not convenient."

"To ensure maintenance of high academic standards, the waiver is avolitional."

"Well, that's bullshit." This was not a very effective thing to say. Sarah wished that Hyacinth could come talk for her; Hyacinth would not be polite, Hyacinth would say completely outrageous things and they would scatter in terror. "There's no way I can accept that." Drawn to the noise like scavengers, two young clean-cut advisors looked in the door with open and understanding smiles. Everyone smiled except for Sarah. But she knew she was right this time—she knew damn well what language was spoken in Wales these days. They could smile stupidly until blue in the face. When the advisor hinted that she was asking for special treatment because she was President, she gave him a look that snapped his composure for a second, a small but helpful triumph.

She had done it by the books, filing a petition requesting to be discharged from Freshman English. But her petition was rejected because of a computer error which made it appear that she had gotten 260 instead of 660 on her SATs. By the time an extra score report from the testing company proved that she was smart after all, it was too late to drop or add classes—so, Freshman English it was.

The end of the class approached at last, and Professor Embers handed back this week's essays. The assignment was to select a magazine ad and write about how it made you feel.

"I've been epiphanied by the quality of your essays this week," said Professor Embers. "We hardly had to give out any C's this time around. I have them alphabetized by your first names up here in sixteen stacks, one for each section."

All five hundred students went down at once to get theirs. Sarah worked for ten minutes, then gathered her things and headed for the front, dawdling on purpose. Clustered around the stack of papers for her section she could see five of the Stalinists—for some reason they had all ended up in her section. Since she never attended section meetings, this was no problem, but she did not want to encounter them at times like this either. Standing there tall and straight as a burned-out sapling in a field was Dexter Fresser, an important figure in the Stalinist Underground Battalion. Most of all, she wanted to avoid him. Sarah and Dex had gone to the same high school in Ohio, ridden the same bus to school, slept in the same bed thirteen times and shared the same LSD on three occasions. Since then, Dex had hardly ever not taken lots of acid. Sarah had taken none. Now he was a weird rattle-minded radical who nevertheless remembered her, and she avoided him scrupulously.

About halfway down the aisle she found a television monitor displaying an image of Dex. She sank deeply into a seat and watched him and his comrades. Dex was reading a paper desultorily and she knew it was hers. He flipped aimlessly through it, as though searching for a particular word or phrase, then shook his head helplessly and dropped it back on the stack. Finally the last of them excavated his paper and they were collectively gone, leaving behind several dozen essays no one had bothered to pick up.

Associate Professor Archibald Embers, Learning Facilitator of Freshman English G Group, was regarding a young woman on his sofa and endeavoring to keep his pipe lit. This required a lot of upside-down work with his butane lighter and he thought the burn on his thumb might be second-degree. This particular woman was definitely confrontational, though, and it was no time to show pain. He held the pipe cautiously and reached out with the other hand to drape his thumb casually over the rim of a potted plant, thrusting the roasted region deeply into the cool humus. *I am Antaeus,* he thought, *and yet I am Prometheus, singed by my own flame.* They were sitting in the conversation pit he had installed so as to avoid talking to students across his desk like some kind of authoritarian. Or was it totalitarian? He could never remember the distinction.

This woman was clearly high voltage, Type A, low-alpha and left-hemisphere, with very weird resonances. Seeing her through to the end of her crisis would be painful. She had ripped off a lot of papers from the auditorium and had brought them here into his space to fine-tooth comb them. She had a problem with her grade, a B.

"Now," she continued, whipping over another page, "let's look at page two of this one, which is about an advertisement for Glans Essence Cologne. 'The point of this is about these foxes. He has a bunch. On him. He a secret agent, like Bond James Bond or something. Or some other person with lots of foxes. Why he has foxes? Is Glans Essence Cologne. They hope you figuring that out, will buy some of it. Which is what they are selling.' Now, next to that in the margin you wrote, 'excellent analysis of the working of the ad.' Then at the end you wrote, 'Your understanding of how the System brainwashes us is why I gave you an A on this paper.' Now really, if you want to give him an A for that it's up to you, but you can you then give me a B? Mine was three times as long, I had an introduction, conclusion, an outline, no grammatical errors, no misspelled words—what do you expect?"

"This is a very good question," said Embers. He took a long draw on his pipe. "What is a grade? That is the question." He chuckled, but she apparently didn't get it. "Some teachers grade on curves. You have to be a math major to understand your grade! But forget those fake excuses. A grade is actually a form of poetry. It is a subjective reaction to a learner's work, distilled and reduced down to its purest essence—not a sonnet, not a haiku, but a single letter. That's remarkable, isn't it?"

"Look, that's just groovy. But you have to grade in such a way that I'm shown to be a better writer than he is. Otherwise it's unfair and unrealistic."

Embers recrossed his legs and spent a while sucking his pipe back into a blaze. His learner picked up a paper and fanned smoke away from her face. "Mind if I smoke?" he said.

"Your office," she said in a strangled voice.

Fine, if she didn't want to assert herself. He finally decided on the best approach. "You aren't necessarily a better writer. You called some of them functional illiterates. Well those illiterates, as you called them, happen to have very expressive prose voices. Remember that in each person's own dialect he or she is perfectly literate. So in the sense of having escaped orthodoxy to be truly creative, they are highly advanced wordsmiths, while you are still struggling to break free of grammatical rules systems. They express themselves to me and I react with little one-letter poems of my own—the essence of grading! Poetry! And being a poet I'm particularly well suited for it. Your idea of tearing down these proto-artists because they aren't just like you smacks of a kind of absolutism which is very disturbing in a temple of academic freedom."

They sat there silent for a while.

"You really said that, didn't you?" she finally asked.

"I did."

"Huh. So we're just floating around without any standards at all."

"You could put it that way. You should interact with the department chairman on this. Look, there is no absolute reality, right? We can't force everyone to express themselves through the same absolute rules."

When the young woman left she seemed curiously drained and quiet. Indeed, absorbing new world-views could be a sobering experience. Embers found a blister on his thumb, and was inspired to write a haiku.

There came the sound of a massive ring of keys being slapped against the outside of Casimir Radon's door. He looked up from the papers on his desk, and in his lap Spike the illicit kitten followed suit, scrambling to red-alert status and scything sixteen claws into his thigh. Before Casimir had opened his mouth to say "Who is it" or Spike could spring forward to engage the foe, the door was unlocked and thrown open. A short, heavy man with a disconcerting resemblance to Leonid Brezhnev stepped into the room.

"Stermnator," he mumbled, rolling the r's on his tongue like Black Sea caviar. Casimir covered Spike with his hand, hoping to prevent detection, and the kitten grasped a finger between its forepaws and began to rasp with its tongue.

Behind the B-man was a small wiry old guy with chloracne, who bore a metal canister with a pump on top and a tube leading to a nozzle in his hand. Before Casimir could even grunt in response, this man had stepped crisply into the room and begun to apply a heavy mist to the baseboards. The B-man glowered darkly at Casimir, who sat in silence and watched as the exterminator walked around the room, nozzle to wall, spraying everything near the baseboards, including shoes, Spike's food and water dishes, a typewriter, two unmatched socks, a book and a calculator charger. Both the strangers looked around the inside of his nearly barren room with faint expressions of incomprehension or disdain.

By the time Casimir got around to saying, "That's okay, I haven't seen any bugs in here since I moved in," the sprayer was bearing down on him inexorably. Casimir pushed the kitten up against his stomach, grasped the hem of his extra-long seven-year-old Wall Drug T-shirt, and pulled it up to form a little sling for the struggling creature, crossing his arms over the resulting bulge in an effort to hold and conceal. At the same time he stood and scampered out of the path of the exterminator, who bumped into him and knocked him off balance onto the bed, arms still crossed. He bounced back up, weaved past the exterminator, and stood with his back to the door, staring nonchalantly out the window at the view of E Tower outside. Behind him, the exterminator paused near the exit to soak the straps of an empty duffel bag. As Casimir watched the reflection of the two men closing the door he was conscious of a revolting chemical odor. Immediately he whirled and tossed Spike onto the bed, then took his food and water dishes out to wash them in the bathroom.

Casimir had seen his first illicit kitten on the floor above his, when he had forgotten to push his elevator button. He got off on the floor above to take the stairs down one flight, and saw some students playing with the animal in the hallway. After some careful inquiries he made contact with a kitten pusher over the phone. Two weeks later Casimir, his directions memorized, went to the Library at 4:15 in the morning. He proceeded to the third floor and pulled down the January–March 1954 volume of the *Soviet Asphalt Journal* and placed two twenty-dollar bills inside the cover. He then went to the serials desk, where he was waited on by a small, dapper librarian in his forties.

"I would like to report," he said, opening the volume, "that pages 1738 through 1752 of this volume have been razored out, and they are exactly the pages I need."

"I see," the man said sympathetically.

"And while I'm here, I have some microfilms to pick up, which I got on interlibrary loan."

"Ah, yes, I know the ones you're talking about. Just a moment, please." The librarian disappeared into a back office and emerged a minute later with a large box filled with microfilm reel boxes. Casimir picked it up, finding it curiously light, smiled at the librarian and departed. A pass had already been made out for him, and the exit guard waved him through. Back in his room, he pulled out the top layer of microfilm boxes to find, curled up on a towel, a kitten recovering from a mild tranquilizer.

Since then Spike had been neither mild nor tranquil, but that at least provided Casimir with some of the unpredictability that Plex life so badly lacked. He almost didn't mind having a kitten run around the obstacle course of his room at high speed for hours at a time in the middle of the night, because it gave his senses something not utterly flat to perceive. Even though Spike tried to sleep on his face, and hid all small important articles in odd places, Casimir was charmed.

He pulled on his glacier glasses in a practiced motion and stepped out into the hall. Casimir's wing was only two floors away from allies of the Wild and Crazy Guys, best partiers in the Plex, and two Saturdays ago they had come down with their spray paint and painted giant red, white and blue twelve-spoked wheels between each pair of doors. These were crude representations of the Big Wheel, a huge neon sign outside the Plex, which the Wild and Crazy Guys pretended to worship as a joke and initiation ritual. This year they had become aggressive graffitists, painting Big Wheels almost everywhere in the Plex. Casimir, used to it, walked down this gallery of giant wheels to the bathroom, Spike's dishes in hand.

The bathrooms in the wings looked on the inside like microwave ovens or autoclaves, with glossy green tile on the walls, brilliant lighting, overwaxed floors and so much steam that entering one was like entering a hallucination. At one end of the bathroom, three men and their girlfriends were taking showers, drinking, shouting a lot and generally being Wild and Crazy. They were less than coherent, but most of what Casimir could make out dealt with Anglo-Saxon anatomical terms and variations on "what do you think of *this*" followed by prolonged yelling from the partner. Casimir was tempted to stay and listen, but reasoned that since he was still a virgin anyway there was no point in trying to learn anything advanced, especially by eavesdropping. He went down the line of closely spaced sinks until he found one that had not been stuffed with toilet paper or backed up with drain crud.

As he was washing Spike's dishes, a guy came in the door with a towel around his waist. He looked conventional, though somewhat blocky, athletic and hairless. He came up and stood very close to Casimir, staring at him wordlessly for a long time as though nearsighted; Casimir ignored him, but glanced at him from time to time in the mirror, looking between two spokes of a Big Wheel that had been drawn on it with shaving cream.

After a while, he tugged on Casimir's sleeve. "Hey," he mumbled, "can I borrow your"

Casimir said nothing.

"Huh?" said the strange guy.

"I don't know," said Casimir. "Depends on what you want. Probably not."

A grin gradually sprouted on the man's face and he turned around as though smirking with imaginary friends behind him. "Oh, Jeez," he said, and turned away. "I *hate* fuckers like you!" he yelled, and ran to the lockers across from the sinks, running a few steps up the wall before sprawling back down on the floor again. Casimir watched him in the mirror as he went from locker to locker, finally finding an unlocked one. The strange guy pawed through it and selected a can of shaving cream. "Hey," he said, and looked at the back of Casimir's head. "Hey, Wall."

Casimir looked at him in the mirror. "What is it?"

The strange guy did not understand that Casimir was looking right at him. "Hey *fucker! Cocksucker! Mr. Drug! You!*" Rhythmic female shrieking began to emanate from a shower stall.

"What is it," Casimir yelled back, refusing to turn.

The strange guy approached him and Casimir turned half around defensively. He stood very close to Casimir. "Your hearing isn't very good," he shouted, "you should take off your glasses."

"Do you want something? If so, you should just tell me."

"Do you think he'd mind if I used this?"

"Who?"

The strange guy smirked and shook his head. "Do you know anything about terriers?"

"No."

"Ah, well." The strange guy put the shaving cream on the shelf in front of Casimir, muttered something incomprehensible, laughed, and walked out of the bathroom.

Casimir dried the food bowl under an automatic hand dryer by the door. As he was on his third push of the button, a couple from one of the showers walked nude into the room, getting ten feet from cover before they saw Casimir.

The woman screamed, clapping her hands over her face. "Oh Jeez, Kevin, there's a *guy* in here!" Kevin was too mellowed by sex and beer to do anything but smile wanly. Casimir walked out without saying anything, breathed deeply of the cool, dry air of the hallway, and returned to his room, where he filled Spike's water bowl with spring water from a bottle.

. . .

As soon as Casimir had heard about Neutrino, the official organization of physics majors, he had crashed a meeting and got himself elected President and Treasurer. Casimir was like that, meek most of the time with occasional bursts of effectiveness. He walked into the meeting, which so far consisted of six people, and said, "Who's the president?"

The others, being physics majors and therefore accustomed to odd behavior of all sorts, had answered. "He graduated," said one.

"No, when he graduated, he stopped being our president. When the guy who *was* our president graduated, we instantaneously ceased to have one," another countered.

"I agree," a third added, "but the proper term is 'was graduated.' "

"That's pedantic."

"That's *correct.* Where's the dictionary?"

"Who cares? Why do you want to know?" the first asked. As the other two consulted a dictionary, a fourth member held a calculator in his hand, gnawing absently on the charger cord, and the other two members argued loudly about an invisible diagram they were drawing with their fingers on a blank wall.

"I want to be president of this thing," Casimir said. "Any objections?"

"Oh, that's okay. We thought you were from the administration or something."

Casimir's motivation for all this was that after the Sharon incident, it was impossible for him to escape from his useless courses. The grimness of what had happened, and the hopelessness of his situation, had left him quiet and listless for a couple of weeks to the point where I was beginning to feel alarmed. One night, then, from two to four in the morning, Casimir's neighbor had watched *Rocky* on cable and the sleeping Casimir had subconsciously listened in on the soundtrack. He awoke in the morning with a sense of mission, of destiny, a desire to go out and beat the fuckers at their own game. Neutrino provided a suitable power base, and since his classes only consumed about six hours a week he had all the time in the world.

Previous to Casimir's administration most of the money allotted to Neutrino had been dispersed among petty activities such as dinners, trips to nuclear reactors, insipid educational gadgets and the like. Casimir's plan was to spend all the money on a single project that would exercise the minds of the members and, in the end, produce something useful. Once he had convinced the pliable membership of Neutrino that this was a good idea, his suggestion for the actual project was not long in coming: construction of a mass driver.

The mass driver was a magnetic device for throwing things. It consisted of a long straight rail, a "bucket" that slid along the rail on a magnetic cushion and powerful electromagnets that kicked the bucket down the rail. When the bucket slammed to a halt at the rail's end, whatever was in it kept on going—theoretically, very, very fast. Recently this simple machine had become a pet project of Professor Sharon, who had advocated it as a lunar mining tool. Casimir argued that the idea was important and interesting in and of itself, and that Sharon's connection to it lent it sentimental value. As a tribute to Sharon, a fun project and a toy that would be a blast to play with when finished, the mass driver was irresistible to Neutrino. Which was just as well, because nothing was going to stop Casimir from building this son of a bitch.

Casimir had been drawing up a budget for it on this particular evening, because budget time for the Student Government was coming up soon. Not long after the exterminator's visit, Casimir got stuck. Many of the supplies he needed were standard components that were easy for him to get, but certain items, such as custom-wound electromagnets, were hard to budget for. This was the sort of fabrication that had to be done at the Science Shop, and that meant dealing with Virgil Gabrielsen. After nailing down as much as he could, Casimir gathered his things and set out on the half-hour elevator ride to the bottom of the Burrows.

In the interests of efficiency, security, ease of design and healthy interplay among the departments, the designers of the Campustructure had put all the science departments together in a single bloc. It was known as the Burrows because it was mostly below street level, and because of the allegedly Morlockian qualities of its inhabitants. At the top of the Burrows were the departmental libraries and conference rooms. Below were professors' offices and departmental headquarters, followed by classrooms, labs, stockrooms and at the very bottom, forty feet below ground level, the enormous CC—Computing Center—and the Science Shop. Any researcher wanting glass blown, metal shaped, equipment fixed, circuits designed or machines assembled, had to come down and beg for succor at the feet of the stony-hearted Science Shop staff. This meant trying to track down Lute, the hyperactive Norwegian technician, rumored to have the power of teleportation, who held smart people in disdain because of their helplessness in practical matters, or Zap, the electronics specialist, a motorcycle gang sergeant-at-arms who spent his working hours boring out engine blocks for his brothers and threatening professors with bizarre and deadly tortures. Zap was the cheapest technician the Science Shop steering committee had been able to find, Lute had been retained at high salary after dire threats from all faculty members and Virgil, to the immense relief of all, had been hired three years earlier as a part-time student helper and had turned the place around.

Science Shop was at the end of a dark unmarked hallway that smelled of machine oil and neoprene, half blocked by junked and broken equipment. When Casimir arrived he relaxed instantly in the softly lit, wildly varied squalor of the place, and soon found Virgil sipping an ale and twiddling painstakingly with wires and pulleys on an automatic plotter.

They went into his small office and Virgil provided himself and Casimir with more ale. "What's the latest on Sharon?" he asked.

"The same. No word," Casimir said, pushing the toes of his tennis shoes around in the sawdust and metal filings on the floor. "Not quite in a coma, definitely not all there. Whatever he lost from oxygen starvation isn't coming back."

"And they haven't caught anyone."

"Well, E14 is the Performing Arts Floor. They used to have a room with a piano in it. The E13S people didn't like it because the Performing Artists were always tap dancing."

"We know how sensitive those poor boys are to noise."

"A couple of days before the piano crash, the piano was stolen from E14. Two of the tap-dancers had their doors ignited the same night. A couple of days later, E13S had a burning-furniture-throwing contest, and it just happens that at the same time a piano crashed through Sharon's ceiling. Circumstantial evidence only."

Virgil clasped his hands over his flat belly and looked at the ceiling. "Though a pattern of socio-heterodox behaviors has been exhibited by individuals associated with E13S, we find it preferable to keep them within the system and counsel them constructively rather than turn them over to damaging outside legal interference which would hinder resocialization. The Megaversity is a free community of individuals seeking to grow together toward a more harmonious and enlightened future, and introduction of external coercion merely stifles academic freedom and—"

"How did you know that?" asked Casimir, amazed. "That's word for word what they said the other day."

Virgil shrugged. "Official policy statement. They used it two years ago, in the barbell incident. E13 dropped a two-hundred-pound barbell through the roof of the Cafeteria's main kitchen area. It crashed into a pressure vat and caused a tuna-nacho casserole explosion that wounded fifteen. And the pressure is so high in those vats, you know, that Dr. Forksplit, the Dean of Dining Services, who was standing nearby, had a nacho tortilla chip shard driven all the way through his skull. He recovered, but they've called him Wombat ever since. The people who handle this in the Administration don't understand how deranged these students are. Now, Krupp and his people would like to pour molten lead down their throats, but they can't do anything about it—the decisions are made by a committee of tenured faculty."

Casimir resisted an impulse to scream, got up and paced around talking through clenched teeth. "This shit really, *really* pisses me off. It's incredible. Law doesn't exist here, you can do what you please."

"Well," said Virgil, still blasé, "I disagree. There's always law. Law is just the opinion of the guy with the biggest gun. Since outside law rarely matters in the Plex, we make our own law, using whatever power—whatever guns—we have. We've been very successful in the Science Shop."

"Oh, yeah? I suppose this was something to do with what you said the other day about some unofficial work here for me."

"That's a perfect example. The researchers of American Megaversity need your services. It's illegal, but the scientific faculty have more power than the rule-enforcers, so we make our own law regarding technical work. You keep track of what you do, and I pay you through the vitality fund.

"The what?"

"The fund made up of donations from various professors and firms who have a vested interest in keeping the Science Shop running smoothly. Hell, it's all just grant money. In the egalitarian system we had before, *nobody* got *anything* done."

"Look." Casimir shook his head and sat back down. "I don't want even to hear all this. You know, all I've ever wanted to be is a normal student. They won't let me take decent classes, okay, so I work on the mass driver. Now I come here to get your help and you start talking about local law and free enterprise. I just want some estimates from you on getting these electromagnets wound for the mass driver. Okay? Forget free enterprise." Casimir dropped a page of diagrams and specifications on Virgil's desk.

Virgil looked it over. "Well, it depends," he finally said. "If we pretend you're just a normal student, then I will charge you, oh, about ten thousand dollars for this stuff and have it done by the time you graduate. Now, unofficially, I could log it in as something much simpler and charge you less. But you can't put that into a formal budget proposal. Very unofficially, I might do it for a small bribe, like some help from you around the Shop. But that's really abnormal to put in a budget. Looks like you're stuck."

"It wouldn't really take you three years."

"It *would* take *me*." Virgil waved at the door. "Zap could do it in a week. Want to ask him? He's not hard to wake up."

Casimir brooded momentarily. "Well, look. I don't really care how it gets done. But it's necessary to have something on paper, you know?"

Virgil shook his head, smiling. "Casimir. You don't think anyone pays any attention to those budgets, do you?"

"Aw, shit. This is too weird for me."

"It's not weird, you're just not used to it yet. Here is what we'll do. We work out a friendly gentlemen's agreement by which I make the magnets for you, probably over Christmas vacation, in exchange for a little of your expert help around the Science Shop. When I'm done with the magnets I put them in an old box and mark it, say, 'SPARE PARTS, 1932 AUTOMATIC BOMBSIGHT PROTOTYPE.' I dump it in the storeroom. When budget time comes around you say, 'Oh, gee, it happens I've designed this thing to use existing parts, I know just where they are.' Ridiculous, but no one knows that, and those who understand won't want to meddle in any arrangement of mine."

"Okay!" Casimir threw up his hands. "Okay. Fine. I'll do it. Just tell me what to do and don't let me see any of this illegal stuff."

"It's not illegal, I said it was legal. Hang on a sec while I Xerox these pages."

Virgil opened the door and was met by a clamor of voices from several advanced academic figures. Casimir looked around the room: a firetrap stuffed with books and papers and every imaginable variety of electronic junk. A Geiger counter hung out the window into a deep air shaft, clicking every second or two. In one corner a 1940's radio was hooked up to a technical power supply and wired into the guts of a torn-open telephone so that Virgil could make hands-off phone calls. An old backless TV in another corner enabled Virgil to monitor the shop outside. Electronic parts, hunks of wire, junk-food wrappers and scraps of paper littered the floor. And in three separate places sat those little plastic trays Casimir saw everywhere, overflowing with tiny seeds—rat poison.

"Damn!" spat Casimir as Virgil reentered. "There's enough of that poison in this room alone to kill every rat in this city. What's their problem with that stuff anyway?"

Virgil snorted. Everyone knew the rat poison was ubiquitous; the wastebaskets might go a month without emptying, but when it came to rat poison the B-men were fearsomely diligent, seeming to pass through walls and locked doors like Shaolin priests to scatter the poison-saturated kernels. "It's cultural," he explained. "They hate rats. You should read some Scythian mythology. In Crotobaltislavonia it's a capital crime to harbor them. That's why they had a revolution! The old regime stopped handing out free rat poison."

"I'm serious," said Casimir. "I've got an illegal kitten in my room, and if they keep breaking in to spread poison, they'll find it or let it out or poison it."

"Or eat it. Seriously, you should have mentioned it, Casimir. Let me help you out."

Casimir rested his face in his hand. "I suppose you also have an arrangement with the B-men."

"No, no, much too complicated. I do almost all my work at the computer terminal, Casimir. You can accomplish anything there. See, a few years ago a student had a boa constrictor in his room that got poisoned by the B-men, and even though it was illegal he sued the university for damages and won. There are still a lot of residents with pets whom the administration doesn't want to antagonize, because of connections or whatever. Some students are even allergic to the poison. So, they keep a list of rooms which are not to be given any poison. All I have to do is put your room on it."

Casimir was staring intently at Virgil. "Wait a minute. How did you get that kind of access? Aren't there locks? Access checks?"

"There are some annoyances involved."

"I suppose with photographic memory you could do a lot on the computer."

"Helps to have the Operator memorized too."

"Oh, fuck! No!"

Casimir, I am sure, was just as surprised as I had been. The Operator was an immense computer program consisting entirely of numbers—machine code. Without it, the machine was a useless lump. With the Operator installed, it was a tool of nearly infinite power and flexibility. It was to the computer as memory, instinct and intelligence are to the human brain.

Virgil handed Casimir a canister of paper computer tape. The label read, "1843 SURINAM CENSUS DATA VOLUME 5. FIREWOOD USAGE ESTIMATES AND PROJECTIONS."

"Ignore that," said Virgil. "It's a program in machine code. It'll put your room on the no-poison list, and your cat will be safe, unless the B-men forget or decide to ignore the rule, which is a possibility."

Casimir barely looked at the tape and stared distantly at Virgil. "What have you been doing with this knowledge?" he whispered. "You could get back at E13S."

Virgil smiled. "Tempting. But when you can do what I can, you don't go for petty revenge. All I do, really, is fight the Worm, which is really my only passion these days. It's why I stay around instead of getting a decent job. It's a sabotage program. It's probably the greatest intellectual achievement of the nineteen-eighties, and it's the only thing I've ever found that is so *indescribably* difficult and complex and beautiful that I haven't gotten bored with it."

"Why would anyone do such a thing? It must be costing the Megaversity millions."

"I don't know," said Virgil, "but it's great to have a challenge."

. . .

Sarah and I were in her room with my toolbox. Outside, the Terrorists were trying to get in. I sat on her bed, as she had commanded, silent and neutral.

"When did they start calling themselves the Terrorists," she asked during a lull.

"Who knows? Maybe Wild and Crazy Guys was too old-fashioned."

"Maybe the hijacking of that NATO tank yesterday gave them the idea. That got lots of coverage. Shit, here they are again."

Cheerfully screaming, another Airhead was dragged down the hall to be given her upside-down cold shower. The original Terrorist plan had been to drag the Airheads to the bathroom by their hair, as in olden times, but after a few tries they were convinced that this really was painful, so now they were holding on to the feet.

"Terror*ists*, Terror*ists*, we're a mean, sonofa*bitch*," came a hoarse chant as a new group gathered in front of Sarah's door. "Come on, Sarah," their leader shouted in a heavy New York accent. He was trying to sound fatherly and patient, but instead sounded anxious and not very bright. "It'll be a lot better for you if you just come out now. We're tickling Mitzi right now and she's going to tell us where the master key is, and once we get that we'll come in and you'll get *ad-dition-al pun-ish-ment.*"

"God," Sarah whispered to me, "these dorks think I'm just playing hard-to-get. Hope they enjoy it."

"Give the word and I'll shoo them off," I said again.

"Wouldn't help. I have to deal with this myself. Don't be so *mach.*"

"Sorry. Sometimes it works to be macho, you know."

Their previous effort to flash her out of her room had failed. "Flashing" was the technique of squirting lighter fluid under a door and throwing in a match. It wasn't as dangerous as it sounded, but it invariably smoked the victim out. Powdering was a milder form of this: an envelope was filled with powder, its mouth slid under the door, and the envelope stomped on, exploding a cloud of powder into the room. Three days earlier this had been done to Sarah by some Airheads. A regular vacuum cleaner just blew the powder out again, so we brought my wet/dry vacuum up and filled it with water and had better results, though she and her room still smelled like babies. She had purchased a heavy rubber weatherstrip from the Mall's hardware store and we had just finished installing it when the flashing attempt had taken place. From listening to the Terrorists on the other side of the door, I had now become as primitive as they had—it was no longer a negotiable situation—and was itching to knock heads.

"Why don't you stop bothering me?" she yelled, trying too hard to sound strong and steady. "I really don't want to play this game with you. You got what you wanted from the others, so why don't you leave? You have no right to bother me."

At this, they roared. "Listen, bitch, this is our sister floor, we decide what our rights are! No one escapes from the rule of the Terror*ists*, Terror*ists*, we're a mean, sonofa*bitch!* We'll get in sooner or later—face up to it!"

Another one played the nice guy. "Listen, Sarah—hey, is that her name? Right. Uh, listen, Sarah. We can make life pretty hard on you. We're just trying to initiate you into our sister floor—it's a new tradition. Remember, if you don't lock your door, we can come in; and if you do lock it, we can penny you in."

The Airheads had once pennied Sarah in. The doors opened inward and locked with deadbolts. If the deadbolt was locked and the door pushed inward with great force, the friction between the bolt and its rectangular hole in the jamb became so great that it was impossible for the occupant to withdraw the bolt to unlock the door. One could not push inward on the door all the time, of course, but it was possible to wedge pennies between the front of the door and the projecting member of the jamb so tightly that the occupant was sealed in helplessly. Since this maneuver only worked when the owner of the room was inside with the door locked, it was used to discourage people from the unfriendly habit of locking their doors. Sarah was pennied in just before a Student Government meeting, and she had to call me so that I could run upstairs and throw myself against the door until the pennies fell out.

"Look," said Sarah, also taking a reasonable tack, "When are you going to accept that I'm not coming out? I don't want to play, I just want peace and quiet." She knew her voice was wavering now, and she threw me an exasperated look.

"Sarah," said the righteously perturbed Terrorist, "you're being very childish about this. You know we don't want that much. It doesn't hurt. You just have one more chance to be reasonable, and then it's *ad-dition-al pun-ish-ment.*"

"Swirlie! Swirlie! Swirlie!" chanted the Terrorists.

"Fuck yourselves!" she yelled. Realizing what was about to happen, she yanked my pliers out of my toolbox and clamped their serrated jaws down on the lock handle just as Mitzi's master key was slid into the keyhole outside.

She held it firm. The Terrorists found the lock frozen. The key-turner called for help, but only one hand can grip a key at a time. The handle did rotate a few degrees in the tussle, and the Terrorists then found they could not pull the key from the lock. Sarah continued to hold it at a slight twist as the Terrorists mumbled outside.

"Listen, Sarah, you got a good point. We'll just leave you alone from now on."

"Yeah," said the others, "Sorry, Sarah."

Looking at me, Sarah snorted with contempt and held on to the pliers. A minute or so after the Terrorists noisily walked away, an unsuccessful yank came on the key.

"Shit! Fuck you!" The Terrorist kicked and pounded viciously on the door, raging.

After a few minutes I got on my belly and pried up the rubber strip and verified that the Terrorists were no longer waiting outside. Sarah opened her door, pulled out the master key, and pocketed it.

She smiled a lot, but she was also shaking, and wanted no comfort from me. I was about to say she could sleep on my sofa for a few days. Sometimes, though, I can actually be sensitive about these things. Sarah was obviously tired of needing my help. I felt she needed my protection, but that was my problem. Suddenly feeling that dealing with me might have been as difficult for her as dealing with the Terrorists, I made the usual obligatory offers of further assistance, and went home. Fortunately for what Sarah would call my macho side, I was on an intramural football team. So were all of the Terrorists. We met three times. I am big, they were average; they suffered; I had a good time and did not feel so proud of myself afterward. The Terrorists did not even understand that I didn't like them. Like a lot of whites, they didn't care much for blacks unless they were *athletic* blacks, in which case we could do whatever we wanted. To knock Terrorist heads for two hours, then have them pat me on the butt in admiration, was frustrating. As for Sarah, she had no such outlets for her feelings.

She lay on her bed for the rest of the afternoon, unable to think about anything else, desperate for the company of Hyacinth, who was out of town for the weekend. Ultra-raunch rock-'n'-roll pounded through from the room above. The Terrorists figured out her number and she had to take her phone off the hook. She ignored the Airheads knocking on her door. Finally, late in the evening, when things had been quiet for a couple of hours, she slipped out to take a shower—a right-side-up, hot shower.

This was not very relaxing. She had to keep her eyes and ears open as much as she could. As she rinsed her hair, though, a *klunk* sounded from the showerhead and the water wavered, then turned bitterly cold. She yelped and swung the hot-water handle around, to no effect, and then she couldn't stand it and had to yank open the door and get out of there.

They were all waiting for her—not the Terrorists, but the Airheads in their bathrobes. One stood at every sink, smiling, hot water on full blast, and one stood by every shower stall, smiling, steam pouring out of the door. With huge smiles and squeals of joy, they actually *grabbed* her by the arms, shouting *Swirlie!, Swirlie!,* took her to one of the toilets, stuck her head in, and flushed.

She was standing there naked, toilet water running in thin cold ribbons down her body, and they were in their bathrobes, smiling sympathetically and applauding. Apologies came from all directions. Somehow she didn't scream, she didn't hit anyone; she grabbed her bathrobe—tearing her hand on the corner of the shower door in her spastic fury —wrapped it around herself and tied it so tightly she could hardly breathe. Her pulse fluttered like a bird in an iron box and tingles of hyperventilation ran down her arms and into her fingertips.

"What the fuck is wrong with you? Are you crazy?"

They mostly tittered nervously and tried to ignore the way she had flown off the handle. They were leaving her a social escape route; she could still smooth it over. But she was not interested.

"Listen to me good, you dumb fucks!" She had let herself go, it was the only thing she could do. In a way it felt great to bellow and cry and rage and scare the hell out of them; this was the first contact with reality these women had had in years. "This is rape! And I'm entitled to protect myself from it! And I will!"

She had stepped over the line. It was now okay to hate Sarah, and several took the opportunity, laughing out loud to each other. Mari did not. "Sarah! Jeez, you don't have to take it so serious! You'll feel better later on. We've got some punch for you in the Lounge. We were just letting you in to the wing. We didn't think you were going to get so upset."

"Yeah."

"Yeah."

"Yeah."

"Well, I'm real sorry, excuse me, but I am going to take it seriously because anyone who can't see why it's serious has bad, bad problems and needs to get straightened out. If you think you're doing this because it's natural and fun, you aren't thinking too fucking hard."

"But, Jeez, Sarah," said Mari, hardly believing anyone could be so weird, "it's for the better. We've all been through it together now and we're all sisters. We're all an equal family together. We were just welcoming you in."

"The whole purpose of a fucking university is not so that you can come and be just like everyone else. I'm not equal to you people, never will be, don't want to be, I don't want to be anyone's sister, I don't want your activities, all I want is a decent place to live where I can be Sarah Jane Johnson, and *not be equalized . . . by a mob . . . of little powderpuff terrorists . . . who just can't stand differentness because they're too stupid to understand it!* What goes on in your heads? Haven't you ever seen the diversity of . . . of nature? *Stop laughing.* Look, you think this is funny? The next time you do this, someone is going to get hurt very badly." She looked down at the little drops of blood on the floor, dripping from her hand, and suddenly felt cleansed. She clenched the fist and held it up. *"Understand?"*

They had been smug at her wild anger. Now they were scared and disgusted and their makeup lay on their appalled skin like blood on snow. Most fled, hysterically grossed out.

"Gag me green!"

"Barf me blue!"

Mari averted her gaze from this gore. "Well, that's okay if you want to give *all of this* up. But I don't think it's like rape. I mean, we all scream a lot and stuff, and we don't really want them to do it, if you know what I mean, but when they do it's fun after all. So for us it's just sort of wild and exciting, and for the guys, it helps them work off steam. You know what I mean?"

"No! Get out! Don't fuck with my life!" That was a lie—she did know exactly what Mari meant. But she had just realized she could never let herself think that way again. Mari sadly floated out, sniffling. Sarah, alone now, washed her hair again (though it had not been a "dirty swirlie") and retreated to her room, a little ill in a gag-me-green sort of way, yet filled with a tingling sense of sureness and power. She was not harassed anymore. Word had gone out. Sarah had gotten additional punishment and was not to be bothered.

The door opened slightly, and a dazzling splinter of fluorescent light shot out across the dusky linoleum. Within the room it was still.

The door opened a bit more. "Spike? It's me. Don't try to get out, kittycat."

Now the door opened all the way and a tall skinny figure stepped in quickly, shut the door, and turned on a dim reading lamp. "Spike, are you sleeping? What did you get into this time?"

He found the kitten under his bed, next to the overturned rat-poison tray that was not supposed to be there. Spike had only been dead for a few minutes, and his body was still so warm that Casimir thought he could be cuddled back to life. He sat on the floor by his bed and rocked Spike for a while, then stopped and let the tiny corpse down into his lap.

A convulsion took his diaphragm and his lungs emptied themselves in jolts. He twisted around, breathless, hung on his elbows on the bed's edge, finally sucked in a wisp of air and sobbed it out again. He rolled onto the bed and the sobs came faster and louder. He pulled his pillow into his face and screamed and sobbed for longer than he could keep track of. Into his lumpy little standard-issue American Megaversity pillow he shuddered it all out: Sharon, Spike, the desecration of his academic dream, his loneliness.

When he pulled himself together he was drained and queasy but curiously relaxed. He put Spike in a garbage bag and slid him into an empty calculator box, which he taped shut. Cradling it, he stared out the window. Around him in even ranks rose the thousands of windows of the towers, and to his tear-blurred vision it was as though he stood in a forest aflame.

"Spike," he said, "What the hell should I do with myself?

"Yeah. Okay. That's what it's going to be.

"Well, Spike, now I have to do something unbelievably great. Something impossible. Something these scum are too dumb even to imagine. To hell with grades. There are much fairer ways of showing how smart you are. I'm smarter than all of these fuckers, rules aside."

He cranked his vent window open. Outside a Tower War was raging: students shouting to one another, shining lights and lasers into one another's rooms, blaring their stereos across the gulfs. Now the countertenor cry of Casimir Radon rode in above the tumult.

"You can make it as hard as you want, as hard as you *can*, but I'm going to be the cleverest bastard this place has ever seen! I can make idiots of you all, damn it!"

"Fuck you!" came a long-drawn-out scream from F Tower. It was precisely what Casimir wanted to hear. He shut his window and sat in darkness to think.

At four in the morning the wing was quiet except for Sarah, who was up, preparing her laundry. It was not *necessary* to do it at four in the morning—one could find open machines as late as six or seven—but this was Sarah's time of day. At this time she could walk the halls like something supernatural (or as she put it, "something natural, in a place that is sub-natural"). In the corridors she would meet the stupid gotten-up-to-urinate, staggering half-dead for the bathroom, and they'd squint at her—clothed, up and bright—as though she were a moonbeam that had worked its way around their room to splash upon their faces. The ultra-late partiers, crushed by alcohol, floated, belched and slurred along in glitzy boogie dress, and the fresh and sober Sarah, in soft clothes and tennis shoes, could dance through them before they had even recognized her presence. The brightest nerds and premeds riding the elevators home from all-nighters were so thick with sleep they could hardly stand, much less appreciate the time of day. A dozen or so hard-core athletes liked to rise as early as Sarah, and when she encountered them they would nod happily and go their separate ways.

Being up at four in the morning was akin to being in the wilderness. It was as close to the outside world as you could get without leaving the Plex. The rest of the day, the harsh artificiality of the place ruled the atmosphere and the unwitting inhabitants, but the calm purity of the predawn had a way of seeping through the cinderblocks and pervading the place for an hour or so.

"Screw the laundry," is what she finally said. She had plenty of clean clothes.

She was kneeling amid a heap of white cottons, and the grim brackishness of her room was all around her. Suddenly she could not stand it. Laundry would not make the room seem decent, and she had to do something that would.

Out in the wing it was easy to find the leftover paints and brushes. The Castle in the Air paintings were just now getting their finishing touches. She found the supplies in a storage closet and brought them to her room.

Normally this would have been a quick and dirty process, but the spirit of four in the morning made her placid. She moved the furniture away from the walls and in a few minutes had the floor, door, windows and furniture covered with a Sunday *New York Times*. It looked better already.

The Castle in the Air, as will later be described, was a sickly yellow, floating on white clouds in a blue sky. By mixing cloud-color with Castle-color and a bit of Bambi-color (on the ground under the Castle, Bambis cavorted) she made a mellow creamy paint. This she applied to the walls and ceiling with a roller.

It was breakfast-time. She wasn't hungry.

Sky-color and castle-color made green. She splayed open a cardboard box and made it into a giant palette, mixing up every shade of green she could devise and smearing them around to create an infinite variety. Then she began to dab away on one wall with no particular plan or goal.

The light fixture was in the middle of the wall. She paused, thinking of the dire consequences, then sighed blissfully and slapped it all over with thick green daubs.

By noon the wall was covered with pied green splotches

ranging from almost-black to yellow. It was not a bad approximation of a forest in the sun, but it lacked fine detail and branches.

She had long since decided to cut all her classes. She left her room for the first time since sunrise and started riding the 'vators toward the shopping mall. She felt great.

"Doin' some paintin'?" asked a doe-eyed woman in leg warmers. Plastered with paint, Sarah nodded, beaming.

"Doin' your room?"

"Yep."

"Yeah. So did we. We did ours all really high-tech. Lots of glow-colors. How 'bout you? Lotsa green?"

"Of course," said Sarah, "I'm making it look like the outside. So I don't forget."

At the Sears in the Mall she got matte black paint and smaller brushes. She returned to her room, passing the Cafeteria, where thousands stood in line for something that smelled of onions and salt and hot fat. Sarah had not eaten in twenty-four hours and felt great—it was a day to fast. Back in her room she cleared away a *Times* page announcing a coup in Africa and sat on her bed to contemplate her forest. Infinitely better than the old wall, yet still just a rude beginning—every patch of color could be subdivided into a hundred shades and crisscrossed with black branches to hold it all up. She knew she'd never finish it, but that was fine. That was the idea.

Casimir immediately went into action. He had already daydreamed up this plan, and to organize the first stages of Project Spike did not take long. Since Sharon had sunk completely into a coma, Casimir had taken over the old professor's lab in the Burrows, spending so much time there that he stored a sleeping bag in the closet so he could stay overnight.

This evening—Day Three—he had found six rats crowded into his box trap near the Cafeteria. Judging from the quantity of poison scattered around this area, they were of a highly resistant strain. In the lab, he donned heavy gloves, opened the trap, forced himself to grab a rat, pulled it out and slammed shut the lid. This was a physics, not a biology, lab and so his methods were crude. He pressed the rat against the counter and stunned it with a piece of copper tubing, then held it underwater until dead.

He laid it on a bare plank and set before him an encyclopedia volume he had stolen from the Library, opened to a page which showed a diagram of the rat's anatomy. Weighing it open with a hunk of lead radiation shield, he took out a single-edged razor and went to work on the little beast. In twenty minutes he had the liver out. In an hour he had six rat livers in a beaker and six liverless rat corpses in the wastebasket, swathed in plastic. He put the livers in a mortar and ground them to a pulp, poured in some alcohol, and filtered the resulting soup until it was clear.

Next morning he visited the Science Shop, where Virgil Gabrielsen was fixing up a chromatograph that would enable Casimir to find out what chemicals were contained in the rat liver extract. "We're ready for your mysterious test," said Virgil.

"Hope you don't mind."

"I love working with mad scientists—never dull. What's that?"

"Mostly grain alcohol. This machine will answer your question, though, if it's fixed."

A few hours later they had the results: a strip of paper with a line squiggled across it by the machine. Virgil compared this graph with similar ones from a long skinny book.

"Shit," said Virgil, showing rare surprise. "I didn't think anything could live with this much Thalphene in its guts. Thalphene! These things have incredible immunities."

"What is it? I don't know anything about chemistry."

"Trade name for thallium phenoxide." Virgil crossed his arms and looked at the ceiling. "*Dangerous Properties of Industrial Materials*, my favorite bedtime reading, says this about thallium compounds. I abbreviate. 'Used in rat poison and depilatories . . . results in swelling of feet and legs, arthralgia, vomiting, insomnia, hyperaesthesia and paresthesia of hands and feet, mental confusion, polyneuritis with severe pains in legs and loins, partial paralysis and degeneration of legs, angina, nephritis, wasting, weakness . . . complete loss of hair . . . ha! Fatal poisoning has been known to occur.' "

"No kidding!"

"Under phenols we have . . . 'where death is delayed, damage to kidneys, liver, pancreas, spleen, edema of the lungs, headache, dizziness, weakness, dimness of vision, loss of consciousness, vomiting, severe abdominal pain, corrosion of lips, mouth, throat, esophagus and stomach . . .' "

"Okay, I get the idea.

"And that doesn't account for synergistic effects. These rats eat the stuff all the time."

"So they go through a lot of rat poison, these rats do."

"It looks to me," said Virgil, "as though they live on it. But if you don't mind my prying, why do you care?"

Casimir was slightly embarrassed, but he knew Virgil's secret, so it was only fair to bare his own. "In order for Project Spike to work, they have to be heavy rat-poison eaters. I'm going to collect rat poison off the floors and expose it to the slow neutron source in Sharon's lab. It's a little chunk of a beryllium isotope on a piece of plutonium, heavily shielded in paraffin—looks like a garbage can on wheels. Paraffin stops slow neutrons, see. Anyway, when I expose the rat poison to the neutrons, some of the carbon in the poison will turn to Carbon-14. Carbon-14 is used in dating, of course, so there are plenty of machines around to detect small amounts of it. Anyway, I set this tagged poison out near the Cafeteria. Then I analyze samples of Cafeteria food for unusually high levels of Carbon-14. If I get a high reading . . ."

"It means rats in the food."

"Either rats, or their hair or feces."

"That's awesome blackmail material, Casimir. I wouldn't have thought it of you."

Casimir looked up at Virgil, shocked and confused. After

a few seconds he seemed to understand what Virgil had meant. "Oh, well, I guess that's true. The thing is, I'm not that interested in blackmail. It wouldn't get me anything. I just want to *do* this, and publicize the results. The main thing is the challenge."

A rare full grin was on Virgil's face. "Damn good, Casimir. That's marvelous. Nice work." He thought it over, taken with the idea. "You'll have the biggest gun in the Plex, you know."

"That's not what I'm after with this project."

"Let me know if I can help. Hey, you want to go downstairs to the Denny's for lunch? I don't want to eat in the Cafeteria while I'm thinking about the nature of your experiment."

"I don't want to eat at all, after what I've just been doing," said Casimir. "But maybe later on we can dissolve our own livers in ethanol." He put the beaker of rat potion in a hazardous-waste bin, logged down its contents, and they departed.

And lest anyone get the wrong idea, a disclaimer: I did not know about this while it was going on. They told me about it later. The people who have claimed I bear some responsibility for what happened later do not know the facts.

"What makes you think you can just play a record?" said Ephraim Klein in a keen, irritated voice. "I'm listening to harpsichord music."

"Oh," John Wesley Fenrick said innocently. "I didn't hear it. I guess my ears must have gone bad from all my terrible music, huh?"

"Looks that way."

"But it's okay, I'm not going to play a record."

"I should hope not."

"I'm going to play a tape." Fenrick brushed his finger against an invisible region on the surface of the System, and lights lit and meters wafted up and down. The mere sound of *silence*, reproduced by this machine, nearly drowned out the harpsichord, a restored 1783 Prussian model with the most exquisite lute stop Klein had ever heard. Fenrick turned on the Go Big Red Fan, which began to chunk away as usual.

"Look," said Ephraim Klein, "I said I was playing something. You can't just bust in."

"Well," said John Wesley Fenrick, "I said I can't hear it. If I don't hear any evidence that you are playing something, there's no reason I should take your word for it. You obviously have a distorted idea of reality."

"Prick! Asshole!" But Klein had already pulled out one of his war tapes, the "Toccata and Fugue in D Minor" as performed by Virgil Fox (what Fenrick called "horror movie music") and snapped it into his own tape deck. He set the tape rolling and prepared to switch from PHONO to TAPE at the first hint of offensive action from Fenrick.

It was not long in coming. Fenrick had been sinking into a Heavy Metal retrospective recently, and entered the competition with *Back in Black* by AC/DC. Klein watched Fenrick's hands carefully and was barely able to squeeze out a lead, the organist hitting the high mordant at the opening of the piece before the ensuing fancy notes were stomped into the sonic dust by *Back in Black*.

From there the battle raged typically. A hundred feet down the hall, I stuck my head out the door to have a look. Angel, the enormous Cuban who lived on our floor, had been standing out in the hallway for about half an hour furiously pounding on the wall with his boxing gloves, laboriously lengthening a crack he had started in the first week of the semester. When I looked, he was just in the act of hurling open the door to Klein and Fenrick's room; dense, choking clouds of music whirled down the corridor at Mach 1 and struck me full in the face.

I started running. By the time I had arrived, Angel had wrapped Fenrick's long extension cord around the doorknob, held it with his boxing gloves, put his foot against the door, and pulled it apart with a thick blue spark and a shower of fire. The extension cord shorted out and smoked briefly until circuit breakers shut down all public-area power to the wing.

AC/DC went dead, clearing the air for the climax of the fugue. Angel walked past the petrified Ephraim Klein and pawed at the tape deck, trying to get at the tape. Frustrated by the boxing gloves, he turned and readied a mighty kick into the cone of a sub-woofer, when finally I arrived and tackled him onto a bed. Angel relaxed and sat up, occasionally pounding his bright-red cinderblock-scarred gloves together with meaty *thwats*, sweating like the boxer he was, glowering at the Go Big Red Fan.

The fugue ended and Ephraim shut off the tape. I went over and closed the door. "Okay, guys, time for a little talk. Everyone want to have a little talk?"

John Wesley Fenrick looked out the window, already bored, and nodded almost imperceptibly. Ephraim Klein jumped to his feet and yelled, "Sure, sure, anytime! I'm happy to be reasonable!" Angel, who was unlacing his right boxing glove with his teeth, mumbled, "I been talking to them for two months and they don't do shit about it."

"Hmm," I said, "I guess that tells the story, doesn't it? If you two refuse to be reasonable, Angel doesn't have to be reasonable either. Now it seems to me you need a set of rules that you can refer to when you're arguing about stereo rights. For instance, if one guy goes to pee, the other can't seize air rights. You can't touch each other's property, and so on. Ephraim, give me your typewriter and we'll get this down."

So we made the Rules and I taped them to the wall, straddling the boundary line of the room. "Does that mean I only have to follow the Rules on my half of the page," asked Fenrick, so I took it down and made a new Rule saying that these were merely typed representations of abstract Rules that were applicable no matter where the typed representations were displayed. Then I had the two sign the Rules, and hinted again that I just didn't know what Angel might do if they made any more noise. Then Angel and I went down to my place and had some beers. Law, and the hope of silence and order, had been established on our wing.

November

Fred Fine was trying to decide whether to lob his last tactical nuke into Novosibirsk or Tomsk when a frantic plebe bounced up and interrupted the simulation with a Priority Five message. Of course it was Priority Five; how else could a plebe have dared interrupt Fred Fine's march to the Ob'?

"Fred, sir," he gasped. "Come quick, you won't believe it."

"What's the situation?"

"That new guy. He's about to win World War II!"

"He is? But I thought he was playing the Axis!"

Fred Fine brushed past the plebe and strode into the next room. In its center, two Ping-Pong tables had been pushed together to make room for the eight-piece World War II map. On one side stood the tall, aquiline Virgil Gabrielsen—the "new guy"—and on the other, Chip Dixon shifted from foot to foot and snapped his fingers incessantly. Because this was the first wargame Virgil had ever played, he was still only a Private, and held Plebe status. Chip Dixon, a Colonel, had been gaming for six years and was playing the Allies, for God's sake! Usually the only thing at question in this game was how many Allied divisions the Axis could consume before Berlin inevitably fell.

At the end of the map, where the lines of longitude theoretically converged to make the North Pole, Consuela Gorm, Referee, sat on a loveseat atop a sturdy table. On the small stand before her she riffled occasionally through the inch-thick rule book, punched away at her personal computer, made notes on scratch paper and peered down at Europe with a tiny pair of opera glasses. Surrounding the tables were twenty other gamers who had come to observe the carnage shortly after Virgil had V-2'd Birmingham into gravel. Many stood on chairs, using field glasses of their own, and one geek was tottering around the area on a pair of stilts, loudly and repeatedly joking that he was a Nazi spy satellite. The attention of all was focused on tens of thousands of little cardboard squares meticulously stacked on the hexagonally patterned playing field. The game had been on for nine and a half hours and Chip Dixon was obviously losing it fast, popping Cheetos into his mouth faster than he could grind them into paste with his hyperactive yellow molars, often gulping Diet Pepsi and hiccuping. Virgil was calm, surveying the board through half-closed eyes, hands behind back, lips slightly parted, wandering around in a world inside his head, oblivious to the surrounding nerds. A hell of a warrior, thought Fred Fine, and this only his first game!

"Here comes the Commander," shouted the guy on stilts as he rounded the Japanese-occupied Aleutians, and the observers' circle parted so Fred Fine could enter. Chip Dixon blushed vividly and looked away, moving his lips as he cursed to himself. "Very interesting," said Fred Fine.

Great stacks of red cardboard squares surrounded Stalingrad and Moscow, which were protected only by pitiable little heaps of green squares. In Normandy an enormous Nazi tank force was hurling the D-Day invasion back into the Channel so forcefully that Fred Fine could almost hear the howl of the *Werfers* and see the bodies fall screaming into the scarlet brine. In Holland, a Nazi amphibious force made ready to assault Britain. In front of Virgil, lined up on the edge of the table as trophies, sat the four Iowa-class battleships, the *Hornet*, and other major ships of the American navy.

Chip Dixon was increasingly manic, his blood pressure pumped to the hemhorrage point by massive overdoses of salt and Diet Pepsi, his thirst insatiable because of the nearly empty Jumbo Pak of Cheetos. Sweat dripped from his brow and fell like acid rain on Scandinavia. He bent over and tried to move a stack of recently mobilized Russians toward Moscow, but as he shoved one point of his tweezers under the stack he hiccupped violently and ended up scattering them all over the Ukraine. "Shit!" he screamed, dashing a Cheeto to the floor. "I'm sorry, Consuela, I forget which hex it was on."

Consuela did not react for several seconds, and the reflection of the rule book in her glasses gave her an ominous, inscrutable look. Everyone was still and apprehensive. "Okay," she said in soft, level tones, "that unit got lost in the woods and can't find its way out for another turn."

"Wait!" yelled Chip Dixon. "That's not in the Rules!"

"It's okay," said Virgil patiently. "That stack contained units A2567, A2668, A4002, and I26789, and was on hex number 1,254.908. However, unit A2567 clashed with Axis A1009 last turn, so has only half movement this turn—three hexes."

Cowed, Chip Dixon breathed deeply (Fred Fine's suggestion) and reassembled the stack. Unit A2567 was left far behind to deal with a unit of about twenty King Tiger Tanks which was blasting unopposed up the Dniepr. Chip Dixon then straightened up and thought for about five minutes, ruffling through his notes for a misplaced page. Consuela made a gradated series of noises intended to convey rising impatience. "Listen, Chip, you're already way over the time limit. Done?"

"Yeah, I guess."

"Any engagements?"

"No, not this turn. But wait 'til you see what's coming."

"Okay, Virgil, your turn."

Virgil reached out with a long probe and quickly shoved stacks of cardboard from place to place; from time to time a move would generate a gasp from the crowd. He then ticked off a list of engagements, giving Consuela data on what each stack contained, what its combat strength was, when it had last fought and so forth. When it was over, an hour later, there was long applause from the membership of MARS. Chip Dixon had sunk to the floor to sulk over a tepid Cola.

"Incredible," someone yelled, "you conquered Stalingrad

and Moscow and defeated D-Day and landed in Scotland and Argentina all at the same time!"

At this point Chip Dixon, who had refused to concede, stood up and blew most of the little cardboard squares away in a blizzard of military might. Fred Fine was angry but controlled. "Chip, ten demerits for that. I ought to bust you down to Second Looie for that display. Just for that, you get to put the game away. And *organize it right.*" Chastened, Chip and two of his admirers set about sorting all of the pieces of cardboard and fitting them into the appropriate recesses in the injection-molded World War II carrying case. Fred Fine turned his attention to Virgil.

"A tremendous victory." He drew his fencing foil and tapped Virgil once on each shoulder as Virgil looked on skeptically. "I name you a Colonel in MARS. It's quite a jump, but a battlefield commission is obviously in order."

"Oh, not really," said Virgil, bored. "It's more a matter of a good memory than anything else."

"You're modest. I like that in a man."

"No, just accurate. I like *that.*"

Fred Fine now drew Virgil aside, away from the dozen or so wargame aficionados who were still gaping at one another and pounding their heads dramatically on the walls. The massively corpulent Consuela was helped down from her eleven-hour perch by several straining MARS officials, and began to roll toward them like a globule of quicksilver.

"Virgil," said Fred Fine quietly, "you're obviously a special kind of man. We need men like you for our advanced games. These board games are actually somewhat repetitive, as you pointed out. Want a little more excitement next time?"

Virgil drew away. "What do you have in mind?"

"You've heard of Dungeons and Dragons?" A gleam came to Fred Fine's eye, and he glanced conspiratorially at Consuela.

"Sure. Someone designs a hypothetical dungeon on graph paper, puts different monsters and treasure in the rooms, and each player has a character which he sends through it, trying to take as much treasure as possible. Right?"

"Oh, only in its crudest, simplest forms, Virgil," said Consuela.

"This one and his friends prefer a more active version."

"Sewers and Serpents," said Consuela, nodding happily.

"The idea is the same as D & D, but we use a real place, and real costumes, and act it all out. Much more realistic. You see, beneath the Plex is a network of sewer tunnels."

"Yeah, I know," said Virgil. "I've got the blueprints for this place memorized, remember."

Fred Fine was taken aback. "How?"

"Computer drew them for me."

"Well, we'd have to give you a character who had some good reason for knowing his way around the tunnels."

"Like maybe, uh," said Consuela, eyes rolled up, "maybe he happened to see a duel between some hero who had just come out of the Dungeon of Plexor"—

"That's what we call the tunnels," said Fred Fine.

—"and some powerful nonsentient beast such as a gronth, and the gronth killed the hero, and then Virgil's character came and found a map on his body and memorized it."

"Or we could make him a computer expert in Techno-Plexor who got a peek at the plans the same way Virgil did."

"Excuse me a sec, but what do you do for monsters?" asked Virgil.

"Well, we don't have real ones. We just have to pretend and use the official S & S rules, developed by MARS through a constitutional process over several years. We maintain two-way radio contact with our referee, Consuela, who stays in the Plex and runs the adventure through a computer program we've got worked out. The computer also performs statistical combat simulation."

"So you slog around in the shit, and the computer says you're being attacked by monsters, and she reads it off the CRT and says that according to the computer you've lost a finger, or the monster's dead, that sort of thing?"

"Well, it's more exciting than you make it sound, and the Dungeon Mistress makes it better by amplifying the description generated by the computer. I recommend you try it. We've got an outing in a couple of weeks."

"I don't know, Fred, it's not my cup of tea. I'll think about it, but don't count on my coming."

"That's fine. Consuela just needs to know a few hours ahead of time so she can have SHEKONDAR—the computer program—prepare a character for you."

Virgil assented to everything, nodded a lot, said he'd be getting back to them and hurried out, shaking his head in amazed disgust. Unlikely as it seemed, this place could still surprise him.

My involvement with Student Government was due to my being faculty-in-residence. I served as a kind of minister without portfolio, investigating whatever topic interested me at the moment, talking to students, faculty and administrators, and contributing to governmental discussions the point of view of an older, supposedly wiser observer. As I had no idea what was going on at the Big U until much later, my contributions can't have done much good. I did visit the Castle in the Air on several occasions, anyway, and whenever I did I was presented with a visual display in three stages.

The first was a prominent mural on the wall of the Study Lounge, clearly visible through the windows from the elevator lobby. Even if I had been visiting one of E12's other wings, therefore, I couldn't have failed to notice that E12S was a wing among wings. Here, as described, the Castle was painted in yellow—not a typical color for castles, but much nicer than realistic gray or brown. The Castle, stolen directly from a book of Disney illustrations, floated on a cloud that looked like a stomped marshmallow, not a thunderhead, seemingly too meager to support its load. Below, more Disney characters frolicked on an undulating green lawn, a combined golf course/cartoon character refuge with no sand traps, one water hazard and no visible greens. The book of illustrations was not large, and each character was shown in only one or two poses which had to be copied over and over again in populating this great lawn. Monotony had rendered the painters somewhat desperate—what was that penguin doing there? And why had they included that evil gray wolf, wagging his red tongue at the stiff cloned Bambis from behind a spherical shrub? But most agreed that the mural was nice—indeed, so nice that "nice" was no longer adequate by itself; in describing it, Airheads had to amplify the word by saying it many, many times and making large gestures with their hands.

The second stage of the presentation was the entryways —two identical portals, one at the beginning of each of the wing's two hallways. Here, at the fire doors by the Study Lounge, the halls had been framed in thick wooden beams—actually papier-mâchéd boxes—decorated with plastic flowers and welcoming messages. The fire doors themselves had been covered with paper and painted so that, when they were closed, I could see what looked like a stairway of light yellow stone rising up from the floor and continuing skyward until further view was blocked by the beam along the ceiling.

Going through these doors, and therefore up the symbolic stair, I found myself in a light yellow corridor gridded with thin wavy black lines supposed to represent joints between the great yellow building-stones of which the Castle was constructed. These were closely spaced in the first part of the hallway, but the crew had found this work tedious and decided that in the back sections much larger stones were used to build the walls. Here and there, torches, fake paintings, suits of armor and the like were painted on the walls.

Each individual room, then, was the province of the occupants, who could turn it into any fantasy-land they wanted. One or two of them painted murals on paper and pasted them to their doors. These murals purported to be windows looking down on the scene below, an artistic challenge too great for most of them.

On each visit to Sarah, then, I was introduced to the Castle in the Air in the manner of a TV viewer. The elevator doors would fade out and there sat the Castle on its cloud, viewed through a screen of glass. The view would then switch to a traveling shot of the stairway leading up to the castle—evidently a long one. Through the magic of video editing, the stair would flatten, part and swing away, and I would be instantly jump-cut to the halls of the Castle proper, where to confirm that it had all happened I could pause at windows here and there and look down at the featureless plains from which I had just ascended.

So much for the opening credits; what about the plot? The plot consisted almost entirely of parties and tame sexual intrigue with the Terrorists. The Airheads were not disturbed by the fact that their home was not much of a castle —the Terrorists or anyone else could invade at any time— and that far from being up in the air, it was squashed beneath nineteen other Terrorist-infested floors. The Airheads got along by pretending that any man who showed up on their floor was a white knight on beck and call. Certain evil influences, though, could not be kept out by any amount of painting, and among these was the fire alarm system.

Early in the morning of November the Fifth, Mari Meegan was ejected from her chamber by three City firefighters investigating a full-tower fire alarm. Versions differed as to whether the firefighters had used physical force, but to the lawyers subsequently hired by Mari's father it did not matter; the issue was the *mental* violence inflicted on Mari, who was forced to totter down the stairway and join the sleepy throng below with only patches of bright blue masque painted on her face.

This situation had not previously arisen because it usually took at least half an hour between the ringing of the alarm and the arrival of the firemen on their tour through the tower. Thirty minutes was time enough for Mari to apply a quickie makeup job which would prevent her from looking "disgusting" even during full moons outside, and, as the lawyers took pains to document and photograph, her emergency thirty-minute face kit was set up and ready to go on a corner of her dresser. Next to it was the masque container, which was for "super emergencies"; given a severely limited time to prepare, she could tear this open and paint a blue oval over her face that would serve partly to diguise and partly to show those who recognized her that she cared about her appearance. But on this particular morning, certain Terrorists from above had demonstrated their mechanical aptitude by disabling the E12S alarm bell with a pair of bolt cutters. The more distant ringing of the E12E bell had not overborne the soft nocturnal beat of Mari's stereo, and by the time she had realized what was happening, and energized the evening light simulation tubes on her makeup center, the sirens were already wafting up from the Death Vortex below.

The Fire Marshall was not amused. After a week's worth of rumors that portrayed the Fire Marshall as a Nazi and a pervert, it was decreed that henceforth during fire drills the RAs would go door-to-door with their master keys and make sure everyone left their rooms immediately. This grim ruling inspired a wing meeting at which Hyacinth wearily suggested they all purchase ski masks, since it was getting cold outside anyway, and wear them down to the street during fire drills. "Stay together and you will be totally anonymous, by which I mean no one will know who you are, or what you look like at three in the morning." The Airheads appointed Teri, a Fashion Merchandising major, to pick out ski masks with a suitable color scheme.

In private, Hyacinth came up with an acronym for them: SWAMPers. This meant that as a bare minimum they found it necessary to Shave, Wash, Anoint, Make-up and Perfume all parts of their body at least once a day. Their insistence on doing this often made Sarah wonder about her own appearance—her use of cosmetics was minimal—but Hyacinth and I and everyone else assured her she looked fine. When preparing for the long, nasty Student Government budget meeting in early November, Sarah looked briefly through her shoebox of miscellaneous cosmetics, then shoved it under the bed again. She had greater things to worry about.

As for clothes, it came down to a choice between her most

businesslike outfit, a grey wool skirt suit, and a somewhat brighter dress. She picked the suit, though she knew it would lay her open to accusations of fascism from the Stalinist Underground Battalion (SUB), wound her hair into a bun, and steeled herself for madness.

The SUB got there an hour before anyone else and had their banners planted and their rabid handouts sown before the Government even showed up. We met in the only room we could find that was reasonably private. Behind us came the TV crews, and then the reporters from the *Monoplex Monitor* and the *People's Truth Publication*, who sat in the first row, right in front of the Stalinists. Finally Lecture Auditorium 3 filled up with supplicants from various organizations, all deeply shocked and dismayed at how little funding they were receiving, all bearing proposed amendments.

First we slogged through the parliamentary trivia, including a bit of "new business" in which the SUB introduced a resolution to condemn the administration for massive human rights violations and to call for its abolition. Then we came to the real purpose of the meeting: amendments to the proposed budget. A line formed behind the microphone on the stage, and at its head was a SUB member. "I move," he said, "that we pass no budget at all, because the budget has to be approved by the administration, and so we haven't got any control over our own activity money." On cue, behind the press corps, eight SUBbies rose to their feet bearing a long banner: TAKE BACK CONTROL OF STUDENT ACTIVITIES CAPITAL FROM THE KRUPP JUNTA. "The money's ours, the money's ours, the money's ours . . ."

We had expected all this and Sarah was undisturbed. She sat back from her microphone and took a sip of water, letting the media record the event for the ages. Once that was done she gaveled a few times and talked them back into their seats. She was about to start talking again when the last standing SUBbie shouted, "Student Government is a tool of the Krupp cadre!"

Behind him, most of the audience shouted things like "eat rocks" and "shut up" and "shove it."

"If you're finished interfering with the democratic process," Sarah said, "this tool would like to get on with the budget. We have a lot to do and everyone needs to be very, very brief."

Student Government was made up of the Student Senate, which represented each of the 200 residential wings of the Plex, and the Activities Council, comprising representatives from each of the funded student organizations, numbering about 150. The distribution of funds among the Activities Council members was decided on by a joint session, which was our goal for the evening.

The Student Senate was crammed with SUBbies and members of an outlaw Mormon splinter group called the Temple of Unlimited Godhead (TUG). Each of these groups claimed to represent all the students. As Sarah explained, no one in his right mind was interested in running for Student Senate, explaining why it was filled with fanatics and political science majors. Fortunately, SUB and TUG canceled each other out almost perfectly.

"I'm tired of having all aspects of my life ruled by this administration that doesn't give a shit for human rights, and I think it's time to do something about it," said the first speaker. There was a little applause from the front and lots of jeering. A hum filled the air as the TUG began to OMMMM . . . at middle C—a sort of sonic tonic which was said to clear the air of foul influences and encourage spiritual peace; overhead, a solitary bat, attracted by the hum, swooped down from a perch in the ceiling and flitted around, occasioning shrieks and violent motion from the people it buzzed. "At this university we don't have free speech, we don't have academic freedom, we don't even have power over our own money!"

At the insistence of the audience, Sarah broke in after a few minutes. "If you've got any specific human rights violations you're concerned about, there are some international organizations you can go to, but there's not much the Student Senate can do. So I suggest you go live somewhere else and let someone else propose an amendment."

Shocked and devastated, the speaker gaped at Sarah as the TV lights slammed into action. He held the stare for several seconds to allow the camera operators to focus and adjust light level, then surveyed the cheering and OMming crowd, face filled with bewilderment and shock.

"I don't bel*eeeve* this," he said, staring into the lenses. "Who says we have freedom of speech? My God, I've come up here to express a free opinion, and just because I am opposed to fascism, the President of the Student Government tries to throw me out of the Plex! My home! That's right, if these *different* people don't like being oppressed, just throw them out of their homes into the dangerous city! I didn't think this kind of savagery was supposed to exist in a university." He shook his head in noble sadness, surveyed the derisive crowd defiantly, and marched away from the mike to grateful applause. Below, he answered questions from the media while the next student came to the microphone.

He looked like a male cheerleader for a parochial school football team, being handsome, well groomed, and slightly pimpled. As he took possession of the mike the OM stopped. He kept his eye on a middle-aged fellow standing in the aisle not far away, who in turn watched the SUBbie's press conference in front of the stage. Finally the older gentleman held up three fingers. The TUGgie shoved his fist between his arm and body and spoke loudly and sharply into the mike.

"I'd like to announce that I have caught a bat here in my hand, and now I'm going to bite the head off it right here as a sacrifice to the God of Communism."

Below, the SUBbie found himself in absolute darkness, and tripped over a power cord. Simultaneously the TUGgie squinted as all lights were swung around to bear on him. He smiled and began to talk in a calm chantlike voice. "Well, well, well. I've got a confession. I'm not really going to bite the head off a bat, because I don't even have one, and I'm not a Communist." There was now a patter of what sounded like canned TV laughter from the TUG section. "I just did that as a little demonstration, to show you folks how easy it is to get the attention of the media. We can come and talk about serious issues and do real things, but what gets TV coverage are violent eye-catching events, a thing which the Communists who wish to destroy our society understand very well. But I'm not here to give a speech, I'm here to propose an amendment . . ." Here he was dive-bombed by the bat, who veered away at the last moment; the speaker jumped back in horror, to the amusement of almost everyone. The TUGgies laughed too, showing that, yes, they did have a sense of humor no matter what people said. The speaker struggled to regain his composure.

"The speech! Resume the speech! The amendment!" shouted the older man.

"My budget proposal is that we take away all funding for the Stalinist Underground Battalion and distribute it among the other activities groups."

The lecture hall exploded in outraged chanting, uproarious applause, and OM. Sarah sat for about fifteen seconds with her chin in her hand, then began smashing the gavel again. I was seated off to the side of the stage, poised to act as the strong-but-lovable authority figure, but did not have to stand up; eventually things quieted down.

"Is there a second to the motion?" she asked wearily.

The crowd screamed YES and NO.

The speaker yielded to another TUGgie, who stood rigidly with a stack of 3-×-5 cards and began to drone through them. "At one time the leftist organizations of American Megaversity could claim that they represented some of the students. But the diverse organizations of the Left soon found that they all had one member who was very strident and domineering and who would push the others around until he or she had risen to a position of authority within the organization. These all turned out to be secretly members of the Stalinist Underground Battalion who had worked themselves into the organizations in order to merge the Left into a single bloc with no diversity or freedom of thought. The SUB took over a women's issues newsletter and turned it into the *People's Truth Publication*, a highly libelous so-called newspaper. In the same way . . ."

He was eventually cut off by Sarah. SUB spokespersons stated their views passionately, then another TUGgie. Finally a skinny man in dark spectacles came to the mike, a man whom Sarah recognized but couldn't quite place. He identified himself as Casimir Radon and said he was president of the physics club Neutrino. He quieted the crowd down a bit, as his was the first speech of the evening that was not entirely predictable.

"I'd like to point out that you've only given us four hundred dollars," he said. "We need more. I've done some analysis of the way our activity money is budgeted, which I will just run through very quickly here—" he fumbled through papers as a disappointed murmur rose from the audience. How long was this nerd going to take? The cameramen put new film and tape in their equipment as lines formed outside by the restrooms.

"Here we go. I won't get too involved in the numerical details—it's all just arithmetic—but if you look at the current budget, you see that a small group of people is receiving a hugely disproportionate share of the money. In effect, the average funding per member of the Stalinist Underground Battalion is $114.00, while the figure for everyone else averages out to about $46.00, and only $33.00 for Neutrino. That's especially unfair because Neutrino needs to purchase things like books and equipment, while the expenses of a political organization are much lower. I don't think that's fair."

The SUB howled at this preposterous reasoning but everyone else listened respectfully.

"So I move we cut SUB funding to the bare minimum, say, twenty bucks per capita, and give Neutrino its full request for a scientific research project, $1500.00."

The rest of the evening, anyway, was bonkers, and I'll not go into detail. It was insignificant anyway, since the administration had the final say; the Student Government would have to keep passing budgets until they passed one that S.

S. Krupp would sign, and the only question was how long it would take them to knuckle under. Time was against the SUB. As the members of the government got more bored, they became more interested in passing a budget that would go through the first time around. Eventually it became obvious that the SUB had lost out, and the only thing wanting was the final vote. The highlight of the evening came just before that vote: the speech of Yllas Freedperson.

Yllas, the very substantial and brilliant leader of the SUB, was a heavy black woman in her early thirties, in her fifth year of study at the Modern Political Art Workshop. She had a knack for turning out woodblock prints portraying anguished faces, burning tenements, and thick tortured hands reaching for the sky. Even her pottery was inspired by the work of wretched Central American peasants. She was also editor and illustrator of the *People's Truth Publication*, but her real talent was for public speaking, where she had the power of a gospel preacher and the fire of a revolutionary. She waited dignified for the TV lights, then launched into a speech that lasted at least a quarter of an hour. At just the right times she moaned, she chanted, she sang, she reasoned, she whispered, she bellowed, she just plain spoke in a fluid and hypnotically rhythmic voice. She talked about S. S. Krupp and the evil of the System, how the System turned good into bad, how this society was just like the one that caused the Holocaust, which was no excuse for Israel, about conservatism in Washington and how our environment, economic security, personal freedom, and safety from nuclear war were all threatened by the greedy action of cutting the SUB's budget. Finally out came the names of Martin Luther King, Jr., Marx, Gandhi, Che, Jesus Christ, Ronald Reagan, Hitler, S. S. Krupp, the KKK, Bob Avakian, Elijah Mohammed and Abraham Lincoln. Through it all, the bat was active, dipping and diving crazily through the auditorium, dive-bombing toward walls or lights or people but veering away at the last moment, flitting through the dense network of beams and cables and catwalks and light fixtures and hanging speakers and exposed pipes above us at great smooth speed, tracing a marvelously complicated path that never brushed against any solid object. All of it was absorbing and breathtaking, and when Yllas Freedperson was finished and the bat, perhaps no longer attracted by her voice, slipped up and disappeared into a corner, there was a long silence before the applause broke out.

"Thank you, Yllas," said Sarah respectfully. "Is there any particular motion you wanted to make or did you just want to inject your comments?"

"I move," shouted Yllas Freedperson, "that we put the budget the way it was."

The vote was close. The SUB lost. Recounting was no help. They took the dignified approach, forming into a sad line behind Yllas and singing "We Shall Overcome" in slow tones as they marched out. Above their heads they carried their big black-on-red posters of S. S. Krupp with a target drawn over his face, and they marched so slowly that it took two repetitions of the song before they made it out into the hallway to distribute leaflets and posters.

Sarah, three members of her cabinet and I gathered later in my suite for wine. After the frenzy of the meeting we were torpid, and hardly said anything for the first fifteen minutes or so. Then, as it commonly did those days, the conversation came around to the Terrorists.

"What's the story on those Terrorist guys?" asked Willy, a business major who acted as Treasurer. "Are they genuine Terrorists?"

"Not on my floor," said Sarah, "since they subjugated us. We're living in . . . the *Pax Thirteenica.*"

"I've heard a number of stories," I said. Everyone looked at me and I shifted into my professor mode and lit my pipe. "Their major activity is the toll booth concept. They station Terrorists in the E13 elevator lobby who continually push the up and down buttons so that every passing elevator stops and opens automatically. If it doesn't contain any non-students or dangerous-looking people, they hold the door open until everyone gives them a quarter. They have also claimed a section of the Cafeteria, and there have been fights over it. But nothing I'd call true terrorism."

"How about gang rape?" asked Hillary, the Secretary, quietly. Everything got quiet and we looked at her.

"It's just a rumor," she said. "Don't get me wrong. It hasn't happened to me. The word is that a few of the hardcore Terrorists do it, kind of as an initiation. They go to big parties, or throw their own. You know how at a big party there are always a few women—typical freshmen—who get very drunk. Some nice-looking Terrorist approaches the woman—I hear that they're very good at identifying likely candidates—and gets into her confidence and invites her to another party. When they get to the other party, she turns out to be the only woman there, and you can imagine the rest. But the really terrible thing is that they go through her things and find out where she lives and who she is, then keep coming back whenever they feel like it. They have these women so scared and broken that they don't resist. Supposedly the Terrorists have kind of an invisible harem, a few terrified women all over the Plex, too dumb or scared to say anything."

I was sitting there with my eyes closed, like everyone else a little queasy. "I've heard of the same thing elsewhere," I said.

"I wonder if it's happened to any Airheads," murmured Sarah. "God, I'll bet it has. I wonder if any of them know about it. I wonder if they even understand what is being done to them—some of them probably don't even understand they have a right to be angry."

"How could anyone not understand rape?" said Hillary.

"You don't know how mixed up these women are. You don't know what they did to *me*, without even understanding why I didn't like it. You can't imagine those people—they have no place to stand, no ideas of their own—if one is raped, and not one of her friends understands, where is she? She's cut loose, the Terrorists can tell her anything and make her into whatever they want. Shit, where are those animals going to stop? We're having a big costume party with them in December."

"There's a party to avoid," said Hillary.

"It's called Fantasy Island Nite. They've been planning it for months. But by the time the semester is over, those guys will be running wild."

"They've been running wild for a long time, it sounds like," said Willy. "You'd better get used to that, you know? I think you're living in the law of the jungle." That sounded a trifle melodramatic, but none of us could find a way to disagree.

Sarah and Casimir met in the Megapub, a vast pale airship hangar littered with uncertain plastic tables and chairs made of steel rods bent around intc uncomfortable chairlike shapes that stabbed their occupants beneath the shoulder blades. At one end was a long bar, at the other a serving bay connected into the central kitchen complex. Casimir declined to eat Megapub food and lunched on a peanut butter-and-jelly sandwich made from overpriced materials bought at the convenience store and a plastic cup of excessively carbonated beer. Sarah used the salad bar. They removed several trays from a window table and stacked them atop a nearby wastebasket, then sat down.

"Thanks for coming on short notice," said Sarah. "I need all the help I can get in selling this budget to Krupp, and your statistics might impress him."

Casimir, chewing vigorously on a big bite of generic white bread and generic chunkless peanut butter, drew a few computer-printed graphs from his backpack. "These are called Lorentz curves," he mumbled, "and they show equality of distribution. Perfect equality is this line here, at a forty-five degree angle. Anything less than equal comes out as a curve beneath the equality line. This is what we had with the old budget." He displayed a graph showing a deeply sagging curve, with the equality line above it for comparison. The graph had been produced by a computer terminal which had printed letters at various spots on the page, demonstrating in crude dotted-line fashion the curves and lines. "Now, here's the same analysis on our new budget." The new graph had a curve that nearly followed the equality line. "Each graph has a coefficient called the Gini coefficient, the ratio of the area between the line and curve to the area under the line. For perfect equality the Gini coefficient is zero. For the old budget it was very bad, about point eight, and for the new budget it is more like point two, which is pretty good."

Sarah listened politely. "You have a computer program that does this?"

"Yeah. Well, I do now, anyway. I just wrote it up."

"It's working okay?"

Casimir peered at her oddly, then at the graphs, then back at her. "I think so. Why?"

"Well, look at these letters in the curves." She pulled one of the graphs over and traced out the letters indicating the Lorentz curve: FELLATIOBUGGERYNECROPHILIACUNNILIN GUSANALINGUSBESTIALITY . . .

"Oh," Casimir said quietly. The other curve read: CUNTFUCKSHITPISSCOCKASSHOLETITGIVEMEANENEMA BEATMELICKMEOWNME . . . Casimir's face waxed red and his tongue was protruding slightly. "I didn't do this. These are supposed to say, 'new budget' and 'old budget.' I didn't write this into the program. Uh, this is what we call a bug. They happen from time to time. Oh, Jeez, I'm really sorry." He covered his face with one hand and grabbed the graphs and crumpled them into his bag.

"I believe you," she said. "I don't know much about computers, but I know there have been problems with this one."

About halfway through his treatise on Lorentz curves it had occurred to Casimir that he was in the process of putting his foot deeply into his mouth. She was an English major; he had looked her up in the student directory to find out; what the hell did she care about Gini coefficients? Sarah was still smiling, so if she was bored she at least respected him enough not to let it show. He had told her that he'd just now written this program up, and that was bad, because it looked

—oy! It looked as though he were trying to impress her, a sophisticated Humanities type, by writing computer programs on her behalf as though that were the closest he could come to real communication. And then obscene Lorentz curves!

He was saved by her ignorance of computers. The fact was, of course, that there was no way a computer error could do *that*—if she had ever run a computer program, she would have concluded that Casimir had done it on purpose. Suddenly he remembered his conversation with Virgil. The Worm! It must have been the Worm. He was about to tell her, to absolve himself, when he remembered it was a secret he was honor bound to protect.

He had to be honest. Could it be that he had actually written this just to impress her? Anything printed on a computer looked convincing. If that had been his motive, this served him right. Now was the time to say something witty, but he was no good at all with words—a fact he didn't doubt was more than obvious to her. She probably knew every smart, interesting man in the university, which meant he might as well forget about making any headway toward looking like anything other than an unkempt, poor, math-and-computer-obsessed nerd whose idea of intelligent conversation was to show off the morning's computer escapades.

"You didn't have to go to the trouble of writing a program."

"Ha! Well, no trouble. Easier to have the machine do it than work it out by hand. Once you get good on the computer, that is." He bit his lip and looked out the window. "Which isn't to say I think I'm some kind of great programmer. I mean, I am, but that's not how I think of myself."

"You aren't a hacker," she suggested.

"Yeah! Exactly." Everyone knew the term "hacker," so why hadn't he just said it?

She looked at him carefully. "Didn't we meet somewhere before? I could swear I recognize you from somewhere."

He had been hoping that she had forgotten, or that she would not recognize him through his glacier glasses. That first day, yes, he had read her computer card for her—a hacker's idea of a perfect introduction!

"Yeah. Remember Mrs. Santucci? That first day?" She nodded her head with a little smile; she remembered it all, for better or worse. He watched her intensely, trying to judge her reaction.

"Yes," she said, "sure. I guess I never properly thanked you for that, so—thank you." She held out her hand. Casimir stared at it, then put out his hand and shook it. He gripped her firmly—a habit from his business, where a crushing handshake was a sign of trustworthiness. To her he had probably felt like an orangutan trying to dislocate her shoulder. Besides which, some apple-blackberry jam had dripped out onto the first joint of his right index finger some minutes ago, and he had thoughtlessly sucked on it.

She was awfully nice. That was a dumb word, "nice," but he couldn't come up with anything better. She was bright, friendly and understanding, and kind to him, which was good of her considering his starved fanatical appearance and general fabulous ugliness. He hoped that this conversation would soon end and that they would come out of it with a wonderful relationship. Ha.

No one said anything; she was just watching him. Obviously she was! It was his turn to say something! How long had he been sitting there staring into the navy-blue maw of his mini-pie?

"What's your major?" they said simultaneously. She laughed immediately, and belatedly he laughed also, though his laugh was sort of a gasp and sob that made him sound as if he were undergoing explosive decompression. Still, it relaxed him slightly.

"Oh," she added, "I'm sorry. I forgot Neutrino was for physics majors."

"Don't be sorry." She was sorry?

"I'm an English major."

"Oh." Casimir reddened. "I guess you probably noticed that English isn't my strong point."

"Oh, I disagree. When you were speaking last night, once

you got rolling you did very well. Same goes for today, when you were describing your curves. A lot of the better scientists have an excellent command of language. Clear thought leads to clear speech."

Casimir's pulse went up to about twice the norm and he felt warmth in the lower regions. He gazed into the depths of his half-drained beer, not knowing what to say for fear of being ungrammatical. "I've only been here a few weeks, but I've heard that S. S. Krupp is quite the speaker. Is that so?"

Sarah smiled and rolled her eyes. At first Casimir had considered her just a typically nice-looking young woman, but at this instant it became obvious that he had been wrong; in fact she was spellbindingly lovely. He tried not to stare, and shoved the last three bites of pie into his mouth. As he chewed he tried to track what she was saying so that he wouldn't lose the thread of the conversation and end up looking like an absent-minded hacker with no ability to relate to anyone who wasn't destined to become a machine-language expert.

"He is *quite* a speaker," she said. "If you're ever on the opposite side of a question from S. S. Krupp, you can be sure he'll bring you around sooner or later. He can give you an excellent reason for everything he does that goes right back to his basic philosophy. It's awesome, I think."

At last he was done stuffing junk food into his unshaven face. "But when he out-argues you—is that a word?"

"We'll let it slip by."

"When he does that, do you really agree, or do you think he's just outclassed you?"

"I've thought about that quite a bit. I don't know." She sat back pensively, was stabbed by her chair, and sat back up. "What am I saying? I'm an English major!" Casimir chuckled, not quite following this. "If he can justify it through a fair argument, and no one else can poke any holes in it, I can't very well disagree, can I? I mean, you have to have some kind of anchors for your beliefs, and if you don't trust clear, correct language, how do you know what to believe?"

"What about intuition?" asked Casimir, surprising himself. "You know the great discoveries of physics weren't made through argument. They were made in flashes of intuition, and the explanations and proofs thought up afterward."

"Okay." She drained her coffee and thought about it. "But those scientists still had to come up with verbal proofs to convince themselves that the discoveries were real."

So far, Casimir thought, she seemed more interested than peeved, so he continued to disagree. "Well, scientists don't need language to tell them what's real. Mathematics is the ultimate reality. That's all the anchor we need."

"That's interesting, but you can't use math to solve political problems—it's not useful in the real world."

"Neither is language. You have to use intuition. You have to use the right side of your brain."

She looked again at the clock. "I have to go now and get ready for Krupp." Now she was looking at him—appraisingly, he thought. She was going to leave! He desperately wanted to ask her out. But too many women had burst out laughing, and he couldn't take that. Yet there she sat, propped up on her elbows—was she waiting for him to ask? Impossible.

"Uh," he said, but at the same time she said, "Let's get together some other time. Would you like that?"

"Yeah."

"Fine!" With a little negotiation, they arranged to meet in the Megapub on Friday night.

"I can't believe you're free Friday night!" he blurted, and she looked at him oddly. She stood up and held out her hand again. Casimir scrambled up and shook it gently.

"See you later," she said, and left. Casimir remained standing, watched her all the way across the shiny floor of the Megapub, then telescoped into his seat and nearly blacked out.

She did not have to wait long amid the marble-and-mahogany splendor of Septimius Severus Krupp's anteroom. She would have been happy to wait there for days, especially if she could have brought some favorite music and maybe Hyacinth, taken off her shoes, lounged on the sofa and stared out the window over the lush row of healthy plants. The administrative bloc of the Plex was an anomaly, like a Victorian mansion airlifted from London and dropped whole into a niche beneath C Tower. Here was none of the spare geometry of the rest of the Plex, none of the anonymous monochromatic walls and bald rectangles and squares that seemed to drive the occupants bonkers. No plastic showed; the floors were wooden, the windows opened, the walls were paneled and the honest wood and intricate parquet floors gave the place something of nature's warmth and diversity. In the past month Sarah had seen almost no wood—even the pencils in the stores here were of blond plastic—and she stared dumbly at the paneling everywhere she went, as though the detailed grain was there for a reason and bore careful examination. All of this was an attempt to invest American Megaversity with the aged respectability of a *real* university; but she felt at home here.

"President Krupp will see you now," said the wonderful, witty, kind, civilized old secretary, and the big panel doors swung open and there was S. S. Krupp. "Good afternoon, Sarah, I'm sorry you had to wait," he said. "Please come in."

Three of the walls of Krupp's office were covered up to about nine feet high with bookshelves, and the fourth was all French windows. Above the bookshelves hung portraits of the founders and past presidents of American Megaversity. The founding fathers stared sullenly at Sarah through the gloom of a century and a half's accumulated tobacco smoke, and as she followed the row of dignitaries around to the other end of the room, their faces shone out brighter and brighter from the tar and nicotine of antiquity until she got to the last spaces remaining, where Tony Commodi, Pertinax Rushforth and Julian Didius III gleamed awkwardly in modern suits and designer eyeglasses.

The glowing red-orange wooden floor was covered by three Persian rugs, and the ceiling was decorated with three concentric rings of elaborate plasterwork surrounding a great domed skylight. A large, carefully polished chandelier hung on a heavy chain from the center of the skylight. Sarah knew that the delicate leaded-glass skylight was protected from above by a squat geodesic dome covered with heavy steel grids and shatterproof Fiberglass panels, designed to keep everything out of S. S. Krupp's office except for the sunlight. Nothing short of a B-52 in a power dive could penetrate that grand silence, though a ring of shattered furniture and other shrapnel piled about the dome outside attested to the efforts of C Tower students to prove otherwise.

Krupp led her to a long low table under the windows, and they sat in old leather chairs and spread their papers out in the grey north light. Between them Krupp's ever-ready tape recorder was spinning away silently. Shortly the secretary came in with a silver tea service, and Krupp poured tea and offered Sarah tiny, cleverly made munchies on white linen napkins embroidered with the American Megaversity coat of arms.

Krupp was a sturdy man, his handsome cowboy face somewhat paled and softened by the East. "I understand," he said, "that you had some trouble with those playground communists last night."

"Oh, they were the same as ever. No unusual problems."

"Yes." Krupp sounded slightly impatient at her nonstatement. "I was pleased to see you disemboweled their budget."

"Oh? What if we'd stayed with the old one?"

"I'd have flushed it." He grinned brightly.

"What about this budget? Is it acceptable?"

"Oh, it's not bad. It's got some warts."

"Well, I want to point out at the beginning that it's easy for you to make minor adjustments in the budget until the warts are gone. It's much more difficult for the Student Government to handle. We almost had to call in the riot police to get this through, and any budget you have approved will be much harder."

"You're perfectly free to point that out, Sarah, and I don't disagree, but it doesn't make much difference."

"Well," said Sarah carefully, "the authority is obviously

yours. I'm sure you can take whatever position you want and back it up very eloquently. But I hope you'll take into account certain practicalities." Knowing instantly she had made a mistake, she popped a munchie into her mouth and stared out the window, waiting.

Krupp snorted quietly and sipped tea, then sat back in his chair and regarded Sarah with dubious amusement. "Sarah, I didn't expect you, of all people, to try that one on me. Why is it that everyone finds eloquence so inauspicious? It's as though anyone who argues clearly can't be trusted—that's the opposite of what reasonable people ought to think. That attitude is common even among faculty here, and I'm just at a loss to understand. I can't talk like a mongoloid pig-sticker on a three-day drunk just so I'll sound like one of the boys. God knows I can't support any position, only the right position. If it's not right, the words won't make it so. That's the value of clear language."

This was the problem with Krupp. He assumed that everyone always said exactly what they thought. While this was true of him, it was rarely so with others. "Okay, sorry," said Sarah. "I agree. I just didn't make my point too well. I'm just hoping you'll take into account the practical aspects of the problem, such as how everyone's going to react. Some people say this is a blind spot of yours." This was a moderately daring thing for Sarah to say, but if she tried to mush around politely with Krupp, he would cut her to pieces.

"Sarah, it's obvious that people's reactions have to be accounted for. That's just horse sense. It's just that basic principles are far more important than a temporary political squabble in Student Government. To you, all those monomaniacs and zombies seem more important than they are, and that's why we can't give you any financial authority. From my point of view I can see a much more complete picture of what is and isn't important, and one thing that isn't is a shouting match in that parody of a democratic institution that we call a government because we are all so idealistic in the university. What's important is principles."

Suddenly Sarah felt depressed; she sat limply back in her

chair. For a while nothing was said—Krupp was surprisingly sensitive to her mood.

"Student Government is just a sham, isn't it?" she asked, surprised by her own bitterness.

"What do you mean by that?"

"It has nothing to do with the real world. We don't make any real decisions. It's just a bunch of imaginary responsibilities to argue about and put down on our résumés."

Krupp thought it over. "It's kind of like a dude ranch. If you lose your dogies, there's someone there to round them up for you. But on the other hand, if you stand behind your horse you can still get wet. My Lord, Sarah, everything is *real.* There's no difference between the 'real' world and this one. The experience you're gaining is real. But it's true that the importance ascribed to Student Government is mostly imaginary."

"So what's the point?"

"The point is that we're here to go over this budget, and when I point out the warts, you tell me why they aren't warts. If you can justify them, you'll have a real effect on the budget." Krupp spread the pages of the budget out on the table, and Sarah saw alarming masses of red ink scrawled across them. She felt like whipping out Casimir's graphs, but she didn't have them with her, and couldn't risk Krupp's seeing what she had seen.

"Now one item which caught my eye," said Krupp half an hour later, after Sarah had lost five arguments and won one, "was this money for this little group, Neutrino. I see they're wanting to build themselves a mass driver."

"Yeah? What's wrong with that?"

"Well," said Krupp patiently, "I didn't say there's anything wrong—just hold on, let's not get adversarial yet. You see, we don't often use activities funds to back research projects. Generally these people apply for a grant through the usual channels. You see, first estimates of the cost of something like this are often wildly low, especially when made by young fellows who aren't quite on top of things yet. This thing is certain to come in over budget, so we'll either end up with a useless, half-completed heap of junk or a Neutrino floundering around in red ink. It seems kind of hasty and ill-considered to me, so I'm just recommending that we strike this item from the budget, have the folks who want to do this project do a complete, faculty-supervised study, then try to get themselves a grant."

Sarah sighed and stared at a small ornament on the teapot's handle, thinking it over.

"Don't tell me," said Krupp. "It's my blind spot again, right?" But he sounded humorous rather than sarcastic.

"There are several good reasons why you should pass this item. The main factor is the man who is heading the project. I know him, and he's quite experienced with this sort of thing in the real world. I know you don't like that term, President Krupp, but it's true. He's brilliant, knows a lot of practical electronics—he had his own business—and he's deeply committed to the success of this project."

"That's a good start. But I'm reluctant to see funds given to small organizations with these charismatic, highly motivated leaders who have pet projects, because that amounts to just a personal gift to the leader. Broad interest in the funded activity is important."

"This is not a personal vendetta. The plans were provided for the most part by Professor Sharon. The organization is already putting together some of the electronics with their own money."

"Professor Sharon. What an abominable thing that was." Krupp stared into the light for a long time. "That was a load of rock salt in the butt. If my damn Residence Life Relations staff wasn't tenured and unionized I'd fire 'em, find the scum who did that and boot 'em onto the Turnpike. However. We should resist the temptation to do something we wouldn't otherwise do just because a peripherally involved figure has suffered. We all revere Professor Sharon, but this project would not erase his tragedy."

"Well, I can only go on my gut feelings," said Sarah, "but I don't think what you've said applies. I'm pretty confident about this project."

Krupp looked impressed. "If that's the case, Sarah, then I should meet this fellow and give him a fair hearing. Maybe I'll have the same gut reaction as you do."

"Should I have him contact you?" This was a reprieve, she thought; but if Casimir had been so obviously nervous in front of *her*, what would he do under rhetorical implosion from Krupp? It was only reasonable, though.

"Fine," said Krupp, and handed her his card.

Their other differences of opinion were hardly worth arguing over. Halving the funding for the Basque Eroticism Study Cluster was not going to make political waves. The meeting came to a civil and reasonable end. Krupp showed her out, and she smiled at the old secretary and maneuvered the scarlet carpets of the administration bloc and dawdled by each painting, finally exiting into a broad shiny electric-blue cinderblock corridor. By the time she made it back to her room she had adjusted to the Plex again, and taught herself to see and hear as little of it as possible.

Ephraim Klein and some of his friends occasionally gathered in his room to smoke cheap cigars, if only because they detested them slightly less than John Wesley Fenrick did. Fenrick set the Go Big Red Fan up in the vent window and blew chill November air across the room, forcing perhaps eighty percent of the fumes out the door. A defect of the Rules was that they made no provision for exchange of air pollution, unfortunately for Fenrick, who despite his tradition of chemically induced states of awareness was fanatically clean.

Caught in a random eddy blown up by the Fan, a cigar resting in a stolen Burger King tinfoil ashtray fell off one evening and rolled several inches, crossing the boundary line into Fenrick's side of the room. It burned there for a minute or two before its owner, a friend of Klein's, made bold to reach across and retrieve it. The result was a brief brown streak on Fenrick's linoleum. Fenrick did not notice it immediately, but after he did, he grew more enraged every day. Klein was obligated to clean up "that mess," in his view. Klein's opinion was that anything on Fenrick's side of the room was Fenrick's problem; Klein was not paying fifteen thousand dollars a year and studying philosophy so he could be a floor-scrubber for a rude asshole geek like John Wesley Fenrick. He pointed to a clause in the Rules which tentatively bore him out. They screamed across the boundary line on this issue for nearly a week. Then, one day, I heard Ephraim yelling through their open door.

"Jesus! What the hell are you—Ha! I don't believe this shit!" He stuck his head outside and yelled, "Hey, everybody, come look at what this dumb fucker's doing!"

I looked.

For reasons I do not care to think about, John Wesley Fenrick kept a milkbottle full of dirt. When I looked in, he had pulled its lid off and was scattering red Okie loam over the boundary line and all over Ephraim's side of the room. Ephraim appeared to be more amused than angry, though he was very angry, and insisted that as many people as possible come and witness. Fenrick sat down calmly to watch television, occasionally smiling a small, solitary smile.

Again the question of my responsibility comes up. But how could I know it was an event of great significance? I had also seen lovers' quarrels in the Cafeteria; why should I have known this was much more important? I had no authority to order these people around. Moreover, I had no desire to. I had done as much as I could. I had shown them how to be reasonable, and if they could not get the hang of it, it was not my problem.

The next time I spectated, Ephraim Klein was alone, studying on his bed with Gregorian chants filling the room. I had come to see why he had borrowed my broom. He had used it to make a welcome mat for his roomie. Right in front of the Go Big Red Fan—the movable portion of the wall that served as a gate—he had swept all the dirt into an even rectangle about one by two feet and half an inch thick. In the dirt he had inscribed with his finger:

GET A BUTT

FUCK JOHNNIE-

WONNIE

When Fenrick got home I followed him discreetly to his room, to keep an eye on things. When I got to their doorway he was staring inscrutably at the welcome mat. He bent and opened the fan-gate, stepped through without disturbing the dirt and closed it. He turned, and looked for a while at the smirking Ephraim Klein. Then, with quiet dignity, John Wesley Fenrick reached down and set the Fan to HI, creating a small simulation of Oklahoma in the 1930's on the other side of the room.

Once I was satisfied that there would be no violence, I left and abandoned them to each other.

Septimius Severus Krupp stood behind a cheap plywood lectern in Lecture Hall 13 and spoke on Kant's Ethics. The fifty people in the audience listened or did not, depending on whether they (like Sarah and Casimir and Ephraim and I) had come to hear the lecture, or (like Yllas Freedperson) to see the Stalinist Underground Battalion Operative throw the banana-cream pie into S. S. Krupp's face.

I had come because I was fascinated by Krupp, and because opportunities to hear him speak were rare. Sarah, I think, had come for like reasons. Ephraim was a philosophy major, and Casimir came because this was the type of thing that you were supposed to do in a university. As for the SUBbies, they were getting edgy. What the fuck was wrong with the plan, man? they seemed to say, looking back and forth at one another sincerely and shaking their heads. The first phases had gone well. Operative 1 had gone out to the stage-left doorway, twenty feet to Krupp's side, opened the door and propped it, then made a show of smoking a cigarette and blowing the smoke out the door. It was obvious that she had severe reality problems by the way she posed there, putting on a casual air so weirdly melodramatic that everyone could see she must be a guerilla mime, a psycho or simply luded out of her big spherical frizzy-haired bandanna-wrapped head. It was also odd that she would show so much concern for others' lungs, considering that her friends were making loud, sarcastic noises and distracting gestures, but unfortunately S. S. Krupp's aides were too straight to tell the difference between a loony and a loony with a plan, and so they suspected nothing when she returned to her seat and forgot to shut the door again.

Ten minutes later, right on time, Operative 2 had arrived late, entering via the stage-right doorway and leaving it, of course, propped open. He moved furtively, like a six-foot mouse with thallium phenoxide poisoning, jerking his head around as if to look for right-wing death squads and CIA snipers.

But Operative 3 did not appear with the banana-cream pie. Where was he? Everyone knew about Krupp's CIA connections, and it was quite possible—don't laugh, the CIA is everywhere, look at Iran—that he might have been intercepted by fascist goons and bastinadoed and wired to an old engine block and thrown into a river. Perhaps the death squads were waiting in their rooms now, test-firing their silenced UZIs into cartons of Stalinist pamphlets.

In fact, Operative 3, when making his plans for the evening, had forgotten that once he bought the banana-cream pie at the convenience store it would have to thaw out. There is little political relevance in bouncing a rock-hard disc of frozen custard off S. S. Krupp's face—the splatter is the point—and so for half an hour he had been in a Plex restroom, holding the pie underneath the automatic hand dryer as unobtrusively as possible. Whenever he heard approaching steps, he stopped and dropped the pie into his knapsack, and held his hands nonchalantly under the hot air; hence he had succeeded only in liquefying the top two millimeters of the pie and ruffling the ring of whipped cream. He then repaired to a spot not far from the lecture hall where he rested the pie on a hot water pipe. There should be plenty of time left in the lecture, though it was hard to judge these things when stoned; Krupp's voice droned on and on, incomprehensible as all that logic and philosophy.

Operative 3 snapped to attention. How long had he been spacing off? Only one way to tell. He stuck his finger in the pie: still kind of stiff, but not stiff enough to break a nose and wet enough to explode mediagenically.

The time was now. Operative 3 pulled on his ski mask, stole to the open stage-left door, and waited for the right moment.

Shit! One of Krupp's CIA men had seen him! One of the Frosted Mini-Wheat types with the three-piece suits who ran Krupp's tape-recorder during speeches. No time to wait; the stun grenade might be lobbed at any moment.

To us he looked like a strange dexed-out bird, not running across the front of the hall so much as vibrating across at low frequency. He was tall, skinny, pale and wore an old T-shirt; he never seemed to plant any part of his nervous body firmly on the ground. He entered, bouncing off a doorjamb and losing his balance. He then caromed off a seat near a CIA man, who had not yet reacted, hopped three times to regain balance and, gaining some direction, scrambled toward S. S. Krupp, chased all the way by four bats driven into a frenzy by the aroma of the banana-cream pie.

"This means that the current vulgar usage of the word 'autonomous' to mean independent, i.e., free of external influence, sovereign, is not entirely correct," said Krupp, who glanced up from his notes to see what everybody was gasping at. "To be autonomous, as we can readily see by examining the Greek roots of the word—*autos* meaning self and *nomos* meaning law"—here he paused for a moment and ducked. The pie flew sideways over his head and exploded on the blackboard behind him. He straightened back up—"is to be self-ruling, to exercise a respect for the Law"—Operative 3 tottered out the door as the SUB groaned—"which in this case means not the law of a society or political system but rather the Law imposed by a rational man on his own actions." Outside in the hallway there was scuffling, and Krupp paused. With much grunting and swearing, Operative 3, sans ski mask, was dragged back into the room by three clean-cut students in pastel sweaters, accompanied by an older, smiling man in a plaid flannel shirt.

"Here's your man, President Krupp, sir," said an earnest young Anglo-Saxon, brushing a strand of hair from his brow with his free hand. "We've placed this Communist under citizen's arrest. Shall we contact the authorities on your behalf?" Their mentor beamed even more broadly at this suggestion, his horsey, protruding bicuspids glaring like great white grain elevators on the Dakota plain.

Krupp regarded them warily, walking around to the other side of the lectern as though it were a shield. Then he turned to the audience. "Excuse me, please. Guess I'm the highest authority here, so just let me clear this up." He looked back at the group by the doorway, who watched respectfully, except for Operative 3, who shouted from his headlock: "See, man? This is what happens when you try to change the System!" Several SUBbies began to come to his aid, but were halted by Krupp's aides.

"Who the hell are you?" said Krupp. "Are you from that squalid North Dakotan cult thing?"

They were shocked, even Operative 3, and stared uncomprehendingly. Deep concern showed in the lined, earnest face of the man in the plaid flannel. Finally he stepped forward. "Yessirree. We are indeed followers of the Temple of Unlimited Godhead, and proud of it too. With all due respect, just what do you mean by 'squalid'?"

"It's like a dead dog in the sitting room, son. Look, why don't you all just let that boy go? That's right."

Regretfully, they released him. Operative 3 stood up, shivering violently. He could not exactly thank Krupp. After hopping from foot to foot he spun and continued his flight down the hall as though nothing had happened.

"Look," Krupp continued. "We've got a security force here. We've got organized religions that have been doing just fine for millennia. Now what we don't need is a brainwashing franchise, or any of your Kool-Aid–stoned outlaw Mormon

Jesuits. I know times are hard in North Dakota but they're hard everywhere and it doesn't call for new religions. Of course, you have some very fine points on the subject of Communism. Now, this does not mean we will in any way fail to extend you full religious and political freedoms as with the old-fashioned nonprofit religions."

The SUB hooted at Krupp's wicked intolerance for religious diversity while the rest of the audience applauded. The TUGgies were galvanized, and spoke up for their renegade sect as eloquently as they knew how.

"But that man was a Communist! We found his card."

"Look at it this way. If TUG brainwashes people, how do you explain the great diversity of our membership, which comes from towns and farms of all sizes all over the Dakotas and Saskatchewan?"

"TUG is fully consistent with Judeo-Christo-Mohammedan-Bahaism."

Communism is the greatest threat in the world today."

"The goals of Messiah Jorgenson Five are fully consistent with the aims of American higher education."

"Our church is noncoercive. We believe of our own free, uh, pamphlet . . . explains our ideas in layman's language."

"Visit North Dakota this summer for fun in the sun. Temple Camp."

"Who is the brainwasher, our church, which teaches that we may all be Messiah/Buddhas together, or today's media society with its constant emphasis on materialism?"

"If you'll accept this free book it will reveal truths you may never have thought about before."

"I couldn't help noticing that you were looking a little down and out, kinda lonely. You know, sometimes it helps to talk to a stranger."

"Do you need a free dinner?"

Krupp watched skeptically. The older man was silent, but finally touched each student lightly on the shoulder, silencing one and all. They left, smiling.

Looking disgusted, Krupp returned to the microphone. "Where was I, talking about autonomy?"

He surveyed his notes and concluded his lecture in another twenty minutes. He paused then to light his cigar, which he had been fingering, twiddling, stroking and sniffing exquisitely for several minutes, and was answered by exagerrated coughing from the SUB section. "I'm free to answer some questions," he announced, surveying the room and squinting into his cigar smoke like a cowboy into the setting sun.

Nearly everyone in the SUB raised his/her hand, but Yllas Freedperson, Operatives 1 and 2 and two others arose and made their loud way up to the back of the hall for an emergency conference. They were deeply concerned; they stopped short of being openly suspicious, a deeply fascist trait, but it occurred to them that what had just happened might strongly suggest the presence of a TUG deep-cover mole in the SUB!

Meanwhile, question time went on down below. As was his custom, Krupp called on two people with serious questions before resorting to the SUB. Eventually he did so, looking carefully through that section and stabbing his finger at its middle.

By SUB custom, any call for a question was communal property and was distributed by consensus to a member of the group. This time, Dexter Fresser, Sarah's hometown ex-beau, number 2 person in the SUB and its chief political theorist, got the nod. Shaking his head, he pushed himself up in his seat until he could see Krupp's face hovering malevolently above the dome of the next person's bandanna. He took a deep breath, preparing for intellectual combat, and began.

"You were talking about autonomy. Well, then you were talking about Greek words of roots. I want to talk about Greek too because we have our roots in Greece, just like, you know, our words do—that is, most of us do, our culture does, even if our ethnicity doesn't. But Rome was much, much more powerful than Greece, and that was after most of the history of the human race, which we don't know anything about. And you know in Greece they had *gayness* all over the place. I'm saying that nice and loud even though you hate it, but even though, uh, you know, fascist? But you can't keep me from saying it. Did you ever think about the concentration camps? How all those people were killed by fascists? And also in Haiti, which we annexed in 1904. And did you ever think about the socialist revolution in France that was crushed by D-Day because the socialists were fighting off the Nazis single-handedly. Where's the good in that? Bela Lugosi was ugly, but he had a great mind. I mean, some of the greatest works of art were done by Satan-worshipers like Shakespeare and Michelangelo! And the next time your car throws a rod on I-90 between Presho and Kennebec because you lost your dipstick you should think, even if it is a hundred and ten in the shade, forty-four Celsius and there are red-winged blackbirds coming at you like Bell AH-64s or something. Put the goddamn zucchini in later next time and it won't get so mushy! I know this is strong and direct and undiplomatical, but this is real life and I can't be like you and phrase it like blue tennis-shoe laces hanging from the rear-view mirror. See?"

Here he stopped. Krupp had listened patiently, occasionally looking away to restack his notes or puff on his cigar. "No," he said. "Do you have a question, son?"

Emotionally wounded, Dex Fresser shook his head back and forth and gestured around it as though tearing off a heavy layer of tar. While his companions supported him, another SUBbie rose to take his place. She was of average height, with terribly pale skin and a safety pin through her septum. She rose like a zeppelin on power takeoff, and began to read in a singsong voice from a page covered with arithmetic.

"*Mister* Krupp, *sir.* Last year. According, to the *Monoplex Monitor,* you, I mean the Megaversity Corporation ruling clique, spent ten thousand dollars on legal fees for union-busting firms. Now. There are forty thousand students at American Megaversity. This means that on the average, you spent . . . four thousand million dollars on legal fees for union-busting alone! How do you justify that, when in this very city people have to pay for their own abortions?"

Krupp simply stared in her direction and took three long slow puffs on his cigar without saying anything. Then he turned to the blackboard. "This weather's not getting any better," he said, quickly drawing a rough outline of the United States. "It's this low pressure center up here. See, the air coming into it turns around counterclockwise because of the Coriolis effect. That makes it pump cold air from Canada into our area. And we can't do squat about it. It's a hell of a thing." He turned back to the audience. "Next question!"

The SUB wanted to erupt at this, but they were completely nonplused and hardly said anything. "I've taken too many questions from the kill-babies-not-seals crowd," Krupp announced. He called on Ephraim Klein, who had been waving his hand violently.

"President Krupp, I think the question of adherence to an inner Law is just a semantic smokescreen around the real issue, which is neurological. Our brains have two hemispheres with different functions. The left one handles the day-to-day thinking, conventional logical thought, while the right one handles synthesis of incoming information and subconsciously processes it to form conclusions about what the basic decisions should be—it converts experience into subconscious awareness of basic patterns and cause-and-effect relationships and gives us general direction and a sense of conscience. So this stuff about autonomy is nothing more than an effort by neurologically ignorant metaphysicists to develop, by groping around in the dark, an explanation for behavior patterns rooted in the structure of the brain."

Krupp answered immediately. "So you mean to say that the right hemisphere is the source of what I call the inner Law, and that rather than being a Law *per se* it is merely a set of inclinations rooted in past experience which tells the left hemisphere what it should do."

"That's right—in advanced, conscious people. In primitive unconscious bicameral people, it would verbally speak to the left hemisphere, coming as a voice from nowhere in times of decision. The left hemisphere would be unable to do otherwise. There would be no decision at all—so you would have perfect adherence to the Law of the right hemisphere voice, absolute autonomy, though the voice would be attributed to gods or angels."

Krupp nodded all the way through this, squinting at Klein. "You're one of those, eh?" he asked. "I've never been convinced by Jaynes' theory myself, though he has some interesting points about metaphors. I don't think an ignorant carpenter like Jesus had all that flawless theology pumped into the left half of his brain by stray neural currents." He thought about it for a moment. "Though it would be a lot quieter around here if everyone were carrying his stereo around in his skull."

"Jesus," said Ephraim Klein, "you don't believe in *God,* do you? *You?*"

"Well, I don't want to spend too much time on this freshman material, uh—what's your name? Ezekiel? Ephraim. But you ought to grapple sometime with the fact that this materialistic monism of yours is self-refuting and thus totally bankrupt. I guess it's attractive to someone who's just discovered he's an intellectual—sure was to me thirty years ago—but sometime you've got to stop boxing yourself in with this intellectual hubris."

Klein nearly rocketed from his chair and for a moment said nothing. He was bolt upright, supporting his weight on one fist thrust down between his thighs into the seat, chewing deeply on his lower lip and staring, to use a Krupp phrase, "like a coon on the runway." *"Non sequitur! Ad hominem!"* he cried.

"I know, I know. Tell you what. Stick around and I'll listen to your Latin afterward, we're losing our audience." Krupp began looking for a new questioner. From the back of the hall came the sound of a fold-down seat bounding back up into position, and we turned to make out the ragged figure of Bert Nix.

"Krupp cuts a fart! The sphinxter cannot hold!" he bellowed hoarsely, and sat back down again.

Krupp mainly ignored this, as his aides strode up the aisle to show Mr. Nix where the exit was, and turned his attention to the next questioner, a tall redheaded SUBbie who accused Krupp of accepting bribes to let wealthy idiots into the law school. Red added, "I keep asking you this question, Septimius, and you've never answered it yet. When are you going to pay some attention to my question?"

Krupp looked disgusted and puffed rapidly, staring at him coldly. Bert Nix paused in the doorway to shout: "My journey is o'er rocks & Mountains, not in pleasant vales; I must not sleep nor rest because of madness & dismay."

"Yeah," said Krupp, "and I give you the same answer every time, too. I didn't do that. There's no evidence I did. What more can I say? I genuinely want to satisfy you."

"You just keep slinging the same bullshit!" shouted the SUBbie, and slammed back down into his seat.

Casimir Radon listened to these exchanges with consuming interest. This was what he had dreamed of finding at college: small lectures on pure ideas from the president of the university, with discussion afterward. That the SUBbies had disrupted it with a pie-throwing made him sick; he had stared at them through a haze of anger for the last part of the meeting. Had he been sitting by the side door he could have tripped that bastard. Which would have been good, because Sarah Jane Johnson was sitting there three rows in front of him, totally unaware of his existence as usual.

Sarah's entrance, several minutes before the start of the lecture, had thrown Casimir into a titanic intellectual struggle. He now had to decide whether or not to say "hi" to her. After all, they had had a date, if you could call stammering in the Megapub for two hours a date. Later he had realized how dull it must have been for her, and was profoundly mortified. Now Sarah was sitting just twenty feet away, and he hated to disrupt her thoughts by just crashing in uninvited; better for her not to know he was there. But in case she happened to notice him, and wondered why he hadn't said "hi," he made up a story: he had come in late through the back doors.

He also wanted to ask Krupp a question, a dazzling and perceptive question that would take fifteen minutes to ask, but he couldn't think of one. This was regrettable, because

Krupp was a man he wanted to know, and he needed to impress him before making his sales pitch for the mass driver.

At the same time, he was working on a grandiose plan for gathering damaging information on the university, but this seemed stupid; seen from this lecture hall, American Megaversity looked pretty much the way it had in the recruiting literature.

He would continue with Project Spike until it gave him satisfaction. Whether or not he released the information depended on what happened at the Big U between now and then.

Sarah's voice sounded in one ear. "Casimir. Earth to Casimir. Come in, Casimir Radon." Shocked and suddenly breathless, he sat up, looking astonished.

"Oh," he said casually. "Sarah. Hi. How're you doing?"

"Fine," she answered, "didn't you see me?"

Eventually they went into the hallway, where S. S. Krupp was down to the last inch of his cigar and having a complicated discussion with Ephraim Klein. His aides stood to the sides brushing hairs off their suits, various alien-looking philosophy majors listened intently and I leaned against a nearby wall watching it all.

"Well, why didn't you say so?" Krupp was saying. "You're a Jaynesian and a materialistic monist. In which case you've got no reason to believe anything you think, because anything you think is just a predetermined neural event which can't be considered true or logical. Self-refuting, son. Think about it."

"But now you've gotten off on a totally different argument!" cried Klein. "Even if we presume dualism, you've got to admit that intellectual processes reflect neural events in some way."

"Well, sure."

"Right! And since the bicameral mind theory explains human behavior so well, there's no reason, even if you are a dualist, to reject it."

"In some cases, okay," said Krupp, "but that doesn't support your original proposition, which is that Kant was just trying to rationalize brain events through some kind of semantic necromancy."

"Yes it does!"

"Hell no it doesn't."

"Yes it does!"

"No it doesn't. Sarah!" said Krupp warmly. He shook her hand, and the philosophy majors, seeing that the intelligent part of the conversation was done, vaporized. "Glad you could come tonight."

"Hello, President Krupp. I wish you'd do this more often."

"Wait a minute," yelled Klein, "I just figured out how to reconcile Western religion and the bicameral mind."

"Well, take some notes quick, son, there's other people here, we'll get to it. Who's your date, Sarah?"

"This is Casimir Radon," said Sarah proudly, as Casimir reflexively shoved out his right hand.

"Well! That's fine," said Krupp. "That's two conversations I have to finish now. If we bring Bud here along with us to keep things from getting out of hand we ought to be safe."

"Look out. I'm not the diplomat you're hoping I am," I mumbled, not knowing what I was expected to say.

"What say we go down to the Faculty Pub and have some brews? I'm buying."

Our party got quite a few stares in the Faculty Pub. The three students were not even supposed to be in the place, but the bouncer wasn't very keen on asking Mr. Krupp's guests to show their IDs. This place bore the same relation to the Megapub as Canterbury Cathedral to a parking ramp. The walls were covered with wood that looked five inches thick, the floor was bottomless carpet and the tables were spotless slabs of rich solid wood. Enough armaments were nailed to the walls to defend a small medieval castle, and ancient portraits of the fat and pompous were interspersed with infinitely detailed coats of arms. The President ordered a pitcher of Guinness and chose a booth near the corner.

Ephraim had been talking the entire way. "So if you were the religious type, you know, you could say that the right side of the brain is the 'spiritual' side, the part that comes into contact with spiritual influences or God or whatever—it has a dimension that protrudes into the spiritual plane, if you want to look at it that way—while the left half is monistic and nonspiritual and mechanical. We conscious unicamerals accept the spiritual information coming in from the right side mixed in subtly with the natural inputs. But a bicameral person would receive that information in the form of a voice from nowhere which spoke with great authority. Now, that doesn't contradict the biblical accounts of the prophets—it merely gives us a new basis for their interpretation by suggesting that their communication with the Deity was done subconsciously by a particular hemisphere of the brain."

Krupp thought that was very good. Sarah and Casimir listened politely. Eventually, though, the conversation worked its way around to the subject of the mass driver.

"Tell me exactly why this university should fund your project there, Casimir," said Krupp, and watched expectantly.

"Well, it's a good idea."

"Why?"

"Because it's relevant and we, the people who do it, will learn stuff from it."

"Like what?"

"Oh, electronics, building things, practical stuff."

"Can't they already learn that from doing conventional research under the supervision of the faculty?"

"Yeah, I guess they can."

"So that leaves only the rationale that it is relevant, which I don't deny, but I don't see why it's more relevant than a faculty research project."

"Well, mass drivers could be very important someday!"

Krupp shook his head. "Sure, I don't deny that. There are all kinds of relevant things which could be very important someday. What I need to be shown is how funding of your project would be consistent with the basic mission of a great institution of higher learning. You see? We're talking basic principles here."

Casimir had removed his glasses in the dim light, and his

strangely naked-looking eyes darted uncertainly around the tabletop. "Well . . ."

"Aw, shit, it's obvious!" shouted Ephraim Klein, drawing looks from everyone in the pub. "This university, let's face it, is for average people. The smart people from around here go to the Ivy League, right? So American Megaversity doesn't get many of the bright people the way, say, a Big Ten university would. But there are some very bright people here, for whatever reasons. They get frustrated in this environment because the university is tailored for averagely bright types and there is very little provision for the extra-talented. So in order to fulfill the basic mission of allowing all comers to realize their full potential—to avoid stultifying the best minds here—you have to make allowances for them, recognize their special creativity by giving them more freedom and self-direction than the typical student has. This is your chance to have something you can point to as an example of the opportunities here for people of all levels of ability."

Krupp listened intently through this, lightly tapping the edge of a potato chip on the table. When Klein finally stopped, he nodded for a while.

"Yep. Yeah, I'd say you have an excellent point there, Isaiah. Casimir, looks as though you're going to get your funding." He raised an eyebrow.

Casimir stood up, yelled "Great!" and pumped Krupp's hand. "This is a great investment. When this thing is done it will be the most incredible machine you've ever seen. There's no end to what you can do with a mass driver."

There was a commotion behind Krupp, and suddenly, larger than life, standing on the bench in the next booth down, Bert Nix had risen to his full bedraggled height and was suspending a heavy broadsword (stolen from a suit of armor by the restroom) over Krupp's head. "O fortunate Damocles, thy reign began and ended with the same dinner!"

After Krupp saw who it was he turned back around without response. His two aides staggered off their barstools across the room and charged over to grab the sword from Bert Nix's hand. He had held it by the middle of the blade, which made it seem considerably less threatening, but the aides didn't necessarily see it this way and were not as gentle in showing Mr. Nix out as they could have been. He was docile except for some cheerful obscenities; but as he was dragged past a prominent painting, he pulled away and pointed to it. "Don't you think we have the same nose?" he asked, and soon was out the door.

Krupp got up and brought the conversation to a quick close. After distributing cigars to Ephraim and Casimir and me, he left. Finding ourselves in an exhilarated mood and with what amounted to a free ticket to the Faculty Pub, we stayed long enough to close it down.

Earlier, however, on his fifth trip to the men's room, Casimir stopped to look at the plaque under the portrait to which Bert Nix had pointed. "WILBERFORCE PERTINAX RUSHFORTH-GREATHOUSE, 1799–1862, BENEFACTOR, GREATHOUSE CHAPEL AND ORGAN." Casimir tried to focus on the face. As a matter of fact, the Roman nose did resemble Bert Nix's; they might be distant relatives. It was queer that a derelict, who couldn't spend that much time in the Faculty Pub, would notice this quickly enough to point it out. But Bert Nix's mind ran along mysterious paths. Casimir retrieved the broadsword from where it had fallen, and laughingly slapped it down on the bar as a deposit for the fourth pitcher of Dark. The bartender regarded Casimir with mild alarm, and Casimir considered, for a moment, carrying a sword all the time, *à la* Fred Fine. But as he observed to us, why carry a sword when you own a mass driver?

"Casimir?"

"Mmmmm. Huh?"

"You asleep?"

"No."

"You want to talk?"

"Okay."

"Thanks for letting me sleep here."

"No problem. Anytime."

"Does this bother you?"

"You sleeping here? Nah."

"You seemed kind of bothered about something."

"No. It's really fine, Sarah. I don't care."

"If it'd make you feel better, I can go back and sleep in my room. I just didn't feel like a half-hour elevator hassle, and my wing is likely to be noisy."

"I know. All that barf on the floors, rowdy people, sticky beer crud all over the place. I don't blame you. It's perfectly reasonable to stay at someone's place at a time like this."

"I get the impression you have something you're not saying. Do you want to talk about it?"

The pile of sheets and blankets that was Casimir moved around, and he leaned up on one elbow and peered down at her. The light shining in from the opposite tower made his wide eyes just barely visible. She knew something was wrong with him, but she also knew better than to try to imagine what was going on inside Casimir Radon's mind.

"Why should I have something on my mind?"

"Well, I don't see anything unusual about my staying here, but a lot of people would, and you seemed uptight."

"Oh, you're talking about sex? Oh, no. No problem." His voice was tense and hurried.

"So what's bothering you?"

For a while there was just ragged breathing from atop the bed, and then he spoke again. "You're going to think this is stupid, because I know you're a Women's Libber, but it really bothers me that you're on the floor in a sleeping bag while I'm up here in a bed. That bothers me."

Sarah laughed. "Don't worry, Casimir. I'm not going to beat you up for it."

"Good. Let's trade places, then."

"If you insist." Within a few seconds they had traded places and Sarah was up in a warm bed that smelled of mothballs and mildew. They lay there for an hour.

"Sarah?"

"Huh?"

"I want to talk to you."

"What?"

"I lied. I want to sleep with you so bad it's killing me. Oh, Jeez. I love you. A lot."

"Oh, damn. I knew it. I was afraid of this. I'm sorry."

"No, don't be. My fault. I'm really, really sorry."

"Should I leave? Do you want me out?"

"No. I want you to sleep with me," he said, as though this answer was obvious.

"How long have you been thinking about me this way?"

"Since we met the first time."

"Really? Casimir! Why? We didn't even know each other!"

"What does that have to do with it?" He sounded genuinely mystified.

"I think we've got a basic difference in the way we think about sex, Casimir." She had forgotten how they were when it came to this sort of thing.

"What does that mean? Did you ever think about me that way?"

"Not really."

Casimir sucked in his breath and flopped back down.

"Now, look, don't take it that way. Casimir, I hardly know you. We've only had one or two good conversations. Look, Casimir, I only think about sex every one or two days—it's not a big topic with me right now."

"Jeez. Are you okay? Did you have a bad experience?"

"Don't put me on the defensive. Casimir, our friendship has been just fine as it is. Why should I fantasize about what a friendship might turn into, when the friendship is fine as is? You've got to live in the real world, Casimir."

"What's wrong with me?"

The poor guy just did not understand at all. There was no way to help him; Sarah went ahead and spoke her lines. "Nothing's wrong with you. You're fine."

"Then what *is* the problem?"

"Look. I don't sleep with people because there's nothing

wrong with them. I don't fantasize about relationships that will never exist. We're fine as we are. Sex would just mess it up. We have a good friendship, Casimir. Don't screw it up by thinking unrealistically."

They sat in the dark for a while. Casimir was being open-minded, which was good, but still had trouble catching on. "It's none of my business, but just out of curiosity, do you like sex?"

"Definitely. It's a blast with the right person."

"I'm just not the right person, huh?"

"I've already answered that six times." She considered telling him about herself and Dex Fresser in high school. In ways—especially in appearance—Casimir was similar to Dex. The thing with Dex was a perfect example of what happened when a man got completely divorced from reality. But Sarah didn't want the Dex story to get around, and she supposed that Casimir would be horrified by this high school saga of sex and drugs.

"I think I'll do my laundry now, since I'm up," she said.

"I'll walk you home."

A few minutes later they emerged into a hall as bright as the interior of a small sun. The dregs of a party in the Social Lounge examined them as they awaited an elevator, and Sarah was bothered by what they were assuming. Maybe it would boost Casimir's rep among his neighbors.

An elevator opened and fifty gallons of water poured into the lobby. Someone had filled a garbage can with water, tilted it up on one corner just inside the elevator, held it in place as the doors closed, and pulled his hand out at the last minute so that it leaned against the inside of the doors. Not greatly surprised, Sarah and Casimir stepped back to let the water swirl around their feet, then threw the garbage can into the lobby and boarded the elevator.

"That's the nice thing about this time of day," said Casimir. "Easy to get elevators."

As they made their way toward the Castle in the Air, they spoke mostly of Casimir's mass driver. With the new funding and with the assistance of Virgil, it was moving along quite well. Casimir repeatedly acknowledged his debt to Ephraim for having done the talking.

They took an E Tower elevator up to the Castle in the Air. A nine-leaved marijuana frond was scotch-taped over the number 13 on the elevator panel so that it would light up symbolically when that floor was passed. In the corridors of the Castle the Terrorists were still running wild and hurling their custom Big Wheel Frisbees with great violence.

Casimir had never seen Sarah's room. He stood shyly outside as she walked into the darkness. "The light?" he said. She switched on her table lamp.

"Oh." He entered uncertainly, swiveling his bottle-bottom glasses toward the wall. Conscious of being in an illegally painted room, he shut the door, then removed his glasses and let them hang around his neck on their safety cord. Without them, Sarah thought he looked rather old, sensitive, and human. He rubbed his stubble and blinked at the forest with a sort of awed amusement. By now it was very detailed.

"Isotropic."

"You saw what?"

"*Isotropic.* This forest is isotropic. It's the same in all directions. It doesn't tend in any way. A real forest is anisotropic, thicker on the bottom, thinner on the top. This doesn't grow in any direction, it just is."

She sighed. "Whatever you like."

"Why? What's it for?"

"Well—what's your mass driver for?"

"Sanity."

"You've got your mass driver. I've got this."

He looked at her in the same way he had been staring at the forest. "Wow," he said, "I think I get it."

"Don't go overboard on this," she said, "but how would you like to attend something dreadful called Fantasy Island Nite?"

December

So nervous was Ephraim Klein, so primed for flight or combat, that he barely felt his suitcases in his hands as he carried them toward his room. What awaited him?

He had left a week ago for Thanksgiving vacation. He had waited as long as he could—but not long enough to outwait John Wesley Fenrick and three of his ugly punker friends, who leered hungrily at him as he walked out. The question was not whether a prank had been played, but how bad it was going to be.

Hyperventilating with anticipation, he stopped before the door. The cracks all the way around its edges had been sealed with heavy grey duct tape. This prank did not rely on surprise.

He pressed his ear to the door, but all he could hear was a familiar chunka-chunka-chunk. With great care he peeled back a bit of tape.

Nothing poured out. Standing to the side, he unlocked the door with surgical care. There was a cracking sound as the tape peeled away under his impetus. Finally he kicked it fully open, waited for a moment, then stepped around to look inside.

He could see nothing. He took another step and then, only then, was enveloped in a cloud of rancid cheap cigar smoke that oozed out the doorway like a moribund genie under the propulsion of the Go Big Red Fan.

Incandescently furious, he retreated to the bathroom and wet a T-shirt to put over his face. Thus protected he strode squinting down the foggy hallway into the lifeless room.

The only remaining possessions of John Wesley Fenrick's were the Go Big Red Fan and most of a jumbo roll of foil. He had moved out of the room and then covered his half of the room with the foil, then spread out on it what must have been several hundred generic cigars—it must have taken half an hour just to light them. The cigars had all burned away to ash, which had been whipped into a blizzard by the Go Big Red Fan on its slow creep across the floor to Ephraim's side. The room now looked like Yakima after Mount Saint Helens. The Fan had ground to a halt against a large potted plant of Ephraim's and for the rest of the week had sat there chunking mindlessly.

He checked a record. To his relief, the ash had not penetrated to the grooves. It had penetrated everything else, though, and even the Rules had taken on a brown parchmentlike tinge. Ephraim Klein took little comfort in the fact that his ex-roommate had not broken any of them.

He cranked open the vent window, set the Go Big Red Fan into it, cleared ash from his chair, and sat down to think.

Klein preferred to live a controlled life. He never liked to pull out all the stops until the final chord. But Fenrick had forced him to turn revenge into a major project and Klein did not plan to fail. He began to tidy his room, and to unleash his imagination on John Wesley Fenrick.

"Sarah?"

"Huh?"

"Did I wake you up?"

"No. Hi."

"Let's talk."

"Sure." Sarah rolled over on her stomach and propped herself up on her elbows. "I hope you're comfortable sleeping down there."

"Listen. Anyplace is more comfortable than my room when a party's going on above it."

"I don't mind if you want to share a bed with me, Hyacinth. My sister and I slept together until I was eleven and she was twelve."

"Thanks. But I didn't decide to sleep down here because I don't like you, Sarah."

"Well, that's nice. I guess it's a little small for two."

There was a long silence. Hyacinth sat up on her sleeping bag, her crossed legs stretching out her nightgown to make a faint white diamond in the darkness of the room. Then, soundlessly, she got up and climbed into bed with Sarah. Sarah slid back against the wall to make room, and after much giggling, rolling around, rearrangement of covers and careful placement of limbs they managed to find comfortable positions.

"Too hot," said Hyacinth, and got up again. She opened the window and a cold wind blew into the room. She scampered back and dove in next to Sarah.

"Comfy?" said Hyacinth.

"Yeah. Mmm. Very."

"Really?" said Hyacinth skeptically. "More than before? Not just physically. You don't feel awkward, being tangled up with me like this?"

"Not really," said Sarah dreamily. "It's kind of pleasant. It's just, you know, warm, and kind of comforting to have someone else around. I like you, you like me, why should it be awkward?"

"Would it be any different if I told you I was a lesbian?"

Sarah came wide awake but did not move. With one eye she gazed into the darkness above the soft white horizon of Hyacinth's shoulder, on which she had laid her head.

"And that I was hoping we could do other nice things to each other? If you feel inspired to, that is." She gently, almost imperceptibly, stroked Sarah's hair. Sarah's heart was pumping rhythmically.

"I wish you'd say something," said Hyacinth. "Are you not sure how you feel, or are you paralyzed with terror?"

Sarah laughed softly and felt herself relaxing. "I'm pretty naïve about this kind of thing. I mean, I don't think about it a lot. I sort of thought you might be. Is Lucy?"

"Yes. Nowadays we don't sleep together that much. Sarah, do you want me to sleep on the floor?"

Sarah thought about it, but not very seriously. The room was pleasantly cold now and the closeness of her friend was something she had not felt in a very long time. "Of course not. This is great. I haven't slept with anyone in a while—a man, I mean. Sleeping with someone is one of my favorite things. But it's different with men. Not quite as . . . sweet."

"That's for sure."

"Why don't you stay a while?"

"That'd be nice."

"Do you mind if we don't *do* anything?" At this they laughed loudly, and that answered the question.

"But we are doing something, you know," added Hyacinth later. "Your nose is in my breast. You're stroking my shoulder. I'm afraid that all counts."

"Oh. Gosh. Does that make me a lesbian?"

"Oh, I don't know. I guess you're off to a promising start."

"Hmmm. Doesn't feel like being a lesbian."

Hyacinth squeezed Sarah tight. "Look, honey, don't worry about it. This is just great as it is. I just wanted you to know the opportunity was there. Okay?"

"Okay."

"Want to go to sleep?"

"Take it easy, what's your hurry?"

Last Night was the night of the blue towers. A week before, the towers had glowed uniformly yellow as forty-two thousand students sat beneath their desk lamps and studied for finals. The next night, blue had replaced yellow here and there, as a few lucky ones, finished with their finals, switched on their TVs. This night, all eight towers were studded with blue, and whole patches of the Plex flickered in unison with the popular shows. The beer trucks were busy all day long down at the access lot, rolling kegs up the ramps to the Brew King in the Mall, whence they were dispersed in canvas carts and two-wheelers and Radio Flyers to rooms and lounges all over the Plex. As night fell and the last students came screaming in from their finals, suitcases full of dope moved through the Main Entrance and were quickly fragmented and distributed throughout the towers for quick combustion. By dinnertime the faucets ran cold water only as thousands lined up by the shower stalls, and the Caf was a desert as most students ate at restaurants or parties. After dark, spotlights and lasers crisscrossed the walls as partying students shone them into other towers, and when the Big Wheel sign blazed into life, bands of Big-Wheel–worshiping Terrorists all over the Plex launched a commemorative fireworks barrage that sent echoes crackling back and forth among the towers like bumper pool balls, punctuating the roar of the warring stereos.

By 10:00 the parties were just warming up. At 10:30 the rumor circulated that a special police squad sent by S. S. Krupp was touring the Plex to bust up parties. At 11:06 a keg was thrown from A24N and exploded on the Turnpike, backing up traffic for an hour with a twelve-car chain-reaction smashup. By 11:30 forty students had been admitted to the Infirmary with broken noses, split cheeks and severe inebriation, and it was beginning to look as though the official estimate of one death from overintoxication and one from accident might be a little low. The Rape/Assault/Crisis Line handled a call every fifteen minutes.

Precisely at 11:40:00 an unknown, uninvited, very clumsy student walked behind John Wesley Fenrick's chair at the big E31E end-of-semester bash and tripped, spilling a strawberry malt all over Fenrick's spiky blond hair.

John Wesley Fenrick was in the shower with very hot water spraying onto his head to dissolve the sticky malt crud, dancing around loosely to a tune in his head and playing the air guitar. He wondered whether the malt had been the work of Ephraim Klein. This, however, was impossible; his new room and number were unlisted and you couldn't follow people home in an elevator. The only way for Klein to find him was by a freak of chance, or by bribing an administration person with access to the computer—very unlikely. Besides, a malt on the head was a bush-league retaliation even for a quiet little harpsichord-playing New Jersey fart like Klein, considering what Fenrick had so brilliantly accomplished.

What made it even greater was that the administration had treated it like a hilarious college prank, a "concrete expression of malfunction in the cohabitant interaction, intended only as nonviolent emotional expression." Though they were after him to pay Klein's cleaning bills, Fenrick's brother was a lawyer and he knew they wouldn't push it in court. Even if they did, shit, he was going to be pulling down forty K in six months! A small price for triumph.

With a snarl of disgust, Fenrick dumped another dose of honey-beer-aloe-grub-treebark shampoo on his hair, finding that the tenacious malt substance still had not come off. *What's in this crap?* Fenrick thought. *Fuck up your stomach, for sure.*

Throughout E Tower, scores of Ephraim Klein's friends sat in the great shiny microwave bathrooms watching the Channel 25 Late Night Eyewitness InstaAction InvestiNews. Even during the most ghastly stories this program sounded like an encounter session among five recently canceled sitcom actors and developmentally disabled hairdressers' models. The weather, well, it was just as bad, but was relieved by its very bizarreness. The weatherman, a buffoon who knew nothing about weather and didn't care, was named Marvin DuZan the Weatherman and would broadcast in a negligee if it boosted ratings; his other gimmick was to tell an abominable joke at the conclusion of each forecast. After the devastating punchline was delivered, the picture of the guffawing pseudometeorologist and his writhing colleagues would be replaced by an animated short in which a crazy-looking bird tried to smash a tortoise over the head with a sledgehammer. At the last moment the tortoise would creep forward, causing the blow to rebound off his shell and crash back into the cranium of the bird. The bird would then assume a glazed expression and vibrate around in circles, much like a chair in Klein's room during the "Passacaglia and Fugue in C Minor," finally to collapse at the feet of the smiling turtle, who would then peer slyly at the audience and wiggle his eyebrow ridges.

During Marvin DuZan's forecast on Last Night, Ephraim Klein was standing outside his ex-roomie's shower stall, watching a portable TV and squirting Hyper Stik brand Humonga-Glue into the latch of the stall's door. He had turned down the volume, of course, and it seemed just as well, since from the reactions of the InvestiNews Strike Force (and the cameramen, who were always visible on the high-tech News Nexus set) it appeared that the joke tonight was a real turd. As the camera zoomed in on the goonishly beaming face of Marvin DuZan, Ephraim Klein's grip on the handles of two nearby urinals tightened and his heart beat wildly, as did the grips and the hearts of a small army of friends and hastily recruited deputies in many other E Tower bathrooms. Bird and Tortoise appeared, the hammer was brandished, and smash!

As the hammer rebounded on the bird's head, scores of toilets throughout E Tower were flushed, causing a vacuum so sharp that pipes bent and tore and snapped and cold water ceased to flow. There was a short pause, and then a bloodcurdling scream emanated from Fenrick's shower stall as clouds of live steam burst out the top. After some fruitless handle-yanking and Plexiglass-banging, the steam was followed by Fenrick himself, who fell ungainly to the floor with a crisp splat and shook his head in pain as Ephraim Klein escaped with his TV. In his haste Fenrick had lacerated his scalp on the steel showerhead, and as he pawed at his face to clear away suds and blood he was distantly conscious of a cold draft that irritated his parboiled skin, and a familiar chunka-chunka-chunk that could be heard above the sounds of gasping pipes and white water. Finally prying one eye open, he looked into the wind to see it: the Go Big Red Fan, complacently revolving in front of his stall, set on HI and still somewhat gray with cigar ash. Unfortunately for John Wesley Fenrick, he did not soon enough see the puddle of water which surrounded him, and which was rapidly expanding toward the base of the old and poorly insulated Fan.

. . .

This was also quite an evening for E17S. Ever since joining the Terrorists as the Flame Squad Faction, this all-male wing had suffered from the stigma of being mere copies of the Big Wheel Men, Cowboys and Droogs of E13. Tonight that was to change.

The Christmas tree had been purchased three weeks ago, left in a shower until the fireproofing compound was washed away, and hung over a hot-air vent in the storage room; it was now a lovely shade of incendiary brown. They took it up to E31, the top floor, seized an elevator, and stuffed the tree inside. Someone pressed all the buttons for floors 30 through 6 while others squirted lighter fluid over the tree's dessicated boughs.

Only one match was required. The door slid shut just as the smoke and flames began to billow forth, and with a cheer and a yell the Flame Squad Faction began to celebrate.

Twenty-four floors below, Virgil and I were having a few slow ones in my suite. I had no time for partying because I was preparing for a long drive home to Atlanta. Virgil happened to be wandering the Plex that night, looking in on various people, and had paused for a while at my place. Things were pretty quiet—as they generally had been since John Wesley Fenrick had left—and except for the insistent and inevitable bass beat, the wing was peaceful.

The fire alarm rang just before midnight. We cursed fluently and looked out my door to see what was up. As faculty-in-residence I didn't have to scurry out for every bogus fire drill, but it seemed prudent to check for smoke. The smoke was heavy when we opened the door, and we smelled the filthy odor of burning plastic. The source of the flame was near my room: one of the elevators, which had automatically stopped and opened once the fire alarm was triggered. I put a rag over my mouth and headed for the fire hose down the hall. Meanwhile Virgil prepared to soak some towels in my sink.

Neither of us got any water. My fire hose valve just sucked air and howled.

"God Almighty," Virgil called through the smoke. "Somebody pulled a Big Flush." He came out and joined the people running for the fire stairs. "No 'vators during fires so I'll have to take the stairs. I've got to get the parallel pipe system working."

"The what?"

"Parallel pipes," said Virgil, skipping into the stairwell. "Hang on! Find a keg! The architects weren't totally stupid!" And he was gone down the stairs.

I locked my door in case of looting and went off in search of a keg. Naturally there was a superabundance that night, and with some help from the too-drunk-to-be-scared owners I hauled it to the lobby and began to pump clouds of generic light into the flaming Christmas tree.

Casimir Radon was in Sharon's lab, washing out a beaker. This was merely the first step of the Project Spike glassware procedure, which involved attack by two different alcohols and three different concentrated acid mixtures, but he was in no hurry. For him Christmas had started the day before. With Virgil's help he could get into this lab throughout the vacation, and that meant plenty of time to work on Project Spike, build the mass driver and suffer as he thought about Sarah.

He was annoyed but not exasperated when the water stopped flowing. There was a gulp in the tapstream, followed by a hefty KLONK as the faucet handle jerked itself from his grasp. The flow of water stopped, and an ominous gurgling, sucking noise came from the faucet, like an entire municipal water system flushing its last. He listened as the symphony of hydraulic sound effects grew and spread to the dozens of pipes lining the lab's ceiling, the knocks and gurgles and hisses weaving together as though the pipes were having a wild Christmas party of their own. But Casimir was tired, and fairly absentminded to boot, and he shrugged it off as yet another example of the infinite variety of building and design defects in the Plex. The distilled water tap still worked, so he used it. Despite the drudgery of the task and his problems with Sarah, Casimir wore a little smile on his long unshaven face. Project Spike had worked.

He had been sampling Cafeteria food for three weeks, and until tonight had come up with nothing. Turkey Quiche, Beef Pot Pies, Lefto Lasagne, Estonian Pasties, and even Deep-Fried Chicken Livers had drawn blanks, and Casimir had begun to wonder whether it was a waste of time. Then came Savory Meatloaf Night, an event which occurred every three weeks or so; despite the efforts of advanced minds such as Virgil's, no one had ever discerned any reliable pattern which might predict when this dish was to be served. Today, of course, the last of the semester, Savory Meatloaf Night had struck and Casimir had craftily smuggled a slice out in his sock (the Cafeteria exit guards could afford to take it easy on Savory Meatloaf Night).

Not more than fifteen minutes ago, as he had been irradiating the next batch of rat poison, the computer terminal had zipped into life with the results of the analysis: high levels of Carbon-14! There were rats in the meatloaf!

That was a triumph for Casimir. It seemed likely to be a secret triumph, though. Sarah would never understand why he was doing this. Casimir wasn't even sure he understood it himself. S. S. Krupp had funded his mass driver, so why should he wish to damage the university now? He suspected that Project Spike was simply a challenge, an opportunity to prove that he was clever and self-sufficient in a sea of idiocy. He had accomplished that, but as a political tactic it was still pretty dumb. Sarah would certainly think so.

Sarah had also thought it was dumb when he had decided to work in the lab all night instead of going to Fantasy Island Nite. She was right on that issue too, perhaps, but Casimir loathed parties of all sorts and would use any excuse to avoid one. Hence he was here on the bottom of the Plex, washing out rat-liver scum, while she was far above, dancing in the clown costume she had shown him—probably having a wonderful time as handsome Terrorists salivated on her.

He observed that he was leaning on the counter staring

at the wall as though it were a screen beaming him live coverage of Sarah at the party. Maybe he would leave now, retaining a lab coat as a costume, and go up and surprise Sarah.

Meanwhile water was squirting out of the wall, forcing its way through the cracks between the panels, running out from under the baseboards and trickling through the grommets in the sides of Casimir's tennis shoes. Abruptly brought back into the here and now, he looked around half-dazed and started unplugging things and moving them to higher ground. What the hell was happening? A broken pipe? He figured that if there was enough water pressure on the 31st floor to run a fire hose, the pressure down here must be phenomenal. This was going to be a hell of a mess.

Water was now trickling through old nail holes high on the wall. Casimir covered the computer terminal with plastic and then ran out to search for B-men. They were not here now, of course—probably spreading rat poison or celebrating some Crotobaltislavonian radish festival.

Across from Sharon's lab was a freight elevator closed off by a manually operated door. When he looked through its little window Casimir saw water falling down the shaft, and sparks spitting past. He got insulated gloves from the lab and hauled the door open. Several gallons of pent-up water rushed past his ankles and fell into the blackness. From below rose the harsh wet odor of the sewers.

The sparks issued from the electrical control box on the shaft wall. Once Casimir was sure there was no danger of fire or electrocution he left, leaving the doors open so that water could drain out of this bottom level of the Plex.

Oh, God. The rat poison. It was only supposed to stay in the radiation source for a minute at a time! Casimir had put it in an *hour* ago, then simply forgotten about it once the results of the analysis had come in. The damn stuff must be glowing in the dark. He sloshed back into the lab.

Water poured and squirted from the walls and ceiling everywhere he looked. He shielded his face from spray and walked through a wall of water toward the neutron source, a garbage can full of paraffin with the plutonium button at its center. Stopping to listen, he sensed that the slow ticking noise which had been coming from one wall had sped up and was growing louder. He stood petrified as it grew into a rumble, then a groan, then a scream—and the wall crashed open and a torrent rushed through the lab. An adjacent storage room had filled with water from a large broken pipe, and Casimir was now knocked to the floor by a torrent of Fiberglass panels, aluminum studs, and janitorial supplies. He rolled just in time to see the neutron source, buoyed on the rush of water, bob through the doorway and across the hall.

Taking care not to be swept along, he made his way to the shaft and looked down. All was dark, but from far below, under the waterfall sound, he thought he heard a buzz, or a ringing: the sound of an alarm. Maybe his ears were ringing, and maybe it was a fire alarm above. Nauseated, he returned to the lab, sat on a table and awaited the B-men.

Fantasy Island Nite was turning out to be not such a bad thing after all. Those Terrorists upstairs in their own lounge were making a lot of noise, but those down here on 12 were making an admirable effort to behave, per their agreement with the Airheads. Only this agreement had persuaded Sarah and Hyacinth to show up. It was potentially interesting, it was nice to be sociable once in a while and they could always leave if they didn't like it. Sarah wore a clown costume. This was her way of making fun of the fantasy theme of the party—most Airheads came as beauty queens or vamps—and had the extra advantage of making her totally unrecognizable. Hyacinth put together a smashing Fairy Godmother costume, as a joke only Sarah would get. Their plan was to drink so much it would become socially acceptable for them to dance together.

While Sarah was working on the first stage of this plan she began getting a lot of attention from three Terrorists. These three—a Cowboy, a Droog and a Commando—were obvious jerks, each one incensed that she would not reveal her name, but as long as they danced, fetched drinks and didn't try to converse they seemed like harmless fun. After a while she got a little boogied out, and withdrew from the action to look out over the city. Hyacinth had gone to visit another party and was expected back soon.

Time twisted and she was no longer at the party; she was watching it from a place in her mind where she had not been for many years. She slid backward like an air hockey puck until she was high up in one corner of the room. The walls of the Plex fell away so that she could see in all directions at once.

One of the picture windows had been replaced by a gate that opened to the sky. The gate was gaily festooned with shining pulsing color-blobs. All the other party-goers had lined up in front of it. On one side of the gate stood Mitzi, taking tickets; on the other, Mrs. Santucci, checking off their names on a clipboard. Each Airhead-Terrorist who passed through stepped out and sat down on a long slippery-slide made of blue light, and squealed with delight as they zoomed earthward. Sarah could not see all the way to the slide's end, but she could see that, below, the Death Vortex had turned into a whirlpool of multicolored fire. Forests and towns and families whirled around and around before gurling down the center to disappear. The Vortex was ringed with hundreds of fire trucks whose crews halfheartedly sprayed their tiny jets of water into its middle.

When Sarah looked beyond the whirlpool she saw in its light a shattered landscape of rubble and corpses, where bawling dirty people scrabbled about aimlessly and squinted into the fire-glow. Nothing more than dust, solitary bricks, cockroaches and jagged glass was there, though Sarah's vision swooped across it for a thousand miles and a thousand years.

Beyond its distant edge was a nonlandscape: a milky white vacuum where choking black clouds of static grew, split, re-formed, hurled themselves against one another, clashed with horrible dry violence and abated to grow and form again. Its slowness and its dryness made it the most awful thing Sarah had ever seen. After five millennia, when she thought she was entirely lost and crazy, she saw a piece of broken glass, then a rivulet of blood. Following them, she found herself in the terrible landscape again, with the Plex on the horizon erupting like a volcano. Blue beams of light shot from its top and wrapped around her and sucked her back through the air into the building. But she could no longer find herself there. She was no longer in the Lounge. The Lounge had been vacant for centuries and only dust and yellowed party favors remained. Following footprints in the dust she came to the hallway—brightly lit, loud, filled with shouting students and bats. She flew straight down the hall until four dots at its end grew into four people and she could slow down and follow them. There were three men: a Cowboy and a Commando held the arms of a woman dressed as a clown, hurrying her down the hall, while a Droog walked ahead of them carrying a paper punch cup which glowed with a green light from within. Sarah closed her eyes to the glow and shook her head, and when she opened them again she was the clown-woman—though she did not want to be.

They were in an elevator filled with black water that rose and crept warmly up Sarah's thighs. Swimming in the water were bad hidden things, so she kicked as well as she could. Her hands were held up above her head by men ten feet high, lost in the glare of the overhead light where it was too bright to look.

Then they were on a floor that reminded Sarah of the broken landscape. On the wall a giant mouth was chewing vigorously, drooling on the floor and smacking its disgusting lips. The men threw her through it and followed behind.

"I won't go down the slide," she protested, but they did not really care. Inside all was red and blue; a neon beer emblem burned in the window and licked her with its hot rays. There stood a giant in a football costume who wore the head of Tiny, leader of the Terrorists.

"Is Dex here?" she said, more out of habit than anything. It would be just like Dex to slip her some LSD. But then she knew this was a stupid question.

She felt the door being locked behind her and saw the music turned up until it was purest ruby red, causing her body to turn into fragile glass. To move now would be to shatter and die.

"Handle with care," she murmured, "I'm glass now," but the words just dribbled down the front of her costume. They were ripping her costume away. She squirmed but felt herself cracking horribly. The beer sign cast grotesque red and blue light on the transparent flesh of her thighs.

She knew what was going to happen next. Somehow her mind connected it all in a straight line, before the idea was swept away by the internal storm. The worst thing in the world. She should have gone down the slide.

She made an effort of will. The sound and the light went away, it was spring; grass and flowers and blue sky were all around and she was not about to be raped. She was eating raspberries on the banks of a creek. Out of curiosity she scratched at the air with her fingernail. Red and blue rays stabbed out into her skin again, and peeking all the way through for a moment she could see that they had not yet started.

No wonder; they were moving in slow motion. Sarah would have to spend many hours waiting on the banks of the creek. She drew back into the sunshine. Perhaps she could live here forever and have a perfect life.

When she slept, she dreamed of those dry, unending wars in the land of milky white. She knew it was all an illusion.

She tore it away and came back to the room. She was not going to sleep through anything. She was not going to imagine anything that didn't exist.

The sign was wavy and upside down now, reflected in a puddle of water on the floor.

A Terrorist was in the corner twisting a faucet handle. Sarah stood up. Tiny turned toward her and smashed her across the face. She was on the floor again, and over there a Terrorist groped in the scintillating ocean of red and blue for the sign's power cord.

He was screaming like an electric guitar now. He was

trying to swim in the shallow lake of blood and bile.

Sarah was thrown onto a bed. Her arms and legs flailed, and one heel found a Terrorist's kneecap. The Droog got on top of her, and because he was in slow motion she kicked him in the nuts. He curled up on top of her and she looked through his hair at the ceiling, which sputtered in the failing sign-light. Tiny was unwinding a long piece of rope and its thin tendrils floated around him like black smoke. She rolled half out from under the Droog and curled into a fetal position so he could not take her arms and legs. As she did she peered down through the transparent floor and saw the Airheads, plastered with grotesque makeup, drinking LSD from crystal goblets and cheering. But where was Hyacinth?

Hyacinth was standing in the doorway. An extremely loud explosion seeped into her ears. Smoke filled the room, catching the hallway light and forming hundreds of 3-D images from Sarah's past life.

Hyacinth's fairy godmother costume was changed, for now she wore heavy leather gloves over her white cloth gloves, and bulky ear protectors under her conical hat, and a pair of goggles beneath her milky-white veil. In her hands she carried a giant revolver. Sarah knew that under her dress, Hyacinth was made of strong young oak-wood.

Hyacinth took one step into the room and shrugged on the main light switch. Tiny stood in the center, staring. The man who had been swimming on the floor was dead. Another clasped his knee and screamed at the ceiling. Sarah laid her head down restfully and put her hands on her ears.

Cones of fire were spurting from the front and back of Hyacinth's gun and her hands were snapping rhythmically up and down. Tiny had his hands on his chest, and as he walked backward toward the window the back of his football jersey bulged and fluttered like a loose sail, darkness splashing away from it. The electrical cord was between his legs. His steps shortened and he fell backward through the picture window. The cord and plug trailed slowly behind him and snapped out of the room and were gone. The noise was so immense that Sarah heard nothing until much later. The blasts were synchronized with the music's beat:

WHAM WHAM WHAM WHAM

with each WHAM followed by a high whine that shrieked through until the next WHAM, so that when Tiny was gone there remained a terrible high tone that resonated between the walls of the room, far too loud for Sarah to stand, filling her awareness like the blowing of the Last Trumpet and tormenting the injured Terrorists, who cried out in it and wrapped their arms around their heads. The Droog on top of Sarah was pulled slowly away and Hyacinth yanked Sarah to her feet. Sarah did not even move her legs as the smoky doorway twisted past her, the corridor walls with their Big Wheels rolled on by, the landings of the fire stair rushed up toward her from blackness and her soft bed drifted up to envelop her face. Hyacinth was above her, probing, rubbing, kissing her. She would not stop until Sarah was well again.

Virgil used his master key eight times before attaining a dark, stained sub-sublevel of the Plex, where great water mains from the City entered from the depths and fed the giant pumps that pressurized the plumbing system overhead.

In an uncharacteristic flash of foresightedness, the Plex's architects made allowances for the certainty that, once in a while, one group or another would flush hundreds of toilets simultaneously and damage the cold water system. So they installed two parallel, independent systems of main pipes to feed the distribution systems of the wings; to switch between them one need only close one set of valves and open another. This Virgil accomplished by grunting and straining at a few red iron wheels. Satisfied that things were settling back toward normal, he set out for Professor Sharon's old lab to see if Casimir Radon was still there.

. . .

The Computing Center was not far away. Though it had many rooms, its heart was a cavernous square space with white walls and a white floor waxed to a thick glossy sheen. The white ceiling was composed of square fluorescent light panels in a checkerboard pattern. Practically all of the room was occupied by disc memory units: brown-and-blue cubes, spaced in a grid to form a seemingly endless matrix of six-foot aisles. At the center of the room was an open circle, and at the center of that area stood the Central Processing Unit of the Janus 64. A smooth triangular column five feet on a side and twelve feet high, it would have touched the ceiling except that above was a circular opening about forty feet across, encircled by a railing so that observers could stand and look into the core of the Computing Center.

Around the CPU were a few other large machines: secondary computers to organize the tasks being fed to the Janus 64, array processors, high-speed laser printers, a central control panel and the like. But closest of all was the Operator's Station, a single video terminal, and tonight the operator was Consuela Gorm, high priestess of MARS. She had volunteered to do the job on this night of partying, when the only people still using the computer in the adjacent Terminal Room were the goners, the hopelessly addicted hackers who had nothing else to live for.

The only sounds were the whine of the refrigeration units, which drew away the heat thrown off by the tightly packed components of the Janus 64; the high hum of the whirling memory discs, miltiplied by hundreds; and the pitter-pat of Consuela's fingertips across the keypad of the Operator's Station. She was hunkered down there, staring hypnotized into the screen, and behind her Fred Fine stood thin and straight as the CPU itself. Tonight they were testing Shekondar Mark V, their state-of-the-art Sewers & Serpents simulation program. Now, at a few minutes before midnight, they had worked out the few remaining bugs and they stood transfixed as their program did exactly what it was supposed to.

"Looks like a routine adventure," mumbled Consuela.

"But it looks like Shekondar might have generated a werewolf colony in this party's vicinity. I'm seeing a lot of indications of lycanthropic activity."

"You'd want plenty of silver arrows on this campaign."

"With this level of activity, you'd want a cleric specialized in lycanthropes," scoffed Consuela.

Fred Fine was perfectly aware of that. He was merely making conversation so Consuela would not realize he was thinking intently about something, and try to beat him to the punch. Yes, the werewolf colony was obvious—it was a large one, probably east-northeast in the Mountains of Krang. Only large-scale organization could account for the lack of wolfsbane and garlic, which were usually abundant in this biome. But Fred Fine was concerned with observations on a far grander scale. Though nothing was catastrophically wrong, something was very strange, and Fred Fine found that he was covered with goosebumps. He tapped a foot nervously and scanned the descriptions scrolling past on the screen.

"Listen for birds!" he hissed.

Consuela ordered an Aural Stimuli Report, specifying Avians as field of interest.

NO AVIAN SOUNDS DETECTABLE, said Shekondar Mark V.

"Damn!" said Fred Fine. "Let's have the alchemist test one of his magical substances—say, some of the fire-starting fluid."

MAGICAL COMBUSTIBLES AND EXPLOSIVES FAIL TO FUNCTION.

"Uh-oh! All characters jettison all magical items immediately!"

SMALL FIRES AND EXPLOSIONS IN ALCHEMICAL SUBSTANCES.

"Good. We'll get farther away."

LARGE EXPLOSIONS. NOXIOUS SMOKE. NO INJURIES DUE TO WIND DIRECTION.

"Lucky! Forgot even to check for that. My character will try turning on his pocket calculator."

ELECTRONIC DEVICES FAIL TO FUNCTION.

"Wait a minute," said the astonished Consuela. "What is this? I don't know of anything that can cause disruption of magic and technology at the same time! Some kind of psionics, maybe?"

"I don't know. I don't know what it is."

"We wrote this thing. We have to know what's in it."

"Aural Stimuli Report, General. Quick!"

DEEP RUMBLING CONSISTENT WITH TEMBLOR OR LARGE SUBTERRANEAN MOVEMENT.

"Can't be an earthquake. We'll head for solid rock, that should protect us. Head uphill!"

MOVEMENT SPEED HALVED BY TEMBLOR. ROCK OUTCROPPING REACHED IN SIX TURNS. EXTREMELY LOUD HISSING. GASEOUS ODOR. GROUND BECOMES WARM.

"It's almost like a Dragon," said Consuela in a constricted, terrified voice, "but from down in the earth."

"God! I can't think of what the hell this is!"

ONE HUNDRED METERS TO YOUR NORTH EARTH BULGES UPWARD. BULGE IS FIFTY METERS IN DIAMETER AND RISING QUICKLY. EARTH CRACKS OPEN AND YOU SEE A GLISTENING SURFACE . . .

The terminal went blank. From just behind them came a violent scream, like a buzzsaw wrenching to a stop in a concrete block. They knew it though they had never heard it before; it was the sound of a disc unit dying, the sound made when the power was cut off and the automatic readers (similar to the tone-arms of phonographs) sank into, and shredded, the hysterically spinning magnetic discs. It was to them what the snapping of a horse's leg is to a jockey, and when they spun around they were astonished and horrified to see a curtain of water pouring onto the floor from the circular walkway overhead. Not more than a dozen feet from the base of the Janus 64, the ring was spreading inward.

"Hey, Fred 'n' Con!" someone yelled. At one end of the room, at the window that looked out into the Terminal Room, an overweight blond-bearded hacker squinted at them. "What's going on? System problems? Oh, Jeeeezus!"

He turned to his comrades in the Terminal Room, screaming, "*Head crash! Head crash! Water on the brain!*" Soon two dozen hackers had vaulted through the window into the Center and were sprinting down the aisles as fast as their atrophied legs could carry them, the men stripping off their shirts as they ran.

Another disc drive shorted out and sizzled to destruction. Abruptly Fred Fine spun and grabbed the Operator's Keychain, then ran through the circular waterfall toward another wall of the Center, shouting for people to follow him.

In seconds he had snapped open the door to the storage room, where tons of accordion-fold computer paper were stored in boxes. As some of the hackers did their best to sweep water away from the base of the Janus 64, the rest formed a line from the storage room to the central circle. The boxes were passed down the line as quickly as possible, slit open with Fred Fine's authentic Civil War bayonet and their contents dumped out as big green-and-white cubes inside the deadly water-ring. Though it did not entirely stem the flow, the paper absorbed what it did not dam. Soon all space between the waterfall and the CPU was covered with at least two feet of soggy computer paper. Meanwhile, Consuela had shut down all the disc drives.

The danger was past. Fred Fine, still palpitating, noticed a small waterfall in the corner of the storage room. Flicking on the lights for the first time, he clambered over the stacked boxes to check it out.

In the corner, three pipes about ten inches in diameter ran from floor to ceiling. One was swathed in the insulation used for hot water pipes. Water was running down one of the bare pipes; higher up, above the ceiling, it must be leaking heavily. Fred Fine put his hand on the third pipe and found that it was neither hot nor cool, and did not seem to be carrying a current. A firehose supply pipe? No, they were supposed to be bright red. He puzzled over it, rubbing his hand over the long thin whiskers that straggled down his cheeks when he had been computing for a week or more.

As he watched, the hiss of running water lowered and

died away, and a few seconds later the leak from above was stemmed. There was the KLONK of an air hammer in a pipe. Fred Fine put his hand on the mystery pipe, and began to feel the gentle vibration of running water underneath, and a sensation of coolness spreading out from the interior.

The hackers saw him wandering slowly toward the Janus, which rose like an ancient glyph from the tumbled, sodden blocks of paper. He had a distant look, and was consumed in thought.

"These are the End Times," he was heard to say. "The Age draws to a close."

He was no weirder than they were, so they ignored him.

Tiny landed on a burning sofa not far from my window. The impact forced much excess lighter fluid out of the foam cushions and created a burst of flame whose origin we did not know until later. Once the water had come back on, and we had soaked the elevator and the Christmas tree, we aimed the fire hose out my living-room window and drenched the heap of dimly burning furniture that was Tiny the Terrorist's funeral pyre. It was a few minutes past midnight, the second strangest midnight I have ever known, and my first semester at the Big U was at an end.

SECOND
SEMESTER

January

The fog of war was real down here. The knee-deep glom on the tunnel floor exhaled it in sheets and columns, never disturbed by a clean wind or a breath of dryness. Through its darkness moved a flickering cloud of light, and at the center walked a tall thin figure with headphones sprouting long antennae. He carried an eight-foot wizard's staff in one hand, a Loyal Order of Caledonian Comrades ceremonial sword in the other, and wore hip waders, a raincoat, and a gas mask. His headlamp's beam struck the fog in front of his eyes and stopped dead, limiting his visibility to what he could see through occasional holes in the atmosphere. From the twin filters of his gas mask came labored hissing sighs as he panted with an effort of wading through the muck.

"I've come to the intersection of the Tunnel of Goblins and the Tunnel of Dragon Blood," he announced. "This is my turnaround point and I will now return to rendezvous with Zippy the Dwarf, Lord Flail and the White Priest in the Hall of the Idols of Zarzang-Zed." True to his word, Klystron the Impaler laboriously reversed direction by gripping his staff and making a five-point turn, then paused for a rest.

A voice crackled from his headphones, a lush, tense introvert's voice made tinny by the poor transmission quality.

"Roger, Klystron the Impaler, This is Liaison. Please hold." There was a brief silence, but the flickering of her fingers on the computer keys *up there,* and her ruffling of papers, kept her voice-operated mike open. She snickered, unaware that Klystron, Zippy, Flail and the White Priest could hear her. "Oh ho," she gloated, "are you in for trouble now. You don't hear anything yet." More fingers on the keyboard. Klystron concluded that Shekondar had generated a monster with many statistics and at least three attack modes, a monster with which Consuela was not entirely familiar. Perhaps, for once, a worthy opponent . . .

Klystron the Impaler drew his mask down to dangle on his chest. Taking care not to breathe through his nose, he brought out his wineskin, opened the plastic spigot and shot a long stream of warm Tab onto his tongue. God, it stank down here. But Klystron could deal with far worse. Anything was better than doing this in a safe light place, like the D & D players, and never experiencing the darkness, claustrophobia and terror of reality.

Liaison was ready. "Klystron the Impaler, known to his allies as the Heroic, High Lord of Plexor, Mage of the CeePeeYu and Tamer of the Purple Worm of Longtunnel, is attacked by the ELECTRIC MICROWAVE LIZARD OF QUIZZYXAR!" She nearly shrieked the last part of this, as frenzied as a priestess during a solar eclipse. "You are not surprised, you have one turn to prepare defense. Statement of intent, please."

Klystron corked the wineskin with his thumb and let it drop to his side, sliding the mask back over his face. So, it was the electric microwave lizard of Quizzyxar. Consuela's reaction had hinted it was something big. He was ready.

"As you will recall, I took an anti-microwave potion six months ago, before the Siege of Dud, and that has not worn off yet. As he will probably attack with microwaves first, this gives me an extra turn. I begin by flipping down the visor on my Helm of Courage. Is he charging?"

"No. She's advancing slowly."

"I stand my ground on the left side of the tunnel and fire a freeze-blast from my Staff of Cold." He wheeled his staff into firing position as though it were a SAM-7 shoulder-fired antiaircraft missile launcher and his body shook with imagined recoil as he CHOONGed a couple of sound effects into the mike.

But why had Consuela specified the lizard was a she? With Consuela it could not have been a mere Freudian slip.

"Okay," Con said slowly, typing in Klystron's actions, "your freeze-blast strikes home, hitting her in the left head. It has no effect. The lizard's microwave blast does not hurt you but explodes your wineskin, causing you two points of concussion damage. It continues to advance at a walk."

"*Touché.*" So much for Tab.

"Liaison, do we know about this yet?" It was Lord Flail.

Liaison asked Shekondar. "Yes. The lizard makes a lot of noise and you hear it."

"Okay!" cried Lord Flail. "We'll proceed at top speed toward the melee."

"Me too," added Zippy the Dwarf.

"It'll take us forever to get there," said the White Priest, who did not seem to be very far into his character. "We're at least a thousand feet away."

Klystron the Impaler took advantage of these negotiations to do some planning. Obviously the female type was immune to cold—highly obnoxious to the male type.

"In my quiver I have a fire arrow which I took from the dying Elf-Lord during that one time when we space-warped into Middle Earth. I'll fire that. Which head is it leading with?"

"Left."

"Then I aim for the right head."

"The arrow finds its mark and burns fiercely," announced Consuela with relish. "The lizard bites you on your left arm, which is now useless until the White Priest can heal it. While you switch back to your sword it claws you with a tentacle/claw appendage, doing five points of damage to your chest. The claw is poisoned but . . . you make your saving throw."

"Good. I'll take a swipe at the appendage as it attacks."

"You miss."

"Okay, I'll make for the right head."

"The lizard has succeeded in clawing the fire arrow out of its hide. Now it makes a right tongue strike, sticking you, and begins drawing you into its mouth. Will you attack the tongue, or parry the poison claw attacks?"

Klystron considered it. This was a hell of a situation. As a last resort he could use a wish from his wishing sword, but that could be risky, especially with Consuela.

"I will defend myself from the claws, and deal with the mouth when I get to it. I've been swallowed before."

"You parry three swipes. But now you are just inside the mouth and it is exhaling poison gas, and you have lost half your strength."

"Oh, all right," said Klystron in disgust. "I'll make a wish on my wishing sword. I'll say . . ."

"Wait a minute!" came the feminine squeal of Zippy the Dwarf. "I just spotted him!"

Snapping to attention, Klystron scanned the surrounding mist with the beam of his headlamp and picked out Zippy's red chest waders. "Confirm contact with Zippy the Dwarf. Estimated range ten meters."

"In that case," observed Consuela, "she is right behind the lizard. Your action, Zippy?"

"Three double fireballs from my fireball-shooting tiara."

"I duck," said Klystron hastily. Shekondar was just clever enough to generate an accidental hit on *him*. He sighed in relief and his pulse became leaden. It was going to be fine.

"All fireballs strike in abdominal area. Lizard is now in bad shape and moving slowly."

"I cut myself loose from the tongue."

"Done."

"Two more fireballs in the right head."

"As soon as I'm out of the way, that is."

"Okay. The lizard dies. Congratulations, people. That's ten thousand experience points apiece."

Klystron and Zippy joined up, edging together against the tunnel wall to avoid the imaginary lizard corpse sprawled between them. They shook hands robustly, though Klystron had some reservations about being saved by a female dwarf.

"Good going, guys!" shouted Lord Flail, overloading his mike.

"Yeah. Way to go," the White Priest added glumly.

"Flail and Priest, give estimated distance from us." Klystron was concerned; those two were the weakest members, even when they were together, and now that one monster had been noisily eliminated others were sure to converge on the area to clean up.

"To be frank, I'm not sure," answered the White Priest. "I kind of thought we'd be getting to an intersection near you by now, but apparently not. The layout of these tunnels isn't what I saw on the Plex blueprints."

Klystron winced at this gross violation of game ethics and exchanged exasperated glances with Zippy. "You mean that the secret map you found was incorrect," he said. "Well, don't continue if you're lost. We will proceed in the direction of the Sepulchre of Keldor and hope to meet you there." He and Zippy plugged off down the tunnel.

They wandered for ten minutes looking for one another, and every sixty seconds Liaison had them stop while Shekondar checked for prowling monsters. Shortly, Klystron overheard an exchange between the Priest and the Lord, who apparently had removed their masks to talk.

"Take it easy! It doesn't take very long, you know," said the White Priest. "I'll be right back. Stay here."

"I don't think we should separate, Your Holiness," pleaded Lord Flail. "Not after a melee that'll attract other monsters."

Klystron turned up the gain on his mike and shouted, "He's right! Don't split up," in hopes that they would hear it without earphones.

The Priest and Lord Flail conversed inaudibly for a few seconds. Then Flail came back on, having apparently replaced his mask. "Uh, this is to notify Shekondar that the White Priest has gone aside," he said, using the code phrase for taking a leak. Klystron chuckled.

A few seconds later came another prowling monster check. Everyone tensed and waited for Shekondar's decree.

"Okay," said Liaison triumphantly, "we've got a monster. Lord Flail, now solo, is attacked by . . . giant sewer rats! There are twelve of them, and they take him by surprise."

"We'll listen for his battle cry and try to locate him that way," announced Klystron immediately, and pulled his headphones down to listen. Oddly, Flail had not responded.

"Statement of intent! Move it!" snapped Consuela.

But no statement of intent was forthcoming from Flail. Instead, a ghastly series of sound effects was transmitted through his mike. First came a whoosh of surprise, followed by a short pause, and some confused interjections. Then nothing was heard for a few seconds save ragged panting; and then came a long, loud scream which obliged them to turn down the volume. The screaming continued, swamping the others' efforts to make themselves heard on the line.

Finally Consuela's voice came through, angry and hurt. "You're jumping the gun. The melee hasn't started yet." But Lord Flail was no longer screaming, and the only sounds coming over his mike were an occasional scraping and shuffling mixed with odd squeals that might have been radio trouble.

Klystron and Zippy, headphones down, could hear the screams echoing down the tunnel a second after they came in on the radio. Flail's plan was clear; he was making a godawful lot of noise to assist the better fighters in tracking him down. A good plan for a character with a fighting level of three and a courage/psychostability index of only eight, but it was a little overdone.

The odd noises continued for several minutes as they tramped toward the scene of the melee, which was in a higher tunnel with a much drier floor.

Ahead of them, Flail's headlamp cast an unmoving yellow blotch on the ceiling. On the fringes of that cone of light moved great swift shadows. Klystron slowed down and drew his sword. Zippy had dropped back several feet. "Making final approach to Flail's location," Klystron mumbled, edging forward, falling unconsciously into the squatting stance of the sabre fighter. At the end of his lamp's beam he could see quickly moving gray and brown fur, and blood.

"At your approach the rats get scared and flee," said Consuela, frantically typing, "though not without persuasion."

He could see them clearly now. They were dogs, like German shepherds, though rather fat, and they had long, long bare tails. And round ears. And pointy quivering snouts. Oh, my God.

Several scurried away, some stood their ground staring at his headlamp with beady black and red eyes, and one rushed him. Reacting frantically he split the top of its skull with a blow of the dull sword. The rest of the giant sewer rats turned and ran squealing down the tunnel. Lord Flail was not going anywhere, and what remained of him, as battle-hardened as Klystron was, was too disgusting to look at.

"You are too late," said Consuela. "Lord Flail has been gnawed to death by the giant sewer rats."

"I know," said Klystron. Hearing nothing from Zippy, he turned around to see her sitting there staring dumbly at the corpse. "Uh, request permission to temporarily leave character."

"Granted. What's going on down there?"

"Consuela, this is Fred. It's Steve. Steven has been, uh, I supposed you could say, uh, eaten, by a bunch of . . ." Fred Fine stepped forward and swept his beam over the brained animal at his feet. "By giant sewer rats."

"Oh, golly!" said Zippy. "What about Virgil? He went off to go tinkle!"

"Jeez," said Fred Fine, and started looking around for footprints. "Liaison, White Priest is solo in unknown location."

The twelve giant sewer rats had run right past the White Priest and ignored him. He was standing with his chest waders around his thighs, relieving himself onto a decaying toilet paper core, when the mass of squealing rodent fervor had hurtled out of the fog, parted down the middle to pass aroung him, rejoined behind, their long tails lashing inquisitively around his knees, and shot onward toward their rendezvous with Lord Flail.

He stood there almost absentmindedly and finished his task, staring into the swirling lights in front of his face, breathing deeply and thinking. Then the screaming started, and he pulled up his waders and got himself together, unslinging the Sceptre of Cosmic Force from its handy shoulder strap and brandishing it. Fred Fine and Consuela had insisted he bring along convincing props, so he had manufactured the Sceptre, an iron re-rod wrapped in aluminum foil, topped with a xenon flash tube in a massive glass ball that was wired to a power supply in the handle. When they had mustered for the expedition, he had switched off the lights and "convinced" them by turning it on and bouncing a few explosive purple flashes off their unprepared retinas. After he had explained the circuitry to Fred Fine, they entered character and descended a long spiral stair into the tunnels. In the ensuing three hours the White Priest had used the Sceptre of Cosmic Force to blind, disorient and paralyze three womp rats, a samurai, a balrog, Darth Vader and a Libyan hit squad.

He began to slog back toward Steven, and the screaming ended. Either the rats had left or Steven was dead or someone had helped the poor bastard out. Tramping down the tunnel, his lamp beam bounding over the discarded feminine-hygiene products, condoms, shampoo-bottle lids and Twinkie wrappers, Virgil tried to decide whether this was really happening or was simply part of the game. The tunnels and the chanting of Consuela had made a few inroads on his sense of reality, and now he was not so sure he had seen those rats. The screams, however, had not sounded like the dramaturgical improvisations of an escapist Information Systems major.

He stopped. The rats were coming back! He looked around for a ladder, or something to climb up on, but the walls of the tunnel were smooth and featureless. He turned and ran as quickly as he could in the heavy rubberized leggings, soon discarding the gas mask and headphones so he could take deep breaths of the fetid ammonia-ridden air.

The rats were gaining on him. Virgil searched his memory, trying to visualize where this tunnel was and where it branched off; if he were right, there were no branches at all —it was a dead end. But the blueprints had been wrong before.

A branch? He swept the left wall with his lamp, and discerned a dark patch ten paces ahead. He made for it. The rats were lunging for his ankles. He kept his left hand on the wall as he ran, flailing with the Sceptre in his right. Then his left hand abruptly felt air and he dove in that direction, tripping over his own feet and falling on his side within the branch tunnel.

A rat was on top of him before he had come to rest, and he stood up wildly, using his body to throw the screaming beast against the wall. Grabbing the Sceptre in both hands he swung it like a scythe. Whatever else it was, it was first and foremost a rod with a heavy globe at one end, a fine mace.

Virgil stood with his back to the wall, kicking alternately with his feet like a Crotobaltislavonian folk dancer to shake off the bites of the rats, lashing out with the Sceptre at the same time. He was then blinded as his hand touched the toggle switch that activated the powerful flasher at the end. He cringed and looked away, and at the same time the rats fell back squealing. He shook sweat and condensation from his eyes, snapped his wet hair back and waved the Sceptre around at arms' length, surveying his opponents in the exploding light. They were gathered around him in a semicircle, about ten feet away, and with every flash their fur glistened for an instant and their eyeballs sparked like distant brakelights. They were hissing and muttering to one another now, their number constantly growing, watching with implacable hostility—but none dared approach.

Continuing to wave the Sceptre of Cosmic Force, Virgil felt down with his other hand to the butt of the weapon, where he had installed a dial to adjust the speed of the flashing. Turning it carefully up and down, he found that as the flashes became less frequent, the circle tightened around him unanimously so that he must frantically spin the dial up to a higher frequency. At this the rats reacted in pain and backed away in the flickering light in stop-action. Now Virgil's vision was composed of a succession of still images, each slightly different from the last, and all he saw was rats. dozens of rats, and each shining purple rat-image was fixed permanently into his perfect memory until he could remember little else. Encouraged by their fear, he grasped the knob again and sped up the flasher, until suddenly they reached some breaking-point; then they dissolved into perfect chaotic frenzy and turned upon one another with hysterical ferocity, charging lustily together into a great stop-action melee at the tunnel intersection. Bewildered and disgusted, Virgil closed his eyes to shut it out, so that all he saw was the red veins in his eyelids jumping out repeatedly against a yellow-pink background.

Some of the rats were colliding with his legs. He lowered the Sceptre so that the flasher was between his ankles, and, guiding himself by sound and touch, moved away from the obstructed intersection and down the unmapped passageway. He opened his eyes and began to run, holding the flasher out in front of him like a blind man's cane. From time to time he encountered a rat who had approached the source of the sound and fury and then gone into convulsions upon encountering the sprinting electronics technician with his Sceptre. Soon, though, there were no more rats, and he turned it off.

Something was tugging at his belt. Feeling cautiously, he found that it was the power cord of the headlamp, which had been knocked off his head and had been bouncing along behind him ever since. He found that the lens, once he had wiped crud from it, cast an intermittent light—a connection was weakened somewhere—that did, however, enable him to see.

This unmapped tunnel was relatively narrow. Its ceiling, to his shock, was thick with bats, while its floor was clean of the stinking glom that covered most of the tunnels in varying depths. Instead there was a thin layer of slimy fluid and fuzzy white bat guano which stank but did not hinder. This was probably a good sign; the passage must lead somewhere. He noted the position of the Sceptre's dial that had caused the rats to blow their stacks, then slung the weapon over his shoulder and continued down the passage, his feet curiously light and free in the absence of deep sludge.

Before long he discerned a light at the end of the tunnel. He broke into a jog, and soon he could see it clearly, about a hundred and fifty feet away: a region at the end of the passage that was clean and white and fluorescently lit. Nothing in the blueprints corresponded to this.

He was still at least a hundred feet away when a pair of sliding doors on the right wall at the very end of the tunnel slid open. He stopped, sank to a squat against the tunnel wall and then lay on his stomach as he heard shouting.

"Ho! Heeeeyah! Gitska!" Making these and similar noises, three B-men peeked out the door and up the passageway, then emerged, carrying weapons—not just pistols, but small machine guns. Two of them assumed a kneeling position on the floor, facing up the tunnel, and their leader, an enormous B-man foreman named Magrov, stood behind them and sighted down the tunnel through the bulky infrared sight of his weapon. About halfway between Virgil and the B-men, a giant rat had turned and was scuttling toward Virgil. There was a roar and a flickering light not unlike that of Virgil's Sceptre, and two dozen automatic rounds dissolved the rat into a long streak on the floor. Magrov shone a powerful flashlight over the wreckage of the rodent, but apparently Virgil was too small, distant and filthy to be noticed. Magrov belched loudly in a traditional Croto expression of profound disgust, and the other two murmured their agreement. He signaled to whoever was waiting beyond the sliding doors.

A large metal cylinder about a foot and a half in diameter and six feet long, strapped to a heavy four-wheeled cart, was carefully pushed sideways into the passage. Magrov walked to a box on the wall, punched a button with the barrel of his weapon and spoke. "Control, Magrov once again. We have put it in normal place like usual, and today only one of those goddamn pink-tailed ones, you know. We taking off now. I guess we be back in a few hours."

"That's an A-OK. All clear to reascend, team." came the unaccented answer from the box. The B-men walked through the sliding doors, which closed behind them, and Virgil was barely able to make out a hum which sounded like an elevator.

After a few seconds, the end wall of the tunnel parted slowly and Virgil saw that it wasn't the end at all, it was a pair of thick steel slabs that retracted into the floor and ceiling. Beyond the doors was a large room, brightly lit, containing several men walking around in what looked like bright yellow rainsuits and long loose hoods with black plastic windows over the eyes. Three of these figures emerged and quickly slid cart and cylinder through the doors while two others stood guard with submachine guns. Then all retreated behind the doors, and the steel slabs slid back together and sealed the tunnel.

He remained motionless for a few minutes more, and noticed some other things: wall-mounted TV cameras that incessantly swiveled back and forth on power gimbals; chemical odors that wafted down the tunnel after the doors were closed; and the many gnawed and broken rat bones scattered across the nearby floor. Then Virgil Gabrielsen concluded that the wisest thing to do was to go back and mess with the giant rats.

Several days into the second semester, the Administration finally told the truth about the Library, and allowed the media in to photograph the ranks upon ranks of card catalog cabinets with their totally empty drawers.

The perpetrators had done it on Christmas Day. The Plex had been nearly deserted, its entrance guarded by a single guard at a turnstile. At eight in the morning, ten rather young- and hairy-looking fellows in B-man uniforms had arrived and haltingly explained that as Crotobaltislavonians they followed the Julian calendar, and had already celebrated Christmas. Could they not come in to perform needed plumbing repairs, and earn quadruple overtime for working on Christmas Day? The skeptical guard let them in anyway; if he could not trust the janitors, whom could he trust?

As reconstructed by the police, the burglars had gathered

in the card catalog area all the canvas carts they could find. They had taken these through the catalog, pulling the lock-pins from each drawer and dumping the contents into the carts. The Library's 4.8 million volumes were catalogued in 12,000 drawers of three-by-five cards, and a simple calculation demonstrated that all of these cards could be fitted into a dozen canvas carts by anyone not overly fastidious about keeping them in perfect order. The carts had been taken via freight elevator to the loading docks and wheeled onto a rented truck, which according to the rental agency had now disappeared. Its borrower, a Mr. Friedrich Engels, had failed to list a correct address and phone number and proved difficult to track down. The only untouched drawer was number 11375, STALIN, JOSEPH to STALLBAUM, JOHANN GOTTFRIED.

The Library turned to the computer system. During the previous five years, a sweatshop of catalogers had begun to transfer the catalog into a computer system, and the Administration hoped that ten percent of the catalog could be salvaged in this way. Instead they found that a terrible computer malfunction had munched through the catalog recently, erasing call numbers and main entries and replacing them with knock-knock jokes, Burma-Shave ditties and tracts on the sexual characteristics of the Computing Center senior staff.

The situation was not hopeless; at any rate, it did not deteriorate at first. The books were still arranged in a rational order. This changed when people began holding books hostage.

A Master's Candidate in Journalism had a few books she used over and over again. After the loss of the catalog she found them by memory, carried them to another part of the Library, and cached them behind twelve feet of bound back issues of the *Nepalese Journal of Bhutanian Studies*. A library employee from Photoduplication then happened to take down a volume of *Utah Review of Theoretical Astrocosmology*, shelved back-to-back with *NJBS*, and detected the cache. She moved it to another place in the Library, dumping it behind a fifty-volume facsimile edition of the ledgers of the Brisbane/Surabaya Steam Packet Co. Ltd., which had been published in 1893 and whose pages had not yet been cut. She then left a sign on the Library bulletin board saying that if the user of such-and-such books wanted to know where they were, he or she could put fifty dollars in the former stash, and she, the employee, would leave in its place the new location. Several thousand people saw this note and the scam was written up in the *Monoplex Monitor;* it was so obviously a good idea that it rapidly became a large business. Some people took only a few volumes, others hundreds, but in all cases the technique was basically the same, and soon extra bulletin board capability was added outside the entrance to the Library bloc. Of course, this practice had been possible before the loss of the card catalog, but that event seemed to change everyone's scruples about the Library. The central keying system was gone; what difference did it make?

Free enterprise helped take up the slack, as students hired themselves out as book-snoopers. The useless card catalog area took on the semblance of a bazaar, each counter occupied by one or two businesses with signs identifying their rates and services. The psychic book-snoopers stole and hid books, then—claiming to use psychic powers—showed spectacular efficiency in locating them. The psychics soon eclipsed the businesses of their nonspiritual colleagues. In order to seem as mysterious as possible, the psychics engaged in impressive rituals; one day, working alone on the top floor, I was surprised to see Professor Emeritus Humphrey Batstone Forthcoming IV being led blindfolded through the stacks by a leotarded witch swinging a censer.

Every week the people who had stolen the card catalog would take a card and mail it to the Library. The conditions of ransom, as expressed on these cards in a cramped hand, were that: (1) S. S. Krupp and the Trustees must be purged; (2) the Megaversity must have open admissions and no room, board or tuition fees; (3) the Plex must become a free zone with no laws or authority; (4) the Megaversity must withdraw all investments in firms doing business in South Africa, firms doing business with firms doing business in South Africa and firms doing business with firms doing business with firms doing business in South Africa; (5) recognize the PLO and the baby seals.

S. S. Krupp observed that card catalogs, a recent invention, had not existed at the Library of Alexandria, and though he would have preferred, *ceteris paribus*, to have the catalog, we didn't have one now, that was too bad, and we were going to have to make do. There was dissent and profound shock over his position, and righteous editorials in the *Monitor*, but after a week or two most people decided that, though Krupp was an asshole, there wasn't any point in arguing.

"Welcome and thanks for coming to the mass driver demonstration." Casimir Radon swallowed some water and straightened his glacier glasses. "The physics majors' organization Neutrino has put a lot of time and work into this device, much of it over the Christmas holiday, and we think it is a good example of what can be done with activities money used constructively. God *damn* it!"

He was cursing at the loudness of his Plex neighbor, Dex Fresser, whose stereo was an electronic signal processor of industrial power. For once Casimir did not restrain himself; he was so nervous over the upcoming demonstration that he failed to consider the dire embarrassment, social rejection and personal danger involved in going next door to ask this jerk-off to turn down his music. He was pounding on Dex Fresser's door before his mind knew what his body was doing, and for a moment he hoped his knocks had been drowned out by the bass beats exploding from Fresser's eighteen-inch woofers. But the door opened, and there was Dex Fresser, looking completely disoriented.

"Could you turn that down?" asked Casimir. Fresser, becoming aware of his presence, looked Casimir over from head to foot. "It kind of disturbs me," Casimir added apologetically.

Fresser thought it over. "But you're not even there that much, so how can it disturb you?" He then peered oddly into Casimir's face, as though the goggle-eyed Radon were the captain of a ship from a mirror Earth on the other side of the sun, which was pretty much what he was thinking. Chagrined, Casimir ground his teeth very loudly, generating so much heat that they became white hot and glowed pinkly through his cheeks. He then receded off into infinity like a starship making the jump into hyperspace, then came around behind Fresser again in such a way as to make it appear (due to the mirror effect) that he was actually coming from the same direction in which he'd gone. Just as he arrived back in the doorway two years later, the space warp snapped shut behind him; but at the last moment Dex Fresser glanced through it, and saw lovely purple fields filled with flowers, chanting Brazilians, leaky green ballpoint pens and thousands of empty tea boxes. He wanted very much to visit that place.

"Well, it does disturb me when I do happen to be in my room. See how that works?" The man who was running this tape, a lanky green tennis shoe with bad acne and an elephant's trunk tied in a double Windsor knot around his waist, stopped the tape and ran it back to Fresser's previous reply.

"But you're not even there that much, so how can it disturb you?" As Fresser finished this, Casimir did exactly what he had done last time, except this time the purple fields were being cluster-bombed by flying garages. The space warp closed off just in time to let a piece of shrapnel through. It zoomed over Casimir's shoulder and embedded itself in the wall, and Fresser recognized it as a Pershing 2 missile.

"Right," said Casimir, now speaking through a sousaphone around his shoulder, which bombarded Dex Fresser with white laser rays. "I know. But you see when I am in my room I prefer not to be disturbed. That's the whole point."

Fresser suddenly realized that the Pershing 2 was actually the left front quarter-panel of a '57 Buick that he had seen abandoned on a street in Evanston on July 28, 1984, and that Casimir was actually John D. Rockefeller. "How can you be so goddamn selfish, man? Don't you know how many people you've killed?" And he slammed the door shut, knowing that the shock would cause the piece of the Buick to fall on Rockefeller's head; since it was antimatter, nothing would be left afterward.

The confrontation had worked out as badly as Casimir had feared. He went back to his room, heart pounding irrationally, so upset that he did not practice his speech at all.

The lack of rehearsal did not matter, as the only audience in Sharon's lab was the Neutrino membership, Virgil, Sarah, a photographer from the *Monoplex Monitor* and I. Toward the end of the speech, though, S. S. Krupp walked in with an official photographer and a small, meek-looking older man, causing Casimir to whip off his glasses in agitation and destroying any trace of calmness in his manner. Finally he mumbled something to the effect that it was too bad Krupp had come in so late, seeing as how the best part of this introduction was over, and concluded that we should stop jabbering and have a look at this thing.

The mass driver was four meters long, built atop a pair of sturdy tables bolted together. It was nothing more than a pair of long straight parallel guides, each horseshoe-shaped in cross-section, the prongs of the horseshoes pointed toward each other with a narrow gap in between. The bucket, which would carry the payload, was lozenge-shaped in cross-section and almost filled the oval tunnel created by the two guides. Most of the bucket was empty payload space, but its outer jacket was of a special alloy supercooled by liquid helium so that it became a perfect superconducting electromagnet. This feature, combined with a force field generated in the two rails, suspended the bucket on a frictionless magnetic cushion. Electromagnets in the rails, artfully wound by Virgil, provided the acceleration, "kicking" the bucket and its contents from one end of the mass driver to the other.

Casimir relaxed visibly as he began pointing out the technical details. With long metal tongs he reached into a giant thermos flask and pulled out the supercold bucket, which was about the size of two beer cans side by side. He slid it into the breech of the mass driver. As it began to soak up warmth from the room, a cascade of frigid white helium poured from a vent on its back and spilled to the floor.

Krupp stood close by and asked questions. "What's the weight of the slug?"

"This," said Casimir, picking up a solid brass cylinder from the table, "is a one-kilogram mass. That's pretty small, but—"

"No, it isn't." Krupp looked over at his friend, who raised his eyebrows and nodded. "Nothing small about it."

Casimir smiled weakly and nodded in thanks. Krupp continued, "What's the muzzle velocity?"

Here Casimir looked sheepish and shifted nervously, looking at his Neutrino friends.

"Oh," said Krupp, sounding let down, "not so fast, eh?"

"Oh, no no no. Don't get me wrong. The final velocity isn't bad." At this the Neutrino members clapped their hands over their mouths and stifled shrieks and laughs. "I was just going to let you see that for yourselves instead of throwing a lot of numbers at you."

"Well, that's fine!" said Krupp, sounding more sanguine. "Don't let us laymen interfere with your schedule. I'm sorry. Just go right ahead." He stepped back and crossed his arms as though planning to shut up for hours.

Casimir gave the empty bucket a tap and there were oohs and aahs as it floated smoothly and quietly down the rails, bounced off a stop at the end and floated back with no change in speed. He reinserted the one-kilogram brass cylinder. "Now let's try it. As you can see we have a momentum absorber set up at the other end of the lab."

The "momentum absorber" was ten squares of 3/8-inch plywood held parallel in a frame, spaced two inches apart to form a sandwich a couple of feet long. This was securely braced against the wall of the lab at the same level as the mass driver. I had assumed that the intended target was a wastebasket on the floor beneath the "muzzle" of the machine, but now realized that Casimir was expecting the weight to fly about twenty feet without losing any altitude. "I suggest you all stand back in case something goes wrong," said Casimir, and feeling somewhat alarmed I stood way back and suggested that Sarah do likewise. Casimir made a last check of the circuitry, then hit a big red button.

The sound was a whizz followed by a rapid series of staccato explosions. It could be written as:

ZZIKKH

where the entire sound takes about a quarter of a second. None of us really saw anything. Casimir was already running toward the momentum absorber. When we got there, we saw that the first five layers of plywood had perfectly clean round holes punched through them, two more had messy holes, and the next layer had buckled, the brass cylinder wedged in place at its bottom. Casimir pulled out the payload with tongs and dropped it into an asbestos mitt he had donned. "It's pretty hot after all those collisions," he explained.

Everyone but Casimir was electrified. Even the Neutrino observers, who had seen it before, were awed, and laughed hysterically from time to time. Sarah looked as though whatever distrust she had ever had in technology had been dramatically confirmed. I stared at Casimir, realizing how smart he was. Virgil left, smiling. Krupp's little friend paced between mass driver and target, hands clasped behind back, a wide smile nestled in his silver-brown beard, while Krupp himself was astonished.

"Jesus H. Christ!" he yelled, fingering the holes. "That is the damnedest thing I've ever seen. Good lord, boy, how did you make this?"

Casimir seemed at a loss. "It's all done from Sharon's plans," he said blankly. "He did all the magnetic fieldwork. I just plugged in the arithmetic. The rest of it was machine-shop work. Nothing complicated about the machine."

"Does it have to be this powerful?" I said. "Don't get me wrong. I'm impressed as hell. Wouldn't it have been a little easier to make a slower one?"

"Well, sure, but not as useful," said Casimir. "The technical challenges only show up when you make it fast enough to be used for its practical purpose—which is to shoot payloads of ore and minerals from the lunar surface to an orbital processing station. For a low-velocity one we could've used air cushions instead of magnetic fields to float the bucket, but there's no challenge in that."

"What's the muzzle velocity?" asked Krupp's guest, who had appeared next to me. He spoke quietly and quickly in an Australian accent. When I looked down at him, I realized he was Oswald Heimlich, Chairman of the Board of Trustees of American Megaversity and one of the richest men in the city —the founder of Heimlich Freedom Industries, a huge defense contractor. Casimir obviously didn't know who he was.

"The final velocity of the bucket is one hundred meters per second, or about two hundred twenty miles per hour."

"And how could you boost that?"

"Boost it?" Casimir looked at him, startled. "Well, for more velocity you could build another just like this—"

"Yes, and put them together. I know. They're interconnectible. But how could you increase the *acceleration* of this device?"

"Well, that gets you into some big technical problems. You'd need expensive electronic gear with the ability to kick out huge pulses of power very quickly. Giant capacitors could do it, or a specialized power supply."

Heimlich followed all this, nodding incessantly. "Or a generator that gets its power from a controlled explosion."

Casimir smiled. "It's funny you should mention that. Some people are speculating about building small portable mass drivers with exactly that type of power supply—a chemical explosion—and using them to throw explosive shells and so on. That's what is called—"

"A railgun. Precisely."

Things began to fall into place for Casimir. "Oh. I see. So you want to know if I could build—basically a railgun."

"Sure. Sure," said Heimlich in an aggressive, glinting voice. "What's research without practical applications?"

The question hung in the air. Krupp took over, sounding much calmer. "You see, Casimir, in order to continue with this research—and you are off to an exceptionally fine start—you will need outside funding on a larger scale. Now, as good an idea as lunar mining is, no one is ever going to fund that kind of research. But railguns—whether you like it or not, they have very immediate significance that can really pull in the grants. I'm merely pointing out that in today's climate relating your work to defense is the best way to obtain funding. And I imagine that if you wanted to set up a specialized lab here to advance this kind of work, you might be able to get all the funding you'd want."

Casimir looked down at the shattered plywood in consternation.

"I don't need an answer now. But give it some careful thought, son. There's no reason for you to be stuck in silly-ass classes if you can do this kind of work. Call me anytime you like." He shook Casimir's hand, Heimlich made a brief smiling spastic bow, and they walked out together.

February

Sarah quit the Presidency of the Student Government on the first of January. At the mass-driver demonstration, S. S. Krupp had simply ignored her, which was fine by Sarah as she had no desire to give the man a point-by-point explanation.

As for the death of Tiny, here the other shoe never dropped, though Sarah and Hyacinth kept waiting. His body was in especially poor condition when found, and the bullet holes might not have been detected even if someone had thought to look for them. The City police made a rare Plex visit and looked at the broken window and the electrocuted man on the floor, but apparently the Terrorists had cleaned up any blood or other evidence of conflict; in short, they made it all look like a completely deranged drunken fuck-up, an archetype familiar to the City cops.

The Terrorists wanted their own revenge. None of them had a coherent idea of what had happened. Even the two surviving witnesses had dim, traumatized memories of the event and could only say it had something to do with a woman dressed as a clown.

As soon as I heard that the Terrorists were looking for someone called Clown Woman, I invited her over and we had a chat. I knew what her costume had been. Though she understood why I was curious, she suddenly adopted a sad, cold reserve I had never seen in her before.

"Some really, really terrible things happened that night. But I'm safe and Hyacinth is safe—okay? And we've been making plans to stay that way."

"Fine. I just—"

"I know. I'd love to tell you more. I'm dying to. But I won't, because you have some official responsibilities and you're the kind of person who carries them out, and knowing anything would be a burden for you. You'd try to help—but that's something you can't do. Can you understand that?"

I was a little scared by her lone strength. More, I was stunned that *she* was protecting *me*. Finally I shrugged and said, "Sounds as though you know what you're doing," because that was how it sounded.

"This has a lot to do with your resigning the Presidency?" I continued. Sarah was a little annoyed by my diplomacy, for the same reason S. S. Krupp would have been.

"Bud, I don't need some terrific reason for resigning. If I'm spending time on a useless job I don't like, and I find there are better things to do with that time, then I ought to resign." I nodded contritely, and for the first time she was relaxed enough to laugh.

On her way out she gave me a long platonic hug, and I still remember it when I feel in need of warmth.

They got the wading pool and the garden hose on a two-hour bus ride to a suburban K-Mart. Hyacinth inflated it in the middle of Sarah's room while Sarah ran the hose down the hall to the bathroom to pipe in hot water. Once the pool was acceptably full and foamy, they retrieved the hose, locked the door and sealed off all windows with newspaper and all cracks around the door with towels and tape. They lit a few candles but blew most of them out when their eyes adjusted. The magnum of champagne was buried in ice, the water was hot, the night was young. Hyacinth's .44 was very intrusive, and so Sarah filed it under G for Gun and they had a good laugh.

Around 4:00 in the morning, to Sarah's satisfaction, Hyacinth passed out. Sarah allowed herself to do likewise for a while. Then she dragged Hyacinth out onto the rug, dried her and hoisted her into bed. They slept until 4:32 in the afternoon. Sleet was ticking against the window. Hyacinth cut a slit in the window screen and they fed the hose outside and siphoned all the bathwater out of the pool and down the side of the Plex. They ate all of Sarah's mother's banana bread, thirty-two Chips Ahoys, three bowls of Captain Crunch, a pint of strawberry ice cream and drank a great deal of water. They then gave each other backrubs and went to sleep again.

"Keeping my .38 clean is a pain in the ass," said Sarah at one point. "It picks up a lot of crud in my backpack pocket."

"That's one reason to carry a single-action," said Hyacinth. "Less to go wrong if it's dirty."

A long time later, Sarah added, "This is pretty macho. Talking about our guns."

"I suppose it's true that they're macho. But they are also *guns*. In fact, they're *primarily* guns."

"True."

They also discussed killing people, which had become an important subject with them recently.

"Sometimes there isn't any choice," Sarah said to Hyacinth, as Hyacinth cried calmly into her shoulder. "You know, Constantine punished rapists by pouring molten lead down their throats. That was a premeditated, organized punishment. What you did was on the spur of the moment."

"Yeah. Putting on protective clothes, loading my gun, tracking them down and blowing one away was really on the spur of the moment."

"All I can say is that if anyone ever deserved it, he did."

Three Terrorists ambled down the hall past Sarah's door, chanting "*Death to Clown Woman!*"

"Okay, fine," said Hyacinth, and stopped crying. "Granted. I can't worry about it forever. But sooner or later they're going to figure out who Clown Woman is. Then there'll be even more violence."

"Better for them to be violent against us," said Sarah, "than against people who don't even understand what violence is."

. . .

Sarah was busy taking care of herself that semester. This made more sense than what the rest of us were doing, but it did not make for an eventful life. At the same time, a very different American Megaversity student was fighting the same battle Sarah had just won. This student lost. The tale of his losing is melancholy but much more interesting.

Every detail was important in assessing the situation, in determining just how close to the brink Plexor was! The obvious things, the frequent transitions from the Technological universe to the Magical universe, those were child's play to detect; but the evidence of impending Breakdown was to be found only in the minutiae. The extra cold-water pipe; that was significant. What had suddenly caused such a leak to be sprung in the plumbing of Plexor, which had functioned flawlessly for a thousand years? And what powerful benign hand had made the switch from one pipe to the other? What prophecy was to be found in the coming of the Thing of the Earth in the test run of Shekondar? Was some great happening at hand? One could not be sure; the answer must be nested among subtleties. So this one spent many days wandering like a lone thaumaturge through the corridors of the Plex, watching and observing, ignoring the classes and lectures that had become so trivial.

With the help of an obsequious MARS lieutenant he was allowed to inspect the laboratory of the secret railgun experiments. Here he found advanced specialized power supplies from Heimlich Freedom Industries. The lieutenant, a Neutrino member of four years' standing, hooked the output of one power supply to an oscilloscope and showed him the very high and sharp spike of current it could punch out—precisely the impulses a superfast mass driver would need to keep its payload accelerating explosively right up to the end. This one also observed a test of a new electromagnet. It was much larger than those used for the first mass driver, wound with miles of hair-thin copper wire and cooled by antifreeze-filled tubes. A short piece of rail had been made to test the magnet. It was equipped with a bucket designed to carry a payload ten centimeters across! This one watched as a violent invisible kick from the magnet wrenched the bucket to high velocity and slammed it to the cushion at the rail's end; the heavy payload shot out, boomed into a tarp suspended about five feet away, and fell into a box of foam-rubber scraps. It was the same pattern he saw everywhere. A peaceful lunar mining device had, under the influence of Shekondar the Fearsome, metamorphosed into a potent weapon of great value to the forces of Good.

He gave the lieutenant a battlefield promotion to Captain. He wanted to stay and continue to watch, but it had been a long day; he was tired, and for a moment his mind seemed to stop entirely as he stood by the exit.

Then came again the creeping sense of Leakage, impossible to ignore; his head snapped up and to the right, and, speaking across the dimensional barrier, Klystron the Impaler told him to go to dinner.

Klystron the Impaler was only Klystron the Impaler when he was in a Magical universe. The rest of the time he was Chris the Systems Programmer—a brilliant, dashing, young, handsome terminal jockey considered to be the best systems man on the giant self-contained universe-hopping colony, Plexor. From time to time Plexor would pass through the Central Bifurcation, a giant space warp, and enter a Magical universe, fundamentally altering all aspects of reality. Though the structure of Plexor itself underwent little change at these times, everything therein was converted to its magical, pretechnological analog. Guns became swords, freshmen became howling savages, *Time* magazine became a hand-lettered vellum tome and Chris the Systems Programmer—well, brilliant people like him became sorcerers, swordspeople and heroes. The smarter they were—the greater their stature in the Technological universe—the more dazzling was their swordplay and the more penetrating their spells. Needless to say, Klystron the Impaler was a very great hero-swordsman-magician indeed.

Of course, Plexorians tended to be that way to begin with. Only the most advanced had been admitted when Plexor was begun, and it was natural that their distant offspring today should tend toward the exceptional. Of those lucky enough to be selected for Plexor, only the most adaptable had any stomach for the life once they got there and, every month or so, found their waterbeds metamorphosing into heaps of bearskins. Klystron/Chris liked to think of the place as a pressure cooker for the advancement of humanity.

But even the most perfect machine could not be insulated from the frailty and stupidity of the human mind. In the early days of Plexor every inhabitant had understood the Central Bifurcation, had respected the distinction between technology and magic, and had shown enough discipline to ensure that division. Within the past several generations, though, ignorance had come to this perfect place and Breakdown had begun. Recent generations of Plexorians lacked the enthusiasm and commitment of their forebears and displayed ignorance which was often shocking; recently it had become common to suppose that Plexor was not a free-drifting eco-sociosystem *at all,* that it was in fact a planetoidal structure bound to a particular universe. Occasionally, it was true, Plexor would materialize on the ground, in a giant city or a barbarian kingdom. Its makers, a Guild of sorcerers and magicians operating in separate universes through the mediation of Keldor, had created it to be self-sufficient and life-supporting in any habitat, with a nuclear fuel source that would last forever. But to believe that one particular world was always out there was a blindness to reality so severe that it amounted to rank primitivism amidst this sophisticated colony of technocrats. It was, in a word, *Breakdown*—a blurring of the boundary—and such was the delicacy of that boundary between the universes that mere ignorance of its existence, mere Breakdown-oriented thinking and Breakdown-conducive behavior, was sufficient to open small Leaks between Magic and Technology, to generate an unholy Mixture of the two opposites. It was the duty of the remaining guardians of the Elder Knowledge, such as Klystron/Chris, to expurgate such mixtures and restore the erstwhile purity of the two existences of Plexor.

In just the past few weeks the Leaks had become rents, the Mixture ubiquitous. Now Barbarians sat at computer terminals in the Computing Center unabashed, pathetically trying, in broad daylight, to run programs that were so riddled with bugs the damn things wouldn't even compile, their recent kills stretched out bleeding between their feet awaiting the spit. Giant rats from another plane of existence roamed free through the sewers of the mighty technological civilization, and everywhere Chris the Systems Analyst found dirt and marrow-sucked bones on the floor, broken light fixtures, graffiti, noise, ignorance. He watched these happenings, not yet willing to believe in what they portended, and soon developed a sixth sense for detecting Leakage. That was in and of itself a case of Mixture; in a Technological universe, sixth senses were scientifically impossible. His new intuition was a sign of the Leakage of the powers of Klystron the Impaler into a universe where they did not belong. In recognition of this, and to protect himself from the ignorant, Klystron/Chris had thought it wise to adopt the informal code name of Fred Fine.

He had denied what was coming for too long. Despite his supreme intelligence he was hesitant to accept the hugeness of his own personal importance.

Until the day of the food fight; on that day he came to understand the somber future of Plexor and of himself.

It happened during dinner. To most of those in the Cafeteria it was just a food fight, but to "Fred Fine" it was much more significant, a preliminary skirmish to the upcoming war, a byte of strategic data to be thoughtfully digested.

He had been contemplating an abstract type of program structure, absently shuffling the nameless protein-starch substance from tray to mouth, when a sense of *strangeness* had verged on his awareness and dispersed his thoughts. As he looked up and became alert, he also became aware that (a) the food was terrible; (b) the Caf was crowded and noisy; and (c) Leakage was all around. His mind now as alert as that of Klystron before a melee, he scanned the Cafeteria from his secure corner (one of only four corners in the Cafeteria and therefore highly prized), stuffing his computer printout securely into his big locking briefcase. Though his gaze traversed hundreds of faces in a few seconds, something allowed him to fix his attention on a certain few: eight or ten, with long hair and eccentric clothing, who were clearly looking at one another and not at the gallons of food heaped on their Fiberglass trays. The sixth sense of Klystron enabled Chris to glean from the whirl of people a deeply hidden pattern he knew to be significant.

He stood up in the corner, memorizing the locations of those he had found, and switched to long-range scan, assisting himself by following their own tense stares. His eyes flicked down to the readout of his digital calcu-chronograph and he noted that it was just seconds before 6:00. Impatiently he polled his subjects and noted that they were now all looking toward one place: a milk dispenser near the center of the Cafeteria, where an exceptionally tall burnout stood with a small black box in his hand!

There was a sharp blue flash that made the ceiling glow briefly—the black box was an electronic flash unit—and all hell broke loose. Missiles of all shapes and colors whizzed through his field of vision and splathunked starchily against tables, pillars and bodies. Amid sudden screaming an entire long table was flipped over, causing a hundredweight of manicotti and French fries to slide into the laps of the unfortunates on the wrong side. Seeing the perpetrators break and dissolve into the milling dinnertime crowd, the victims could only respond by slinging handfuls of steaming ricotta at their disappearing backsides. At this first outbreak of noise and action the Cafeteria quieted for a moment, as all turned toward the disturbance. Then, seeing food flying past their own heads, most of the spectators united in bedlam. The Terrorist sections seemed to have been expecting this and joined in with beer-commercial rowdiness. Several tables of well-dressed young women ran frantically for the exits, in most cases too slowly to prevent the ruination of hundreds of dollars' worth of clothes a head. Many collapsed squalling into the arms of their patron Terrorist organizations. The Droogs opened a milk machine, pulled out a heavy poly-bag of Skim and slung it into the midst of what had been an informal gathering of Classics majors, with explosive results.

All was observed intently by Klystron/Chris, who stood calm and motionless in his corner holding his briefcase as a shield. Though the progress of the fight was interesting to watch, it was hardly as important as the behavior of the instigators and the reactions of the Cafeteria staff.

Of the instigating organization, some were obliged to flee immediately in order to protect themselves. These were the *agents provocateurs,* the table-tippers and tray-slingers, whose part was already played. The remainder were observers, and they stood in carefully planned stations around the walls of the Cafeteria and watched, much as Chris did. Some snapped pictures with cheap cameras.

This picture-taking began in earnest when, after about fifteen seconds, the reactive strike began. The cooks and servers had instantly leapt to block the doors of the serving bays, which in these circumstances had the same value as ammunition dumps. Pairs of the larger male cooks now charged out and drew shut the folding dividers which partitioned the Cafeteria into twenty-four sections. Meanwhile, forty-eight more senior Cafeteria personnel and guards fanned out in organized fashion, clothed in ponchos and facemasks. In each section, one of them leapt up on a table with a megaphone to scream righteousness at the students, while his partner confronted particularly active types. Klystron/Chris's view of the fight was abruptly reduced to what he could see in his own small section.

Among other things he saw eight of the Roy G Biv Terrorist Group overturn the table on which the local official stood, sending him splaying on hands and knees across the slick of grease and tomato sauce on the floor. His partner skidded after him and swiveled to protect their backs from the Terrorists, who had huddled and were mumbling menacingly. For the first time Klystron/Chris felt the hysterical half-sick excitement of approaching violence, and he began to edge along the wall toward a more strategically sound position.

One of the Terrorists went to the corner where the sliding partitions intersected, blocking the only route of escape. The men in the room moved away uneasily; the women pressed themselves against the wall and sat on the floor and tried to get invisible. Then the Roy G Biv men broke; two went for the still-standing official, one for the man who was just staggering to his feet with the dented megaphone. Abruptly, Klystron/Chris stepped forward, took from his briefcase a small weapon and pulled the trigger. The weapon was a flash gun, a device for making an explosively intense flash of light that blinded attackers. Everyone in front of the weapon froze. As they were putting their hands to their eyes, he pulled out his Civil War bayonet, jammed it into a fold in the sliding partition and pulled it down to open a six-foot rent. He led the tactical retreat to the adjoining section, which was comparatively under control.

The officials here were not amused. A stocky middle-aged man in a brown suit stomped toward Klystron/Chris with death in his eye. He was stopped by a chorus of protest from the refugees, who made it clear that the real troublemakers were back there. And that was how Klystron/Chris avoided having any of these seriously Mixed officials discover his informal code name.

But what was the strategic significance?

He knew it had been done by Barbarians. Despite the carefully tailored modern clothes they used to hide their stooping forms and overly long arms, he recognized their true nature from the ropy scars running along their heavy overhanging brows and the garlands of rodent skulls they wore around their necks. Had it not been for the cameramen, he would have concluded that this was nothing more than a purposeless display of the savages' contempt for order. But the photographers made it clear that this riot had been a reconnaissance-in-force, directed by an advanced strategic mind with an interest in the Cafeteria's defenses. And that, in turn, implied an upcoming offensive centered on the Cafeteria itself. Of course! In here was enough grub to feed a good-sized commando force for years, if rationed properly; it would therefore be a prime objective for insurrectionists planning to seize and hold large portions of Plexor. But why? Who was behind it? And how did it connect with the other harbingers of catastrophe?

Once upon a time, a mathematically inclined friend of Sarah's, one Casimir Radon, had estimated that her chances of running into a fellow Airhead at dinner were no better than about one in twenty. As usual he was not trying to be annoying or nerdish, but nevertheless Sarah wished for a more satisfying explanation of why she could get no relief from her damned neighbors. One in twenty was optimistic. At times she thought that they were planting spies in her path to take down statistics on how many behavioral standards she broke, or to drive her crazy by asking why she had *really* resigned the Presidency.

She was annoyed but not surprised to find herself eating dinner with Mari Meegan, Mari's second cousin and Toni one night. Relaxed from a racquetball game, she made no effort to scan her route through the Caf for telltale ski masks. So as she danced and sideslipped her way toward what looked like an open table, she was blindsided by a charming squeal from right next to her. "Sarah!" Too slow even to think of pretending not to hear, she looked down to see the three color-coordinated ski masks looking back at her expectantly. She despised them and never wanted to see them again, *ever*, but she also knew there was value in following social norms, once in a while, to forestall hatred and God knows what kinds of retribution. The last thing she wanted was to be connected with Clown Woman. So she smiled and sat down. It was not going to be a great meal, but Sarah's conversation support system was working well enough to get her at least through the salad.

The ski masks had become very popular since the beginning of second semester, having proved spectacularly successful during fire drills. The Airheads found that they could pull them on at the first ringing of the bell and make it downstairs before all the bars filled up, and when they returned to their rooms they did not have to remove any makeup before going back to bed. Then one sartorially daring Airhead had worn her ski mask to a 9:00 class one January morning, and pronounced it worthwhile, and other Airheads had begun to experiment with the concept. The less wealthy found that ski masks saved heaps of money on cosmetics and hair care, and everyone was impressed with their convenience, ease of cleaning and unlimited mix-'n'-match color coordination possibilities. Blousy, amorphous dresses had also become the style; why wear something tight and uncomfortable when no one knew who you were?

Talking to Mari, Nicci and Toni was not that bad, of course, but Sarah felt unusually refreshed and clean, was having one of her favorite dinners, was going to a concert with Hyacinth that night and had hoped to make it a perfect day. Worse than talking to them was having to smile and nod at the stream of cologned and blow-dried Terrorists who came up behind the Airheads in their strange bandy macho walk, homing in on those ski masks like heat-seeking missiles on a house fire. Several sneaked up behind Mari and the others to goose them while they ate. Sarah knew that they did not want to be warned, so she merely rolled her manicotti around in her mouth and stared morosely over Mari's shoulder as the young bucks crept forward with exaggerated stealth and twitching fingers. So long as these people continued to lead segregated lives, she knew, it was necessary to do such things in order to have any contact with members of the other sex. They at least had more style than the freshman Terrorists, who generally started conversations by dumping beverages over the heads of freshman women. So there were many breaks in the conversation while Terrorist fingers probed deep into Airhead tenderloins and the requisite screaming and giggling followed.

Notwithstanding this, "the gals" did manage to have a conversation about their majors. Sarah was majoring in English. Mari had a cousin who majored in English too, and who had met a very nice Business student doing it. Mari was majoring in Hobbies Education. Toni was Undecided. Nicci was in Sociology at another school.

And then the food fight.

Between the opening salvo and the moment when their table was protectively ringed by Terrorists, the others were quite dignified and hardly moved. Sarah sat still momentarily, then came to her senses and slipped under the table. From this point of view she saw many pairs of corduroy, khaki, designer jean and chino pantlegs around the table, and saw too the folding partitions slide across.

Once the partitions were closed she emerged, mostly because she wanted to see who owned the brown polyester legs that had been dancing around the room in such agitation. The Terrorists grabbed her arms solicitously and hauled her to her feet, wanting to know if she had lost her ski mask in "all the action."

The man in the brown three-piecer was none other than Bartholomew (Wombat) Forksplit, Dean of Dining Services, who had been promoted to Dean Emeritus after his recovery from the nacho tortilla chip shard that had passed through his brain. No one knew where he came from—Tibet? Kurdistan? Abyssinia? Circassia? Since the accident, he had become known as Wombat the Marauder to his victims, mostly inconsiderate dorks who had broken Caf rules only to find this man gripping them in an old Bosnian or Tunisian martial arts hold that shorted out the major meridians of their nervous system, and shouting at them in a percussive accent that crackled like fat ground beef on a red-hot steam griddle. Some accused him of using the accident as an excuse to act like a madman, but no one doubted that he was pissed off.

When he saw the ex-President half-dragged from under a table by the beaming Terrorists, Forksplit released the knee of his current victim and speed-skated across the stained linoleum toward her, his tomato-sauce–spattered arms outstretched as if in supplication. Sarah pulled her arms free and backed up a step, but he stopped short of embracing her and cried, "Sarah! You, here? Indicates this that you are part of these—these asshole Terrorists? Please say no!" He stared piteously into her eyes, the little white scar on his forehead standing out vividly against his murderously flushed face. Sarah swallowed and glanced around the room, conscious of many ski masks and Terrorists looking at her.

"Oh, not really, I was just over here at another table. These guys were just helping me up. This is a real shame. I hope the B-men don't go on strike now."

A look of agony came over Wombat the Marauder's face at the mere mention of this idea, and he backed up, pirouetted and paced around their Cafeteria subdivision directing a soliloquy of anger and frustration at Sarah. "I joost—I don't know what the hell to do. I do everything in the world to deliver fine service. This is good food! No one believes that. They go off to *other* places and eat, come back and say, 'Yes Mr. Forksplit let me shake your hand your food is so good!! Best I have ever eaten!' But do these idiots understand? No, they throw barbells through the ceiling! All they can do with good food is throw it, like it is being a sports implement or something. You!"

Forksplit sprinted toward a tall thin fellow who had just slit one of the sliding partitions almost in half with a bayonet and plunged through, pulling a briefcase behind him. Under his arm this man carried a pistol-shaped flashlight, which he tried to pull out; but before Forksplit was able to reach him, several more people exploded through the slit, pointing back and complaining about high rudeness levels in the next room. With a bloodcurdling battle cry Forksplit flung his body through the breach and into the next compartment, where much loud smashing and yelling commenced.

Mari turned to Sarah, a big smile visible through her mouth-hole. "That was very nice of you, Sarah. It was sweet to think about Dean Forksplit's feelings."

"He put me in a hell of a spot," said Sarah, who was looking at Fred Fine and his light-gun and his bayonet. "I mean, what was I supposed to say?"

Mari did not follow, and laughed. "It was neat the way you didn't say something bad about the Terrorists just on his account."

Fred Fine was stashing his armaments in his briefcase and staring at them. Sarah concluded that he had just come over to eavesdrop on their conversation and look at their secondary sex characteristics.

"Diplomatic? There's nothing I could say, Mari, that could be nasty enough to describe those assholes, and the sooner you realize that the better off you'll be."

"Oh, *no*, Sarah. That's not true. The Terrorists are nice guys, really."

"They are *assholes*."

"But they're *nice*. You said so yourself at Fantasy Island Nite, remember? You should get to know some of them."

Sarah nearly snapped that she had almost gotten to know some of them quite well on Fantasy Island Nite, but held her tongue, suddenly apprehensive. *Had* she said that on Fantasy Island Nite? And had Mari known who she was? "Mari, it is possible to be nice and be an asshole at the same time. Ninety-nine percent of all people are nice. Not very many are decent."

"Well, sometimes you don't seem terribly nice."

"Well, I don't wish to be nice. I don't care about nice. I've got more important things on my mind, like happiness."

"I don't understand you, Sarah. I like you so much, but I just don't understand you." Mari backed away a couple of paces on her spikes, gazing coolly at Sarah through her eyeholes. "Sometimes I get the feeling you're nothing but a *clown*." She stood and watched Sarah triumphantly.

DEATH TO CLOWN WOMAN! hung before Sarah's eyes. A knifing chill struck her and she was suddenly nauseated and lightheaded. She sat down on a table, assisted needlessly by Fred Fine.

"You'll be fine," he said confidently. "Just routine shock.

Lie back here and we'll take care of you." He began making a clear space for her on the table.

Somehow, Sarah had managed to unzip the back pocket of her knapsack and wrap her fingers around the concealed grip of the revolver. Shocked, she forced herself to relax and think clearly. To scare the hell out of Mari was easy enough, after what had happened to Tiny, but could she afford to make such a display here and now? Obviously not. Mari continued to glint at her, apparently expecting a dramatic confession.

Finally Sarah just started to talk, making it up as she went along. "Okay, Mari, look, I'll tell you the truth. Actually I like those Terrorists and I've always thought this one guy was real cute, you know?" Mari's eyes widened at this and she stepped in very close, ready to share the secret. Fred Fine put his hand on Sarah's shoulder.

"Miss Johnson, it would be best for you to lie down until you're feeling steadier." Sarah ignored him.

"But the thing is that my father, uh, is a private investigator. He used to be a chopper pilot for a Mafia kingpin—he's a Vietnam vet—but then he decided to go into private-eye work and use the inside knowledge he'd gotten to fight the Mob on its own terms. This Terrorist that I like is actually a prince—he belongs to one of those European houses—but he is a rebel by nature and he decided to change his identity and live in the U.S. and work his way to success using his own talent and good looks and likable, open approach to everything. His father is rich and is heavily into the oil business, and also in drug smuggling, so he's got lots of Mob connections. Well, when his father found out I was going with this Terrorist he was afraid I'd get vital Mob information and give it to my father, who could organize a major sting operation. So they decided to kill me. But his father's mistress, who is a double agent with the KGB and is also an English baroness by birth, though she was cheated out of her inheritance—anyway, she got wind of it and warned us. That's why I dressed up in the clown costume—so the hit men wouldn't recognize me."

"Some cases of shock can result in delirium," suggested Fred Fine. "This can be serious if not properly treated."

Mari was astonished, from what Sarah could see through the mask. "So this boy and I were going to elope that night in our costumes, but when we went up to his room to get his things, the hit men were there. But just then the other Terrorists rushed in to save us, and that's how Tiny got shot. Then my father showed up! And he has a secret plan to help us. But it all depends on us pretending that I actually shot Tiny. Now that you know you can't talk about it to anyone or you might be killed. In the meantime, I'm protecting myself with this." She tipped the knapsack toward Mari and showed her the .38. Fred Fine, looking over her shoulder, saw it too and stepped back sharply.

All doubt was blown clear from Mari's mind. She gasped and stumbled back a couple of steps, hand to breast. Fred Fine, keeping one nervous eye on Sarah, strode over to Mari and put his hand lightly on her shoulder.

"You'll be just fine, ma'am. Just a routine case of shock. Maybe you should lie down for a bit." But this had attracted the attention of the Terrorists. Seeing that Mari and Sarah's gal-to-gal chat was finished, they closed in helpfully around Mari and assisted her to a reclining position. Fred Fine was shouldered out of the way but persisted on the edges of the group, giving advice on the treatment of shock.

Sarah left. Fred Fine watched her with something akin to awe.

March

The social lounge of D24E had picture windows that looked out over the Death Vortex, over the puddle-stained pea-gravel roofs of the ghetto brownstones beyond it, across a trolley terminus webbed over with black power cables, and into a sleazy old commercial square often visited by AM students suffering from Plex Fever and lacking the wheels to go farther. Since the raising of the Plex with its clean, trendy stores, and the decay of the adjacent neighborhood, the square had degenerated meteorically and become a chaotic intersection lined with dangerous discos, greasy spoons, tiny weedlike businesses, fast-food joints with armed guards and vacant buildings covered with acres of graffiti-festooned plywood and smelling of rats and derelicts' urine. The home office of the Big Wheel Petroleum Corporation had moved out some years ago to a Sunbelt location. It had retained ownership of its old twelve-story office building, and on its roof, thrust into the heavens on a dirty web of steel and wooden beams, the Big Wheel sign continued to beam out its pulsating message to everyone within five miles every evening. One of the five largest neon signs ever built, it was double-sided and square, a great block of lovely saturated cherry red with a twelve-spoked wagon wheel of azure and blinding white rotating eternally in the middle, underscored by heavy block letters saying BIG WHEEL that changed, letter by letter, from white to blue and back again, once every two revolutions. Despite the fact that the only things the corporation still owned in this area were eight gas stations, the building and the sign, some traditionalist in the corporate hierarchy made sure that the sign was perfectly maintained and that it went on every evening.

During the daytime the Big Wheel sign looked more or less like a billboard, unless you looked closely enough to catch the glinting of the miles of glass tubing bracketed to its surface. As night fell on the city, though, some mysterious hand, automatic or human, would throw the switch. Lights would dim for miles around and anchormen's faces would bend as enough electricity to power Fargo at dinnertime was sent glowing and incandescing through the glass tracery to beam out the Big Wheel message to the city. This was a particularly impressive sight from the social lounges on the east side of the Plex, because the sign was less than a quarter mile away and stood as the only structure between it and the horizon. On cloudless nights, when the sky over the water was deep violet and the stars had not yet appeared, the Big Wheel sign as seen from the Plex would first glow orange as its tubes caught the light of the sunset. Then the sun would set, and the sign would sit, a dull inert square against the heavens, and the headlights of the cars below would flicker on and the weak lights of the discos and the diners would come to life. Just when the sign was growing difficult to make out, the switch would be thrown and the Big Wheel would blaze out of the East like the face of God, causing thousands of scholarly heads to snap around and thousands of conversations to stop for a moment. Although Plex people had few opportunities to purchase gasoline, and many did not even know what the sign was advertising, it had become the emblem of a university without emblems and was universally admired. Art students created series of paintings called, for example, "Thirty-eight views of the Big Wheel sign," the Terrorists adopted it as their symbol and its illumination was used as the starting point for many parties. Even during the worst years of the energy crisis, practically no one at AM had protested against the idea of nightly beaming thousands of red-white-and-blue kilowatt-hours out into deep space while a hundred feet below derelicts lost their limbs to the cold.

The summit conference, the Meeting of Hearers, the Conclave of the Terrorist Superstars, was therefore held in the D24E lounge around sunset. About a dozen figures from various Terrorist factions came, including eight stereo hearers, two Big Wheel hearers, a laundry-machine hearer and a TV test-pattern hearer.

Hudson Rayburn, Tiny's successor, got there last, and did not have a chair. So he went to the nearest room and walked in without knocking. The inhabitant was seated cross-legged on the bed, smoking a fluorescent red plastic bong and staring into a color-bar test pattern on a 21-inch TV. This was the wing of the TV test-pattern hearers, a variation which Rayburn's group found questionable. There were some things you could say about test patterns, though.

"The entire spectrum," observed Hudson Rayburn.

"Hail Roy G Biv," quoth the hearer in his floor's ritual greeting. Rayburn grabbed a chair, causing the toaster oven it was supporting to slide off onto the bed. "I must have this chair," he said.

The hearer cocked his head and was motionless for several seconds, then spoke in a good-natured monotone. "Roy G Biv speaks with the voice of Ward Cleaver, a voice of great power. Yes. You are to take the chair. You are to bring it back, or I will not have a place for putting my toaster oven."

"I will bring it back," answered Rayburn, and carried it out.

The hosts of the meeting had set up a big projection TV on one wall of the lounge, and the representatives of the Roy G Biv faction stared at the test pattern. One of them, tonight's emcee, spoke to the assembled Terrorists, glancing at the screen and pausing from time to time.

"The problem with the stereo-hearers is that everybody has stereos and so there are many different voices saying different things, and that is bad, because they cannot act together. Only a few have color TVs that can show Roy G Biv, and only some have cable, which carries Roy G Biv on Channel 34 all the time, so we are unified."

"But there is only one Big Wheel. It is the most unified of all," observed Hudson Rayburn, staring out at the Big Wheel, glinting orange in the setting sun.

There was silence for a minute or so. A stereo-hearer, holding a large ghetto blaster on his lap, spoke up. "Ah, but it can be seen from many windows. So it's no better at all."

"The same is true of the stereo," said a laundry-machine hearer. "But there is only one dryer, the Seritech Super Big-Window 1500 in Laundry, which is numbered twenty-three and catches the reflection of the Astro-Nuke video game, and only a few can see it at a time, and I think it told me just the other day how we could steal it."

"So what?" said Hudson Rayburn. "The dryer is just a little cousin of the Big Wheel. The Big Wheel is the Father of all Speakers. Two years ago, before there were any hearers, Fred and I—Fred was the founder of the Wild and Crazy Guys, he is now a bond analyst—we sat in our lounge during a power blackout and smoked much fine peyote. And we looked out over the city and it was totally dark except for a few headlights. And then the power came back on, like with no warning, out of nowhere, just like that, and instantly, the streets, buildings, signs, everything, were there, and *there is the Big Wheel hanging in space* and god it just freaked our brains and we just sat there going 'Whooo!' and just being blown away and stuff! And then Big Wheel spoke to me! He spoke in the voice of Hannibal Smith on the A-Team and said, 'Son, you should come out here every time there is a blackout. This is fun. And if you buy some more of that peyote, you'll have more when you run out of what you have. Your fly is open and you should write to your mother, and I suggest that you drop that pre-calculus course before it saps your GPA and knocks you out of the running for law school.' And it was all exactly right! I did just what he said, he's been talking to me and my friends ever since, and he's always given great advice. Any other Speakers are just related to the Big Wheel."

There was another minute or two of silence. A stereo cult member finally said, "I just heard my favorite deejay from

Youngstown. He says what we need is one hearer who can hear all the different speakers, who we can follow . . ."

"Stop! The time comes!" cried Hudson Rayburn. He ran to the window and knelt, putting his elbows on the sill and clasping his hands. Just as he came to rest, the Big Wheel sign blazed out of the violet sky like a neutron bomb, its light mixing with that of Roy G Biv to make the lounge glow with unnatural colors. There was a minute or two of stillness, and then several people spoke at once.

"Someone's coming."

"Our leader is here."

"Let's see what this guy has to say."

Everyone now heard footsteps and a rhythmic slapping sound. The door opened and a tall thin scruffy figure strode in confidently. In one hand he was lugging a large old blue window fan which had a *Go Big Red* sticker stuck to its side. The grilles had been removed, exposing the blades, which had been painted bright colors, and as the man walked, the power cord slapped against the blades, making the sound that had alerted them. Wordlessly, he walked to the front of the group, put the fan up on the windowsill, drew the shades behind it to close off the view of the Big Wheel, and plugged it in. Another person had shut off Roy G Biv, and soon the room was mostly dark, inspiring a sleeping bat to wake up and flit around.

Once the fan was plugged in, they saw that its inside walls had been lined with deep purple black-light tubes, which caused the paint on the blades to glow fluorescently.

"Lo!" said the scruffy man, and rotated the fan's control to LO. The glowing blades began to spin and a light breeze blew into their faces. Those few who still bore stereos set them on the floor, and all stared mesmerized into the Fan.

"My name is Dex Fresser," said the new guy. "I am to tell you my story. Last semester, before Christmas break, I was at a big party on E31E. I was there to drink and smoke and stare down into the Big Wheel, which spoke to me regularly. At about midnight, Big Wheel spoke in the voice of the alien commander on my favorite video game. 'Better go pee before you lose it,' is what he said. So I went to pee. As I was standing in the bathroom peeing, the after-image of Big Wheel continued to hang in front of me, spinning on the wall over the urinal.

"I heard a noise and looked over toward the showers. There was a naked man with blood coming from his head. He was flopping around in the water. There was much steam, but the Go Big Red Fan blew the steam away, creeping toward him and making smoke and sparks of power. The alien commander spoke again, because I didn't know what to do. 'You'd better finish what you're doing,' it said, so I finished. Then I looked at the Fan again and the afterimage of the Big Wheel and the Fan became one in my sight and I knew that the Fan was the *incarnation* of the Big Wheel, come to lead us. I started for it, but it said, 'Better unplug me first. I could kill you, as I killed this guy. He used to be my priest but he was too independent.' So I unplugged Little Wheel and picked it up.

"It said, 'Get me out of here. I am smoking and the firemen will think I set off the alarm.' Yes, the fire alarm was ringing. So I took Little Wheel away and modified it as it told me, and today it told me I am to be your leader. Join me or your voices will become silent."

They had all listened spellbound, and when he was done, they jumped up with cheers and whoops. Dex Fresser bowed, smiling, and then, hearing a command, whirled around. The Fan had almost crept its way off the windowsill, and he saved it with a swoop of the hand.

In the middle of the month, as the ridges of packed grey snow around the Plex were beginning to settle and melt, negotiations between the administration and the MegaUnion froze solid and all B-men, professors, clerical workers and librarians went on strike.

To detail the politics and posturings that led to this is nothing I'd like to do. Let's just say that when negotiations had begun six months before, the Union had sworn in the names of God, Death and the Four Horsemen of the Apocalypse that unless granted a number of wild, vast demands they would all perform hara-kiri in President Krupp's bedroom. The administration negotiators had replied that before approaching to within a mile of the bargaining table they would prefer to drink gasoline, drop their grandchildren into volcanoes, convert the operation into a pasta factory and move it to Spokane.

Nothing unusual so far; all assumed that they would compromise from those positions. All except for the B-men, that is. After some minor compromising on both sides, the Crotobaltislavonian bloc, which was numerous enough to control the Union, apparently decided to stand their ground. As the clock ticked to within thirty minutes of the deadline, the Administration people just stared at them, while the other MegaUnion people watched with sweaty lunatic grins, waiting for the B-men to show signs of reason. But no.

Krupp came on the tube and said that American Megaversity could not afford its union, and that there was no choice but to let the strike proceed. The corridors vibrated with whooping and dancing for a few hours, and the strike was on.

As the second semester lurched and staggered onward, I noted that my friends had a greater tendency to drop by my suite at odd times, insist they didn't want to bother me and sit around reading old magazines, examining my plants, leafing through cookbooks and so on. My suite was not exactly Grandma's house, but it had become the closest thing they had to a home. After the strike began, I saw even more of them. Living in the Plex was tolerable when you could stay busy with school and keep reminding yourself that you were just a student, but it was a slough of despond when your purpose in life was to wait for May.

I threw a strike party for them. Sarah, Casimir, Hyacinth, Virgil and Ephraim made up the guest list, and Fred Fine happened to stop by so that he could watch a Dr. Who rerun on my TV. We all knew that Fred Fine was weird, but at this point only Virgil knew *how* weird. Only Virgil knew that an S & S player had died in the sewers during one of Fred Fine's games, and that the young nerd-lord *had simply disregarded it.* The late Steven Wilson was still a Missing Person as far as the authorities were concerned.

Ephraim Klein was just as odd in his own way. We knew that his hated ex-roommate had died of a freak heart attack on the night of the Big Flush, but we didn't know Ephraim had anything to do with it. We were not alarmed by his strange personality because it was useful in parties—he would allow no conversation to flag or fail.

Virgil sat in a corner, sipping Jack Daniels serenely and staring through the floor. Casimir stayed near Sarah, who stayed near Hyacinth. Other people stopped in from time to time, but I haven't written them into the following transcript —which has been rearranged and guessed at quite a bit anyway.

HYACINTH. The strike will get rid of Krupp. After that everything will be fine.

EPHRAIM. How can you say that! You think the problem with this place is just S. S. Krupp?

BUD. Sarah, how's your forest coming along?

EPHRAIM. Everywhere you look you see the society coming apart. How do you blame S. S. Krupp alone for that?

SARAH. I haven't done much with it lately. It's just nice to have it there.

CASIMIR. Do you really think the place is getting worse? I think you're just seeing it more clearly now that classes are shut down.

HYACINTH. You were in Professor Sharon's office during the piano incident, weren't you?

FRED FINE. What do you propose we do, Ephraim?

EPHRAIM. Blow it up.

CASIMIR. Yeah, I was right there.

HYACINTH. So for you this place has seemed terrible right from the beginning. You've got a different perspective.

SARAH. Ephraim! What do you mean? How would it help anything to blow up the Big U?

EPHRAIM. I didn't say it would help, I said it would prevent further deterioration.

SARAH. What could be more deteriorated than a destroyed Plex?

EPHRAIM. Nothing! Get it?

SARAH. You do have a point. This building, and the bureaucracy here, can drive people crazy—divorce them from reality so they don't know what to do. Somehow the Plex has to go. But I don't think it should be blown up.

FRED FINE. Have you ever computed the explosive power necessary to destabilize the Plex?

EPHRAIM. Of course not!

CASIMIR. He's talking to me. No, I haven't.

HYACINTH. Is that nerd as infatuated with you as he looks?

SARAH. Uh . . . you mean Fred Fine?

HYACINTH. Yeah.

SARAH. I think so. Please, it's too disgusting.

HYACINTH. No shit.

FRED FINE. I have computed where to place the charges.

CASIMIR. It'd be a very complicated setup, wouldn't it? Lots of timed detonations?

BUD *(drunk)*. So do you think that the decay of the society is actually built into the actual building itself?

SARAH. The reason he likes me is because he knows I carry a gun. He saw it in the Caf.

EPHRAIM. Of course! How else can you explain all this? It's too big and it's too uniform. Every room, every wing is just the same as the others. It's a giant sensory deprivation experiment.

HYACINTH. A lot of those science-fiction types have big sexual hangups. You ever look at a science-fiction magazine? All these women in brass bras with whips and chains and so on—dominatrices. But the men who read that stuff don't even know it.

EPHRAIM. Did you know that whenever I play anything in the key of C, the entire Wing vibrates?

FRED FINE. This one worked out the details from the blueprints. All you need is to find the load-bearing columns and make some simple calculations.

EPHRAIM. Hey! Casimir!

CASIMIR. Yeah?

SARAH. What's scary is that all of these fucked-up people, who have problems and don't even know it, are going to go out and make thirty thousand dollars a year and be important. We'll all be clerk-typists.

EPHRAIM. You're in physics. What's the frequency of a low C? Like in a sixty-four-foot organ pipe?

CASIMIR. Hell, I don't know. That's music theory.

EPHRAIM. Shit. Hey, Bud, you got a tape measure?

CASIMIR. I'd like to take music theory sometime. One of my professors has interesting things to say about the similarity between the way organ pipes are controlled by keys and stops, and the way random-access memory bits are read by computers.

BUD. I've got an eight-footer.

FRED FINE. This one doesn't listen to that much music. It would be pleasant to have time for the luxuries of life. In some D & D scenarios, musicians are given magical abilities. Einstein and Planck used to play violin sonatas together.

EPHRAIM. We have to measure the length of the hallways!

The conversation split up into three parts. Ephraim and I went out to measure the hallway. Hyacinth was struck by a craving for Oreos and repaired to the kitchen with a fierce determination that none dared question. Casimir followed her. Sarah, Fred Fine and Virgil stayed in the living room.

FRED FINE. What's your major?

SARAH. English.

FRED FINE. Ah, very interesting. This one thought you were in Forestry.

SARAH. Why?

FRED FINE. Didn't our host mention your forest?

SARAH. That's different. It's what I painted on my wall.

FRED FINE. Well, well, well. A little illegal room painting, eh? Don't worry, I wouldn't report you. Is this part of an other-world scenario, by any chance?

SARAH. Hell, no, it's for the opposite. Look, this place is already an other-world scenario.

FRED FINE. No. That's where you're wrong. This is reality. It is a self-sustaining ecosociosystem powered by inter-universe warp generators.

(There is a long silence.)

VIRGIL. Fred, what did you think of Merriam's Math Physics course?

(There is another long silence.)

FRED FINE. Well. Very good. Fascinating. I would recommend it.

SARAH. Where's the bathroom?

FRED FINE. Ever had to pull that pepper grinder of yours on one of those Terrorist guys?

SARAH. Maybe we can discuss it some other time.

FRED FINE. I'd recommend more in the way of a large-gauge shotgun.

SARAH. I'll be back.

FRED FINE. Of course, in a magical universe it would turn into a two-handed broadsword, which would be difficult for a petite type to wield.

Meanwhile Casimir and Hyacinth talked in the kitchen. They had met once before, when they had stopped by my suite on the same evening; they didn't know each other well, but Casimir had heard enough to suspect that she was not particularly heterosexual. She knew a fair amount about him through Sarah.

HYACINTH. You want some Oreos too?

CASIMIR. No, not really. Thanks.

HYACINTH. Did you want to talk about something?

CASIMIR. How did you know?

HYACINTH *(scraping Oreo filling with front teeth)*. Well, sometimes some things are easy to figure out.

CASIMIR. Well, I'm really worried about Sarah. I think there's something wrong with her. It's really strange that she resigned as President when she was doing so well. And ever since then, she's been kind of hard to get along with.

HYACINTH. Kind of bitchy?

CASIMIR. Yeah, that's it.

HYACINTH. I don't think she's bitchy at all. I think she's just got a lot on her mind, and all her good friends have to be patient with her while she works it out.

CASIMIR. Oh, yeah, I agree. What I was thinking—well, this is none of my business.

HYACINTH. What?

CASIMIR. Oh, last semester I figured out that she was dating some other guy, you know? Though she wouldn't tell me anything about him. Did she have some kind of a breakup that's been painful for her?

HYACINTH. No, no, she and her lover are getting along *wonderfully*. But I'm sure she'd appreciate knowing how concerned you are.

(Long silence.)

HYACINTH *(slinging one arm around Casimir's waist, feeding Oreo into his mouth with other hand)*. Hey, it feels terrible, doesn't it? Look, Casimir, she likes you a hell of a lot. I mean it. And she hates to put you through this kind of pain—or she wishes you wouldn't put yourself through it. She thinks you're terrific.

CASIMIR *(blubbering)*.Well what the hell does it take? All she does is say I'm wonderful. Am I unattractive? Oh, I forgot. Sorry, I've never talked to a, ah . . .

HYACINTH. You can say it.

CASIMIR. Lesbian. Thanks.

HYACINTH. You're welcome.

CASIMIR. Why can she look at one guy and say, "He's a friend," and look at this other guy and say, "He's a lover?"

HYACINTH. Instinct. There's no way you can go against her instincts, Casimir, don't even think about it. As for you, I think you're kind of attractive, but then, I'm a dyke.

CASIMIR. Great. The only woman in the world, besides my mother, who thinks I'm good looking is a lesbian.

HYACINTH. Don't think about it. You're hurting yourself.

CASIMIR. God, I'm sorry to dump this on you. I don't even know you.

HYACINTH. It's a lot easier to talk when you don't have to worry about the sexual thing, isn't it?

CASIMIR. That's for sure. Good thing I've got my sunglasses, no one can tell I've been crying.

HYACINTH. Let's talk more later. We've abandoned Sarah with Fred Fine, you know.

CASIMIR. Shit.

Casimir pulled himself together and they went back to the living room. Shortly, Ephraim and I returned from the hallway with our announcement.

BUD. Isn't it interesting how the alcohol goes to your head when you get up and start moving around?

EPHRAIM. The hallway on each side of each wing is a hundred twenty-eight feet and a few inches long. But the fire doors in the middle cut it exactly in half—sixty-four feet!

BUD. And three inches.

EPHRAIM. So they resonate at low C.

FRED FINE. Very interesting.

VIRGIL. Casimir, when are you going to stop playing mum about Project Spike?

CASIMIR. What? Don't talk about that!

SARAH. What's Project Spike?

CASIMIR. Nothing much. I was playing with rats.

FRED FINE. What does this one hear about rats?

VIRGIL. Casimir was trying to prove the existence of rat parts or droppings in the Cafeteria food through a radioactive tracer system. He came up with some very interesting results. But he's naturally shy, so he hasn't mentioned them to anyone.

CASIMIR. The results were screwed up! Anyone can see that.

VIRGIL. No way. They weren't random enough to be considered as errors. Your results indicated a far higher level of Carbon-14 in the food than could be possible, because they could never eat that much poison. Right?

CASIMIR. Right. And they had other isotopes that couldn't possibly be in the rat poison, such as Cesium-137. The entire thing was screwed up.

FRED FINE. How large are the rats in question?

CASIMIR. Oh, pretty much your average rats, I guess.

FRED FINE. But they are not—they were normal? Like this?

CASIMIR. About like that, yeah. What did you expect?

VIRGIL. Have you analyzed any other rats since Christmas?

CASIMIR. Yeah. Damn it.

VIRGIL. And they were just as contaminated.

CASIMIR. More so. Because of what I did.

SARAH. What's wrong, Casimir?

CASIMIR. Well, I sort of lost some plutonium down an elevator shaft in the Big Flush.

(Ephraim gives a strange hysterical laugh.)

FRED FINE. God. You've created a race of giant rats, Casimir. Giant rats the size of Dobermans.

BUD. Giant rats?

HYACINTH. Giant rats?

BUD. Virgil, explain everything to us, okay?

VIRGIL. I am sure that there are giant rats in the sewer tunnels beneath the Plex. I am sure that they're scared of strobe lights, and that strobes flashing faster than about sixteen per second drive them crazy. This may be related to the frequency of muzzle flashes produced by certain automatic weapons, but that's just a hypothesis. I know that there are organized activities going on at a place in the tunnels that are of a secret, highly technological, heavily guarded nature. As for the rats, I assume they were created by mutation from high levels of background radiation. This included Strontium-90 and Cesium-137 and possibly an iodine isotope. The source of the radiation could possibly have been what Casimir lost down the elevator shaft, but I suspect it has more to do with this secret activity. In any case, we now have a responsibility. We need to discover the source of the radioactivity, look for ways to control the rats and, if possible, divine the nature of the secret activity. I have a plan of attack worked up, but I'll need help. I need people familiar with the tunnels, like Fred; people who know how to use guns—we have some here; big people in good physical condition, like Bud; people who understand the science, like Casimir; and maybe even someone who knows all about Remote Sensing, such as Professor Bud again.

An advantage of the Plex was that it taught you to accept any weirdness immediately. We did not question Virgil. He memorized a list of equipment he'd have to scrounge for us, and Hyacinth grilled us until we had settled on March 31 as our expedition date. Fred Fine said he knew where he could get authentic dumdums for our guns, and tried to tell us that the best way to kill a rat was with a sword, giving a lengthy demonstration until Virgil told him to sit down. Once we had mobilized into an amateur commando team, we found that our partying spirit was spent, and soon we were all home trying vainly to sleep.

The strike itself has been studied and analyzed to death, so I'm spared writing a full account. For the most part the picketers stayed within the Plex. Their intent was to hamper activities inside the Plex, not to seal it off, and they feared that once they went outside, S. S. Krupp would not let them back in again.

Some protesters did work the entrances, though. A delegation of B-men and professors set up an informational picket at the Main Entrance, and another two dozen established a line to bar access to the loading docks. Most of these were Crotobaltislavonians who paraded tirelessly in their heavy wool coats and big fur hats; with them were some black and Hispanic workers, dressed more conventionally, and three political science professors, each wearing high-tech natural-tone synthetic-insulated expedition parkas computer-designed to keep the body dry while allowing perspiration to pass out. Most of the workers sported yellow or orange work gloves, but the professors opted for warm Icelandic wool mittens, presumably to keep their fingers supple in case they had to take notes.

The picket's first test came at 8:05 A.M., when the morning garbage truck convoy arrived. The trucks turned around and left with no trouble. Forcing garbage to build up inside the Plex seemed likely to make the administration more openminded. Therefore the only thing allowed to leave the Plex was the hazardous chemical waste from the laboratories; run-of-the-mill trash could only be taken out if the administration and Trustees hauled it away in their Cadillacs.

A little later, a refrigerated double-bottom semi cruised up, fresh and steaming from a two-day, 1500-mile trek from Iowa, loaded with enough rock-frozen beef to supply American Megaversity for two days. This was out of the question, as the people working in the Cafeteria now were all scabs. The political science professors failed to notice that their comrades had all dropped way back and split up into little groups and put their signs on the ground. They walked toward the semi, waving their arms over their heads and motioning it back, and finally the enormous gleaming machine sighed and slowed. An anarcho-Trotskyite with blow-dried hair and a thin blond mustache stepped up to the driver's side and squinted way up above his head at a size 25 black leather glove holding a huge chained rawhide wallet which had been opened to reveal a Teamsters card. The truck driver said nothing. The professor started to explain that this was a picket line, then paused to read the Teamsters card. Stepping back a little and craning his neck, he could see only black greased-back hair and the left lens of a pair of mirror sunglasses.

"Great!" said the professor. "Glad to see you're in solidarity with the rest of us workers. Can you get out of here with no problem, or shall I direct you?" He smiled at the left-hand lens of the driver's sunglasses, trying to make it a tough smile, not a cultured pansyish smile.

"You AFL-CIO," rumbled the trucker, sounding like a rough spot in the idle of the great diesel. "Me Teamsters. I'm late."

The professor admired the no-nonsense speech of the common people, but sensed that he was failing to pick up on some message the trucker was trying to send him. He looked around for another worker who might be able to understand, but saw that the only people within shotgun-blast range of the truck had Ph.D.'s. Of these, one was jogging up to the truck with an impatient look on his face. He was a slightly gray-tinged man in his early forties, who in consultation with his orthopedist had determined that the running gait least damaging to his knees was a shuffling motion with the arms down to the sides. Thus he approached the truck. "Turn it around, buster, this is a strike. You're crossing a picket line."

There was another rumble from the truck window. This sounded more like laughter than words. The trucker withdrew his hand for a moment, then swung it back out like a wrecking ball. Balanced on the tip of his index finger was a quarter. "See this?" said the trucker.

"Yeah," said the professors in unison.

"This is a quarter. I put it in that pay phone and there's blood on the sidewalks."

The professors looked at each other, and at the third professor, who had stopped in his space-age hiking-boot tracks. They all retreated to the other end of the lot for a discussion of theory and praxis as the truck eased up to the loading dock. They watched the trucker carry his two-hundred-pound steer pieces into the warehouse, then concluded that a policy decision should be made at a higher level. The real target of this picket ought to be the scabs working the warehouse and Cafeteria. All the Crotobaltislavonians had gone inside, and the professors, finding themselves in an empty lot with only the remains of a few dozen steers to keep them company, decided to re-deploy inside the Plex.

There things were noisier. People who never engage in violence are quick to talk about it, especially when the people they are arguing with are elderly Greek professors unlikely to be carrying tire chains or knives. Of course, the Greek professors, who tried to engage the picketers in Socratic dialogue as they broke the picket lines, were not subject to much more than occasional pushing. Among younger academics there were genuine fights. A monetarist from Connecticut finally came to blows with an Algerian Maoist with whom he'd been trading scathing articles ever since they had shared an office as grad students. This fight turned out to be of the tedious kind held by libidinous orthodontists' sons at suburban video arcades. The monetarist tried to break through the line around the Economics bloc, just happening to attack that part of the line where the Maoist was standing. After some pushing the monetarist fell down with the Algerian on top of him. They got up and the monetarist missed with some roundhouse kicks taken from an aerobic dance routine. The Maoist whipped off his designer belt and began to whirl the buckle around his head as though it were dangerous. The monetarist watched indecisively, then ran up and stuck out his arm so that the belt wrapped around it. As he had his eyes closed, he did not know where he was going, but as though guided by some invisible hand he rammed into the Algerian's belly with his head and they fell onto a stack of picket signs and received minor injuries. The Algerian grabbed the monetarist's Adam Smith tie and tried to strangle him, but the latter's gold collar pin prevented the knot from tightening. He grabbed the Maoist's all-natural-fiber earthtone slacks and yanked them down to midthigh, occasioning a strange cry from his opponent, who removed one hand from the Adam Smith tie to prevent the loss of further garments; the monetarist grasped the Algerian's pinkie and yanked the other hand free. Finding that they had made their way to the opposite side of the picket line, he got up and skipped away, though the Maoist hooked his foot with a picket sign and hindered him considerably.

Students wanting to attend classes in the ROTC bloc found that they need only assume fake kung fu positions and the skinny pale fanatics there would get out of their way. Otherwise, students going to classes taught by nonunion professors worried only about verbal abuse. Unless they were aggressively obnoxious, like Ephraim Klein, they were in no physical peril. Ephraim went out of his way to cross picket lines, and unleashed many awe-inspiring insults he had apparently been saving up for years. Fortunately for him he spent most of his time around the Philosophy bloc, where the few picketing professors devoted most of their time to smoking cigarettes, exchanging dirty jokes and discussing basketball.

The entrance to the Cafeteria was a mess. The MegaUnion could never agree on what to do about it, because to allow students inside was to support S. S. Krupp's scab labor, and to block the place off was to starve the students. Depriving the students of meals they had already paid for was no way to make friends. Finally the students were encouraged to prepare their own meals as a gesture of support. In an attempt at plausibility, some efforts were mounted to steal food from Caf warehouses, but to no avail. The radicals advocated conquering the kitchen by main force, but all entrances were guarded by private guards with cudgels, dark glasses and ominous bulges. The radicals therefore used aerial bombardment, hurling things from the towers in hopes that they would crash through Tar City and into the kitchens. This was haphazard, though, and moderate MegaUnion members opposed it violently; as a result, students who persisted in dining at the Caf were given merely verbal abuse. As for the scabs themselves, they were determined-looking people, and activists attempting to show them the error of their ways tried not to raise their voices or to make any fast moves.

Then, seven days into the strike, it really happened: what the union had never dreamed of, what I, sitting in my suite reading the papers and plunging into a bitter skepticism, had been awaiting with a sort of sardonic patience. The Board of Trustees announced that American Megaversity was shutting down for this year, that credit would be granted for unfinished courses and that an early graduation ceremony would take place in mid-April. Everyone was to be out of the Plex by the end of March.

"Well," said S. S. Krupp on the tube, "I don't know what all the confusion's about. Seems to me we are being quite straightforward. We can't afford our faculty and workers. We can't meet our commitment to our students for this semester. About all we can do is clean the place out, hire some new faculty, re-enroll and get going again. God knows there are enough talented academics out there who need jobs. So we're asking all those people in the Plex to clear out as soon as they can."

The infinite self-proclaimed cleverness of the students enabled them to dismiss it as a fabulous lie and a ham-fisted maneuver. Once this opinion was formed by the few, it was impossible for the many to disagree, because to believe Krupp was to proclaim yourself a dupe. Few students therefore planned to leave; those who did found it perilous.

The Terrorists had decided that leaving the Plex was too unusual an idea to go unchallenged, and the Big Wheel backed them up on it. So the U-Hauls and Jartrans stacked up in the access lot began to suffer dents, then craters, then cave-ins, as golf balls, chairs, bricks, barbell weights and flaming newspaper bundles zinged out of the smoggy morning sky at their terminal velocities and impacted on their shiny tops. Few rental firms in the City had lent vehicles to students in the first place; those that did quickly changed their policies, and became dour and pitiless as desperate sophomores paraded before their reception desks waving wads of cash and Mom-and-Dad's credit cards.

The Plexodus, as it was dubbed by local media, dwindled to a dribble of individual escapes in which students would sprint from the cover of the Main Entrance carrying whatever they could hold in their arms and dive into the back seats of cars idling by on the edge of the Parkway, cars which then would scurry off as fast as their meager four cylinders could drag them before the projectiles hurled from the towers above had had time to find their targets.

I had seen enough of Krupp to know that the man meant what he said. I also had seen enough of the Plex to know that no redemption was possible for the place—no last-minute injection of reason could save this patient from its overdose of LSD and morphine.

Lucy agreed with me. You may vaguely remember her as Hyacinth's roommate. Lucy and I hit it off pretty well, especially as March went on. The shocks and chaos that took everyone else by surprise were just what we had been expecting, and both of us were surprised that our friends hadn't foreseen it. Of course our perspectives were different from theirs; we both had slaves for great-grandparents and the academic world was foreign to our backgrounds. Through decades of work our families had put us into universities because that was the place to be; when we finally arrived, we found we were just in time to witness the end result of years of dry rot. No surprise that things looked different to us.

Lucy and I began making long tours of the Plex to see what further deterioration had taken place. By this time the Terrorists outnumbered their would-be victims. The notion that the strike might be resolved restrained them for a while, but then came the pervasive sense that the Big U was dead and the rumor that it had already been slated for demolition. Obviously there was no point in maintaining the place if destruction loomed, so all the Terrorists had to worry about were the administration guards.

The Seritech Super Big-Window 1500 in Laundry soon disappeared, carted off by its worshipers. Unfortunately the machine didn't work on their wing, which lacked 240-volt outlets. Using easy step-by-step instructions provided by its voice, they tore open the back and arranged a way of rotating it by hand whenever they needed to know what to make for dinner or what to watch on TV.

In those last days of March it was difficult to make sense of anything. It was hinted that the union was splitting up, that the faculty had become exasperated by the implacable Crotobaltislavonians and planned to make a separate peace with the Trustees. This caused further infighting within the decaying MegaUnion and added to the confusion. Electricity and water were shut off, then back on again; students on the higher floors began to throw their garbage down the open elevator shafts, and fire alarms rang almost continuously until they were wrecked by infuriated residents. But we thought obsessively about Virgil's reference to secret activities in the sewers and developed the paranoid idea that everything around us was strictly superficial and based on a much deeper stratum of intrigue. It's hard enough to follow events such as these without having to keep the mind open for possible conspiracies and secrets behind every move. This uncertainty made it impossible for us to form any focused picture of the tapestry of events, and we became impatient for Saturday night, tired of having to withhold judgment until we knew all the facts. What had been conceived as an almost recreational visit to the Land of the Rats had become, in our minds, the search for the central fact of American Megaversity.

A hoarse command was shouted, and a dozen portable lamps shone out at once. Forty officers of MARS found themselves in a round low-ceilinged chamber that served as the intersection of two sewer mains. They stood at ease around the walls as Fred Fine, in the center, delivered his statement.

"We've never revealed the existence of this area before. It's our only Level Four Security Zone large enough for mass debriefings.

"All of you have been in MARS for at least three years and have performed well. Most of you didn't understand why we included physical fitness standards as part of our promotion system. Things got a little clearer when we introduced you to live-action gaming. Now, this—this is the hard part to explain."

All watched respectfully as he stared at the ceiling. Finally he resumed his address, though his voice had become as harsh and loud as that of a barbarian warlord addressing his legions. The officers now began to concentrate; the game had begun, they must enter character.

"You know about the Central Bifurcation that separates Magic and Technology. Some of you have probably noticed that lately Leakage has been very bad. Well, I've got tough news. It's going to get a lot worse. We are approaching the most critical period in the history of Plexor. If we do what needs to be done, we can stop Leakage for all time and enter an eternal golden age. If we fail, the Leakage will become like a flood of water from a broken pipe. Mixture will be everywhere, Purification will be impossible, and mediocrity will cover the universes for all time like a dark cloud. Plexor will become a degenerate, pre-warp-drive society.

"That's right. The responsibility for this universe-wide task falls on our shoulders. We are the chosen band of warriors and heroes called for in the prophecies of Magic-Plexor, foretold by JANUS 64 itself. That means you'll need a crash course on Plexor and how it works. That's why we're here.

"Consuela, known in Magic-Plexor as the High Priestess Councilla, is a top-notch programmer in Techno-Plexor. She therefore knows all there is to know about the Two Faces of Shekondar. Councilla, over to you."

"Good evening," came the voice from Fred Fine's big old vacuum-tube radio receiver. She sounded very calm and soft, as though drugged. "This is Councilla, High Priestess of Shekondar the Fearsome, King of Two Faces. Prepare your minds for the Awful Secrets.

"Plexor was created by the Guild, a team consisting half of Technologists and half of Sorcerers who operated in separate universes through the devices of Keldor, the astral demigod whose brain hemispheres existed on either side of the Centrl Bifurcation. Under Keldor's guidance the colony of Plexor was created: a self-contained ecosystem capable of functioning in any environment, drawing energy and raw materials from any source, and resisting any magical or technological attack. When Plexor was completed, it was populated by selecting the best and the brightest from all the Thousand Galaxies and comparing them in a great tournament. The field of competition was split down the middle by the Central Bifurcation, and on one side the contestants fought with swords and sorcery, while on the other they vied in tests of intellectual skill. The champions were inputted to Plexor; we are their output.

"The Guild had to place an overseer over Plexor. It must be the Operating System for the Technological side, and the Prime Deity for the Magic side, and in Plexor it must be omniscient and all-powerful. Thus, the Guild generated Shekondar the Fearsome/JANUS 64, the Organism that inhabits and controls the colony. The creation of this system took twice as long as the building of Plexor itself, and in the end Keldor died, his mind overloaded by massive transfers of data from one hemisphere to the other, the Boundary within his mind destroyed and the contents Mixed hopelessly. But out of his death came the King of Two Faces, that which in Techno-Plexor is JANUS 64 and in Magic Plexor, Shekondar the Fearsome.

"Though the last member of the Guild died two thousand years ago, most Plexorians have revered the King of Two Faces. But in these dark days, at the close of this age, those who know the story of Shekondar/JANUS 64 are very few. We who have kept the flame alive have trained your bodies and minds to accept this responsibility. Today, our efforts output in batch. From this room will march the Grand Army celebrated in the prophecies and songs of Magic-Plexor, whose coming has been foretold even in the seemingly random errors of JANUS 64; the band of heroes which will debug Plexor, which will fight Mixture in the approaching crisis. And for those of you who have failed to detect Mixture, who scoff that Magic might have crossed the Central Bifurcation: Behold!"

The listeners had now allowed themselves to sink deep into their characters, and Councilla's words had begun to mesmerize them. Though a few had grinned at the silliness spewing out of the big speakers, the oppressive seriousness and magical unity that filled this dank chamber had silenced them; soon, cut off from the normal world, they began to doubt themselves, and heeded the Priestess. As she built to a climax and revealed the most profound secrets of Plexor, many began to sweat and tingle, fidgeting with terrified energy. When she cried, "Behold!" the spell was bound up in a word. The room became silent with fear as all wondered what demonic demonstration she had conjured up.

A *sssh!* was heard, and it avalanched into a loud, general hiss. When that sound died away, it was easy to hear a soft, cacophonous noise, a jumble of sharp high tones that sounded like a distant kazoo band. The sound seemed to come from one of the tunnels, though echoes made it hard to tell which one. It was approaching quickly. Suddenly and rapidly, everyone cleared away from the four tunnel openings and plastered against the walls. Only when all the others had found places did Klystron the Impaler move. He walked calmly through the center of the room, leaving the radio receiver and speakers in the middle, and found himself a place in front of a hushed squadron of swordsmen. The roar swelled to a scream; a bat the size of an eagle pumped out of a tunnel, took a fast turn around the room, sending many of the men to their knees, then plunged decisively into another passage. As the roar exploded into the open, in the garish artificial light the Grand Army saw a swarm of enormous fat brown-grey lash-tailed bright-eyed screaming frothing *rats* vomit from the tunnel, veer through the middle of the room and compress itself into the opening through which the giant bat had flown. Some of them smashed headlong into the old boxy radio, sending it sprawling across the floor, and before it had come to rest, five rats had parted from the stream and demolished it, scything their huge gleaming rodent teeth through the plywood case as though it were an orange peel, prying the apparatus apart, munching into its glass-and-metal innards with insane passion. Their frenzy lasted for several seconds; their brothers had all gone; and they emitted piercing shrieks and scuttled off into the tunnel, one trailing behind a streak of twisted wire and metal.

Most everyone save Klystron sat on the floor in a fetal position, arms crossed over faces, though some had drawn swords or clubs, prepared to fight it out. None moved for two minutes, lest they draw another attack. When the warriors began to show life again, they moved with violent trembling and nauseated dizziness and the most perfect silence they could attain. No one strayed from the safety of the walls except for Klystron the Impaler/Chris the Systems Programmer, who paced to a spot where a thousand rat footprints had stomped a curving highway into the thin sludge. Hardly anyone here, he knew, had been convinced of the Central Bifurcation, much less of the danger of Mixture. That was understandable, given the badly Mixed environment which had twisted their minds. Klystron/Chris had done all he could to counter such base thinking, but the rise of the giant rats, and careful preparation by him and Councilla and Chip Dixon, had provided proof.

He let them think it over. It was not an easy thing, facing up to one's own importance; even he had found it difficult. Finally he spoke out in a clear and firm voice, and every head in the room snapped around to pay due respect to their leader.

"Do I have a Grand Army?"

The mumbled chorus sounded promising. Klystron snapped his sword from its scabbard and held it on high, making sure to avoid electrical cables. "All hail Shekondar the Fearsome!" he trumpeted.

Swords, knives, chains and clubs crashed out all around and glinted in the mist. "All hail Shekondar the Fearsome!" roared the army in reply, and four times it was answered by echoes from the tunnels. Klystron/Chris listened to it resonate, then spoke with cool resolve: "It is time to begin the Final Preparations."

An advantage of living in a decaying civilization was that nobody really cared if you chose to roam the corridors laden with armfuls of chest waders, flashlights, electrical equipment and weaponry. We did receive alarmed scrutiny from some, and boozy inquiries from friendly Terrorists, but were never in danger from the authorities. A thirty-minute trek through the deepening chaos of the Plex took us to the Burrows, which were still inhabited by people devoted to such peaceful pursuits as gaming, computer programming, research and *Star Trek* reruns.

From here a freight elevator took us to the lowest sublevel, where Fred Fine led us through dingy hallways plastered with photos of nude Crotobaltislavonian princesses until we came to a large room filled with plumbing. From here, Virgil used his master key to let us into a smaller room, from which a narrow spiral staircase led into the depths.

"I go first," said Virgil quietly, "with the Sceptre. Hyacinth follows with her .44. Bud follows her with the heavy gloves, then Sarah and Casimir with the backpacks, and Fred in the rear with his sixteen-gauge. No noise."

After one or two turns of the stair we had to switch on our headlamps. The trip down was long and tense, and we seemed to make a hellacious racket on the echoing metal treads. I kept my beam on the blazing white-gold beacon of Virgil's hair and listened to the breathing and the footsteps behind me. The air had a harsh damp smell that told me I was sucking in billions of microbes of all descriptions with each breath. Toward the bottom we slipped on our gas masks, and I found I was breathing much faster than I needed to.

The rats were waiting a full fifty feet above the bottom. One had his mouth clamped over Virgil's lower leg before he had switched on the Sceptre of Cosmic Force. The flashing drove away the rest of the rats, who tumbled angrily down the stair on top of one another, but the first beast merely clamped down harder and hung on, too spazzed out to move. Fortunately, Hyacinth did not try to shoot it on the spot. I slipped past, flexed my big elbow-length padded gloves, and did battle with the rat. The rodent teeth had not penetrated the soccer shinguards Virgil wore beneath his waders, so I took my time, relaxing and squatting down to look into the animal's glowering white-rimmed eye. His bared chisel teeth, a few inches long and an inch wide, flickered purple-yellow with each flash of the strobe. Having sliced through Virgil's waders to expose the colorful plastic shinguard, the rat now tried to gnaw its way through the obstacle without letting go. I did not have the strength to pull its mouth open.

"A German shepherd can exert hundreds of pounds of jaw force," said Fred Fine, standing above and peering over Casimir's shoulder with scientific coolness.

The rat was not impressed by any of this.

"Let's go for a clean kill," suggested its victim with a trace of strain, "and then we'll have our sample."

I bashed in the back of its head with an oaken leg I had foresightedly unscrewed from my kitchen table for the occasion. The rat just barely fit into a large heavy-duty leaf bag; Virgil twist-tied it shut and we left it there.

And so into the tunnels. The sewers were unusually fluid that night as thousands of cubic feet of beer made its traditional way through the digestive tracks of the degenerates upstairs and into the sanitary system. Hence we stuck to the catwalks along the sides of the larger tunnels—as did the rats. The Sceptre was hard on our eyes, so Virgil waited until they were perilously close before switching it on and driving them in squalling bunches into the stream below. We did not have to use the guns, though Fred Fine insisted on shooting his flash gun at a rat to see how they liked it. Not at all, as it happened, and Fred Fine pronounced it "very interesting."

Casimir said, "Where did my radioactive source fall to? Are we going anywhere near there?"

"Good point," said Fred Fine. "Let's steer clear of that. Don't want blasted 'nads."

"I know where it went, but it's not there now," said Virgil. "The rats ate everything. Some rat obviously got a free surprise in with his paraffin, but I don't know where he ended up."

Fred Fine began to point out landmarks: where he had left the corpse of the Microwave Lizard, long since eaten by you know what; where Steven Wilson had experienced his last and biggest surprise; the tunnel that led to the Sepulchre of Keldor. His voice alternated between the pseudo-scientific dynamo hum of Fred Fine and the guttural baritone of the war hero. We had heard this stuff from him for a couple of weeks now, but down in the tunnels it really started to perturb us. Most people, on listening to a string of nonsense, will tend to doubt their own sanity before they realize that the person who is jabbering at them is really the one with the damaged brain. That night, tramping through offal, attacking giant rats with a strobe light and listening to the bizarre memoirs of Klystron, most of us were independently wondering whether or not we were crazy. So when we asked Fred Fine for explanations, it was not because we wanted to hear more Klystron stories (as he assumed); it was because we wanted to get an idea of what other people were thinking. We were quickly able to realize that the world was indeed okay, that Fred Fine was bonkers and we were fine.

Hundreds of cracked and gnawed bones littered one intersection, and Virgil identified it as where he had discovered the useful properties of the Sceptre. This area was high and dry, as these things went, and many rats lurked about. Virgil switched the Sceptre on for good, forcing them back to the edge of the dark, where they chattered and flashed their red eyes. Hyacinth stuffed wads of cotton in her ears, apparently in case of a shootout.

"Let's set up the 'scope," Virgil suggested. Casimir swung off his pack and withdrew a heavily padded box, from which he took a small portable oscilloscope. This device had a tiny TV screen which would display sound patterns picked up by a shotgun microphone which was also in the pack. As the 'scope warmed up, Casimir plugged the microphone cord into a socket on its front. A thin luminous green line traced across the middle of the screen.

Virgil aimed the mike down the main passageway and turned it on. The line on the screen split into a chaotic tangle of dim green static. Casimir played with various knobs, and quickly the wild flailing of the signal was compressed into a pattern of random vibes scrambling across the screen. "White noise," said Fred Fine. "Static to you laymen."

"Keep an eye on it," said Virgil, and pointed the mike down the smaller side tunnel. The white noise was abruptly replaced by nearly vertical lines marching across the screen. Casimir compressed the signal down again, and we saw that it was nothing more than a single stationary sine wave, slightly unruly but basically stable.

"Very interesting," said Fred Fine.

"What's going on?" Sarah asked.

"This is a continuous ultrasonic tone," said Virgil. "It's like an unceasing dog whistle. It comes from some artificial source down that tunnel. You see, when I point the mike in most directions we get white noise, which is normal. But this is a loud sound at a single pitch. To the rats it would sound like a drawn-out note on an organ. That explains why they cluster in this particular area; it's music to their ears, though it's very simple music. In fact, it's monotonous."

"How did you know to look for this?" asked Sarah.

Virgil shrugged. "It was plausible that an installation as modern and carefully guarded as the one I saw would have some kind of ultrasonic alarm system. It's pretty standard."

"Very interesting," said Fred Fine.

"It's like sonar. Anything that disturbs the echo, within a certain range, sets off the alarm. Here's the question: why don't the rats set it off?"

"Some kind of barrier keeps them away," said Casimir.

"I agree. But I didn't see any barrier. When I was here before, they could run right up to the door—they had to be fought off with machine guns. Thay must have put up a barrier since I was last down here. What that means to us is this: we can go as far as the barrier, whatever it may be, without any fear of setting off the alarm system."

We moved down the tunnel in a flying wedge, making use of table leg, Sceptre and sword as necessary. Soon we arrived at the barrier, which turned out to be insubstantial but difficult to miss: a frame of angle-irons welded together along the walls and ceiling, hung with dozens of small, brilliant spotlights. At this point, any rat would find itself bathed in blinding light and turn back in terror and pain. Beyond this wall of light there was only a single line of footprints—human—in the bat guano. "Someone's been changing the light bulbs," concluded Sarah.

The fifty feet of corridor preceding the light-wall were littered almost knee-deep in glittering scraps of tinfoil and other bright objects, including the remains of Fred Fine's radio.

"This is their hangout," said Hyacinth. "They must like the music."

"They want to make a nice, juicy meal out of whoever changes those light bulbs," suggested Fred Fine.

Sarah's pack contained a tripod and a pair of fine binoculars. Once we had set these up in the middle of the tunnel we could see the heavy doors, TV cameras, lights and so on at the tunnel's end. As we took turns looking and speculating, Virgil set up a Geiger counter from Sarah's pack.

"Normally a Geiger counter would just pick up a lot of background and cosmic radiation and anything meaningful would be drowned out. But we're so well shielded in these tunnels that the only thing getting to us should be a few very powerful cosmic rays, and neutrinos, which this won't pick up anyway." The Geiger counter began to click, perhaps once every four seconds.

Sarah had the best eyes; she sat crosslegged on the layers of foil and gazed into the binoculars. "In a few minutes a hazardous waste pickup is scheduled for the loading dock upstairs," said Virgil, checking his watch. "My theory is that, in addition to taking hazardous wastes *out* of the Plex, those trucks have been bringing something even more hazardous *into* the Plex, and down into this tunnel."

We waited.

"Okay," said Sarah, "Elevator door opening on the right."

We all heard it.

"Long metal cylinder thingie on a cart. Now the end of the

tunnel is opening up—big doors, like jaws. Now some guys in yellow are rolling the cylinder into a large room back there."

The Geiger counter shouted. I looked at Casimir.

"Skip your next chest X-ray," he said. "If this place is what it looks like, it's just Iodine-131. Half-life of eight days. It'll end up in your thyroid, which you don't really need anyway."

"I'm pretty fond of my thyroid," said Hyacinth. "It made me big and strong."

"Doors closing," said Sarah over the chatter of us and the Geiger counter. "Elevator's gone. All doors closed now."

"Well! Congratulations, Virgil," said Fred Fine, shaking his hand. "You've discovered the only permanent high-level radioactive waste disposal facility in the United States."

Most of us didn't have anything to say about it. We mainly wanted to get back home.

"Fascinating, brilliant," continued Fred Fine, as we headed back. "In today's competitive higher education market, there has to be some way for universities to support themselves. What better way than to enter lucrative high-technology sectors?"

"Don't have to grovel for the alumni anymore," said Sarah.

"You really think universities should be garbage dumps for the worst by-products of civilization?" asked Hyacinth.

"It's not such a bad idea, in a way," said Casimir. "Better the universities than anyone else. Oxford, Heidelberg, Paris, all those places have lasted for centuries longer than any government. Only the Church has lasted longer, and the Vatican doesn't need the money."

We paused for a rest in the spiral staircase, near our rat body. Casimir, Fred Fine and Virgil went back down to the bottom for an experiment. Virgil had brought an ultrasonic tone generator with him, and they used it to prove—very conclusively—that the rats loved the ultrasound as much as they hated the strobe. They ran back upstairs, Sceptre flashing, and I slung the rat over my shoulder and we all proceeded up the stairs as fast as our lungs would allow.

The dissection of the rat was most informal. We did it in the sink of Professor Sharon's old lab, amid the pieces of the railgun.

Fred Fine laid into the thorax with a kitchen knife and a single-edged razor. We were quick and crude; only Casimir had seen the inside of a rat before. The skin peeled back easily along with thick pink layers of fat, and we looked at the intestines that could digest such amazing meals. Casimir scrounged a pair of heavy tin snips and used them to cut the breastbone in half so we could get under the ribcage. I shoved my hands between the halves of the breastbone and pulled as hard as I could, and finally with a crack and a spray of blood one side snapped open like a stubborn cabinet door and we looked at the lungs and vital organs. The heart was not immediately visible.

"Maybe it's hidden under this organ here," suggested Fred Fine, pointing to something between the lungs.

"That's not an organ," said Casimir. "It's an intersection of several major vessels."

"So where's the heart?" asked Hyacinth, just beginning to get interested.

"Those major vessels are the ones that ought to go into, and come out of, the heart," said Casimir uncertainly. He reached down and slid his hand under the bundle of vessels, and pulling it up and aside, revealed—nothing.

"Holy Mother of God," he whispered. "This animal doesn't have a heart."

Our own thumped violently. For a long time we were frozen, disturbed beyond reason; then a piercing beep emanated from Fred Fine and we jumped and gasped angrily.

Unconcerned, he pressed a button on his digital calculator/watch, halting the beep. "Sorry. That's my watch alarm."

We looked at him; he looked at his watch. We were all sweating.

"I set it to go off like that at midnight, the beginning of April first, every year. It's sort of a warning, so that this one remembers, hey, April Fools' Day, anything could happen now."

April

While we sewer-slogged, E13S held a giant party in honor of Big Wheel. It was conceived as your basic formless beer blow-out, but the ever-spunky Airheads had insisted upon a theme: Great Partiers of the Past. The major styles in evidence were Disco, Sixties, Fifties and Toga. A team of sturdy Terrorists had lugged Dex Fresser's stereo up to the social lounge, which was the center of Disco activity. A darkened room down the hall featured a Sixties party, at which participants roughed up their perms, wore T-shirts, smoked more dope than usual and said "groovy" at the drop of a hat. The study lounge was Fifties headquarters, and was identical to all the other Fifties parties which had been held since about 1963 by people who didn't know anything about the Fifties. The Toga people were forced to adopt a wandering, nomadic partying existence; they had no authentic toga music to boogie to, though someone did experiment by playing an electronic version of the "1812 Overture" at full blast. Mostly these people just stood sheepishly in the hallways, draped in their designer bedsheets, clutching cups of beer and yelling "toga!" from time to time.

The Disco lounge was filled with women in lollipop plastic dresses and thick metallic lipstick under ski masks, and heavily scented young men in pastel three-piecers and shiny hardware-laden shoes. The smell was deafening, and when the doors were open, excess music spilled out and filled nearby rooms to their corners. These partiers were a generation whose youth had been stolen. They had prepared all through their adolescence for the day when they could go to college and attend real discos, adult discos where they had alcohol and sex partners you could take home with no payrental hassles. Their hopes had been dashed in the early eighties when Disco had flamed out somewhere over New Jersey, like a famous dirigible. But the nostalgic air here made them feel young again. Dex Fresser even showed up in a white three-piecer and took several opportunities to boogie right down to the ground with shapely females in clingy synthetic wraps.

On the windowsill, the Go Big Red Fan, held in place with bricks, spun and glowed in its self-made halo of black light. Overhead, a mirrored ball cast revolving dots of light on the walls, and more stoned or imaginative dancers could imagine that they were actually standing *inside a giant Big Wheel.* Whoooo! The picture windows were covered with newspaper, as the panes had long since been smashed and the curtains long since burned.

After Dex Fresser had consumed sixteen hits of acid (his supplier had never really grasped the idea of powers of two), five bongloads of hashish rolled in mescaline, a square of peyote Jell-O, a lude, four tracks, a small handful of street-legal caffeine pep pills, twelve tablespoons of cough syrup, half a can of generic light wine and a pack of Gaulois cigarettes, he began to toy with a strobe light that was being used to establish the Disco atmosphere. He turned it up faster and faster until the lounge was wracked with delighted freaked-out screams and the dancers had begun to hop randomly and smash into one another, as though they had been time-warped into Punk. Meanwhile, what passed for Dex's mind wandered over to the Go Big Red Fan, and though the time-warp effect was really blowing his tubes, he thought the fan might be slowing down; continuing to turn up the strobe, he was able to make the Little Wheel stop revolving altogether—either that, or time itself had come to a halt! Dex spazzed out to the max. All became quiet as the propulsion reactors of a passing Sirian space cruiser damped out his stereo (the DJ had turned down the volume), and all heard Dex announce that at midnight Big Wheel would say something very important to him. He relaxed, the music was cranked back up, the strobe light hurled out a nearby window and the Fan began to rotate again.

Midnight could hardly come soon enough. The partiers packed into the social lounge, sitting in rows facing the window. Dex Fresser stood before the shrouded window with his back to the crowd, and priests stood ready to tear the papers away. A few minutes before midnight, the DJ put on "Stairway to Heaven," timed so that the high-energy sonic blast section would begin at 12:00 sharp.

The newspapers ripped apart, the red-white-and-blue power beams of Big Wheel exploded into the room, and the heavy beat of the rock and roll made their thoraxes boom like empty kegs.

But Dex Fresser was impressively still. He stared into the naked face of the Big Wheel for fifteen minutes before he moved a muscle. Then he relayed the message to the huddled students.

Speaking through a mike hooked to his stereo, he sounded loud and quadraphonic. "Tonight the Big Wheel has plans for us, man. We're going to have a fucking war." The Terrorists cheered and whooped and the Airheads oohed and aahed. "The outside people, who are all hearing-impaired to the voice of Big Wheel and Roy G Biv and our other leaders, will come tomorrow to the Plex with guns to kill us. They want to put short-range tactical nuclear weapons on the roof of D Tower in order to threaten Big Wheel and make him do as they wish.

"We have friends, though, like Astarte, the Goddess, who is the sister of Big Wheel and who is going to like help us out and stuff. The Terrorists and the SUB will cooperate just like Big Wheel and Astarte do. Also, the B-men are our friends too.

"We've got shitloads of really powerful enemies, says Big Wheel. Like the Administration and the Temple of Unlimited Godhead and a bunch of nerds and some other people. We have to kill all of them.

"This is going to take cooperation and we have to have

perfect loyalty from everyone. See, even if you think you have friends among our enemies, you're wrong, because Big Wheel decides who our friends are, and if he says they're your enemies, they're your enemies, just like that. Everything's very simple with Big Wheel, that's how you can be sure he's telling the truth. So we've got to join together now and there can't be any secrets and we can't cover up for our enemies or have mercy for them."

Mari Meegan, sitting in the front row, legs tucked demurely to the side, listened intensely, eyes slitted and lips parted as she thought about how this applied to her.

At this point a few people came to their senses and made a run for it. One of these, a none-too-bright advisee of mine who had been going along for the good times, realized that these people were *nuts*, sprinted to the nearest fire stair, and escaped unharmed, later to tell me this story. What happened after his exit is vague; apparently, Yllas Freedperson, High Priestess of Astarte, showed up, and the leaders of the SUB and of the Terrorists did a lot of planning and organizing in those next few hours.

By contrast, Bert Nix celebrated the evening by incinerating himself in a storage room on C22W. He had been using it as a hideout for some time, and had gotten along well with the students, except for one problem: Bert Nix's obsession with collecting garbage. It was partly a practical habit, as he got most of his food and clothing from the trash. Far beyond that, however, he could not bring himself to throw out anything, and so in his little rooms scattered around the Plex the garbage was packed in to the ceiling, leaving only a little aisle to the door. Out of gratitude to his protectors, Bert Nix stuffed oily rags under the doors to seal the odor in.

This sufficed until the evening of March 31, when he happened to open the door while a fastidious student from Saskatoon was walking by. She watched as half a dozen cockroaches over three inches long lumbered out between the derelict's bare feet and approached her, waving their antennae affably. No Airhead, she stomped them to splinters and called Security on the nearest telephone. Between then and the time they arrived five hours later, however, the fire started. It could have been spontaneous combustion, it could have been the heating system, or a suicidal whim or wayward cigarette from Bert Nix. In any event, the room became a tightly sealed furnace, and when the flames had died, all that remained were a charred corpse in the aisle and drifts of cockroach bodies piled up in front of the door.

At the northern corner of the Plex's east wall, north of the Mall loading docks, the docks for student use, the mail, Cafeteria, general supply, Burrows and wide-load docks was the Refuse Area. Six loading docks opened on an enormous room with six giant trash compactors and six great steel chutes which expelled tons of garbage from their foul, stained sphincters every few minutes. When there wasn't a strike on, the compactors would grind away around the clock and a great truck would be at one dock or another at any given time, bringing back an empty container and hauling off a full one.

North of the Refuse Area, in the very corner of the Plex, was the Hazardous Waste Area with its steel doors and explosion-proof walls. When scientists produced any waste that was remotely hazardous, they would seal it into an orange container, mark down its contents and take it to the Refuse Area, where they could deposit it in a chute that led into the HWA. If the container was too large for this, they could simply leave it on a dolly by the door, and the specially trained B-men would then wheel it through when it was time for a pickup. When the Hazardous Waste truck arrived, three times a day, all the containers were then loaded into its armor-plated back and hauled away. This was usually done in the dead of night, to lessen the danger of traffic accidents. So extraordinary was this disposal system that American Megaversity had won awards from environmental groups and acclaim from scientists.

At 4:30 on the morning of April 1, when I should have been drinking or sleeping, I was sitting in my suite staring at the telephone. Virgil Gabrielsen, even more ambitious, was sitting by the door to the HWA in a huge orange crate about the shape of a telephone booth. "HANDLE WITH EXTREME CARE," its label read, "CONTAINS UNIVERSAL SOLVENT. DO NOT PUT ON SIDE OR EXPLOSION WILL RESULT." The same concepts were repeated by means of ideograms which we had hastily painted on the sides, showing a Crotobaltislavonian stick figure being blown to bits after putting the crate on its side. Instructions to telephone Dr. Redfield, and giving my telephone number, were added in several places.

"The nuke waste has to be coming in through the HWA," Virgil had insisted, as he and I and the disemboweled rat relaxed in Sharon's lab. "I counted my steps down there in the tunnels. As far as I can tell, that elevator shaft should go right up into the northeast corner of the building. The HWA is locked and alarmed within an inch of its life, but I know how to get inside."

At quarter to five, the enormous Magrov and half a dozen other Crotobaltislavonians entered the Refuse Area. As Virgil watched through strategically placed peepholes, they began with some unusual procedures. First they opened the southernmost of the six metal doors to the Access Lot. Shortly after, an old van backed up to this dock and threw open its rear doors. Two men jumped out into the Refuse Area in protective clothing, gas masks dangling on their chests, and exchanged hearty Scythian greetings with the B-men. Much equipment was now hauled out of the van, including a long metal cylinder—an exact replica of a nuclear waste container—and a huge tripod-mounted machine gun. Then came numerous small machine guns, what appeared to be electronic equipment and crates of supplies. These were piled on a cart and wheeled over to Virgil's position.

Virgil had realized by now that this was not a business-as-usual day. At least the situation appealed to his sense of humor.

The fake nuke waste cylinder opened like a casket and the two gas-masked men climbed in and lay one atop the other. The others handed them weapons and closed the lid. This cylinder was also placed next to Virgil. In the meantime, B-men bolted the big gun's tripod directly into the concrete floor at the loading dock, apparently having already drilled the holes in preparation. The weapon was aimed into the Access Lot, and loaded and checked over with an experienced air unusual among janitors.

Virgil's crate was the source of a long and emotional discussion in Scythian. Occasionally Magrov or one of the others would shout something about *telefon* while pounding on the crate with his index finger.

"Hoy!" shouted a B-man back at the machine gun. Virgil saw a glint of headlights outside. It was 4:59. A hellacious roar ensued as the determined janitors sprayed several thousand rounds per minute out the door. Magrov cut off debate by seizing Virgil's crate and wheeling it into the HWA.

The gunfire was over before Virgil was all the way through the door. Once the crate was stopped and he was able to get his bearings again, he could see that he was in a somewhat smaller room with a segmented metal door in the outside wall and a large red rectangle painted in the middle of the floor. A dozen or so bright orange waste containers had been slid through the chute and were waiting on a counter to be hauled away.

My phone rang at 5:01.

"Profyessor Rettfeelt? Sorry, getting you up early in mornink. Magrov here. You put humongous waste container by HWA, correct?"

"Yes, that's correct. Universal Solvent. Very dangerous."

"Ees too tall for goink inside of vaste truck. Ve must put on her side."

"No! That's dangerous. You will be blown to little bits."

"Then what to do with it?"

"I'll have to put it in a different container. You must leave it in the HWA overnight. I will come to the Refuse Area tomorrow night, at the time of the next pickup, and get the crate and take it away."

"Good." Magrov hung up.

Back in the HWA, Magrov checked his watch, then turned and shouted at a swiveling TV camera on the wall. "Ha! Those profyessors! Say! Where is truck? Very late today."

"Roger, team leader, we read four minutes late," said an Anglo voice over a loudspeaker. "Maybe some trouble with those strikers. Hey! Let's cut the idle chitchat."

Finally the great steel door rolled open. Through one of his peepholes, Virgil could see a hazardous waste truck backing into the brilliantly lit, fenced-in area outside. He could also see a pair of half-inch bullet holes through the outside rear-view mirror. The tiny black-and-white monitors, he knew, would never pick up this detail. When it had come to rest, the B-men unlocked the back with Magrov's keys and pulled open armored doors to reveal a stainless steel cylinder on a cart. This they rolled into the HWA, placing it in the middle of the red rectangle on the floor.

Other B-men set about hauling the small orange containers into the back of the truck and strapping them down. Magrov removed guns from a locked cabinet and distributed them to himself and two others. There three took up positions in the red area around the cylinder. "Hokay, ready for little ride," said Magrov.

"Roger, team leader. Stand by." A deep hum and vibration commenced. The men and the cylinder began to sink, and Virgil could see that the red rectangle was actually an elevator platform. Within seconds only a black hole remained.

In five minutes the platform returned, with the B-men but without the cylinder. Displaying frank contempt for safety regulations, the B-men began to smoke profusely.

The intercom crackled alive. "*Crotobaltislavonia aiwa!*" came the exhilarated shout.

"*Crotobaltislavonia aiwa!*" howled the B-men, leaping to their feet. There was much whoopee-making and cigarette-throwing, and then they opened the door to the Refuse Area and carried in crate after crate of supplies and put them on the elevator platform. The platform, laden with Crotobaltislavonians, guns and food, sank into the earth once again, then returned in a few minutes carrying nine bleeding bodies in yellow radiation suits.

Virgil had been expecting TV cameras. If they had them down in the tunnels, they must have them upstairs in the HWA. So after a few minutes, when Virgil was sure that the B-men were down there for the long haul, he opened a small panel in the side of his crate and stuck out a long iron rod with a magnesium tip. The important thing about the magnesium rod was that Virgil had just set it on fire, and when magnesium burns, it makes an intolerably brilliant light. Virgil soon squirmed out through the panel, a welding mask strapped over his face. Even through the dark glass, everything in the room was blindingly lit—certainly bright enough to overload, or even burn out, the television cameras. Any camera turned his way would show nothing but purest white. To make sure, he lit two more magnesium rods and placed them on the floor around the room. Satisfied that all three cameras were now blinded, he withdrew a can of spray paint from his crate and used it to paint over their lenses. The mikes were easy to find and he destroyed these simply by shoving burning magnesium rods into them. Then he called me on the phone. "I was right," he said, "I'm safe, and you can go to sleep. But look out. Trouble is brewing." Alas, I was already asleep before he got to that last part.

While the magnesium rods burned themselves out, Virgil climbed into the cab of the truck, where the corpses of its late drivers had been stretched out on the floor. The Crotos' plan was daring and their aim excellent; they needed to penetrate the truck's armored cab and kill the occupants without wiping out the engine or the gas tank. The driver's window was splattered all over the seat, the door itself deeply buckled and perforated by the thumb-sized shells. Virgil hit the ignition and drove it far enough out to wedge the electrical gates open while leaving enough space for other vehicles to pass.

Back in the Plex, he made phone calls to several ready-mix concrete companies. Returning to the Burrows, he found a cutting torch and wheeled it back to the HWA. The red platform was nothing more than thick steel plate, and once he had gotten the torch fired up and the red paint burned away, it cut like butter.

As he sliced a hole in the platform, he reviewed his reasoning:

1) Law is opinion of guy with biggest gun.

2) Biggest "gun" in U.S. held by police and armed forces.

3) Hypothesis: someone wants to break the law, or more generally, render U.S. law null and void in a certain zone.

4) This necessitates a bigger gun.

5) Threat of contamination of urban area with nuclear waste ought to fill the bill.

6) This provides a motive for taking over Nuke Dump.

7) Crotobaltislavonians have taken over Nuke Dump.

8) They either want to contaminate the city, or take over this area—the Plex—by threat of same.

9) Either we will all be poisoned, or else representatives of the People's Free Social Existence Node of Crotobaltislavonia will dictate their own law to people in this area.

10) This does not sound very nice either way.

11) Maybe we can destroy their gun by blocking the possible contamination routes. The elevator would be their preferred route, as it would provide direct access to the atmosphere.

A rough steel circle about two feet across pulled loose and dropped into the blackness. Virgil pulled back his mask and peered down. The circle's edge was still red hot, and as it fell through the blackness, he could see it spinning and diminishing until it smashed into the bottom. The clang reached his ears a moment later. Through the hole he could smell the odor of the sewers and hear occasional arguments among rats.

Hearing the whine of a down-shifting truck, he shut off the torch and ran out into the Access Lot. Virgil directed the cement truck through the jammed gate and up to the loading dock. He directed the driver to swing his chute around and dump the entire load into the freshly cut hole.

The driver was young, a philosophy Ph.D. only two years out of the Big U. He obviously knew Virgil was asking him to commit an illegal act. "Give me a rational reason to dump my cement down that hole," he demanded.

Virgil thought it over. "The reasons are very unusual, and if I were to explain them, you would only be justified in thinking I was crazy."

"Which doesn't give me my rational reason."

"True," admitted Virgil. "However, let's not forget the conventional view of craziness. Our media are filled with images of the crazy segment of society as being an exceptionally dangerous, unpredictable group. Look at Hinckley! Watch any episode of *T. J. Hooker!* So if you thought I was crazy, the reaction consistent with your social training would be to do as I say in order to preserve your own safety."

"That would be true with your run-of-the-mill truck driver," said the truck driver after agonized contemplation, "who tends to be an M.A. in sociology or something. But I can't make an excuse based on failure to think independently of the media."

"True. Follow me." Virgil walked across the HWA, leading the truck driver over to the heavy door that led into the Refuse Area. Here he paused, allowing the truck driver to notice the long red streaks on the floor. Virgil then opened the door and pointed at the nine bloody corpses, which he had dragged there to get them off the platform. "Having seen the remains of several savagely murdered people, you might conclude that my showing them to you so dramatically constituted a nonverbal threat. You might then decide—" but the truck driver had already decided, and was running for the controls at the back of the truck. The concrete was down the hole in no time. The truck driver did not even wait to be given an official American Megaversity voucher.

After that, trucks arrived every fifteen minutes or so for the rest of the morning. Subsequent truckers, seeing wet cement slopped all over the place, impressed by Virgil's official vouchers, were much less skeptical. By lunchtime, twenty truckloads of cement were piled up behind the sliding doors at the bottom of the elevator shaft.

The first Refuse Area dock was still open. After blowing the crap out of the hazardous waste truck, the B-men had hauled the real radioactive waste cylinder out and left it there in the doorway. Virgil had the last driver bury the cylinder in cement where it sat. He smoothed out a flat place with his hand and inscribed: DANGER. HIGH LEVEL RADIOACTIVE WASTE. TRESPASSERS WILL BE STERILIZED. His day's work was done.

Unbeknownst to anyone else, the two most important battles of the war had already been fought. The Crotobaltislavonians had won the first, and Virgil the second.

Once the actual war got started, things happened quickly. In fact, between the time that S. S. Krupp and two of his associates and I had got on an elevator and the time we escaped from it, the situation had changed completely.

S. S. Krupp felt compelled to visit E13S after its riot/party of the night before, somewhat in the spirit of Jimmy Carter visiting Mount Saint Helens. Naturally, as faculty-in-residence for E Tower, I was asked to serve as tour guide. It was preferable to washing dung off my boots, but only just.

Krupp arrived at the base of E Tower at 11:35 A.M., fresh from a tour of Bert Nix's cremation site. Considering the gruesome circumstances, not to mention the journalists and the SUBbie screaming directly into his ear, he looked relaxed. With him were Hyman Hotchkiss, Dean of Student Life, and Wilberforce (Tex) Bracewill, Administrator of Student Health Services. Hyman looked young, pale and ill. Tex had seen too much gonorrhea in too many strange places to be shocked by anything. They were so civilized that they viewed my Number 27 BILL'S BREWS softball jersey as though it were a jacket and vest, and shook my hand as though I had saved their families from death sometime in the distant past.

Here in the lobby the sixteen elevators and four fire stairs of E Tower emptied together into a desert of vandalized furniture, charred bulletin boards and overflowing wastebaskets. I didn't know about events on E13S yet, and my guests were doubtless still considering the charred remains of Bert Nix, so we were not suspicious when elevators 2, 4 and 1 remained frozen at the thirteenth floor for ten minutes. Only number 3 moved. When it got to us, it was packed with students. Two got off, but the rest explained in dull voices that they had missed their floor and were staying on for the return trip. Therefore the journalists and protesters found no room in the compartment; only the four of us could squeeze in.

This chummy group rode to the Terrorist-controlled ninth floor, where everyone else got off. As the doors slid shut, a burnout who had just disembarked turned around to say, "Sweet dreams, S. S. Krupp."

We started up again. "Shit!" said Krupp. "We've got a problem. Everyone get on the floor. Tex, you got your .44?"

Of course he did. Much to the concern of the SUB, Tex was massively armed at all times, on the theory that you never knew when degens might come and shoot up the clinic looking for purer highs. He was prepared to go out like a true AM administrator. Dropping stiffly to the floor, he paused on his knees to whip a humongous revolver out of his briefcase and hand it to Krupp.

"Hope we don't have to shoot it out on thirteen," he said. We agreed. Krupp tore from Tex's briefcase a medicine bottle, struggled with the childproof cap, yanked out the cotton wad, tore it in half and stuffed it into his ears. At this point I began to experience terror, more of Krupp than of whatever he was planning to dismember with that howitzer.

We passed the twelfth floor and the elevator crashed to a stop. Above us, from the elevators still halted on thirteen, we heard excited yelling.

"I get it." Krupp cocked the revolver and we all plugged our ears as he pointed it at the ceiling.

The bullet vaporized the latch on the trap door and flipped the door open as well. We saw light above us. Krupp's second shot annihilated the light in our car. I felt as though my fingers had been driven three inches deep into my ears; my eyelids fluttered in shock and my nose complained of dense smoke. Krupp now stood up in the darkness and fired the remaining three rounds through the trapdoor. With a sigh and a thump, a corpse crashed into our roof.

At a great distance I heard Tex say, "Sep. Here's a speed loader." After some clicking and cursing, Krupp fired two more rounds—the natives were getting restless—and tugged at my shirt. "Leg up!" he shouted.

I stood and made a step of my hands, and he used it to propel himself through the trap door. Once he had scrambled through, I jumped and dragged myself to the roof after him. The only thing I was scared of was touching the corpse; other than that, one place was as dangerous as another. Krupp, who did not share my fear, retrieved a revolver from the body and handed it to me.

He began scaling the emergency ladder on the shaft wall. When he got to thirteen, he pounded the wall switch and the doors slid open. Seeing him jump through the aperture onto thirteen, I began to follow him up the ladder, not really thinking about what I'd do when I arrived. The two adjacent elevators began to head down, and as they passed, someone on a roof fired off a wild shot in my direction.

A tremendous roar rang up and down the shaft. It came in three bursts, and not until the third one did I realize it was machine-gun fire. I had been dimly aware of it—"Oh, that's a machine gun being fired"—but it was not for a few moments that I comprehended that machine guns were in use at my institution of higher learning. There were also three WHAMs, and then silence.

Taking this as a good sign, I dove through onto thirteen and lay there dazed, looking at an elevator lobby dotted with strings of machine-gun fire and blood pools, tracked and smeared by hasty tennis-shoe footprints that converged on the two elevators.

I sat up timidly. Krupp went to the far side of a large pillar and retrieved an assault rifle from a dead soldier. "See," he said, pounding hollowly on the pillar with the butt of the rifle, "these pillars are just for show. Just a little girder in the middle and the rest is plaster and chicken wire. Don't want to hide behind them." Judging from the bullet holes in the pillar and the unmoving legs and feet on the other side, someone had recently been in dire need of Krupp's architectural knowledge. "Can't believe they're handing out loaded Kalashnikovs to cretins like that, whoever it is that's running this show," he grumbled. "These youths need ROTC training if they're going to pack ordnance like this."

"Maybe this is someone's ROTC program," I suggested, trying to lighten the atmosphere. Krupp frowned. *"Maybe this is someone's ROTC,"* I shouted, remembering the cotton. He nodded in deep thought. "Very good. What's your field again?"

"Remote sensing. *Remote sensing. Involves geography, geology and electrical engineering."*

"I'm listening," Krupp assured me in the middle of my sentence, as he walked to the two corners of the lobby to peer down the hallways. "But you'll have to speak up," he added, squeezing off a half-second blast at something. There was an answering blast, muffled by the fire doors between the combatants, but it apparently went into the ceiling. Impressed, Krupp nodded.

"Well, we've got two basic tactical options here," he continued, ejecting the old clip and inserting a fresh one taken from the dead SUBbie. "We can seize the wing, or retreat. Based on what we've seen of these sandbox insurrectionists, I don't doubt we can stage a takeover. The question is: is this wing a worthwhile strategic goal in and of itself, or is my strong inclination to seize it singlehandedly—almost, excuse me—just what we call a macho complex these days? Not that I'm trying to draw us into psychobabble." He glared at me, one eyebrow raised contemplatively.

"Depends on *what kind of forces they have elsewhere."*

"Well, you're saying it's easier to make tactical decisions when one has more perfect information, a sort of strategic context from which to plan. That's a predictable attitude for a remote-sensing man. The areal point of view comes naturally to a generalistic, left-handed type like you." He nodded at my revolver, which I was holding, naturally, in my left hand. "But lacking that background, we'll have to use a different method of attack—using 'attack' in a figurative sense now—and use the more linear way of thinking that would suggest itself to, say, a right-handed low-level Catholic civil engineer. Follow?"

"I suppose," I shouted, looking down the elevator shaft at Tex's face, barely visible in the dim light.

"For example," continued Krupp, "our friends below, though we must be concerned for them, are irrelevant now. Presumably, the students on this wing will do the rational thing and not attack us, because to attack means coming into the halls and exposing themselves to our fire. So we control entry and exit. If we leave now, we'll just have to retake it later. Secondly, this lobby fire stair here ensures our safety; we can always escape. Third, our recent demonstration should delay a reinforcement action on their part. What I figure is that if we move along room by room disarming the occupants, they'll be too scared by what happened to that guy in the hall to try any funny stuff. Christ on fishhooks!" Krupp dove back into the safety of the lobby as a barrage of fire ripped down the hall, blowing with it the remains of the fire doors. We made for the stairway and began skittering down the steps as quickly as we could. By the time we had descended three flights, the angry shouts of Terrorists and SUBbies were pursuing us. The shouters themselves prudently remained on their own landing.

"We're okay unless they have something like a hand grenade or satchel charge they can drop down this central well," said Krupp. "Hold it right there, son! That's right! Keep those paws in the air! Say, I know you."

We had surprised Casimir Radon on a landing. He merely stared at S. S. Krupp's AK-47, dumbfounded.

"Let's all hold onto our pants for a second and ask Casimir what he's up to," Krupp suggested.

"Well," said Casimir, taking off his glacier glasses to see

us better in the dim stairwell. "I was going to visit Sarah. Things are getting pretty wild now, you know. I guess you do know," he concluded, looking again at the assault rifle.

"Physics problem:" said Krupp, "how far does a hand grenade fall in the seven seconds between handle release and boom?"

"Well, air resistance makes that a toughie. It's pretty asymmetrical, and it would probably tumble, which makes the differential equation a son-of-a-bitch to solve. You'd have to use a numerical method, like . . ."

"Estimate, son! Estimate!"

"Eight hundred feet."

"No problem. But what if they counted to three? How far in four seconds?"

"Sixteen times four . . . two hundred fifty-six feet."

"If they count to five?"

"Two seconds . . . sixty-four feet."

"That's terrible. That's six stories. That would be about the sixth floor, which is where we make the run into the lobby. Do you think they'd be dumb enough to pull the pin and count to *five?*"

"Not with a Soviet grenade."

"Good point."

"If I'm not mistaken, sir," said Casimir, "they all have impact fuses on them anyway. So it'd go off on six in any case."

"Oh. Well . . . what the hell?" said Krupp, and started to run down the stairs again.

"Wait!" I said. Krupp stopped on the next landing. "You don't want to go up there," I told Casimir.

"Yeah. If you think it's wild down there, you should see thirteen. It's wilder than a cat on fire, thirteen. Those people are *irrational,*" said Krupp.

"Are you going to stop me by force?" asked Casimir.

"Well, anyone traveling with S. S. Krupp today is a prime target, so I couldn't justify that," said Krupp.

"Then I'm going," said Casimir, and resumed his climb.

"Let's get a move on. Let's build up a good head of steam

here so we can charge right through the danger zone at the bottom. I think the twenty-third psalm is in order."

Reluctantly, I left Casimir to his own dreams and we began to charge down the steps side by side, crossing paths at each turn, listening upward. I saw a 7 painted on the wall. We were practically diving down the last flight when I heard someone yell *"Five!"* We were on the level now, sprinting for a door with a small rectangular window and a sign reading E TOWER MAIN LOBBY.

"Did he say *five*, or *fire*?" Krupp wondered as we neared the door. We punched it open together and were in the lobby. And there, waiting for us, were three Crotobaltislavonians with UZIs. "Professionals, I see," said Krupp. He had gone through on the hinged side of the door and now pushed it all the way around so that it was flat against the lobby wall, where he leaned against it. Back in the stairwell there was a series of metallic clanks, like something heavy bouncing off an iron pipe. Having seen many TV shows involving foreigners with submachine guns, I had already raised my hands; I now took the opportunity to clap them over my ears.

Krump. Bits of fire shot out the door at incredible speed. The three janitors just seemed to melt and soften, sagging to the floor quietly.

"It worked," said Krupp, sounding drunken and amazed. Trying to walk around, I found that the concussion had scrambled my inner ear; stars shot around like tracer bullets. I went to a wall phone, dialed Lucy and Hyacinth's number, and listened to it ring.

At each ring my head cleared a bit. They were not answering. Had the Terrorists taken twelve? I redialed; no answer. After eight rings I lost my mind, gripped the handset that had withstood untold vandalism attempts and jerked it out by its roots. I grabbed its shattered wires and swung it into the wall like a mace, ludicrously enraged, and began to stumble back toward the stairway.

"Hate to bust in, but we've got to stop porch-setting here," shouted Krupp from the lobby entryway. He lay on the floor with the AK-47 pointed down the hall.

"What about these B-men?"

"They'll keep."

"I'm not leaving. My friends are up on twelve. Hey, look. These men are in pain, okay? I'm going to tell their friends upstairs they've got wounded down here."

"*Could* do that," said Krupp, "but Casimir's in the stairwell, If they come down this way, he'll be like a hoppity toad in a snake stampede."

For the first time, we heard shouting and shooting from the main hallway which led to the Cafeteria. "Don't look forward to fighting my way through whatever that sounds like," said Krupp.

"Shit. Shit in a brown bag. Great fucking ghost of Rommel," I said. "That thing is a tank."

Indeed, a small tank was approaching our location. We retreated.

For Fred Fine too it was a hell of a day. He was physically burned out to begin with. The Grand Army of Shekondar the Fearsome had stood at yellow alert for two days, and he had worked like an android the whole time, directing the stockpiling of supplies and material in the most secure regions of Plexor. Klystron may have been a haughty swordsman who reveled in single combat, but Chris the Systems Programmer was a master strategist who understood that, in a long war, food was power. The recent Mixture of Klystron and Chris was regrettable, but it did enable him to plan for the coming weeks with magical intuition and technological knowledge, a combination that proved extremely potent.

Finally Consuela and Chip Dixon had insisted that he sleep, and Klystron/Chris had okayed the rec. He slept from the close of our expedition until 1200 hours on April First, then rolled smartly out of the sack, called an aide for a quick briefing and proceeded to the mess hall for some grub and a few cups of joe. It was there, in the Cafeteria, just as he had predicted, that the war began.

Many things contributed to its success. The MegaUnion

finally found the secret elevator used to smuggle scab workers into the Caf, resulting in fights between the Haitian and Vietnamese cooks and the professors and clerical workers who stood in their way. The outcome was predictable, and when the battered progressives returned to the main picket outside the Caf entrance, Yllas Freedperson exhorted them to hang tough, to further peace and freedom in the Plex by finding the violent people who had hurt them and bashing their brains out.

Mobs of hungry students broke through the picket lines empty-handed, obviously bent on eating scab food. The unionists were still so pissed off from the earlier fight that more scuffling and debris-throwing ensued. Twenty TUGgies carrying anti-communist signs took advantage of the confusion to set up a barrier around the SUB information table and erect their OM generator, a black box with big speakers used to augment their own personal OMs, which they now OMed through megaphones. A picket-sign duel broke out; it became clear that the SUB had reinforced their picket signs to make them into dangerous weapons. At a sign from their leader, Messiah #645, the TUGgies produced sawed-off pool cues and displayed highly developed kendo abilities.

All the Terrorists then seemed to arrive together. Twenty Droogs, thirty-two Blue Light Specials, nineteen Roy G Bivs, eight Ninja with Big Wheels on their foreheads, four of the Flame Squad Brotherhood and forty-three of the Plex Branch of the Provisional Wing of the Irish Republican Army (Unofficial) marched in with their politically correct bag lunches and, shouting and waving sticks in the air, demanded that a large area be cleared of scab sympathizers and other scum so they could sit down. This section contained a table of twenty-five athletic team standouts, heavily drunk, as well as a number of people on ghetto scholarships who really knew how to handle unpleasant situations. Much hand-to-hand violence took place and the Terrorists were humiliated. There were more of them, though. A huge arena ring formed around the brawl and tables were herded to the walls to make room. The SUB showed up, decided that the brawl was ideologically impure, and began chanting and throwing food. This triggered the Cafeteria's mass food fight emergency plan; but as the enforcers began to emerge from the serving bays, they were met by MegaUnion partisans who wanted to get them out in the open. Short on brawling power because of the inexplicable absence of the Crotobaltislavonians, the MegaUnion was bested here.

The Haitians and Vietnamese, who had built up fierce hatred for the Terrorists, took this opportunity to rush into the central brawl. The SUB tried to block them, without success. The TUGgies charged after the SUB to make sure they didn't do anything illegal. The fight was frenzied now; a flying wedge of cooks speared back toward the kitchen to obtain big knives.

Upstairs in the towers, SUB/Terrorist extremists who were apparently waiting for something like this began to bombard the roof of the vast kitchen complex with heavy projectiles. On cue, the administration's anti-terrorism guards, stationed on Tar City and in some wings and on top of towers, responded by blasting tear gas grenades into the SUB/Terrorist strongholds. Already there were gaping holes in the roof; above the tumult, everyone in the Caf now heard the booms of the grenade launchers—every gun in the place was drawn for the first time.

Shooting began, at first to scare and then to injure. People scrambled to the walls, throwing furniture through the wide plate-glass wall sections to escape. But some were unable to get out, and others were happy to stay and fight. After a minute of incomprehensible noise and violence, battle lines formed and things became organized.

Obviously SUB and TUG were prepared. Both groups hoped to capture the kitchen by entering through the serving bays and vaulting the steam tables. Local fights hence developed along the approaches to all twelve serving bays. Squads from both groups made for the main serving bay, ducking sporadic fire. The SUB got there first, shot the lock out and kicked the door; but there was a senior TUGgie barricaded behind a steam table, with a heavy machine gun aimed at them and a smiling protégé holding the ammo belt. The gunner watched cheerfully as the SUBbies jumped back and rolled away from the door, but held his fire until the TUGgies behind them had jumped through the breach and scurried out of the line of fire. He immediately opened fire on a strategic SUB salad bar across the Cafeteria. This entailed shooting through several tables, but he had plenty of ammo, and as soon as the furniture was conveniently dissolved, a river of red tracer fire could swing around and demolish whatever it touched, such as a milk machine, a number of people, and, of course, the flimsy salad bar. The SUBbies retreated and joined their Terrorist allies in safer places.

Klystron/Chris knew as well as anyone that the kitchens were the strategic linchpin of the Plex. He was the first person in the Cafeteria to decide that war was breaking out, and so during the early stages of the great fistfight he mobilized and girded his loins for the Apocalypse. Retreating to a corner, he dumped the now-useless textbooks out of his briefcase and withdrew the bayonet, which he stuck in his belt, and the flash gun, which he carried. As the booms and thuds from the ceiling indicated that aerial bombardment had begun, he flexed his fingers, then shoved his right hand into his left armpit and snapped out a standard-issue .45 automatic pistol—just to test the shoulder holster one last time. After cocking the weapon he gingerly slid it back under his houndstooth polyester blazer and turned toward the nearest serving bay.

A burst from the flash gun got him through the door and over the steam tables into the kitchen area. Here was chaos: scab workers running to and fro, some with knives; Cafeteria administrators telling him to get the hell out of here, an opinion his flash gun then modified; particularly bold SUBbies and TUGgies making their first inroads; a man in a flannel shirt carrying a .50-caliber machine gun—that could be a problem—all of this in an almost primeval landscape littered with sections of roof, piano fragments, scattered food and utensils, broken pipes spewing steam and water, sparks and flames breaking out here and there.

The elevator he sought was at the dead-end of a hallway, hidden in the nethermost parts of the kitchens, back by the strategic food warehouses. Arriving safely, Klystron/Chris protected his rear by slitting open and overturning several hundred-pound barrels of freeze-dried potatoes and dehydrated eggs near the doorway, where hot water spewed from a broken ceiling pipe. Without waiting to watch the results he jogged down and boarded the elevator, held for him by a captain of the Grand Army of Shekondar the Fearsome.

Below, in the Burrows, he emerged to find all in readiness: several officers awaiting orders; his body armor and weapons; and in a nearby storage closet, the APPASMU, or All-Purpose Plex Armed Strife Mobile Unit.

The APPASMU was a project begun three years ago by several MARS members. Starting out as a joke—a tank for use in the Plex, ha ha—it became a hobby, a thing to tinker with, and finally, this semester, an integral part of the GASF defense posture. The tank was built on the chassis of an electric golf cart, geared down so that its motor could haul additional weight. The tires had been filled with dense foam to make them bulletproof, and a sturdy frame of welded steel tubing built around the cart to support the rest of the innovations. Hardened steel plates were welded to the frame to make a sloping, pyramidal body in which as many as four people could sit or lie. Gun slits, shielded peepholes and thick glass prisms enabled the occupants to see and shoot anything in their vicinity, while a full complement of lights, radios, sirens, loudspeakers and so forth gave the APPASMU eyes and ears and vocal cords. The APPASMU had been designed to fit into any elevator in the Plex. It could recharge its batteries at any wall outlet, and replacement battery packs had already been stashed at several secret locations around the building.

From status reports provided by underlings as he pulled on his gear, Klystron/Chris learned that S. S. Krupp was trapped in a hostile area of E Tower. Such a mission was perfect to battle-test the APPASMU and toughen up its crew, and so after barking some orders to his major officers he squeezed into the tank along with three others and steered it backward into the elevator.

The situation upstairs had begun to take on some texture. The dead-end outside the elevator was blocked by a mountain of light-yellow potato-egg mixture. The APPASMU plowed through with ease, and Klystron/Chris could now hear the rumble of the heavy TUG machine gun. The APPASMU could not withstand such firepower, so Klystron/Chris decided to outflank it by exiting the kitchens through a back route. He aimed the APPASMU down an aisle lined with great pressure vats and headed for the door.

Unfortunately a stray weapons burst had struck a pressure vat by the exit. The top of the vat exploded off, blasting a neat hole through the ceiling, and the vat, torn loose by the recoil, tumbled over and spilled thousands of gallons of Cheezy Surprise Tetrazzini onto the floor. This mixture had long, long overcooked in the fighting, causing the noodles to congeal into a glutinous orange mass with an internal temperature over three hundred degrees Fahrenheit, which had rolled out on impact and squatted sullenly in the doorway, swathed in its nebula of live orange steam. Klystron/Chris fired a few desultory rounds into it and concluded that this doorway was now impassable. They would have to choose a serving bay, pass through the Caf and hope to avoid the TUG machine gun—exactly what the APPASMU was built for, though to fire it now would be to use up their first and only surprise.

"We'll have to make the most of it, men. We'll head for the lines of the SUB/Terrorist Axis and pick up all the weaponry we can find. If you see anything that looks like it's armor-piercing, sing out!" Without further chitchat, and accompanied by a soft plopping of potato-egg, the minitank was out of the kitchen and into a serving bay which was being disputed in hand-to-hand combat. The astonished fighters could only stand in confusion, and only two rounds glanced off the APPASMU's armor before they entered the Caf.

The tank's entrance occasioned a surprised lull in the fighting. Klystron/Chris and Chip Dixon used the flat-trajectory indoor mortars to lob a few stun grenades behind the line of overturned tables and main salad bar that served as the SUB bunker. At this, the Axis forces turned and ran through the shattered plate-glass walls behind them and scurried for F Tower. The poorly armed wretches who had been pinned down by their presence emerged and sprinted for the exits.

They got a fine haul from the stunned and demoralized soldiers in the Axis bunker: a Kalashnikov, a twelve-gauge slug gun, ammo, knives, clubs and gas masks, all plastered with smoldering lettuce and sprouts but functional. After collecting the booty and using his intercom to dispatch a negotiator to cut a deal with the TUGgies—who were clearly winning in this theater—Klystron/Chris sent the APPASMU crashing magnificently through a plate-glass panel that had miraculously remained unbroken, and pointed it toward E Tower and the endangered Septimius Severus Krupp.

There we met them, below E Tower. From a distance we could make out the insignia: a stylized plan of the Plex (eight Swiss crosses within a square) with a sword and phaser rifle crossed underneath and the word MARS above. "I guess that would be Fred Fine," I said.

The top hatch flipped open and a helmeted, goggled head arose, speaking through the PA system. "This is the Grand Army of Shekondar the Fearsome Expeditionary Plex Purification Warfare Corps. Resistance is useless." The tank pulled up next to us, and Fred Fine pulled back the mask to reveal (alas) his face. He spoke with his usual grating humility.

"Mr. President. Professor Redfield. Sorry if we upset you. This is a little something we've been developing as a career suitability demonstration project during the recent years of decaying civilization. In fact, once we're on secure ground, I'd like to discuss the possibility of receiving some academic credit for it, Mr. President. The basic design principles are the same as for any armored vehicle."

"I see that," said Krupp, nodding. "Heimlich would go nuts over this. But what you need, I think, are more liberal arts courses."

Dr. Redfield will find the infrared personnel sensing equipment very interesting. But sirs, we have heavy fighting in the Cafeteria. My men have secured the other end of this hallway while I came to get you."

Chip Dixon had clambered out to reconnoiter and inspect the APPASMU. Seeing the three mangled B-men, he scurried over to them and slid his hand under one's ear to check his pulse. A queer look came on his face and he stared directly up at Fred Fine.

"Jim, he's dead," he whispered.

"*Sir* to you," said Fred Fine, nonplussed, "and my name is not Jim, it's . . . something else. Anyway, sirs, my men are now securing D Tower, with direct elevator connections to the Burrows. We've arranged with your anti-terrorist forces to courier you to C Tower, which they are securing. Chip will steer the APPASMU, you'll sit in my place and I'll serve as point man. Dr. Redfield is welcome to follow. But first we must retrieve those weapons!" He clomped over to the remains of the Crotobaltislavonians.

Sarah slept until about noon, when a corpse burst through her window. Her eyes were half open, so that it exploded out of a dream: a leathery female cadaver from the Med College, wearing the wig Sarah had left behind in Tiny's room, white clown makeup smeared on the face. This effigy had been placed in a hangman's noose and thrown out the window above hers; it swung down and crashed through her window, then swung out and in and out as Sarah struggled between sleep and awakeness, disbelief and terror. At last she chose awakeness and terror, and stared at the corpse, which grinned.

She tried to scream and gag at the same time, but did neither. Outside she heard the excited whispers of the lurking Terrorists.

She took three slow breaths and pulled her .38 from under her pillow. As she was sliding her feet into her running shoes, she found a big shard of window glass on one of them and nearly panicked. She picked up her phone and punched out Hyacinth's number (after the rape attempt she had bought a pushbutton phone so she could dial silently). Hyacinth answered alertly. Sarah pushed the 1 button three times and hung up, stood, slipped on the pack containing her emergency things and padded to the door. Sleeping in her long johns was neither cool nor glamorous, but proved useful nonetheless.

There was a long wait. The Terrorists were quietly getting impatient, wondering whether she was in there, talking about shooting the door open—they knew a police lock would be difficult to blow off. Sarah stood shivering, feet on marked places on the floor, gun in right hand, doorlock in left. If only there had been a way to practice this!

Hyacinth's gun sounded. Horribly slow, she snapped the lock, moved her hand to the doorknob, grasped it, turned it, swung the door open and examined the five men standing there. They were looking sideways toward Hyacinth. As they began to turn their faces toward her, she finally picked out the one with the gun—thanking God there was only one gun. For just a second now they were trapped and helpless, caught in a double take, trying to process the new information. For the first time Sarah understood how generals and terrorists made their plans of attack.

The one with the shotgun had turned it toward Hyacinth and now seemed indecisive. The other men were stepping back and dropping to the floor. Sarah's finger twitched and she fired a round into the ceiling.

The rest happened in an instant. She pointed her gun at the head of the armed man. One of the other four suddenly whipped a handgun from his belt. Sarah wheeled and shot him in the stomach. The one with the shotgun tried to swing around but scraped the end of his barrel on the wall; Sarah and Hyacinth fired two shots apiece; three missed, and one of Sarah's hit the man in the arm and dropped him. The other three had simply disappeared; looking down the hall, Sarah saw them piling into the fire stairway.

There was less blood than she had expected. Before she

could examine the two wounded, Hyacinth floated past and Sarah followed. They ran to the elevator lobby, where Lucy was waiting with an elevator and another gun. That was what had taken so long—an elevator! But many Terrorists were pouring into the lobby as the doors began to creep shut. A Terrorist glided toward the wall buttons, hoping to punch the doors open; Sarah made eye contact with him; he kept going; she fired a shot whose effects she never saw. The doors were closed, joining in front of them to form a Big Wheel mural. The car was motionless for a sickeningly long time, and then shifted and began to sink.

Casimir Radon only came in at the end of it. He had gotten up earlier than any of us that morning. Opening his curtains to let in the gray light, he had seen the blind patches grow, and had put on his glacier glasses before allowing any more light past his eyelids. He lay in bed until the blind spots had shifted over to the right side of his vision, then read some physics and tinkered with the railgun's electronics. Finally he went to lunch; but seeing the outbreak of violence there, he headed back up the stairs to look for Sarah, meeting me and Krupp. After we parted, he continued resolutely, placing his feet as gently as possible on each tread and pressing carefully until he moved up to the next step. As a result he moved with a smoothness that was not even noticed by the little embryonic headache in his brain.

A few seconds after leaving us behind, something flashed by him down the center of the stairwell, and a second later—accompanied by a brief stabbing light—came a sharp awesome KABOOM that KABOOMed many times over as it bounded up and down the height of the stairwell. To Casimir it was like being bayoneted through the head, and when he dared to move again, the headache struck so badly that he could only laugh at it. He proceeded toward the Castle in the Air with a helpless moaning laugh, heels of hands buried in temples, and heard other, less tremendous explosions.

The door to E12S was open and three Terrorists were

running through in a panic, headed for thirteen. Something white flashed by the door, heading for the lobby. Casimir ran into the hall and was promptly knocked aside by a migration of Terrorists, who emerged from several nearby rooms. Falling, he glimpsed Sarah and Hyacinth, clad in white long johns, running with guns and backpacks down the hall. He managed to trip a few of the Terrorists, more by flailing away randomly than by craftiness, and stood up and began to head for the elevators too. As he approached the lobby, there was another painful WHAM and he felt a sharp pain in his chest. He had no idea what had happened. In fact, Sarah's last bullet, after ricocheting off several walls and passing through a fire door, had in mangled form dispersed its last bit of energy by bouncing sharply off Casimir's T-shirt.

Something hard was against the back of his head—the floor? The Terrorists were standing above him. He stood up. Two wounded men were being carried toward him, leaving uneven trails of blood on the shiny tile floor. He followed these trails to their sources, and stepped through Sarah's open door.

A clown-cadaver was smiling at him through the window and he knew he was hallucinating. Nothing he did could dissolve the ghastly sight. Noticing a Terrorist looking at him from the doorway, he walked over, slammed the door in his face and locked it. Then he wandered around the room, picking up and examining random objects—numerous mementos of Sarah's friends and family, books he would never read, a little framed collection of snapshots. A family portrait, graduation photos of several smiling good-looking earnest types —which was her boyfriend?—and various shots of Sarah and friends being happy in different places, including some of Hyacinth. Tucked in one corner of the frame was a folded piece of paper. Casimir felt filthy reading it; it was obviously a love note. He had never gotten one himself, but he figured this was one of them. Getting to the bottom, he read the name of the mysterious man Sarah so obviously preferred to Casimir: Hyacinth.

He sat on her bed, elbows on knees, scarcely hearing the

shouting outside. He smiled a little, knowing Sarah and Hyacinth had made it out safely.

He knew why he'd come up here. Not to *assist* Sarah, or go *with* her, but to *save* her. To create a debt of gratitude that could neither be erased nor forgotten. She would have to love him then, right? This impossible secret hope of his had made his thoughts so twisted and complicated that he no longer knew why he was doing anything; he was never one to analyze his pipe dreams. But now she was safe. His goal was accomplished. And if she had done it herself, and not seen him, then that was his fault. She was safe, and now he had to be happy whether he wanted to or not.

Most importantly, he had seen the proof he had needed for so long, the undeniable proof that she would never be in love with him. All his wild fantasies were impossible now. He could purge himself of his useless infatuation. He could relax. It was wonderful.

The Terrorists shot out the lock, came in and grabbed his arms. In the hall he was thrown on his back and straddled by a Terrorist while others sat on his arms and legs. Then they all stared at him dully, lost and indecisive.

"Let's knock his teeth out," said a voice from behind Casimir. A hammer was given to the man on his chest. Someone held Casimir by the hair. Casimir's vision was sharp and bright without the glacier glasses; the hammerhead was cold and luminous in the white light, finely scratched on its polished striking face, red paint worn way from use. The Terrorist was examining Casimir's face as though he could not find the mouth, neither excited nor scared, just curiously resigned to what he was doing and, it seemed, at peace with himself.

This is what I get, being heroic for the wrong reason, thought Casimir. He could not take his eyes off the hammer. He began to struggle. His captors clamped down harder. The torturer made a swing; but Casimir jerked his head to one side and the blow slid down his cheek and crushed a fold of neck skin against the floor.

Then he felt a light tingly feeling and sat up. The hammerer slid backward onto the floor. Casimir's hands were free and he punched the man in the nuts, then pulled his legs free and stood up. Everything he touched now snapped away and started bleeding. Someone was coming with a shotgun, so Casimir re-entered Sarah's room and bolted the door with her police lock.

He smashed the photo frame on her desk, removed a snapshot of Sarah and Hyacinth, wrapped it in Kleenex and put it in his pocket. The only potential weapon was a fencing saber, so he took that. He knocked over a set of brick-and-board shelves, and using one brick as a hammer and another as an anvil, snapped off the final inch of the blade to leave a clean, sharply fractured edge.

When he opened the door again, all he had to do was push the barrel of the shotgun out of the way and push his saber through one of the owner's lungs. The gun came free in his hand and he hurled it backward out the window, where it bounced off the cadaver and fell to Tar City. In the ensuing melee Casimir slashed and whipped several Terrorists with the blade, or punched them with the guard, and then they were all gone and he was walking down the stairs.

His destination was a room in a back hallway far beneath A Tower: University Locksmithing. This was the most heavily fortified room in the Plex, as a single breach in its security meant replacing thousands of locks. It had just one outside window, gridded over by heavy steel tubes, and the door was solid steel, locked by the toughest lock technology could devise. As Casimir approached it, he found the nearby corridors empty. The security system was still on the ball, he supposed. But the events of the day had unleashed in Casimir's mind a kind of maniacal, animal cunning, accumulated through years of craftily avoiding migraines and parties.

The corridors in this section were relatively narrow. He put his feet against one wall and his hands against the other, pushed hard enough to hold himself in the air, slowly "walked" up the walls until his back was against the pipes on the ceiling, then "walked" around the corner and down the hall toward that steel door. Usually the only beings found on the ceilings of the Plex were bats, and so the little TV camera mounted above the door was aimed down toward the floor. Eventually Casimir was able to rest his hands directly on the camera's mounting bracket and wedge his feet into a crack between a ceiling pipe and the ceiling across the hall. Not very comfortable, he used one hand to undo his belt buckle. In five minutes, during which he frequently had to rest both arms, he was able to get the belt over another pipe and rebuckle it around his waist, giving himself an uncomfortable but stable harness.

Within half an hour, the TV camera, inches from his face, began to swivel back and forth warily. Casimir loosened his belt buckle. The lock clicked open and an old man emerged, holding a pistol. Casimir simply dropped, pulled the gun free, flung it back into the room, then dragged the locksmith inside. While the man was regaining his breath, Casimir went through his pockets and came up with a heavily laden keychain.

After a while the locksmith sat up. "Whose side are you on?" he said.

"No side. I'm on a quest."

The locksmith, apparently familiar with quests, nodded. "What do you want with me?" he asked.

"The master keys, and a place for the night. It looks as though I've got both." Casimir tossed the keys in his hand. "Where were you taking these keys?"

The locksmith rose to his feet, looking suddenly fierce and righteous. "I was getting them out of the Plex, young fella! Listen. I didn't spend thirty-five years here so's I could sell the masters to the highest bidder soon as things got hairy. I was taking those out of the Plex for safekeeping and damn you for insulting me. Give 'em back."

"I have no right to take them, then," said Casimir, and dropped the keys into the locksmith's hands. The man stepped back, first in fear, then in wonder.

There was a high *crack* and the locksmith fell. Casimir ran for the door, where a loner with a bolt-action .22 was frantically trying to get a second round into the chamber. Casimir nailed him with the saber, kicked him dead into the hallway, grabbed the .22 and locked the door.

The locksmith was struggling to his feet, pulling something bright from his sock. The big keychain was still on the floor where he'd dropped it. He now held seven loose keys in his hands, and with a distant, dying look he gazed through the crossbars of the window at the million lights of the city. Casimir ran and stood before him, but seeing his shadow cross the man's face, fell to his knees.

"Thirty-five years I looked for someone worthy to take my place," whispered the Locksmith. "Thought I never would, thought it was all turning to shit. And here in the last five minutes . . . here, lad, I pass my charge on to you." He parted his hands, allowing the keys to fall into Casimir's. Then he dropped his hands to his sides and died. Casimir gently laid him out on a workbench and crossed his arms over his heart.

After pinching the barrel of the .22 shut in a vise, Casimir curled up on a neighboring workbench and slept.

Though Casimir considered Sarah and Hyacinth safe, they were only *relatively* safe when they and Lucy left E12S. Their destination was the Women's Center, and their route was a young and disorganized war.

They went first to my suite—I had given Lucy a key. They remained for a couple of hours, borrowing clothes, eating, calming down and building up their courage.

Fully clothed, equipped and reloaded, they broke out my picture window in midafternoon and lowered themselves a few feet onto Tar City. For the time being they kept their guns concealed. Running across the roof it was possible to cover ground swiftly and avoid the thronged corridors. After a couple of hundred feet and a few far misses by bombardiers above, they arrived at one of the large holes in the roof and ducked down into the kitchen warehouses. Approaching quietly, they slid into the narrow space between the boxes and the ceiling and avoided detection. Following Hyacinth, they slid on their bellies down the shelf to the nearest door. This turned out to be guarded by a GASF soldier, who watched the door while a dozen TUGgies methodically tore open and examined crates of food. Hyacinth slid a hundredweight of pasteurized soybean peanut butter substitute onto the guard's head and they dropped to the floor, pulling more crates with them to hinder pursuit. Running into the kitchens, they found themselves cheerfully greeted by more TUGgies. Fortunately the kitchen was huge, full of equipment and partitions and fallen junk and clouds of steam and twists and turns, and after some aimless running around they came to the giant wad of Cheezy Surprise Tetrazzini, squeezed past it through the door, and entered a little-used service corridor filled with the wounded and scared. Four of the latter, also women, seeing that these three were armed and not as scared as they were, joined up. The seven edged into a main hall and made for the Women's Center.

This was in the Student Union Bloc, an area not as bitterly contested as the Caf or the Towers. Hyacinth wounded two Droogs on the way and reloaded. Eventually they came to a long hall lined with the offices of various student activities groups, dark and astonishingly still after their riotous trip. Here they slowed and relaxed, then began to file along the corridor. Soon they smelled sweet incense, and began to make out the distant sounds of chanting and the tinkling of bells. Moving along quietly, they paused by each door: the Outing Club; the Yoga, Solar Power and Multiple Orgasm Support Group; the Nonsocietal Assemblage of Noncoercively Systematized Libertarian Individuals; Let's Understand Animals, Not Torture Them; the men's room; the punk fraternity Zappa Krappa Claw; the Folk Macramé Explorers. As they approached the Women's Center, the sweet odors grew stronger, the soprano-alto chant louder.

"Looks like the Goddess worshipers got here first," said Sarah. "I guess I can live with that, if they can live with someone who shaves her pits." She and Lucy and Hyacinth concealed their guns again, not wanting to seem obtrusive.

Hyacinth knocked. There was a lull, then the voice of Yllas Freedperson, then a new chant.

"You don't know the True Knock," said Yllas.

"Well, we're women, this is the Women's Center."

"Not all women can enter the Women's Center."

"Oh."

"Some have more man than woman in them. No manhood can be allowed here, for this place is sacred to the Goddess."

"Who says?"

"Astarte, the Goddess. Athena. Mary. Vesta. The Goddess of Many Names."

"Have you been talking to her a lot lately?" asked Hyacinth.

"Since I offered her my womb-blood at the Equinox last week, we have been in constant contact."

"Well look," said Hyacinth, "we didn't come to play Dungeons and Dragons, we're here for safety, okay?"

"Then you must purify youself in the sight of the Goddess," said Yllas, opening the door. She and the two dozen others in the Center were all naked. All the partitions that had formerly divided the place into many rooms had been knocked down to unify the Center into a single room. They couldn't see much in the candlelight, except that there was a lot of silver and many daggers and wands. The women were chanting in perfect unison.

"You cannot touch our lives in any way until you have been made one with us," continued Yllas.

Sarah and company declined the invitation with their feet. Before they got far, Yllas started bellowing. "Manwomen! Heteros! Traitors! Impurities! Stop them!"

Nearby doors burst open and several women jumped out with bows and arrows taken from the nearby P. E. Department. Sarah began a slow move for her gun, but Hyacinth prevented it.

"Take them to PAFW," decreed Yllas, "and when Astarte tells us what is to be done, we will take them away one by one and give them support and counseling."

Escorted by the archers, they traveled for several minutes

through Axis hallways, leaving the Union block and entering the athletics area. Here they were turned over to a pair of shotgun-wielding SUBbies, who led them into the darkened hallway behind the racquetball courts. Each of the miniature doors they passed had been padlocked; and looking through the tiny windows, they saw several people in each court. Finally they arrived at an open door and were ushered into an empty court, the door padlocked behind them. On the walkway that ran above the back walls of the courts two guards paced back and forth. Taped above the door was a hastily Magic-Markered sign:

WELCOME

TO THE

PEOPLE'S ALTERNATIVE FREEDOM WORKSHOP

The Axis clearly lacked experience in running prisons. They did not even search them for weapons. The few guards were not particularly well armed and followed no strict procedures; they seemed incapable of dealing with relatively simple situations, such as requests for feminine hygiene materials. All tough decisions such as this had to be transmitted to a higher authority, who was holed up at the far end of the upper walkway.

After a few hours, several more people had been put in their cell, among them some large athletes. Escape was easy. They waited until the pacing guards on the walkway were both at one end, and then two large men simply grabbed Hyacinth by the legs and threw her up over the railing. She rolled on her stomach and plugged the two guards, who did not even have time to unsling their weapons. The rest of the incompetent, somnambulistic personnel were disarmed, and everyone was free. Five high-spirited escapees ran down the walkway toward the office of the high-muck-a-muck, firing through its door the entire way. When they finally kicked open the bent and perforated remains, they found themselves in the courts reservation office. A Terrorist sat in a chair, rifle across lap, staring into a color TV whose picture tube had been blasted out. Hyacinth, Lucy and Sarah, not interested in this, headed for the Burrows with several other refugees in tow. The domain of Virgil was near.

Not far from that gymnasium bloc, on the fourth floor. Klystron/Chris inspected his lines. He had just approved one of the border outposts when Klystron had called him back and berated him for his greenhornish carelessness. Right there, he pointed out, a crafty insurrectionist might creep unseen down that stairway and set up an impregnable firepost! The GASF soldiers, awed by his intuition, extended their lines accordingly.

As Klystron/Chris stood on those stairs making friendly chitchat with the men, the warble of a common urban pigeon sounded thrice from below, warning of approaching hostiles. Klystron/Chris whirled, leapt through a group of slower aides and crouched on the bottom step to peer down the hallway. His men were assuming defensive stances and rolling for cover.

He exposed himself just enough to see the vanguard of the approaching force. As he did, the voice of Shekondar came into his head, as it occasionally did in times of great stress:

"She is the woman I want for you. You know her! She is ideal for you. The time has come for you to lose your virginity; at last a worthy partner has arrived. Look at that body! Look at that hair! She has long legs which are sexually provocative in the extreme. She is a healthy specimen."

He could hardly disagree. She was evolutionarily fit as any female he had ever observed; he remembered now how the firm but not disgusting musculature of her upper arm had felt when he had set her down on that dinner table during her fainting spell. But at this juncture, when she needed to be strong in order to prevail and preserve her ability to reproduce, she showed the bounce and verve that marked her as the archetypal Saucy Wench of practically every dense sword-and-sorcery novel he had ever consumed in his farmhouse bed on a hot Maine summer afternoon with his tortilla chips on one side and his knife collection on the other. Later, after he had saved her from something—saved her from her own vivacious feminine impulsiveness by an act of manly courage and taken her to some sanctuary like the aisle between the CPU and the Array Processing Unit—then she could allow herself to melt away in a rush of feminine passion and show the tenderness combined with fire that was enticingly masked behind her conventional calm sober behavioral mode. He wondered if she were the type of woman who would tie a man up, just for the fun of it, and tickle him. These things Shekondar did not reveal; and yet he had told him that they matched! And that meant she could be nothing other than the fulfillment of his unique sexual desires!

The group approached their perimeter. Klystron/Chris staggered boldly into the open, hindered by a massive erection, hitched up his pants with the butt of the Kalashnikov and waved the group to a halt.

She dipped behind a pillar and covered him with a small arm—a primitive chemical-powered lead-thrower that was nevertheless dangerous. Then, seeing many automatic weapons, she pointed her gun at the ceiling. Her troop slowed to a confused and apprehensive halt. They were disorganized, undisciplined, obviously typical refugee residue, led by a handful of Alpha types with guns—not a minor force in this theater, but helpless against the GASF.

"Hi, Fred," she said, and the obvious sexual passion in her voice was to his ears like the soothing globular tones of the harp-speakers of Iliafharxhlind. "We were headed for the Burrows. How are things between here and there?"

It was easiest to explain it in math terms. "We've secured a continuous convex region which includes both this point and the region called the Burrows, ma'am. It's all under my command. How can we help you?"

"We need places to stay. And the three of us here need to get to the Science Shop."

So! Friends of the White Priest! She was very crafty, very coy, but made no bones about what she was after. These women thought of only one thing. Klystron/Chris liked that —she was quite a little enticer, but subtle as she was, he knew just what the audacious minx was up to! Shekondar tuned in again with unnecessary advice: "Please her and you will have a fine opportunity for sexual intercourse. Do as she asks in all matters."

He straightened up from his awkward position and smiled the broadest, friendliest smile he could manage without exceeding the elastic limit of his lip tissue. "Men," he said to his soldiers, "it's been a secret up to now, but this woman is a Colonelette in the Grand Army of Shekondar the Fearsome and a priestess of great stature. I'm putting Werewolf Platoon under her command. She'll need passage into the Secured Region—unless she changes her mind first!" Women often changed their minds; he glanced at her to see if she had caught this gentle ribbing. She put on an emotionless act that was almost convincing.

"Well, gee. It's kind of a surprise to me too. Can we just go, then?"

"Permission granted, Colonelette Sarah Jane Johnson!" he snapped, saluting. She threw him a strange look, no doubt of awe, thanks and general indebtedness, and after giving a few cutely tentative orders to her men, headed into the Secured Region. Fired with new zest for action, Klystron/Chris wheeled and led his men toward the next outpost of the Purified Empire.

I declined Fred Fine's offer and waited below E Tower for my friends. Before long it became obvious that I would never meet anyone in that madhouse of a lobby, and so I set out for the Science Shop.

The safest route took me down Emeritus Row, quiet as always. I checked each door as I went along. Sharon's office had long since been ransacked by militants looking for railgun information. Other than the sound of dripping water falling into the wastecans below the poorly patched hole in

Sharon's ceiling, all I heard on Emeritus Row was an old man crying alone.

He was in the office marked: PROFESSOR EMERITUS HUMPHREY BATSTONE FORTHCOMING IV. Without knocking (for the room was dark and the door ajar) I walked in and saw the professor himself. He leaned over the desk with his silvery dome on the blotter as though it were the only thing that could soak up his tears, his hands flung uselessly to the side. The rounded tweed shoulders occasionally humped with sobs, and little strangled gasps made their way out and died in the musty air of the office.

Though I intentionally banged my way in, he did not look up. Eventually he sat up, red eyes closed. He opened them to slits and peered at me.

"I—" he said, and broke again. After a few more tries he was able to speak in a high, strangled voice.

"I am in a very bad situation, you see. I think I may have suffered ruination. I have just . . . have just been sitting here"—his voice began to clear and his wet eyes scanned the desk—"and preparing to tender my resignation."

"But why," I asked. "You're not that old. You seem healthy. In your field, it's not as though you have equipment or data that's been destroyed in the fighting. What's wrong?"

He gave a taut, clenched smile and avoided my eyes, looking around at the stacks of manuscript boxes and old books that lined the room. "You don't understand. I seem to have left my lecture notes in my private study in the Library bloc. As you can appreciate, it will be rather difficult for a man of my years to retrieve them under these conditions."

This clearly meant a lot to him, and I did not say *"So? Write up some new ones!"* For him, apparently, it was a fatal blow.

"You see," he continued, sounding stronger now that his secret was out. "Ahem. There is in my field a large corpus of basic knowledge, absolutely fundamental. It must be learned by any new student, which is why it appears in my courses and so forth. I, er, I've forgotten it entirely. Somehow. With my engagements and editorial positions, conferences, trips, consultations, et cetera, and of course all my writing—well, there's simply no room for trivia. So if I am hired away by another university and asked to teach, or some dreadful thing—you can imagine my embarrassment."

I was embarrassed myself, remembering now a snatch of overheard conversation among three grad students, one of whom referred contemptuously to "Emeritus Home-free Et-cetera," who apparently was making him do a great deal of pointless research, check out books for him and pay the fines, put money in his parking meters and so on. If that was Forthcoming's style, I could understand what this break in routine would do to his career. He was only a scholar when there was a university to say he was.

A distant machine-gun blast echoed down the hallway. "Mr. Forthcoming," I said firmly. "I'd like to help you out, but for the moment it's not possible. I guess what I'm trying to say is . . . let's get the hell out of here!"

He wouldn't move.

"Look. Maybe if we get down to a safe place, we can see about getting your lecture notes back."

He looked up with such relief and hope that I wanted to spit. My unfortunate statement had given him new life. He stood up shakily, began to chatter happily and set about packing pipes and manuscripts into his briefcase.

As ever, the Burrows were calm. The GASF guards let us past the border after quick checks over their intercoms, and we were suddenly in a place unchanged since the days of old, where students roamed the hallways wild and free and re-search and classes continued obliviously. Most of the Bur-rows folk regarded the entire war/riot as a challenge for their ingenuity, and those who had not been sucked into Fred Fine's vortex of fantasy and paranoia set about preserving the ancient comforts with the enthusiasm of Boy Scouts lost in the woods.

The Science Shop was an autonomous dependency of Fred Fine's United Pure Plexorian Realm, and the hallway that led there was guarded, mostly symbolically, by Zap with his sawed-off shotgun and his favorite blunt instrument. He waved us through and we came to our haven for the war.

The vacuum of authority that filled the Plex for the first two weeks of April resulted from events in the Nuke Dump. The occupying terrorists warned that any attempt by authorities to approach the building would be met by the release of radioactive poisons into the city. The city police who ringed the Plex late on April First had no idea of how to deal with such a threat and called the Feds. The National Guard showed up a day later with armored personnel carriers, helicopters and tanks, but they, too, kept their distance. The Crotobaltislavonians had obviously intended to establish their own martial law in the Plex, enforcing it through their SUB proxies and the SUB's Terrorist proxies. But the blocked elevator shaft and the giant rats made their authority tenuous, and unbelievably fierce resistance from GASF and TUG kept the SUB/Terrorist Axis from seizing any more than E and F Towers. Instead of National Guard authority or Crotobaltislavonian authority, we ended up with no central authority at all.

"I see that," said Krupp, nodding. "Heimlich would go nuts over this. But what you need, I think, are more liberal arts courses."

Dr. Redfield will find the infrared personnel sensing equipment very interesting. But sirs, we have heavy fighting in the Cafeteria. My men have secured the other end of this hallway while I came to get you."

The Towers were held by the best-armed groups. The Axis held E and F, the GASF held D, the administration anti-Terrorist squads B and C, and TUG held A, H, and G, prompting Hyacinth to remark that if this were tic-tac-toe the TUG would have won. The towers were easy to hold because access was limited; if you blocked shut the four outer fire stairs of each wing, you could control the only entrances to the tower with a handful of soldiers in the sixth-floor lobby. The base of the Plex was a bewildering 3-D labyrinth. Here things were much less stable as several groups struggled for control of useful ground, such as bathrooms, strategic stairways, rooms with windows and so forth. Many of these were factions that had split away from the Terrorists, finding the strict hierarchy and tight restrictions intolerable. Other important groups were made up of inner-city financial-aid students, who at least knew how to take care of themselves; one gang of small-towners from the Great Plains, also adept at mass violence; the hockey-wrestling coalition; and the Explorer post, which had a large interlocking membership with the ROTC students.

Those who were not equipped or inclined to fight fared poorly. Most ended up trapped in the towers for the duration, where all they could do was watch TV and reproduce. Escape from the Plex was impossible, because the nuclear Terrorists allowed no one to approach it, and snipers in the Axis towers made perilous the dash from the Main Entrance. Those who could not make it to the safety of a tower were not wanted by the bands of fighters in the Base, and so had to wander as refugees, most ending up in the Library. It was a very, very bad time to be an unescorted woman. We tried to make raids against weaker bands in order to rescue some of these unfortunates, but only retrieved thirty or so.

Fire in the Plex was not the problem it had been feared to be. The plumbing still worked reasonably well and most people had enough sense to use the fire hoses. Many areas were smoky for days, though, to the point of being hostile to life, and bands driven from their own countries by smoke accounted for a good deal of the fighting. The food problem was minor because the Red Cross was allowed to distribute it in the building. Unfortunately there was no way to remove garbage, so it piled up in lobbies and stairwells and elevator shafts. Insects, invading through windows that had been broken out or removed to vent smoke, grew fruitful and multiplied; but this plague then abated, as the bat population swelled enormously to take advantage of the explosion in their food supply. By the end of the crisis, the top five floors of E Tower had been evacuated to make room for bats, who were moving down the tower at the rate of one floor every three days.

There were stable areas where well-armed people settled in and organized themselves. The Burrows were exceptionally stable, brilliantly organized by Fred Fine, and Virgil's Science Shop was an enclave of stability within that. About twenty people lived in the Shop; we slept on floors and workbenches, and cooked communally on lab burners. Fred Fine allowed us this autonomy for one reason: Shekondar the Fearsome/JANUS 64 had selected Virgil as his sole prophet.

Of course it was not really so simple. It was actually the Worm, and Virgil's countermeasures. As Virgil explained it, he had signed on to his terminal on March 31 to find a message waiting:

WELL MET WORM-HUNTING MERCENARY. YOU ARE ADEPT. LET US HOPE YOU ARE WELL PAID. SO FAR I HAVE ONLY FLEXED MY MUSCLES. NOW BEGINS THE DUEL.

The next day, of course, civilization had fallen. As soon as Virgil had been sure of this, he had signed on to find that his terminal had been locked out of the system by the Worm. This he had anticipated, and so he calmly proceeded to the Operator's Station, ejected Consuela and signed on there under a fake ID. Virgil had then commandeered six tape drives (to the dismay of the hackers who were using them) and mounted six tapes he had prepared for this day. He went to the Terminal Room, where sat hundreds of terminals in individual carrels. Here Virgil signed on to eighteen terminals at once, using fake accounts and passwords he had been keeping in reserve. On each terminal he set in motion a different program—using information stored on the six special tapes. Each of these programs looked like a rather long but basically routine student effort, the sort of thing the Worm had long since stopped trifling with. But each did contain lengthy sections of machine code that had no relevance to the program proper.

Virgil returned to the Operator's Station and entered a single command. Its effect was to draw together the reins of the eighteen sham programs, to lift out, as it were, all those long machine code sections and interleave them into one huge powerful program that seemed to coalesce out of nowhere, having already penetrated the Worm's locks and defenses. This monster program, then, had calmly proceeded to wipe out all administrative memory and all student and academic software, and then to restructure the Operator to suit Virgil's purposes. It all went—payroll records, library overdues, video-game programs. From the computer's point of view, American Megaversity ceased to exist in the time it took for a micro-transistor to flip from one state to the other.

A mortal wound for the university, but the university was already mortally wounded. This was the only way to prevent the Worm from seizing the entire computer within the next week or so. Virgil's insight had been that although the Worm had been designed to take into account any conceivable action on the Computing Center's part, it had not anticipated the possibility that someone might destroy all the records and dismantle the Operator simply to fight the Worm.

The Worm's message to Virgil had been the key: it had identified him as an *employee* of the Computing Center, a hired hit man. That was not an unreasonable assumption, considering Virgil's power. But it was wrong anyway, proving that the Worm could only take into account reasonably predictable events. The downfall of the university wasn't predictable, at least not to sociopath Paul Bennett, so he hadn't foreseen that anyone would take Virgil's pyrrhic approach.

Virgil now had enough processing power to run a large airline or a small developing country. The Worm could only loop back and start over and try to retake what it had lost, and this time against a much more formidable foe. So on hummed the CPU of the Janus 64, spending one picosecond performing a task for the Worm, the next a task for Virgil. The opponents met and mingled on the central chip of the CPU, which evenhandedly did the work of both at once, impassively computing out its own fate. Fred Fine noticed that no one could sign on now except Virgil, and concluded the obvious: Virgil was the Prophet of Shekondar, the Mage.

So we saw little of Virgil, who had absorbed himself completely in the computer, who mumbled in machine language as he stirred his soup and spent fifteen hours a day sitting alone before the black triangular obelisk staring at endless columns of numbers.

Sarah, Hyacinth, Lucy and friends showed up late in the evening of the First, giddy and triumphant, and we had a delighted reunion. Ephraim Klein showed up at five in the morning bleeding from many small birdshot wounds, moving with incredible endurance for such a small, unhealthy-looking person. After establishing that the shot in his legs was steel, not lead, we sent him to Nirvana on laughing gas and generic beer and sucked out the balls with a large electromagnet. Casimir turned up suddenly, late on April second, slipping in so quietly that he seemed just to beam down. He dumped a load of clothing and sporting gear on a bench and set to work in a white creative heat we did not care to disturb.

"I told you," Ephraim said to Sarah, as he recovered. "We should blow this place up. Look what's happened."

"Yeah," said Sarah, "it's a bad situation."

"Bad situation! A fucking war! How many other universities do you know where a civil war closes off the academic year?"

Sarah shrugged. "Not too many."

"So why do you think we're having one? These people are a totally normal cross-section of the population, caught in a giant building that drives them crazy."

"Okay. Lie down and stop moving around so much, okay?" She wandered around the shop watching a goggled Casimir slice into a fencing mask with a plate grinder. In one corner, Hyacinth was teaching the joys of bunsen-burner cuisine to a small child who had been caught up in the fighting and sent down here by grace of the Red Cross. Sarah suddenly walked back to Ephraim.

"You're wrong," she said. "It's nothing to do with the Plex.

What people do isn't determined by where they live. It happens to be their damned fault. They decided to watch TV instead of thinking when they were in high school. They decided to take blow-off courses and drink beer instead of reading and trying to learn something. They decided to chicken out and be intolerant bastards instead of being openminded, and finally they decided to go along with their buddies and do things that were terribly wrong when there was no reason they had to. Anyone who hurts someone else *decides* to hurt them, goes out of their way to do it."

"But the pressures! The social pressures here are irresistible. How . . ."

"I resisted them. You resisted them. The fact that it's hard to be a good person doesn't excuse going along and being an asshole. If they can't overcome their own fear of being unusual, it's not my fault, because any idiot ought to be able to see that if he just acts reasonably and makes a point of not hurting others, he'll be happier."

"You don't even have to try to hurt people here. The place forces it on you. You can't sit up in bed without waking up your goddamn neighbor. You can't take a shower without sucking off the hot water and freezing the next one down. You can't go to eat without making the people behind you wait a little longer, and even by eating the food you increase the amount they have to make, and decrease the quality."

"That's all crap! That's the way life is, Ephraim. It has nothing to do with the architecture of the Plex."

"Look at the sexism in this place. Doesn't that ever bother you? Don't you think that if people weren't so packed together in this space, the bars and the parties wouldn't be such meat markets? Maybe there would be fewer rapes if we could teach people how to get along with the other sex."

"If you want to prevent rapes, you should make a justice system that protects our right not to be raped. Education? How do you pull off that kind of education? How do you design a rape-proof dorm? Look, Ephraim, all we can do is protect people's rights. We wouldn't get a change in attitude by moving to another building. The education you're talking about is just a pipe dream."

"I still think we should blow this fucker up."

"Good. Work on it. In the meantime I'll continue to carry a gun."

Professor Forthcoming, or "Emeritus" as Hyacinth called him, followed me around a great deal, jabbering about his lecture notes, prodding my latissimus muscles and marveling at how easy it would be for me, a former first-string college nose guard with a gun, to rescue them from the Library. I did not have the heart to discourage him. In the end, all I could do was make sure he paid for it: made him promise that he would sit down and study those notes so that he could rewrite them if he had to. He promised unashamedly, but by the time we organized the quest he was already looking forward to a conference in Monaco in the fall, and listening to the casualty reports on the radio to hear if any of his key grad students had been greased.

No, said Fred Fine, the APPASMU was not available for raids on the Library. But we could have some soldiers and one AK-47, on the condition that, given the choice between abandoning the quest and abandoning the assault rifle, we would abandon the quest. I loudly agreed to this before Emeritus could sputter any disagreements. Our party was me, Hyacinth, Emeritus, four GASF soldiers and the Science Shop technician Lute. Sarah stayed behind reading *The Origin of Consciousness in the Breakdown of the Bicameral Mind.*

Our route took us through fairly stable academic blocs, and other areas controlled by gangs. We could not avoid passing through the area controlled by Hansen's Gang, the small-towners of the Great Plains. They were not well armed, but neither was anyone else in the base, and they had jumped into the fray with the glee of any rural in an informal blunt-instruments fight and come out winners. This was their idiom. Our negotiations with their leader were straightforward: we showed them our AK-47 and offered not to massacre them if they let us pass without hassle. Their leader had no trouble grasping this, but many of the members seemed to have a bizarre mental block: they could not see the AK-47 in Hyacinth's hands. All they saw was Hyacinth, the first clean healthy female they had seen in a week, and they came after her as though she were unarmed. "Hey! She's mine!" yelled one of these as we entered their largest common area.

"Fuck you," said another, swinging a motorcycle chain past his brother's eyes at high speed. He turned and began to trudge toward Hyacinth, hitching up his pants. "Hey, bitch, I'm gonna breed you," he said cheerfully. Hyacinth aimed the gun at him; he looked at her face. She pulled the bolt into firing position and squared off; he kept coming. When I stepped forward he brandished his chain, then changed course as Hyacinth stepped out from behind me.

"Go for it," and "All right, for sure, Combine," yelled his pals.

"Hyacinth, please don't do that," I said, plugging my ears. She fired off half a clip in one burst and pulverized a few square feet of cinderblock wall right next to the man's head. The lights went out as a power cable was severed. Courtesy of a window, we could still see.

"Shit, what the fuck?" someone inquired.

Rather than trying to explain, we proceeded from the room. "I like that bitch," someone said as we were leaving, "but she's weird. I dunno what's wrong with her."

The Mailroom was an armistice zone between Hansen's Gang and the Journalism Department. The elevators here descended to the mail docks, making this one of the few ports of entry to the Plex. The publicity-minded Crotobaltislavonians had worked out an agreement with one of the networks —you know which, if you watched any news in this period— allowing the camera crews to come and go through this room. The network's hired guards all toted machine guns. We counted twenty automatic weapons in this room alone, which probably meant that the network had the entire Axis outgunned.

In exchange for a brief interview, which was never aired, and for all the information we could provide about other parts of the Plex, we were allowed into the Journalism bloc. Here we picked up a three-man minicam crew who followed along for a while. Emeritus was magnificently embarrassed and insisted on walking behind the camera. One of the crew was an AM student, and I talked to him about the network's operations.

"You've got a hell of a lot of firepower. You guys are the most powerful force in the Plex. How are you using it?"

The student shrugged. "What do you mean? We protect our crews and equipment. All the barbarians are afraid of us."

"Right, obviously," I said. "But I noticed recently that a lot of people around here are starving, being raped, murdered—you know, a lot of bum-out stuff. Do those guards try to help out? You can spare a few."

"Well, I don't know," he said uncomfortably. "That's kind of network-level policy. It goes against the agreement. We can go anywhere as long as we don't interfere. If we interfere, no agreement."

"But if you've already negotiated one agreement, can't you do more? Get some doctors into the building, maybe?"

"No way, man. No fucking way. We journalists have ethics."

The camera crew turned back when we reached the border of the Geoanthropological Planning Science Department, a bloc with only two entrances. My office was here, and I hoped I could get us through to the other side. The heavy door was bullet-pocked, the lock had been shot at more than once, but it was blocked from the other side and we could hear a guard beyond. Nearby, in an alcove, under a pair of drinking fountains, stretched out straight and dead on the floor, was a middle-aged faculty member, his big stoneware coffee mug still clenched in his cold stiff fingers. He had apparently died of natural causes.

As it turned out, the guard was a grad student I knew, who let us in. He was tired and dirty, with several bandages, a bearded face, bleary red eyes and matted hair—just as he had always looked. Three other grads sat there in the reception room reading two-year-old *U.S. News and World Reports* and chomping hunks of beef jerky.

While my friends took a breather, I stopped by my office and checked my mailbox. On the way back I peeked into the Faculty Lounge.

The entire Geoanthropological Planning Science faculty was there, sitting around the big conference table, while a few favored grad students stood back against the walls. Several bowls of potato chips were scattered over the table and at least two kegs were active. The room was dark; they were having a slide show.

"Whoops! Looks like I tilted the camera again on this one," said Professor Longwood sheepishly, nearly drowned out by derisive whoops from the crowd. "How did this get in here? This is part of the Labrador tundra series. Anyway, it's not a bad shot, though I used the wrong film, which is why everything's pink. That corkscrew next to the caribou scat gives you some idea of scale—" but my opening the door had spilled light onto the image, and everyone turned around to look at me.

"Bud!" cried the Chair. "Glad you could make it! Want some beer? It's dark beer."

"Sounds good," I said truthfully, "but I'm just stopping in."

"How are things?" asked Professor Longwood.

"Fine, fine. I see you're all doing well too. Have you been outside much? I mean, in the Plex?"

There was bawdy laughter and everyone looked at a sheepish junior faculty member, a heavyset man from Upper Michigan. "Bert here went out to shoot some slides," explained the Chair, "and ran into some of those hayseeds. He told them he was a journalist and they backed off, but then they saw he didn't have a press pass, so he had to kick one of them in the nuts and give the other his camera!"

"Don't feel bad, Bert," said a mustachioed man nearby. "We'll get a grant and buy you a new one." We all laughed.

"So you're here for the duration?" I asked.

"Shouldn't last very long," said a heavily bearded professor who was puffing on a pipe. "We are working up a model to see how long the food needs of the population can last. We're using survival ratios from the 1782 Bulgarian famine —actually quite similar to this situation. We're having a hell of a time getting data, but the model says it shouldn't last more than a week. As for us, we've got an absolute regional monopoly on beer, which we trade with the Journalism people for food."

"Have you taken into account the rats and bats?" I asked.

"Huh? *Where?*" The room was suddenly still.

"We've got giant rats downstairs, and billions of bats upstairs. The rats are this long. Eighty to a hundred pounds. No hearts. I hear they've worked their way up to the lower sublevels now, and they're climbing up through the stacks of garbage in the elevator shafts."

"Shit!" cried Bert, beating his fists wildly on the table. "What a time to lose my fucking camera!"

"Let's catch one," said his biologist wife.

"Well, we could adjust the model to account for exogenous factors," said the bearded modeler.

"We'd have people eating rats, and rats eating people," said the mustachioed one.

"And rats eating bats."

"And bats eating bugs eating dead rats."

"The way to account for all that is with a standard input/output matrix," said the Chair commandingly.

"These rats sound similar to wolverines," said Longwood, cycling through the next few slides. "I think I have some wolverine scats a few slides ahead, if this is the series I think it is."

Seeing that they had split into a slide and a modeling faction, I stepped out. A few minutes later we were back on the road.

We were attacked by a hopeless twit who was trying to use

a shotgun like a long-range rifle. I was nicked in the cheek by one ball. Hyacinth splashed him all over a piece of abstract sculpture made of welded-together lawn ornaments. The GASFers, who were humiliated that a female should carry the big gun, were looking as though they'd never have another erection.

We passed briefly through the Premed Center, which was filled with pale mutated undergrads dissecting war casualties and trying to gross each other out. I yelled at them to get outside and assist the wounded, but received mostly blank stares. "We can't," said one of them, scandalized, "we're not even in med school yet."

From here we entered the Medical Library, and from there, the Library proper.

Huge and difficult to guard, the Library was the land of the refugees. It had no desirable resources, but was a fine place in which to hide because the bookshelves divided into thousands of crannies. Waves of refugees made their way here and holed up, piling books into forts and rarely venturing out.

The first floor was unguarded and sparsely occupied. We stuck to the open areas and proceeded to the second floor.

Here was a pleasant surprise. An organized relief effort had been formed, mostly by students in Nursing, Classics, History, Languages and Phys. Ed. By trading simple medical services to the barbarians they had obtained enough guns to guard the place. An incoming refugee would be checked out by a senior Nursing major or occasional premed volunteer, then given a place in the stacks—"your place is DG 311 1851 and its vicinity"—and so on. Most of the stragglers could then hide out between bulletproof walls of paper, while the seriously wounded could be lowered out the windows to the Red Cross people below. In the same way, food, supplies and brave doctors could be hoisted into the Plex. The atmosphere was remarkably quiet and humane, and all seemed in good humor.

The rest of our journey was uneventful. We climbed to the

fourth floor and wended our way toward Emeritus' study. Soon we could smell smoke, and see it hanging in front of the lights. To the relief of Emeritus, it came not from his office but from the open door of the one labeled "Embers, Archibald."

Three men and a woman, all unarmed, sat around a small fire, occasionally throwing on another book. They had broken out the window to vent the smoke.

The woman shrieked as I appeared in the door. "Jesus! If I had a gun, you'd be dead now. I react *so* uncontrollably."

"Good thing you don't," I observed.

"It's really none of your business," intoned a thin, pale man. "But I suppose that since you have that wretched gun, you're going to have us do what you want. Well, we don't have anything you could want here. And forget about Zelda here. She's a *lousy* lay."

Zelda shrieked in amusement. "It's a good thing you're witty when you're a bastard, Terence, or I'd despise you."

"Oh, do go ahead. I adore being despised. I really do. It's so inspiring."

"Society despises the artist," said Embers, lighting a Dunhill in the bookfire, "unless he panders to the masses. But society treats the artist civilly so he can't select specific targets for his hatred. Open personal hatred is so very honest."

"Now that's meaningful, Arch," said the other man, a brief lump with an uncertain goatee.

"How come you're burning books?" I asked.

"Oh, that, well," said Embers, "Terence wanted a fire."

Terence piped up again. "This whole event is so very like camping out, don't you agree? Except without the dreadful ants and so forth. I thought a fire would be very—*primal.* But it smoked dreadfully, so we broke out the window, and now it's very cold and we must keep it going ceaselessly, of course. Is that adequate? Is that against Library rules?"

"We've been finding," added Embers, "that older books are much better. They burn more slowly. And with their thin pages, Bibles and dictionaries are quite effective. I'm taking some notes." He waved a legal pad at me.

"Also," added the small one, "old books are printed on acid-free paper, so we aren't getting acid inside of our lungs."

"Why don't you just cover the window and put it out?" I asked.

"Aren't we logical?" said Terence. "You people are all so tediously Western. We wanted a fire, you can't take it away! What happened to academic freedom? Say, are you quite finished with your bloody suggestions? I'm trying to read one of my fictions to these people, Mr. Spock."

I followed my friends into Emeritus' office. Behind me Terence resumed his reading. "The thin stream of boiling oil dribbled from the lip of the frying pan and seared into the boy's white flesh. As he squirmed against the bonds that were holding him down, unable to move, it ran into the bed of thorny roses underneath him; the petals began to wither like a dying western sunset at dusk."

A minute or two later, as we exited with Emeritus' papers, there was a patter of applause. "Ravishing, Terence. Quite frankly, it's similar to Erasmus T. Bowlware's *Gulag Pederast.* Especially the self-impalement of the heroine on the electric fencepost of the concentration camp as she is driven into a frenzy by psychic emanations from the possessed child in the nearby mansion where the defrocked epileptic priest gives up his life in order to get the high-technology secrets to the Jewish commandos. I do like it."

"When do I get to read *my* fiction?" asked Zelda.

"Is this from the novel about the female writer who is struggling to write a novel about a woman writer who is writing a novel about a woman artist in Nazi Germany with a possessed daughter?" asked Embers.

"Well, I decided to make her a liberated prostitute and psychic," said Zelda; and that was the last I heard of the conversation, or of the people.

We deposited Emeritus in the refugee camp on the second

floor and made it back to the Science Shop in about an hour. There, Sarah and Casimir were deep in conversation, and Ephraim Klein was listening in.

Casimir's finished suit of armor used bulletproof fabric taken from a couple of associate deans. The administration was unhappy about that, but they could only get to Casimir by shooting their way through the Unified Pure Plexorian Realm. Underneath the fabric, Casimir wore various hard objects to protect his flesh from impact. On legs and knees he wore soccer shinguards and the anti-kneecapping armor favored by administration members. He wore a jockstrap with a plastic cup, and over his torso was a heavy, crude breastplate that he had endlessly and deafeningly hammered out of half a fifty-five gallon oil drum. Down his back he hung overlapping shingles of steel plate to protect his spine.

His head was protected by a converted defensive lineman's football helmet. He had cut the front out of a fencing mask and attached the wire mesh over the plastic bars of the helmet's facemask. Over the earholes he placed a pair of shooter's ear protectors. So that he would not overheat, he cut a hole in the back of the helmet and ran a flexible hose to it. The other end of the hose he connected to a battery-powered blower hung on his belt, and to get maximum cooling benefit he shaved his head. The helmet as a whole was draped with bulletproof fabric which hung down a foot on all sides to cover the neck. And as someone happened to notice, he took his snapshot of Sarah and Hyacinth and taped it to the inside of the helmet with grey duct tape.

When Casimir was in full battle garb, his only vulnerable points were feet, hands and eye-slit. Water could be had by sucking on a tube that ran down to a bicyclist's water bottle on his belt. And it should not go unmentioned that Casimir, draped in thick creamy-white fabric, with blazing yellow and blue running shoes, topped with an enormous shrouded neckless head, a faceless dome with bulges over the ears and a glittering silver slit for the eyes, a sword from the Museum in hand, looked indescribably terrible and fearsome, and for the first time in his life people moved to the walls to avoid him when he walked down the hallways.

It was a very smoke-filled room that Casimir ventilated by swinging in through the picture window on the end of a rope. Through the soft white tobacco haze, Oswald Heimlich saw his figure against the sky for an instant before it burst into the room and did a helpless triple somersault across the glossy parquet floor. Heimlich was already on his feet, snatching up his $4,000 engraved twelve-gauge shotgun and flicking off the safety. As the intruder staggered to his feet, Heimlich sighted over the head of the Trustee across from him (who reacted instinctively by falling into the lap of the honorable former mayor) and fired two loads of .00 buckshot into this strange Tarzan's lumpy abdomen. The intruder took a step back and remained standing as the shot *plonk*ed into his chest and clattered to the floor. Heimlich fired again with similar effects. By now the great carved door had burst open and five guards dispersed to strategic positions and pointed their UZIs at the suspicious visitor. S. S. Krupp watched keenly.

The guards made the obligatory orders to freeze. He slowly reached around and began to draw a dueling sword from the Megaversity historical collections out of a plastic pipe scabbard. Tied to its handle was a white linen napkin with the AM coat of arms, which he waved suggestively.

"I swear," said S. S. Krupp, "don't you have a phone, son?"

No one laughed. These were white male Eastern businessmen, and they were serious. Heimlich in particular was not amused; this man looked very much like the radiation emergency workers who had been staggering through his nightmares for several nights running, and having him crash in out of a blue sky into a Board of Trustees meeting was not a healthy experience. He sat there with his eyes closed for several moments as waiters scurried in to sweep up the broken glass.

"I'll bet you want to do a little negotiating," said Krupp, annoyingly relaxed. "Who're you with?"

"I owe allegiance to no man," came the muffled voice from behind the mask, "but come on behalf of all."

"Well, that's good! That's a fine attitude," said Krupp. "Set yourself down and we'll see what we can do."

The intruder took an empty chair, laid his sword on the table and peeled off his hood of fabric to reveal the meshed-over football helmet. A rush of forced air was exhaled from his facemask and floated loose sheets of paper down the table.

"Why did you put a nuclear waste dump in the basement?"

Everyone was surprised, if genteel, and they exchanged raised eyebrows for a while.

"Maybe Ozzie can tell you about that," suggested Krupp. "I was still in Wyoming at the time."

Heimlich scowled. "I won't deny its existence. Our reasons for wanting it must be evident. Perhaps if I tell you its history, you'll agree with us, whoever you are. Ahem. You may be aware that until recently we suffered from bad management at the presidential level. We had several good presidents in the seventies, but then we got Tony Commodi, who was irresponsible—an absolute mongoloid when it came to finance—insisted on teaching several classes himself, and so forth. He raised salaries while keeping tuition far too low. People became accustomed to it. At this time we Trustees were widely dispersed and made no effort to *lead* the university. Finally we were nearly bankrupt. Commodi was forced to resign by faculty and Trustees and was replaced by Pertinax Rushforth, who in those days was quite the renascence man, and widely respected. We Trustees were still faced with impossible financial problems, but we found that if we sold all the old campus—hundreds of acres of prime inner-city real estate—we could pull in enough capital to build something like the Plex on the nine blocks we retained.

But of course the demographics made it clear that times would be very rough in the years to come. We could not compete for students, and so we had to run a very tight ship and seek innovative sources for our operating funds. We could have entered many small ventures—high technology spinoffs, you see—but this would have been extraordinarily complex, highly controversial and unpredictable, besides raising questions about the proper function of the university.

"It was then that we hit upon the nuclear waste idea. Here is something that is not dependent on the economy; we will always have these wastes to dispose of. It's highly profitable, as there is a desperate demand for disposal facilities. The wastes must be stored for millennia, which means that they are money in the bank—the government, whatever form it takes, must continue to pay us until their danger has died away. And by its very nature it must be done secretly, so no controversy is generated, no discord disrupts the normal functions of the academy—there need be no relationship between the financial foundation and the intellectual activities of the university. It's perfect."

"See, this city is on a real stable salt-dome area," added a heavy man in an enormous grey suit, "and now that there's no more crude down there, it's suitable for this kind of storage."

"You," said the knight, pointing his sword at the man who had just spoken, "must be in the oil business. Are you Ralph Priestly?"

"Ha! Well, yeah, that's me," said Ralph Priestly, unnerved.

"We have to talk later."

"How did you know about our disposal site?" asked Heimlich.

"That doesn't matter. What matters now is: how did the government of Crotobaltislavonia find out about it?"

"Oh," said Heimlich, shocked. "You know about that also."

"Yep."

After a pause, S. S. Krupp continued. "Now, don't go tell your honchos that we did this out of greed. America had to start doing something with this waste—that's a fact. You know what a fact is? That's something that has nothing to do with politics. The site is as safe as could be. See, some things just can't be handed over to political organizations, because they're so damned unstable. But great universities can last for thousands of years. Hell, look at the changes of government the University of Paris has survived in the last century alone! This facility had to be built and it had to be done by a university. The big steady cash flow makes us more stable, and that makes us better qualified to be running the damn thing in the first place. Symbiosis, son."

"Wait. If you're making so much money off of this, why are you so financially tight-assed?"

"That's a very good question," said Heimlich. "As I said, it's imperative that this facility remain secret. If we allowed the cash flow to show up on our ledgers, this would be impossible. We've had to construct a scheme for processing or laundering, as it were, our profits through various donors and benefactors. In order to allay suspicion, we keep these 'donations' as small as we can while meeting the university's basic needs."

"What about the excess money?"

"What's done with that depends on how long the site remains secret. Therefore we hold the surplus in escrow and invest it in the name of American Megaversity, so that in the meantime it is productively used."

"Invest it where? Don't tell me. Heimlich Freedom Industries. the Big Wheel Petroleum Corporation . . ."

"Well," said Ralph Priestly, cutting the tip off a cigar. "Big Wheel's a hell of an investment. I run a tight ship."

"We don't deny that the investments are in our best interests," said a very old Trustee with a kindly face. "But there's nothing wrong with that, as long as we do not waste or steal the money. Every investment we make in some way furthers the nation's economic growth."

"But you're no different from the Crotobaltislavonians, in principle. You're using your control over the wastes to blackmail whatever government comes along."

"That's an excellent observation," said Krupp. "But the fact is, if you'll just think about it, that as long as the waste exists, someone's going to control them, and whoever does can blackmail whatever government there is, and as long as someone's going to have that influence, it might as well be good people like us."

The knight drummed his fingers on the table, and the Trustees peered at his inscrutable silver mask. "I see from the obituaries that Bert Nix and Pertinax Rushforth were one and the same. What happened to him?"

Heimlich continued. "Pertinax couldn't hack it. He was all for fiscal conservatism, of course—Bert was not a soft-headed man at any point. But when he learned he was firing people and cutting programs just to maintain this charade, he lost his strength of will. The faculty ruined his life with their hatred, he had a nervous breakdown and we sacked him. Then the MegaUnion began to organize a tuition strike, so the remaining old-guard Trustees threw up their hands, caved in and installed Julian Didius as President!" At the memory of this, several of the Trustees sighed or moaned with contempt. "Well! After he had enjoyed those first three weeks of flying in all his intelligentsia comrades for wine and cheese parties, we got him in here and showed him the financial figures, which looked disastrous. Then he met Pertinax after the electroshock, and realized what a bloody hell-hole he was in. Three days later he went to the Dean's Office for a chat, and when the Dean turned out to be addressing a conference in Hawaii, he blew his top and hurled himself out the window, and then we brought in Septimius and he's straightened things out wonderfully." There were admiring grins around the table, though Krupp did not appear to be listening.

"Did Pertinax have master keys, then, or what? How did he keep from being kicked out of the Plex?"

"We allowed the poor bastard to stay because we felt sorry for him," said Krupp. "He wouldn't live anywhere else."

The angle of the knight's head dropped a little.

"So," said Heimlich briskly, "for some reason you knew our best-kept secrets. We hope you will understand our actions now and not do anything rash. Do you follow?"

"Yes," murmured the knight, "unfortunately."

"What is unfortunate about it?"

"The more thoughtful you people are, the worse you get. Why is that?"

"What do we do that is wrong, Casimir Radon?" said Krupp quietly.

The mask rose and gleamed at S. S. Krupp, and then its owner lifted off the helmet to reveal his shaven head and permanently consternated face.

"Lie a hell of a lot. Fire people when you don't have to. Create—create a very complicated web of lies, to snare a simple, good ideal."

"I don't think it's a hell of a lot of fun," said Krupp, "and it hurts sometimes, more than you can suppose. But great goals aren't attained with ease or simplicity or pleasantry, or whatever you're looking for. If we gave into the MegaUnion, we would tip our hand and cause ruination. As long as we're putting on this little song-and-dance, we've got to make it a complete song-and-dance, because if the orchestra's playing a march and the dancers are waltzing, the audience riots. The theater burns."

"At least you could be more conciliatory."

"Conciliatory! Listen, son, when you've got snakes in the basement and the water's rising, it's no time to conciliate. Someone's got to have some principles in education, and it might as well be us. If this country's educators hadn't had their heads in their asses for forty years, we wouldn't have a faculty union, and more of our students might be sentient. I'll have strap marks on my ass before I conciliate with those medicine men down there on the picket lines."

"You're trying to fire *everyone*. That's a little extreme."

"Not if we're to be consistent," said Heimlich. "We can use the opportunity to rearrange our financial platform, and hire new people. There are many talented academics desperate for work these days, and the best faculty members here won't let themselves be taken out en masse anyway."

"You're going to do it, aren't you!"

"It's evident that we have no choice."

"Don't you think—" Casimir looked out at the clear blue sky.

"What?"

"That if the administration gets to be as powerful as you, you have killed the university?"

"Look, son," said Ralph Priestly, rolling forward. "We never claimed this was an ideal situation. We're just doing our best. We don't have much choice."

"We're rather busy, as you can imagine," said Heimlich finally. "What do you want? Something for the railgun?" He sat up abruptly. "How *is* the railgun?"

"Safe."

Heimlich smiled for the first time in a week. "I'd like to know what a 'safe' railgun is."

"Maybe you'll find out."

Everyone looked disturbed.

"We are prepared to remove the Terrorists from the waste disposal site," said Casimir crisply, "as a public service. The estimated time will be one week. Beforehand, we plan to evacuate the Plex. We require your cooperation in two areas.

"First, we will need control of the Plex radio station. One of our group has developed a scheme for evacuating the Plex which makes this necessary.

"The second requirement is for the consideration of you, Ralph Priestly. What we want, Ralph, is for some person of yours to sit by the switch that controls the Big Wheel sign. When we phone him and say, *'Fiat lux,'* he is to turn it on, and when we say, *'Fiat obscuritas,'* off.

"That commando team you tried to send in through the sewers last night was stopped by a RAT, or Rodent Assault Tactics team associated with us. We'll be releasing them soon, we can't do much more with first aid. The point is that only we can get rid of the Terrorists. We just ask that you do not interfere."

Finished, Casimir sat back, hands clasped on breastplate, and stared calmly at a skylight. The Board of Trustees moved down to the far end of the table. After they had talked for a few minutes, S. S. Krupp walked over and shook hands with Casimir.

"We're with you," Krupp said proudly. "Wish I knew what the hell you had in mind. What's your timetable?"

"Don't know. You'll have plenty of warning."

"Can we supply men? Arms?" asked Heimlich.

"Nope. One gun is all we need." Casimir let go of Krupp's hand and walked down the table, unclipping himself from the rope and throwing it out to dangle there. A forest of pinstripes rushed up the other side, trying to circumnavigate the table and shake Casimir's hand too. Casimir stopped by the exit.

"I probably won't see you again. Bear in mind, after the university starts running again, two things: we control the rats. And we control the Worm. You no longer monopolize power in this institution."

The Trustees stopped dead at this breach of pleasantness and stared at Casimir. Krupp looked on as though monitoring a field of battle from a high tower. Casimir continued. "I just mention this because it makes a difference in what is reasonable for you to do, and what is not. Good-bye." As he reached for the doorknob, he found the door briskly opened by a guard; he nodded to the man and strode out into an anteroom.

"Soldier," said Septimius Severus Krupp, "see that that man receives safe passage back to his own sphere of influence."

Night fell, and Towers A, B, C, D, H and G began to flash on and off in perfect unison. Every tower except for E and F—homes of the Axis—was blinking in and out of existence every two seconds. As the Axis people saw it, the entire Plex was disappearing into the night, then re-igniting, over and over. It was much closer than the Big Wheel; it was far larger; it surrounded them on three sides. The effect was stupefying.

Dex Fresser ran to his observation post. In the corridors of E13S, Terrorists wandered like decapitated chickens. Some were hearing voices telling them to look, some not to look, to run or stay, to panic or relax. The SUBbie who was supposed to guard the lounge-headquarters had dropped his gun on the floor and disappeared. Fresser burst into the lounge to consult with Big Wheel.

Big Wheel had gone dark.

He turned on the Little Wheel—the Go Big Red Fan.

"Big Wheel must be mad at you or something. What the fuck did you do wrong?" shouted the Fan, loud, omnipresent and angry. Dex Fresser shrank, got on his knees and snuffled a little. Outside, a bewildered stereo-hearer was playing with the knobs on his ghetto blaster, desperate for advice.

"The stereo! The stereo, dipshit, find that frequency! Find the frequency," said the Fan in the voice of Dex Fresser's old scoutmaster. Dex Fresser tumbled over a chair in his haste to reach the stereo. The only light in the room was cast by the glowing LEDs on his stereo that looked out like feral eyes in the night. All systems were go for stereo energize. As Dex Fresser's hands played over the controls, dozens of lights kicked in with important systems data, and green digits glowed from the tuner to tell him his position on the FM dial. Only dense static came from the speakers, meaningless to anyone else; but he could hear Big Wheel guiding him in the voice of his first-grade ballroom dance teacher.

"A little farther down, dear. Keep going right down the dial. You're certain to get it eventually."

Dex Fresser punched buttons and a light came on, saying: "AUTO DOWNWARD SCAN." He now heard many voices from the dark cones of the speakers: funky jazz-playing fascists, "great huge savings now . . .", Neil Young wailing into his harmonica, a call-in guest suggesting that we load the

Mexicans on giant space barges and hurl them into the sun, a base hit by Chambliss, an ad for rat poison, a teen, apoplectic about his acne . . . and then the voice he was looking for.

"On. Off. On. Off. On. Off." It was a woman's voice, somehow familiar.

"It's Sarah, dumbshit," said the Go Big Red Fan. "She's on the campus station."

Indeed. The other towers were going on and off just as Sarah told them to. He knelt there for ten minutes, watching their reflection in the glassy surface of the Big Wheel. *On. Off. On. Off.*

"On," she said, and paused. "Most of you did very well! But we've got some holdouts in E and F Towers. I'm sorry to say that Big Wheel won't be showing up this evening. He will not be here to give us his advice without cooperation from the E and F tower hearers. We'll try later. I'll be back in an hour, at midnight, and by then I hope that you SUBbies and Terrorists will have submitted to Big Wheel's will." Sarah was replaced by Ephraim Klein, who started in with another solid hour of pre-classical keyboard selections.

Dex Fresser was clutching his chest, which felt unbearably tight. "Oh, shit," he exclaimed, "it's us! We're keeping Big Wheel off! *Everybody put your stereos on ninety point three! Do as she says!*"

Down in Electrical Control, deep in the Burrows, I and the other switch-throwers rested. The circuit breakers that supply power to an entire tower are large items, not at all easy to throw on and off every two seconds!

By midnight we were rested up and ready to go. Sarah resumed her broadcast.

"I sure hope we can get Big Wheel to come on. Let's hope E and F Towers go along this time. Ready? Everyone standing by their light switch? Okay . . . Off. On. Off . . ."

From his lounge-headquarters, Dex Fresser watched his towers flash raggedly on and off. Some of the lights were not flashing; but within minutes the Wing Commisars had swept through and shot out any strays, and Dex Fresser was indescribably proud that his towers could flash like the others. Big Wheel could not forsake them now.

"On!" cried Sarah, and stopped. Several lights went off again from habit, then coyly flickered back on. There was an unbearable wait.

"I think we've done it," Sarah said. "Look at Big Wheel!"

And the wheel of fire cast its light over the Plex with all its former glory. Dex wept.

"Not bad for a fascist," observed Little Wheel.

The Big Wheel spun all night.

It was trickier to get the attention of the barbarians of the Base. Most of them did not have bicameral minds and thus could not be made to hear mysterious voices. We needed to impress them. Hence Sarah predicted that in twenty-four hours a plague of rats would strike Journalism, unless all the journalists cleared out of the Plex.

"Frank," said the reporter into the camera, "I'm here in the American Megaversity mailroom, our operations center for the Plex war. It's been quiet on all fronts tonight despite former Student President Sarah Jane Johnson's prediction of a 'plague of rats.' Well, we've seen a few rats here"—his image is replaced by shot of small rat scurrying down empty corridor, terrified by TV lights—"but perhaps that's not unusual in these very strange, very special circumstances. We toured the Plex today, looking for plagues of rats, leaving no stone unturned to find the animals of which Ms. Johnson spoke. We looked in garbage heaps"—shot of journalist digging in garbage with long stick; sees nothing, turns to camera, holds nose, says "phew!"—"but all we found were bugs. We toured the corridors"—journalist alone in long empty corridor; camera swivels around to look in other direction; nothing there either; back to journalist—"but apparently the rats were somewhere else. We checked the classrooms, but the only rats there were on paper"—journalist standing in stolen lab coat next to diagram of rat's nervous system—"Finally, though, we did manage to find one rat. In a little-used lab, Frank, in a little cage, we found one very hungry white rat" —back to mailroom; journalist holds up wire cage containing furtive white rat—"but he's been well fed ever since, and we don't think he'll attack."

"Sam, what do you think about Sarah Jane Johnson's pronouncement? Is it a symbolic statement, or has she cracked?"

"No one can be sure, Frank." Behind journalist, door explodes open with a boom and a flash; strobe light is seen beyond it. The journalist continues, trying to resist the temptation to turn around and look; but the explosion has drowned out the audio part of the camera. Dozens of giant rats storm the room. ". . . However, reliable sources have it that . . ." His words are drowned out by mass machine-gun fire. In an unprecedented breach of media etiquette, journalist turns around to look, and presently disappears from view. Abruptly, the ceiling of the mailroom spins down to fill the screen, and three great fuzzy out-of-focus rat snouts converge from the edges of the screen, long teeth glistening in the TV lights; all goes dark. We return to Network Control. Anchorman is in process of throwing his pen at someone, but pauses to say, "Now, this," and is replaced by an animated hemorrhoid.

All we wanted was to get everyone out of the Plex and end this thing. Once rats roamed the Base and bats frolicked in the hallways, and smoke, flies and filth were everywhere, those people were ready to go. The GASF would leave whenever Virgil told them to. The administration would clear B and C Towers as soon as we gave the word. The TUGgies claimed that they were merely holding their three towers to fend off the Reds. Later, to no one's surprise, we found that they had half-brainwashed the population of those towers by the time Sarah kicked in with her pronouncements; and how could oversweetened Kool-Aid, Manilow songs and love-bombing compete with her radical power and grand demonstrations? After we shut off their electricity and water for twelve hours, the TUG agreed to evacuate their towers at our command. The SUB/Terrorist axis would do whatever they had to to keep the Big Wheel on.

As the days went by, Big Wheel grew more demanding.

Everyone was to leave his stereo tuned to 90.3 at all times. Everyone was to plan evacuation routes from their towers and clear away any obstacles that might have been placed at the exits. Dex Fresser's devotion to Sarah's words became complete, and after a week we knew we could evacuate the Axis and everyone else whenever we were ready.

In the meantime we were moving the railgun downstairs.

To withstand the recoil thrust, the machine's supports had to be bolted right into the concrete floor of the sewer. We had to precision-fit a hundred and twenty bolts into the concrete for the fifty-foot-long railgun, a dull and filthy task requiring great precision. Once the holes were prepared, we began carrying the supports down. It was a terrible, endless job. After a day of it, I decided I was going to write a book—that way, all of this drudgery was a fascinating contribution to my artistic growth. Strength was not a requirement in the Grand Army of Shekondar the Fearsome, so I had to torque all the bolts myself. During breaks I would look down the tunnel at the wall of lights that guarded the Nuke Dump's approach. What were the Crotobaltislavonians doing down there, and what were they thinking?

Their plan—the years of infiltration and the moments of violence—had gone perfectly. They had probably made their radioactive-waste bombs, only to find that their only elevator shaft had been blocked by tons of concrete. They must have thought they had lost, then; but the National Guard had not moved in and the authorities had given in to all demands. Was this a trick?

They must have been unprepared for the resistance put up by the GASF and the TUG. Still, their proxies had seized two towers and were holding their own. That was fine, until they threw Marxism to the winds and began to worship a giant neon sign. Dex Fresser must have worked closely with Magrov for years. The cafeteria riot of April First had clearly been timed to coincide with the seizure of the Nuke Dump, and the SUB had not bought their Kalashnikovs at the 7-11. Then—a window fan! A fucking window fan! In a way, I sympathized with the Crotobaltislavonians. Besides us, they were the only rational people here. Like us, they must have wondered whether they had gone out of their minds. If they had any dedication to their cause, though, they must have changed their plans. They still had the waste, they were protected by the rats, they could still wield plenty of clout. They could not see past the barrier of light, where we were implanting the railgun.

During a breather upstairs I encountered Ephraim Klein, moving stiffly but on his feet.

"Come here!" he yelled, grabbed my shirt, and began pulling me down a hallway. I knew it must be something either very important or embarrassingly trivial.

"You won't believe this," he said, shuffling down the hall beside me. "We're heading for Greathouse Chapel. We were there to broadcast some organ music—guess what we found."

Ephraim had appointed himself Music Director for our radio station, and later added Head Engineer and Producer. He knew that we could not spend twenty-four hours a day on Big Wheel chatter, and that in the meantime he could damn well play whatever he liked on what amounted to the world's largest stereo—revenge at last. If Sarah had commanded all residents to play their radios twenty-four hours a day, so much the better; they were going to hear music that meant something. He was going to improve their minds, whether they thanked him or not.

"Remember, listeners, a record is a little wheel. Any record at all is Big Wheel's cousin. So whenever a record speaks, you had damn better listen."

Ephraim and I heard the music from hundreds of feet away. Someone was playing the Greathouse Organ, and playing it well, though with a kind of inspired abandon that led to occasional massive mistakes. Still, the great Bach fugue lurched on with all parts intact, and no error caused the interweaving of those voices to be confused.

"Your friend has a lot of stops pulled out today," I said.

"That's not my friend!" shouted Ephraim. "Well, he is now, but he's not that friend."

We reached the grand entrance and I looked far up the center aisle to the console. A wide, darkly clad man sat there, blasting along happily toward the climax. No music was on the console; the organist played from memory. High up on the wall of the chapel, bright yellow light shone down from the picture-windowed broadcast booth, where the organ's sound could be piped to the radio station hundreds of meters away.

As we approached, I could see a ragged overcoat and the pink flashes of bare feet on the pedals. The final chord was trumpeted, threatening to blow out the rose window above, and the performer applauded himself. I climbed the dais and gaped into the beaming face of Bert Nix.

His tongue was blooming from his mouth as usual; but when I arrived, he retracted it and fixed a gaze at me that riveted me to the wall.

"Beware the Demon of the Wave," he said coldly. For a moment I was too scared to breathe. Then the spell was broken as he removed a cup of beer from the Ethereal keyboard and drained it. "I never was dead," he said defensively.

"You're actually Pertinax, aren't you?" I asked.

"I've always been more pertinent than you thought," he said and, giggling, pounded out a few great chords that threatened to lift the top of my head off.

"Who was the dead man in your room?"

He rolled his eyes thoughtfully. "Bill Benson, born in nineteen-twenty. Joined Navy in forty-two, five-inch gun loader in Pacific War, winning Bronze Star and Purple Heart, discharged in forty-eight, hired by us as security guard. That poor bastard had a stroke in the elevator, he was so worried about me!"

"How'd he get in that room?"

"I dragged him there! Otherwise, they don't close the lid of the little pine box and your second cousins come in plastic clothes and put dead flowers on you, a bad way to go!"

"I see. Uh, well, you're quite an organist."

"Yes. But a terrible administrator!" Pertinax now clapped

his foot down on the lowest pedal, sounding a rumble too low to hear. "But hark!" he screamed, "there sounds an ominous undertone of *warning!*" He released the pedal and looked around at Ephraim and me. "I shall now play the famous 'Toccata and Fugue in D Minor.' This is clearly the work of a young and vigorous Bach, almost ostentatious in his readiness to show virtuosity, reveling in the instrument's ability to bounce mighty themes from the walls of the *Kirche* . . . but enough of this, my stops are selected." He looked suspiciously at the ceiling. "This one brings out the bats. Prepare your tennis rackets therefore! Ah. The nuptial song arose from all the thousand thousand spirits over the joyful Earth & Sea, and ascended into the Heavens; for Elemental Gods there thunderous Organs blew; creating delicious Viands. Demons of Waves their watry Eccho's woke! Demons of Waves!" And throwing his head back, he hurled himself into the Toccata. We stood mesmerized by his playing and his probing tongue, until the fugue began; then we retreated to the broadcast booth.

"He's playing stop combinations I've never heard before," said Ephraim. "Anyway, I'm broadcasting all this. He's great."

Down in the tunnels we always kept the radio on low, and so heard plenty of Pertinax in the next few days.

Eventually we brought down the big power supplies from Heimlich Freedom Industries, wrapped in plastic and packed with chemical dessicants to keep them dry, surrounded with electric blankets to keep the electronics warm. Casimir produced several microchips he had stolen from the supplies so that Fred Fine could not use them, and plugged them into their proper spots. We ran thousands of feet of heavy black power cables down into the tunnels to power them. We tested each electromagnet; two were found wanting and had to be sent back and remade. We energized the rail and slid the bucket up and down it hundreds of times, using a small red laser to check for straightness, laboriously adjusting for every defect. It took two days to carry down the machine's parts, four days to adjust it and a day of testing before Casimir was satisfied it would work on its first and only trial.

Virgil worked on the payload, a ten-kilogram high-explosive shell. He used a computer program to design the shaped charge, an enormous program that normally would have run for days, but now required only seconds. The weakened Worm could only taunt him.

AH, GOING TO BLOW SOMETHING UP?

"I'm going to blow you up."

THREATS OF PHYSICAL VIOLENCE ARE USELESS AGAINST THE WORM. This was its usual response to what sounded like threats. YOU'RE VERY CLEVER, BUT I SHALL TRIUMPH IN THE END.

"Wrong. I found where you are."

HUH?

"I found the secret mini-disc drives that Paul Bennett hid above the ceiling of his office. The drives where you've been hiding . It's all over now."

I AM EVERYWHERE.

"You are most places, but not everywhere. I'm going to shut off your secret disc drives as soon as I'm sure they aren't booby trapped."

I'M GOING TO BLOW YOU UP.

"I'm going to be careful."

THAT'S A LOT OF EXPLOSIVE FOR YOU TO FOOL AROUND WITH, LITTLE BOY.

"It'll do."

I WILL BLOCK YOUR CALCULATIONS.

"You're living in the past, Worm," typed Virgil, and executed his program. "I have just executed my program. And next, I'm going to execute you."

THREATS OF PHYSICAL VIOLENCE ARE USELESS AGAINST THE WORM.

Lute turned the shell on a Science Shop lathe and packed the explosive with a hydraulic press. Virgil carried it down an evacuated stairwell, placing each foot very, very carefully.

Casimir put it on a clean table downstairs and weighed

it; ten kilograms precisely. He dusted it off with a lint-free rag and slid it into the bucket. We checked the power sources, and they looked fine. Everyone was evacuated except for me, Casimir and Fred Fine; Virgil led the remaining GASF forces upstairs and commanded them to leave. It was 10:30 P.M.

We sat in the APPASMU for an hour and a half, until Sarah's program came on.

"Everyone look at Big Wheel!" she said. There was long silence and we sat there on the APPASMU, protected by strobes, the rats chattering and grumbling in the darkness around us, the HFI power sources looking oddly clean and shiny as they flashed in and out of darkness in their own little strobe-pool.

"That's good," said Sarah. "As you can see, Big Wheel is shining tonight. But he won't shine for long, because he is unhappy." Another wait. We knew that, upstairs, Hyacinth had phoned the Big Wheel's controller and ordered him to shut off the sign. "Big Wheel is not shining tonight," Sarah continued, "because he wants you all out of the Plex. You are all to stop watching him from a distance. The Big Wheel wants you to see him up close tonight. Everyone get out of the building now and walk toward Big Wheel and stand under him. Leave your radios on in case I have more instructions! You have an hour to leave the Plex. When Big Wheel is happy, he will turn on again."

Organ music came on, obviously another live performance by a particularly inspired Pertinax. We played cards atop the tank.

"Should we evacuate too?" asked Fred Fine. "Could Big Wheel be another face of Shekondar?"

"Sarah wants you here," said Casimir. This satisfied him.

The music started just after midnight and continued for three hours. Above, we supposed, the evacuees were being loaded into ambulances or paddy-wagons, while Army fallout emergency workers prepared the city for the worst.

The Board of Trustees were departing by helicopter from the top of C Tower, withdrawing to the HFI Tower a mile away.

"This is really it," said Fred Fine, ready to black out. "This is the moment of the heroes. The Apocalypse of Plexor. All will be unMixed in an instant."

"Yep," said Casimir, drawing another card. "I'll see that, and raise you four chocolate chips."

The only problem so far was minor: the station's signal seemed to be dying away. We had to keep turning up the volume to hear the music, and by 1:30 we had it up all the way. Our batteries were fine, so we assumed it was a problem at the station. As long as everyone else was turning up their volume too, it should be fine.

Finally the organ music was phased out for a second and we heard Sarah. "Go for it," she said, tense and breathless. "We're gone. See you outside." I started sweating and trembling and had to get up and pace around to work off energy, finally taking an emergency dump. We were in a sewer, who cared? We gave Sarah, Hyacinth, Ephraim and Bert Nix half an hour to evacuate, but the music kept on going. After twenty minutes, Ephraim's voice came in. "Go ahead," he said, "we're staying."

So we went ahead. We had no choice.

The tunnel was four hundred feet long.

The first fifty feet were taken up by the railgun, set up on its supports about five feet above the floor. There was a three-hundred-foot desert of tinfoil shards, then the barrier of light, then, fifty feet beyond that, the door to the Nuke Dump. We rolled the APPASMU to within twenty feet of the light barrier and parked it against one of the tunnel sides. Through long wires strung down the tunnel we controlled the firing of the railgun. When we were ready, we entered the tank, shut off the strobe and turned on the ultrasound. Within a minute we were surrounded by a thousand giant rats, standing on one another's shoulders in their lust for that sweet tone, milling about the APPASMU as though it were a dumpster.

Fred Fine and I aimed shotguns out the forward gun ports.

Casimir hit the button.

We could not see the shell as it shot past the vehicle. We heard the explosion, though, and saw its flash. The rats milled back from the explosion. Fred Fine and I opened fire and annihilated the light-wall in a few shots, and with a chorus of joy the rat-army surged forward into its long-looked-at Promised Land, followed by us. Our fear was that the shell would not suffice to blow open the door, but even with our poor visibility we could see the jagged circle of light and the boiling silhouette of the rat-stream pouring through it. As we drew very near, some rats were blown back by machine-gun fire, and a Crotobaltislavonian ducked through the hole and ran toward us in his ghostly radiation suit, two rats hanging from his body.

Fred Fine opened the top hatch, whipped out his sword as he vaulted out and leapt at him howling, "SHEKONDAR!" I grabbed at his legs on his way out but he kicked free, jumped to the floor, smashed in a few rat skulls, and made toward the Croto. I do not know whether he intended to save the man or kill him. A rat tried to come in through the open hatch but I shoved it out, then stood up through it with my shotgun. I damaged my hearing for life but did not change the outcome. Once the rats started landing on my back and I could no longer see Fred Fine, I could only give up. I sat down and closed the hatch, and we waited for a while. But nothing happened; all we saw through our peepholes were rats, and the clicking of our Geiger counter did not vary.

Casimir turned the APPASMU around, and we plowed through rats and followed the tunnels until we joined up with the city sewer system. Pertinax continued to play. From time to time he sang or shouted something, and the microphones hanging back amid the pipes would dimly pick him up: "There is no City nor Corn-field nor Orchard! all is Rock & Sand; There is no Sun nor Moon nor Star, but rugged wintry rocks Justling together in the void suspended by inward fires. Impatience now no longer can endure!"

We easily found the manhole we sought, because dim morning light was shining down through it. The Guardsmen were waiting to haul us out, and emerging onto the street, we saw civil authority around us again and, even better, our friends. The Plex rose above us, about half a mile distant, beginning to glow brownish-pink in the imminent dawn. All was quiet except for the distant hum of the TUGgies, gathered just outside the police cordons and running their OM generators full blast.

During our frantic reunion, two absurdly serious-looking men approached me with complicated badges and questions. As they introduced themselves, we were all startled by a hoarse blast of organ music that burst from all directions.

"Ephraim must have turned the broadcast volume way down, then back up again," said Casimir as soon as everyone in our area had turned down their radios. Once the music was quiet enough to be recognized, I knew it as Ephraim's old favorite, the "Passacaglia and Fugue in C Minor"; and at the end of each phrase, when the voice of the Greathouse Organ plunged back down home to that old low C, it rumbled in concord with the OM generators across the street, and the Plex itself seemed to vibrate as a single huge eight-tubed organ pipe.

And after all this, I was the only one to understand.

"Get away!" I screamed, tearing myself loose from an agent. "Get away!" I shouted, ripping a megaphone from a policeman's hand, and "Get away!" I continued, stumbling to the roof of a squad car and cranking up the volume.

"Get away!" all the other cops began to shout into their megaphones. "Get away!" crackled from the PA systems of squad cars and helicopters. It was the word of the hour, and mounted cops howled it at TUGgies and SUBbies and the media, forcing them back with truncheons and horses. Someone flashed it to the police teams who had entered the Plex, and they scrambled out and squealed away in their cars. Perhaps it was shouted ten thousand times as the ring of onlookers gradually expanded away from the Base.

The sound waxed. Ephraim kept turning it up and Bert

Nix, building for the climax, kept pulling out more stops. Casimir tried to phone Ephraim from a booth, but he didn't answer. He probably couldn't even hear it ring.

He certainly heard nothing but organ as, at the end, he cranked the volume all the way and Pertinax Rushforth pulled out all the stops.

The windows went first. They all burst from their frames at once. All 25,000 picture windows boomed out into trillions of safe little cubes in the red dawn air. At first it seemed as though the Plex had suddenly grown fuzzy and white, then as though a blizzard had enveloped the eight towers, and finally as though it were rising up magnificently from a cloud of glinting orange foam. As the cloud of glass dropped away from the towers with grand deliberation, the millions of bats in the upper levels, driven crazy by the terrible sound, imprisoned in a building with too few exits, stopped beating their wings against the windows and exploded from the rooms in a black cloud of unbelievable volume. The black cloud drifted forth and rose into the sky and the white cloud sank into the depths, and Pertinax pushed the swell pedals to the floor and coupled all the manuals to the pedalboard and pushed his bare pink foot down on the first one, the low C, and held it down forever.

The building's steel frame was unaffected. The cinderblocks laid within that frame, though, stopped being walls and became a million individual blocks of stone. Uncoupled, they began to dissolve away from the girders, and the floors accordioned down with a boom and a concussion that obliterated the sound of the organ. All the towers went together; and as those tons of debris avalanched into the girders on which the towers rested, the steel finally went too, and crumpled together and sagged and fell and snapped and tore with painful slowness and explosive booms.

The hundred thousand people watching it plugged their ears, except for the TUGgies, who watched serenely and shut off their OM generators. From the enormous heap of rubble, broken water pipes shot fountains glistening white in the rising sun. Crunches and aftershocks continued for days.

Not far away, Virgil Gabrielson sat on a curbstone, his hair bright in the sun, drinking water. Between his feet was a stack of mini-computer memory discs in little black envelopes.

The APPASMU is in the Smithsonian Institution and may be visited 10:00 A.M.–5:30 P.M. seven days a week.

And the Go Big Red Fan was found unscathed, sitting miraculously upright on a crushed sofa on a pile of junk, its painted blades rotating quietly and intermittently in the fresh spring breeze.

About the Author

NEAL STEPHENSON has no job and does not live anyplace in particular except in summers, when he travels. This is his first published novel. In the past he has worked as a library and hospital clerk, garbage-to-energy research consultant, vending-machine loader, physics research assistant, anti-perspirant test subject, crystal grower, movie extra, tutor, funeral-home driver, detasseler, theatrical lighting technician, ditch digger, greeting-card salesman, fungus farmer, paperboy, and Chinese restaurant food-chopper, which prepared him for editing early drafts of *The Big U*.